Warp World

Truth, Triumph, Universe.

Inquiries should be addressed to
Morhawven@gmail.com or Morhawven.tumblr.com

Printed by CreateSpace, an Amazon.com company.
Printed on planet Earth.
The official word count for this story is 132,733.

The really fun part about publishing this novel myself is that I have total control over all this stuff. There's only a little official business here. This paragraph is just a lot of text to make it look like all the other books. In reality, this book wants to make it perfectly clear that it doesn't feel a need to conform to standards. I, the author, personally think this is amusing and the opinions here do not necessary reflect the views or opinions of Amazon.com, their affiliated companies, the US government, the Rurrians, DSHU, the Illuminati, or anyone else.

Library of Congress recommended Cataloging for when they decide to catalog this.

Ramm, Jacob H.
    Warp World / Jacob H Ramm.—1st ed.
        p. cm.
        1. Warping!—Fiction. 2. Space and shit—Fiction. 3. QUILTBAG+—Fiction.
4. Philosophy—Fiction. I. Title.

PS1234.12345678 2013
666'.6—lk33
Whaaa, I have to apply for this thing?

ISBN: 1492703877
ISBN-13: 978-1492703877

Edition 1.1

Warp World

A Concordant Book
Unsettled Realm
Single

Jacob H Ramm

Dedicated To

My first Philosophy Teacher,
and
Joshua Harris who provided a wealth
of insight and idea refinement,
and
All my First Readers.

Direct Inspirations
(a.k.a. – stuff I stole stuff from)

Doctor Who
Star Wars: Knights of the Old Republic II
Portal 2
Halo 2
Death Note
Minecraft
xkcd
NCM FirstLook

Contents

The sun has set and now betrays
decreasing breath from worlds without
a shape, precast in molds of clay.

Stability long lost. Reset
my troubled mind without so much
as fear for me. Subdue your fret

for me. These words are your belief;
a hollow answer to nothing
I can say, because of you, thief.

But dare, you do, against the strife
and run to us, acknowledged pleas,
for you so claim to fight for life,
will your assurance shelter me?

Chapter 1
Before It Had a Name

My name's Ethan Stroud and my life had been mostly normal, the only problem was things had a habit of disappearing, or worse, changing completely. The first time I can remember such a strange occurrence is actually my earliest memory. I was barely a year old and was playing with a set of building blocks. I happened to sneeze, and once I recovered I found that the blocks had somehow multiplied and covered the entire floor.

When I woke up on my fifth birthday my family's single story house in Utah had inexplicably become a two story house. I didn't complain; I had always wanted a two story house. I could finally throw my parachuting army men over the railing of the stairs and race down to try catching them. Halfway through my sixth grade year, the color orange apparently disappeared from existence. The Californian Poppies that grew in my mother's garden had become a speckled yellow and the Buddhist Monks I once saw on TV had worn reddish-brown robes. It wasn't until nearly the end of eighth grade that orange finally found its way back into the world.

The day I started high school when I was fourteen the bus had blurred into a hovercraft that lacked a driver but had realistic eyes where the front widow should have been. This eyed hovercraft had never said anything throughout the school year, though I had had a strong suspicion that it did have the ability to speak. The next year a shiny, red convertible appeared in the driveway for me on the first day of school, along with a parking permit that only the juniors and seniors could have, *and* a driver's license even though I wouldn't turn sixteen until next summer.

You might be wondering what everyone else had thought about these strange incidents. I always wondered too. No one ever said anything or gave any notion that they thought the changes were abnormal. In fact, when I would ask them "Where did orange go?" or "Did you just see that bus change?" they would laugh at first and think I was making a joke. But when I persisted they said there was no such color as orange or that the bus had always been like that. It was unsettling, this softness of the world. After I had gotten the new car and license I had told everyone I could that this had to be some mistake, that it was impossible. No one listened. In the end they all just waved me off after growing greatly impatient with me. That's when I gave up trying.

Over the sophomore year my car keys tended to be skittish, disappearing even if I tied them to my bed post. Luckily I would always find them somewhere before I had to leave in the morning. In winter all the snow was blue, and I continuously got A's on all my tests even if I didn't write down a single answer. Over summer the president switched genders, and my desktop computer turned into a laptop that would start up to the original Pong and do absolutely nothing else. New York and Paris also switched places, and that didn't return to normal until almost the end of senior year.

There was a hiatus over junior year in which nothing really happened except the disappearance of broccoli from Earth and an increase of me finding my keys in my cereal bowl, but only after I had poured the milk in.

The beginning of senior year I met Peter Sanville, who eventually became my boyfriend, though sometimes I worried about how stable he would be. That year all my teachers at school also turned into dwarves, oddly enough, and a new constellation shaped like a fork appeared in the sky. I guess a couple other small things happened, but they aren't really worth mentioning.

Now that's all background, more-or-less. This story didn't really get started until the day of my eighteenth birthday, a few weeks after graduating high school. I was hurrying home in my car, and I raced into an intersection that had just turned green. A horn blared and the suggestion of a truck flitted in the corner of my right eye, and that was the last thing I remember.

No crash, no jolt. Just instant change, like the snap of your fingers. No scene transition.

I fell into a bed, a hospital bed. Bland patient room: white walls, a heart monitor, footsteps echoing on linoleum outside the door. I sat up, heart racing. A tremor danced up my arms and jittered into my brain. What was this? Was I, actually here? Was I dead?

The possibility of death had an oddly calming effect on me. I looked around the room again and a laugh forcepopped out of my lips. A hospital? Really? Some afterlife this was. I closed my eyes and flopped back in the bed. Dying hadn't even hurt. But really, a hospital?

That was when I started considering I might not actually be dead. Not being dead would mean my car was totaled would mean I couldn't get to work would mean I couldn't pay for college would mean medical bills on top of no job. My stomach churned as my whole future unraveled before my mind's eye. I needed this to not be happening. I really needed this to not be happening. Dying would have actually been simpler. My heart picked up speed again and my head started pounding and I think I fell asleep or blacked out for a moment.

"Are you feeling any better, Ethan?"

It was Peter's voice. I opened my eyes and that was when I decided I needed a word that was about twelve times stronger than "weird." I was in some new room, which was bad enough, but worse still it was filled with *my* things. My room's furniture, my posters, my clothes left strewn on the floor. But it wasn't my room. It wasn't even a room in my house. I started to sit up, but Peter stopped me with a hand on my shoulder.

"Hey, the doctors said you need to take it easy, remember?"

"What?"

"You've been out for almost two whole days."

"What?"

"Don't you remember anything?"

"No. No..."

He stoked my cheek. "You were in a car crash, but it's okay now."

"No. That, but, that just happened. *Just* happened."

Peter kinda grinned and licked his lips. "Geez. They said you might not remember."

"But what happened? Nothing happened. Didn't it?"

"No. You were in a wreck, and insanely lucky too. You didn't even get a scratch. But you wouldn't... I mean, you were asleep, and..." He tugged at the fabric of his pant leg. "But now you're awake. You don't remember it, but that's okay, right? You've always forgotten things."

I furrowed my eyebrows. That wasn't true. A wreck? Whatever, fine. But this wasn't okay: not knowing here I was. I looked around again, and that was when I saw out the window properly. Over Peter's shoulder was the strangest tree I'd ever seen, and beyond the tree was a view of the ocean.

"Where... are we?" I asked.

"You're home. Don't you recognize it?"

I was about to say no, but I decided against it. I pulled the covers aside and stood up from the bed to see for myself.

"Hey, what are you doing?" Peter grabbed my wrist.

"I feel fine, stop. I just, just want to get some air." I pulled my hand away and went down not one flight of stairs, but two, in order to reach the ground floor.

It was evening and chilly outside and I didn't recognize a single thing. Not one flower, not one car model parked in the few driveways on the street, not the name of the road, not even the architecture of the houses around me. Each one was kind of squashy and curved around the sides but had incredibly steep roofs that were six stories high. The tree I had seen earlier looked like something you might make out of paper. The trunk was a narrow cone and the leaves were long, flat shoots that all originated from the cone's point at the top of the trunk.

I ran down to the beach and Peter followed me. The waves were roaring and crashing, roaring and crashing, and all I could do was stare at them.

"Ethan! What is *wrong* with you?"

"The sun is blue."

It was low on the horizon, dipping into the ocean and staining the sky lavender and amethyst.

"Of course it is, come on. The frost is about to settle in." He tugged on my arm.

"Frost? What frost?"

"The frost that comes every night. Don't you remember? It's fatal." Peter tugged harder on my arm.

"No... no." I shook my head. "Maybe."

This would be the easiest way to get everything explained to me. Pretend it was my memory that was the worst, just like all the times before:

"Wait, I'm sorry, when was the president elected?"

"Three years ago, how can you forget that?"

"And she's been in office the whole time?"

"*Yes*. Do you live under a rock?"

"No..."

Always me, never the world. Impossible, but there it was.

Back inside the house Peter sat me down on the couch and started telling me all these things from my life, trying to jog my memory. But none of it was real. My home schooling, our first meeting at a political rally, the grand opening of the space elevator just last year. My focus left him, his words fading from my ears as I watched the world freezing outside. A small flurry of snow drifted through the air as frost crept over the windows. The long leaf-branches of the tree snapped under the weight of ice and fell to the ground. Peter told me that the tree regrew them every morning.

That night Peter slept over and in the morning I was awoken by my parents calling. I sat up in bed, my back against the wall, holding the phone with both hands as I talked to them. They were in some country on the other side of the planet I had never heard of before, but I knew it had never existed before yesterday. They wanted to make sure I was recovering well, and they told me the convention for the family business was going fine. When we finally said goodbye the phone slipped from my fingers and fell into the blanket's folds. The changes had never been this drastic before.

Peter was awake now. He was lying silently on the other half of the bed, looking up at me. His red hair was a mess, and I tried to comb it down with my fingers.

"Feeling better?" he asked.

"Not really."

"Want me to cook us some breakfast?"

"You can cook?"

"Yes. What do you mean 'can I cook?' "

"Since when?"

"Since always. Come on. It'll help you feel better."

Down in the kitchen Peter started preparing a pair of ham, cheese, and spinach omelets. I watched him for several minutes; he was still only wearing his boxers. Outside the window new leaf-branches were already growing out from the top of the strange cone tree. I got up from the kitchen table and told Peter I had to go to the bathroom, but really I just wanted to look around the new house.

"House" wasn't an accurate name for it though; it was more of a mansion but with an illogical floor plan. Most rooms were connected not by hallways but by other rooms, so after passing through just a few it became difficult to backtrack. This degradation of direction was only worsened by the number of pointless rooms that either had no furniture or merely a few chairs. After a few minutes I stumbled upon a library that was more vertical than horizontal, spreading all three stories and down into the basement.

I heard Peter calling my name from somewhere in the house. I followed his voice as well as I could, but he found me in one of the few hallways that the mansion did have.

"Where'd you go? The omelets are getting cold," Peter said.

"I got lost."

"Oh, Ethan, Ethan, Ethan." He took my hand and led me back to the kitchen.

He watched me during the whole meal, and we didn't talk much. After finishing I fidgeted with my fork, pushing the few remaining crumbs of egg around my plate.

"What is it?" Peter asked.

"I... I can't explain it."

"Is something hurting?" He scooted his chair around next to me and put a hand on my shoulder.

"No, not really." I looked into his eyes. "I love you."

"I love you too, darling. But, you're really worrying me."

"I know, I'm sorry. It's not...it's the world. The whole world is wrong."

"Wrong? What are you talking about?"

"Yeah. Look. I, I remember everything completely differently. None of this is right." I pointed up. "I've never been homeschooled. I've never lived in this house. And the world never froze before."

Peter stared at me. "Why are you doing this again? This

isn't funny, okay? Okay? You're really freaking me out. You 'forgetting' has been kind of funny before, but stop doing it now. How am I supposed to know if you're actually okay?"

"*Peter*, it's not *me*. It's the world."

He started tapping his knees together. "Ethan. I think, maybe, I should call your doctor, okay?"

I took a deep breath. How was I supposed to explain this? I had never been able to before. I was grasping at words, trying to find some arrangement that could explain this. Someone rang the doorbell.

It was faint from the distance, but we both heard it and looked up.

"Are we expecting anyone?" I asked.

"No. Your parents don't get back 'til this weekend." Peter paused. "Maybe it's a package. Have you ordered anything?"

"I dunno."

The doorbell rang again, followed by several quick knocks.

"I'm gonna go get it." I stood.

"No, they can come back later. I really don't think you should be going anywhere right now." He reached to grab my arm, but I stepped away.

"It'll only take a minute."

Now the person was knocking and ringing the doorbell at the same time.

"Ethan, I'm not even dressed!"

"Then stay here." I left the kitchen and followed the sound.

"Wait, Ethan," Peter called after me but didn't follow.

I approached the door slowly. It was different, an airlock to fight back the cold of night. The inner door stood open as the person outside knocked on the outer door. Who would try to get your attention like this? But with the world so changed, I supposed it could be for any reason. The person was still knocking as I looked through the peephole.

It was another guy who looked about my own age. I'd never seen him before, but I didn't suppose that would count for much of anything now. I opened the door.

His arm swung forward in mid-knock as the door opened, and he looked slightly surprised. "Ah, you finally got the door." He rubbed his wrist before extending his hand back out to shake hands. "Kris Abdel-Rumos."

I eyed him for a moment, not taking his hand. He was wearing black boots, a pair of loose, black jeans, and a form fitting white sleeveless t-shirt. To top it all off his black hair had that ruffed just-got-out-of-bed look. And his face. For a second I thought he might be related to Peter, but I couldn't tell.

He smiled. "You look so adorably confused."

I blinked. "And, who... are you?"

"I told you, Kris Abdel-Rumos. And that's one last name. It's got a little dashy thing in it." He still hadn't lowered his hand.

I shook my head. "You must really have the wrong address."

"Is this not the lovely abode of Ethan Stroud? Newest son of millionaires?"

"Ne-newest? What do you mean?"

"Can I come in?"

"No."

Kris grinned and dropped his arm. "Good thing I'm not a vampire then." He slid right past me.

"Hey!" I turned around, keeping my gaze on him.

"Such a unique world you made here, you know that?" Kris started walking right down the hallway like he owned the place. "A freeze every night, because of an atmosphere that can't properly retain heat!" He laughed. "That coupled with a blue sun that's a hell of a lot colder than a blue sun is supposed to be. Even colder than a yellow sun."

"Wait, wait. You *know* this is different?"

Kris turned his body partway and grinned at me over his shoulder. "Of course."

"Who the hell is this?" Peter was standing at the end of the hallway.

Kris turned forward and a small jolt jumped through his body when he saw Peter. "Whoa."

"I said, 'who are you?' Ethan, who is this? Do you know him?"

I shook my head. I didn't know him, but did he know me?

Kris swept forward and turned so he was standing shoulder to shoulder with Peter, and he put an arm around his shoulders. "Alright, boxer boy, I think you need to just take a chill pill. I'm here to see Ethan, because he's in a bit of a spot right now. Comprende, chico?"

"Get your arm off me!" Peter knocked Kris's arm away from him and stepped towards me. "Ethan, *who* is this?"

"I don't know, I don't know. He just showed up."

"Now as uncanny as this whole situation is, I need Peter to stop yelling." Kris snapped his fingers and Peter stopped in place. "There. Now. Ethan." He paused. "Yeah, that's a good name. I like that name. Simple." He spun around and looked out a window. "Now where was I? This world, right? You made it. Fun stuff. Dangerous. Icy, but, eh, details." He shrugged. "You know the first thing I did accidently was turn my house into cake. Messy to say the least, but deliciously moist. And hell, you warped a whole planet. Shit. That's a lot for a first time. Did it hurt?"

Each word he had said I could understand on its own but not in the order he had placed them. My face was blank as I looked between him and Peter who hadn't moved the whole time.

Kris forced a chuckle. "Yeah... it's like this the first time. Wow. And Radcliff had to do this five times over. Holy balls. Well, come on. I guess, um, stuff. I'll show you stuff." He held out his hand.

"I'm, not going anywhere," I said slowly.

Kris tilted his head to the side. "Huh?"

"What'd you do to Peter?" I pointed at him.

"Froze him."

"What do you mean, you froze him? How?"

"Like, not moving frozen. I guess like a stasis? I did it with reality warping. Same way you scrambled the planet. Congratulations. You got the jackpot."

"Reality what? Warping? What even is that? Unfreeze him right now."

"Aw, man, really? This planet doesn't have reality warping as even a story thing? Or have you just never heard of it before?"

"Unfreeze Peter now!" I repeated.

"Alright, alright, geez." Kris flicked his wrist and Peter immediately became animated again.

"I'm not going to stop yelling just because you 'need me to,' "

Peter said. "And actually I think you'd better leave right now. We'll call the cops if you don't."

"See?" Kris pointed at Peter. "This is exactly why I needed him to stop yelling. He won't even listen for one minute."

"Get out of this house right now!"

"Oh my god, stop, stop!" I raised my hands to both of them. "Peter, we're not calling the cops. Kris, stop antagonizing Peter."

"*Me*? I'm the antagonizer?" Kris asked.

"Yes. Now, Peter, look, he knows something about the world being changed."

"The world hasn't changed!" Peter yelled. "What the hell is going on? Is this supposed to be a joke or something?"

"It's *not* a joke," I said.

"You know that isn't really gonna get you anywhere," Kris said.

"There's nowhere to get. Ethan, we need to call the cops," Peter said.

Kris ignored Peter and continued talking to me. "You don't have to explain this to him. He can't get it. The whole universe is yours now if you just go and have it." He paused. "I'll come back, I guess. After you've thought about it." He turned and walk out of the house.

"Go lock the door," Peter said. "I'll grab the phone."

"You're really calling the cops?"

"Yes." Peter left for the kitchen.

Kris had left the door opened, and I glanced out before closing it. He was nowhere to be seen outside. The only thing active out on the street was a trash-truck of some sort and two men collecting the leaf-branches that had fallen from the tree.

I shut the door and followed Peter.

"Now, this guy. Have you ever seen him before?" Peter asked, phone in his hand. "He could be a stalker."

"No. No, I never have." I sat down at the kitchen table.

"You knew his name."

"He told me it when he came in."

"Hmm. Well what was his last name?" Peter dug a pad of paper out of a junk drawer.

"Abdel-Rumos."

"How in the world do you spell that?"

"I dunno." I was silent a moment, thinking about what Kris had said. "Do you know what 'reality warping' is?"

Peter looked up. "Reality warping? Why?"

"He mentioned it."

"When?"

I didn't want to try explaining that he had been frozen for part of the conversation. "Before you came into the hall."

"I've heard about it in comics, but that's it. It's a super power."

"What kind? What does it do?"

"It lets you change reality anyway you want. Hang on, I'm calling them now."

"How does it work?"

"What? I don't know." He pressed the phone between his ear and shoulder. "It would depend on the comic or whatever it's in.—Oh, yes, hi. I want to report a suspicious person, maybe a stalker, how do I do that?"

I got up. I needed to move; I couldn't sit still.

"He was just here. I've got his name and I can describe him," Peter was saying.

I paced over to the window, back to the table, to the window again.

"Yeah. Kris Abdel-Rumos. Black hair, pretty close to my height, I think, so at least 5'10"-ish."

Changing reality at will? Changing reality yes, but not at will.

"Ethan, they want to speak with you."

I didn't notice him talking to me. The things that have happened: my car, the president, this *world*. Could it really be? I pressed my hand against the wall, pushing on it slightly, imaging it was like clay. Soft. Changeable.

And it happened.

Just as I was imagining the change I felt a deep something within me, a surge upwards, and my hand sank softly into the plaster. I gasped and jerked my hand away. The indentation remained.

"Ethan... what, is that?" Peter pointed at the wall.

I stated to shake, badly too. I didn't know what to say. I shook my head, tried to speak, but I didn't want to be here. I didn't want to have to explain what I didn't know. My vision started to blur, almost as if I were trying to see something else. Peter's mouth open wide with surprise or terror or both as he dropped the phone. And I was gone.

Chapter 2
Here Is How the World Is

The house was gone. I was on the beach again. It was overcast and the waves were crashing behind me. The planet must have still been the same, because there was another one of those cone shaped trees at the edge of the sand. The leaf-branches hadn't been collected from this one.

"First teleport. Cool. Good. Impressive really. I mean, you didn't go very far, but still." It was Kris.

I didn't turn around. I was hoping maybe this was actually a dream, maybe I actually was dead. I took a deep breath and faced him.

"It's real then? It's true?" I ask.

Kris nodded.

"But I don't understand." I was still shaking. I thought I might cry. I really didn't want to cry.

"Come on now, it'll be okay." He put his arms around me, holding me.

A second passed; I pushed him off. "Where am I?" I rubbed my eye with the heel of my palm.

"About a kilometer down the beach from your house. Now, you're gonna be fine. Just talk to me. When was your eighteenth birthday?"

"Huh?"

"Your birthday. The most recent one. When was it? Do you remember?"

I closed my eyes. "Yesterday? Two days ago? I dunno. It's changing."

Kris smiled slightly. "It's okay. One day, two days, no big deal whichever it is."

"How did I...? How did I do that?"

"I told you: reality warping. You're a reality warper. Here, sit down." He helped me sit on the sand, and he sat down beside me.

"But I don't..." I started crying.

"It's okay. It's gonna be just fine, Ethan." Kris pulled me lightly so I was leaning on his shoulder. "Your power is pretty crazy."

I saw my tears falling into the sand, wetting it, indenting it. I closed my eyes.

Slowly the tears started to slow. It was still a number of minutes before they stopped, a number more before I wanted to move. Finally I sat up and looked out at the waves and the ocean.

"It's not okay," I said.

"Why not?"

"I don't know what's going on. I don't even know if this is really real. It's so much worse than ever before."

"This is real. Believe me. This is finally real."

"I don't even know you. How can I trust you?"

"But I'm—" His mouth hung open a moment. "I'm..." He looked away. "You don't know yet."

"Know what?"

"Look." He pointed out at the ocean. "These are all yours. The waves. Each grain of sand. Every tree and every person. Here, on this new version of the planet. You made them and they're all yours."

I grasped up a handful of sand and let it slip between my fingers. "No..."

"Yes." He looked at me. "You really did. You know it."

"But not on purpose. I didn't mean to change *everything*. I don't want to change anything."

"But it's perfectly okay." He took my hand in his. "Perfectly okay. This is what you do now."

I scoffed and pulled my hand away. "So who are you then?"

"The same as you. One day, many years ago, I was told the same thing I'm telling you. Different words though, of course. You and I. We're both lucky, that's what."

"You can warp reality too?"

"Yes." Kris held out his hand and a small blue towel appeared in it. "Here."

14

I just stared for a few moments before taking it to wipe my eyes. "Where do you live?"

"What? Why?"

"Did I change your house? Mess up... everything? When I changed this world? Is that why you had to come tell me I'm a reality warper?"

Kris looked confused for a moment, then laughed. "Oh! Oh, oh, no. Not at all. It's fine. I don't live here. This is just one planet you changed. It's still a lot for your first real warp, but... oh man." He smiled. "Man, there's so much more for you to see. I can't wait to finally show you."

I shook my head; I couldn't understand him. "This wasn't my first, uh, *warp*."

"Of course not. We all get little spurts in the beginning, but it's not until you turn eighteen that the power becomes fully manifested." He stood up. "Come on, we should go now." He offered his hand to me.

"Go where?"

"Everywhere."

I took his hand, expecting to pull myself up, but that's not what happened. The world blurred a moment, followed by rushing colors, and stopped less than a second later.

The first thing I noticed was the black sky and stars above, next the silver and gray ground beneath us. Then I saw the Earth. We were on the Moon, standing perfectly safe in a bubble of air in the emptiness of space. I couldn't move or think of anything to say, I was so dumbfounded. The Earth was almost exactly like the photos: blue and green and brown with white swirling pastels over the expanse. The continents were unrecognizable—I must have done that too—but it was still very much Earth. Home, surrounded in blackness. It seemed so fragile.

"I thought I'd start you off slow," Kris said.

"*Slow*? Slow?" I forced a laugh as I tried to catch my breath. "How, in the world, is this slow?"

Kris grinned very widely. "You wanna see?"

"Uh, I don't know."

"Baby steps then."

He was still holding my hand. We lifted off the surface of the Moon, flying straight up and away from it, traveling so fast that both spheres shrank away from us at an alarming speed; yet I couldn't feel us moving. It was as if we had no momentum. For a dizzying moment it almost seemed like the Earth and Moon were the ones moving away, and we were standing still. In no time at all the Earth was but a blue point of light and the Moon was invisible. The sun was to our left with a light filter across the bubble allowing me to stare into the fiery orb with impunity. I could see its flairs and several small black flecks across its surface.

"Don't forget to breath," Kris said softly.

I meant to retort him, but found myself needing to take a breath first. I did so and lost the words I had been preparing to say. I just ran a hand through my hair, and my voice trembled as I muttered, "Oh lord."

"Jupiter's coming up."

At first I didn't see anything, then I noticed a small point of blanched orange. It was rapidly growing larger too. We flew straight towards the planet; within a minute we were close enough to see its individual moons.

"I don't see Io," Kris said. "Probably on the other side. Your Jupiter does have an Io, right?"

"Uh, the name sounds right. I dunno off hand."

"Let's find out."

We flew past three smaller moons and zoomed closer to the planet. In seconds we were above the clouds of Jupiter, skimming them like waves and leaving a swirling wake as we arced around the planet. It was so strange. I knew we were flying around Jupiter, but all the clouds around us just looked flat like an ocean. Then I realized we were effectively on a different planet. The sheer immensity of the fact was mindboggling.

A few seconds later the sun set behind us and the ocean of clouds became dark. Every now and then I saw flashes of lightning in the clouds below, but Kris didn't notice any of them. He was too busy looking up at the sky, scanning for Io.

"How can you tell which moon is which?" I asked.

"I can't tell all of them, but Io is obvious. You'll see what I mean."

Another minute passed before Kris pointed up at the stars and told me to look. Above us and a bit to the left was a moon that looked smaller than ours and shown with a yellowish-orange glow.

"Io?" I asked.

"Yep."

And with that we pulled up from Jupiter's clouds and headed straight towards the natural satellite. It rapidly grew closer and larger until it seemed like me might smash into its surface. Kris flipped us so our feet were towards the moon and almost all our acceleration instantly disappeared. We landed gently with a gust of yellow dust around us.

"Okay, don't move yet. Gotta set up a perimeter." Kris put his hands together and closed his eyes. There was a rush of wind that swept up a ring of dust around us and quickly pushed it out and away in a circle. Grass started to grow around Kris's feet and spread instantly out to the limits of the perimeter. A huge oak tree appeared behind him and flowers of all colors outlined the edge of the grass. Kris took in a deep breath of satisfaction and sat down with his back resting on the tree.

"Come on, have a seat." Kris patted the ground beside him.

"How can the grass grow here?"

"Because I made it grow."

I shook my head as I sat down. "That's insane."

Kris smiled. "You think that's insane? You should see the pockets of the universe where the laws of physics have been changed. *That's* some weird shit. Wouldn't recommend actually going in most of them though."

"Wait, wait. You've changed the laws of physics?"

"Oh, no, not me. Some other warper or warpers did a long time ago. It's not very practical though. You'll rarely see places with physics permanently changed unless it's to do something really specific."

"We aren't the only two?"

"Nope. There's never only one anomaly. Or in this case, two. There's always six of us at any one time. Six powers and six warpers. And when one of us dies the very next Human to be conceived receives the warping power. There's some technicalities to it though, but... well, I think it would be better if Radcliff explained that part and told you it's actually a thing."

"Who's Radcliff?"

"He's interesting." Kris scratched the back of his head. "Kinda overbearing and he's the oldest of us right now. About 420 some years, can't remember exactly."

"But, how? Is he an alien?"

Kris laughed. "Nah, only Humans can become warpers. But we live really long, around 660 years. Once we age to about 24-ish we kinda stop. It's a really nice plus."

I was silent for a moment. "How old are you?"

"Me? 117 as of three months ago." He smiled. "It was kind of a lame birthday though. No one really wanted to do anything, and besides I'd been looking for you."

I blinked. "For me?"

"Yeah. After... well, after the last warper with your power died we knew you'd be coming along in about nineteen years. I started looking a little while ago in the off chance that I'd find you early."

"But why? Why were you looking for me early?"

Kris stood up and I couldn't see his face. "Eh. A few reasons." He walked away from me and raised his hand up to Jupiter with one finger pointing at the planet. "There's still so much you need to know, and I really don't think I'll be the best at explaining them." He was tracing something in the air.

"You could just *try* to explain it." I stood up behind him.

He continued tracing in the air, and it wasn't until I looked at the planet that I realized what he was doing. On the surface of Jupiter a bearded man holding a lightning bolt was being drawn. Kris wasn't the best artist, but the image was clear enough.

"Jupiter himself," Kris said quietly as he finished.

I watched as the image slowly rotated away from us. "The people on Earth are gonna freak out when they see that."

"So?"

"So is it okay to change it like that?"

Kris turned to me, looking slightly confused. "Yeah. Of course it is. We can change whatever we want. That's how it goes."

"Just like that? Whatever we want?"

"Yep."

"But... there's no, like, rules?"

Kris laughed. "That'd be like the canvas trying to put rules on the artist."

I felt a bit of heat rising up in my cheeks, and I realized was nervous. "I don't– But, how? I mean, aren't there reasons why–?"

"Ha! *No*. No." He looked away, back at the planet. "There's no reason for anything. No 'why.' " He snapped his fingers and the entire planet shrank down to a single point and disappeared like turning off an old TV.

"Holy shit!" I stared where Jupiter had been. "You just..."

"Yeah. Gone. Just like that." Kris walked away from me, back towards the tree.

I kept staring into the newly emptied space. "Earth needs Jupiter."

"Why?"

"It blocks comets and things. Things that could hit Earth."

"No big deal. It's just another Earth."

"That's my *home*." I turned to face him.

He was lounging on the grass, head leaned back, looking up at the leaves of the tree. "Not really anymore."

I narrowed my eyes and turned back to the empty place where a planet should have been. The wall in my house popped into my mind: how easily I had changed it. I'll just make a change again; I'll put it back. I stretched my arms out, focusing on the missing planet. Nothing happened for several long moments, but slowly, slowly, I felt the deep something within me again. I followed it, pressed after it. I reached it. It was like breaking through a layer of ice and sinking into an infinite ocean of possibilities. The center of my chest had opened up to the core of the universe, and pure energy was surging through. My whole body started shaking and my vision blurred. For a brief second I thought I saw the outline of Jupiter. I was overcome.

The next thing I knew I was on my back, staring up at the stars. I blinked a few times and looked to my side. Kris was crouched down next to me.

"Jumped right into it then?" He shook his head. "You're gonna have to start out with smaller things first. Less complex stuff. At least until you get the hang of your warping power." He stood and offered his hand to help me up.

I didn't take it; I remained where I was. "That was so... weird."

"But exhilarating too, wasn't it?"

I held up my hands and looked at them. "I've never– never felt anything like, *it*."

"The warp energy."

"Huh?" I looked at him.

"It's warp energy. It's what we use to change reality. The universe is full of it. We just have to draw on it. And actually, speaking of drawing on it, I need to refill my reserve." He took a step back and held out both hands. A silver sphere with a plethora of thin black cables extending from all over its surface appeared and fell into his grasp. It was slightly smaller than a bowling ball, and at the end of each cable was a different attachment apparatuses. There were clamps, hooks, plugs for electric outlets, large and small pins, type A and B USB plugs, both sides of Velcro, loops, rubber bands, trident shaped spikes, countless other technological connectors that I didn't recognize, and more.

"What is that?"

"My Reality Converter. It's how I get warp energy. I just plug this into three different things and I can draw in the warp energy and store it within myself. Like this." He clipped a clap onto a flower, drove a spike into the ground, and fixed a hook into the bark of the tree. "Whenever I warp something I use up some of my stored energy in proportion to the warp."

"Where'd it come from? The Converter?"

"Nowhere. I just bring it in and out of existence anytime I want. And oh man, if only you knew how much I freaked out the first time I popped it into existence. That's a story. You know the random spurts are more likely to happen when you're excited?"

"Do I have one?"

"A Reality Converter? No. Each power works a little differently. Yours is possibility warping. You don't have to worry about storing energy, you just have to jump through more mental hoops to use the energy around you and 'find' what you want possible."

"Huh?"

"Radcliff has a perfect way to explain it using dots." Kris

detached the Reality Converter and tossed it up in the air. It disappeared before falling back down. "But now we should probably go. This moon is careening through space now. No telling where it'll end up. Let's go back to my place. We can relax there as you get used to things." He held out his hand again.

"I dunno." I didn't want to go with him. I wanted to go back home, and be alone, and be with Peter, and not have to worry about all this, and figure it out so I could put my planet back. I didn't really know what I wanted to do. I felt overwhelmed.

"Come on, you gotta," he said.

"Why?"

Kris titled his head to the side. "Well we can't stay here."

"I want to go back home."

"But you don't have to go back immediately. Come get lunch with me. I can make anything you want to eat."

"Look, I appreciate the offer, but I need to get home. I need to set my planet back."

"And how do you plan on doing that?"

"I'm a warper now, aren't I? I'll just, warp it." I shrugged.

"Like you warped Jupiter?" Kris smirked.

"I'll figure it out. I can do it."

Kris shook his head. "I dunno about that. But I can teach you. Come on. It'll be a lot easier than fumbling around in the dark."

I hesitated a moment and sighed. "Fine."

A real smile spread across Kris's face now, wrinkling his eyes. "Awesome." He teleported us away.

Chapter 3
Dearly Departed

We sat together on the second floor patio of Kris's house, eating *brylat* which was a unique pasta dish from Kris's native planet. It had a fairly standard meat sauce, but the pasta was cut into frilled triangles and hexagons. The house itself was uncanny, because it seemed as if it was missing half of its furniture. A living room with an armchair, TV stand, and coffee table, but no couch or TV. A china cabinet in the kitchen but not a single dish or glass inside. A shoe rack by the door that could hold at least six pairs of shoes but only had one. A dining room with fancy chairs but no table.

Beyond the inside of the house, its location was incredible. The structure jutted off the side of a steep mountain face overlooking a wide valley cut into the mountain range long ago. The clouds were no higher than sixty meters above our heads, but an invisible bubble around the house kept the air from being too thin or too cold. All in all it was so strange but so irresistible as well.

"I really need to move the house soon," Kris was saying. "It's been here too long. Needs something different. Something more vibrant. More fitting now."

"But this is an amazing view."

"I suppose. Not actually as awesome as the planet with the floating islands I had the house on once. That was something."

"Floating islands? Like in the ocean?"

"Nope. In the sky."

"But... how?"

Kris shrugged. "Something about the trapped gases in the rocks. Don't remember. It's Alicia's home planet, so she knows the details."

"Who's Alicia?"

"One of the other warpers. You'll meet her soon. You'll meet everyone soon. She's an Elf."

"What?"

"She's an Elf."

"An Elf? Really? Like archery and trees and everything?"

Kris laughed. "Well, not really really, otherwise she wouldn't be a warper since it's only us Humans, like I said. She's just got the pointy ears and the face for it. She's a bit taller too, but not by much. Some warper long ago made a bunch of Humans look like elves on Alicia's home planet, and oh man! Her home planet!" Kris shook his head back and forth in excitement. "It's really funny though, because her home country was basically just Spain with a different name."

"Why's that so funny?"

"Because the rest of her planet is so insane and crazy and awesome. Not to say Spain can't be those things, but it's a little out of place on her planet." Kris laughed again. "That planet has literally everything. You name it, it's there. Dragons, werewolves, zombies, di'orts, vampires, krakens, helfraks." He took a breath. "Bigfoot, Lelarís, unicorns, Click-Clacks, djinn, real Furries, Corbellin slugs... Yeah, it's really something. Someone had a hell of a time making it. And, that's just the stuff *living* there. Just wait 'til you see the scenery. I already mentioned the floating islands, but there's also glaciers kilometers high, inverted mountains, giant citadel cities. Unimaginable underground crystal chambers, boiling seas, migrating forests. There's even lakes so dense you can walk on them. Oh! And there's these rainforests with more water in the air than actual air... Oh man... This really takes me back." He sighed.

"That sounds so, *unreal*."

"You'll get used to it. Though I guess that is a bit sad: when the fantastic-ness wears off."

I thought on that for a moment. "Like spider webs."

"Huh?"

"Spider webs. How spiders know how to make them just right. People never think twice about that. Or the Moon. How it always faces the Earth. Well... assuming I didn't change that too."

Kris leaned forward. "Yes. Yes, exactly. We always miss..." He looked down quickly and then back up at me. "Those are such things to find."

"I guess so." I kinda half smiled and picked up my glass and finished my drink. "I'm gonna go get some water." I stood.

"Where are you going?"

"To the kitchen. If you don't mind, I mean."

"No, no. Don't go anywhere. You gotta start thinking like a warper now." He took the glass from my hand and set it back on the table. "Just *make* water." He snapped his fingers and the glass was instantly full.

"Oh. Didn't think of that."

"Obviously." Kris chuckled.

I sat down and drank from the glass. It was delicious water.

Kris leaned back in his chair and stretched. "So for tomorrow, I'll start you off slow. We can go to my home planet first. It's pretty cool. See, I was born in London, well, *a* London, and it's a pretty unique one. Already has robots and it's only, um, oh, well, I guess it's about 2035 there now." He sighed. "What a letdown. Can't see how it was back in the 1930's." He was silent a moment. "Oh! I could make a copy! Just like from my childhood! See, back in eighteen-fifty...one? Yeah. Yeah, 1851, long before I was born, there was this giant robot that appeared right out of the Thames, trying to attack everything. Lucky it was defeated, but most of its body was gone afterwards. But enough of it was left over that they took it and made robots–"

"Wait, wait. How will this help me learn warping?"

"Oh. Uh... hmm. Background?"

"O-kay," I said slowly. "Maybe, later. But right now I just want to know how to warp."

"But don't you want to see everything first? We literally have the *whole* universe at our fingertips. There's so much to see. So many planets, art made from stars and nebulas, those places where physics have been rewritten."

"I said maybe later." I paused, waiting to see how he would respond. After a few seconds of silence I added, "What about Radcliff? You said he's the oldest warper. Can he teach me?"

"I don't wanna go see Radcliff." Kris looked away.

"Why?"

"He's boring. And stuffy."

"Why's that?"

"He just is. Besides, he's kinda busy. Making a planet from scratch and all."

"From scratch?"

"Yeah. Takes a lot more time than just copy-pasting or auto-making one."

"What's auto-making? And how do you copy-paste a planet?"

"You know, I feel like this conversation is becoming way too fractally."

"You're the one who keeps saying things that I don't know about."

Kris groaned. "If you want to make something, you can just make it. You don't worry about the details too much. That's auto-making. If you copy-paste, you just find something you like, look at it, decide to copy it, and put the copy somewhere else. There are some restrictions to that, but not important right now. To make it from scratch, you worry about all the little details. Like Radcliff. He made the planet core, then the surface, then the continents, the mountains, the rivers, and all that land stuff. He's probably still making all the plants now. Does that answer all your questions?"

"Everything except why you don't like him."

"He just– just, he..." Kris scratched behind his ear vigorously for a second then flung his hand back down. "Like, like I'll be talking about this big important thing, okay? And he'll just listen with this weird smile on his face. Just listening, whatever, you know. Then he'll just cut me off or not even answer my question." He paused. "I just don't like it."

I considered this for a moment. "Is he really all that bad?"

"I mean, kinda, yeah. Also, if he ever gets upset then he's just all like, *hrrgh!*" Kris pantomimed pulling a glove on his left hand as he flexed his fingers out.

" 'Hrrgh?' " I repeated.

"Yeah. Exactly."

"Well... I guess I'll just see for myself. Where is he? How do I get to him?"

"Just teleport there. You don't know how to yet though, so I guess I'll have to take you. But I won't stay."

"Fine. Let's go then."

"*Now?*"

"Yeah. Now. Why not?"

"Not today. Please, not today. I don't want to today. Today is just you."

"Then when?"

"I don't know. Next week?"

"How about tomorrow?"

He looked at me for several seconds and sighed. "Such a catch-22."

"What's the catch-22?"

"Nothing. Fine. I'll take you tomorrow. But you'd probably like to see Alicia better though."

"The Elf warper?"

"Yeah. She's booking it up at the Grand Library and she knows just as much as Radcliff. She's actually a whole lot better in my opinion. True, she's changed a little, a little reclusive now, but she was absolutely amazing before. The parties we'd go to! We'd spend *months* in them. Her power lets her loop things, like in time, so it would never die down. It'd keep going and going at full throttle until we got bored of it. Then we'd just go make some other party and do it all over again! Everyone was together then." He smiled, his gaze drifting into the distance. "Such great times, with everyone."

Spending months at a party sounded exhausting to me, but I was more curious with the last thing he'd said. "Who's 'everyone?' The other two warpers you haven't mentioned?"

"How'd you know there are six?"

"You told me."

"I did?"

"Yeah. On Io."

"Oh." He paused. "Yeah. The other two."

"Who are they?"

Kris licked his lips. "Jett and Erika."

"And what are they both doing now?"

"Stuff. Like whatever, I guess."

"What do you mean?"

"Not now. It's too... cumbersome."

"When then?"

"Later. Just, later."

I sighed. "Why won't you just answer anything?"

He didn't reply. Instead he stood and disappeared into the house with his plate and cup. I remained on the patio and crossed my arms. I felt surprisingly frustrated as I looked out over the valley. I decided to follow him. I grabbed my dining implements and slid the patio door open. In the kitchen Kris was holding his plate under hot water in the sink, steam rising up between his hands.

"I thought you said you should do things like a warper," I said.

"Huh?" He didn't look up.

"Couldn't you warp them clean?"

"...Yeah."

"So why aren't you?"

Kris turned off the water, left the plate in the sink, and walked over to me. He took my plate and cup and threw them over his shoulders, aiming for the sink. They shattered on the floor.

"Kris! What–!"

"Don't worry. It's no big deal. But..." He looked down and shook his head. "I'm really sorry. Really sorry. Things are shit now."

"What?"

"Erika and Jett. You're gonna find out soon enough, and then you'd probably get upset if I didn't tell you now." He took a deep breath and looked me in the eyes. "They're, they... there's these Stages, okay? After booking it up and thinking you're a badass, you start, well, god-moding, basically. And, Jett. Jett's off committing genocide."

"Genocide–?"

"It's bad! It's bad, I know." He held up his hands. "It's really bad. But, it– it's kinda not *that* bad, because they're not real. The people aren't real. And Erika, she's, she's put herself in a cage so she can't do the same when she starts god-moding. You see, so she won't hurt anyone. Do– do you understand?"

"*No.* I sure as hell do not understand. The people aren't real? What does that even mean?"

"It means they're not real." Kris shook his head. "I'm gonna go take a walk, or something." He disappeared down the hallway, heading towards the front door.

"Wait! Wait, Kris!" I ran after him.

The front door was swinging shut, but he wasn't outside when I shoved it open. Outside was just chilled mountain air with nothing to see but eroded rocks and clouds, the wind whistling as it passed me.

"Kris? Kriiis?" I called out, but he was gone. "Dammit."

I rubbed my hands down my face and went back inside.

*　　*　　*

For the rest of the afternoon I practiced conjuring up items of my own. It was difficult to focus, and for the longest time I couldn't create a single thing. Finally I successfully made up a wooden block with the letter L on it. By the time Kris returned late in the evening I had covered the living room floor with dozens of items: some recreations of items I had owned before, others were things I remembered from stores or movies.

Kris walked into the room wearing a new set of clothes: a pair of forest-camo cargo shorts and a black mesh tank top.

"Been busy?" he asked.

I stood up. "Why'd you leave?"

"What's this?" He picked up a red and white ball.

"Just something from a show. Where were you?"

He dropped the ball on the floor and glanced at a few of the other items. He stayed silent for so long I was just about to ask him again, then he said, "At a rave." He left, walking towards the kitchen.

"A *rave*?" I repeated quietly to myself before following. "You just went off to some rave?" I asked upon entering the kitchen.

"Why not?" He was holding a water bottle now and drank from it.

I raised my hands halfway and dropped them again "Why did you even leave? What were you talking about?"

Kris lifted the lid of a pizza box that was sitting on the table and looked inside at the three remaining slices. "I guess you had this for dinner?"

"That's not really important, is it?" I asked.

"Food's important. Good diet and all."

I crossed my arms. "Take me back home."

Kris turned his head to me. He looked hurt. "But, why?"

"Because this isn't helping me learn warping and you haven't answered my questions. I want to go home, so I can sleep in my own bed and just... you know, try to process all of this."

"I'm sorry, please. I'm sorry." He took my hands in his. "You can't expect me to show you how to warp in one night though. And what do you want to know? I'm here. I'm here now."

"Really? You're gonna answer things now? Fine. What did you mean that the people aren't real?"

Kris let go of my hands and looked away, drinking from the water bottle again. As he leaned back slightly I noticed his chest through the mesh fabric. The white light from the kitchen ceiling gave a better contrast than the light in the living room. He was by no means muscular, but his chest did have an appealing definition to it.

"We can change them," he said.

"Huh?"

"People. Humans. We can change them. They aren't solid. They aren't real."

"But we come from them. You said only Humans become warpers."

"And only warpers become real, because we can't be changed."

I crossed my arms and turned away from him. "This is stupid. Take me home, I want to sleep."

"You, you don't have to go. I mean, you can stay with me. My bed's really soft. Look." He teleported us upstairs, into his bedroom. It was nearly empty. There was a king sized bed against a wall with a large picture window over it, but aside from that the only other item in the room was a rectangle on the wall covered by a cloth.

"What? Why would I do that?" I asked.

"Why wouldn't you?"

"I'm with *Peter*."

"But... but, he's not real." Kris looked confused.

"Of course he's *real*. We've been together years now, and who are you? Just some crazy guy I met this morning. Warper or not, that doesn't change anything."

Kris winced. "No, no. That changes everything. It can't work anymore, you and Peter. It can never work anymore."

"Don't tell me what can and can't work." I stepped away from him. "You don't know."

"But I do."

I scowled and left the room, slamming his door shut behind me. How could he know? He didn't know anything about me or Peter. I clenched my fists and realized I still needed him to get back home tonight. That did nothing to help my mood.

But forget him, I thought, I'll just go make a bed tonight and in the morning I'll leave. I sulked down the hallway, looking for a room to use. I passed one that had bookshelves but no books; another room had only a desk in the center of the floor. At the opposite end of the house I found an empty room and claimed it as mine for the night.

I wasn't completely sure if I could make a bed yet, but I could probably make a mattress. I closed my eyes and focused on the possibility, remembering my own mattress from back home. I stretched my hands out towards the floor and slowly felt the right state. I sank down, for a second I felt a surging connection to my room, my Earth; I almost thought I was actually there. I opened my eyes, breathing heavily, and saw I had succeeded in creating a mattress. I wasn't completely certain though. A part of me wondered if I had instead pulled my actual mattress here.

I didn't completely care at the moment. I was exhausted and felt completely drained. I had enough will left to create a blanket and pillow before falling atop the bed and into sleep almost instantly.

Chapter 4
Things That Gnaw

When I awoke in the morning, before I opened my eyes, I wondered if it really had all been a dream. Of course it wasn't though. I knew it. The house was quiet. I still felt too tired, and I stretched before opening my eyes. Something about the sunlight outside seemed different, but I didn't fully consider it yet.

Sometimes in the morning, before I got out of bed, I would ask myself: Am I happy? I asked myself right now. The answer didn't come immediately.

I considered what I could do now. I thought I should probably be happy—ecstatic even—but everything revolving around the warping power seemed so complicated. I thought about Kris. He *seemed* normal enough, didn't he? I wasn't sure. And what about those other too: Erika and Jett? I remembered countless movies and books where characters went insane or lost themselves in power. Wasn't that the age old saying? Absolute power corrupts absolutely? Apparently it was true. And now I was one of them.

I sat up. I wasn't happy. I was nervous. Understatement. Correction: I was scared.

But what could I do? I scratched my head and realized my hair was greasy. It was a good enough distraction, and I mused about warping myself clean. I decided to give it a go, folded my hands and focused on myself. The warp energy slowly start to build, but I couldn't direct it at myself. It was like a tightly coiled spring that I couldn't bend back far enough to make the ends meet. I broke off my concentration and exhaled. At least I could make clean clothes.

After changing into new jeans and t-shirt I stood up and

31

finally realized why the sunlight seemed different. The house
was sitting on a bright beach with white sand and prefect palm
trees lining the dunes. A few clouds floated lazily not far above
the house. I pushed the window open and the cascade of waves
filled the room.

"Wow," I whispered to myself.

I heard a noise downstairs and quietly descended the
staircase. Kris was in the kitchen, sitting cross-legged on the
top of the island counter. He was only wearing a pair of black
sweatpants and had a thick blanket shrouded over his head
and shoulders. A plate of spaghetti and meatballs rested in his
lap.

"Well, good morning, my fine friend!" He smiled broadly,
swaying back slightly and correcting his balance.

"Uh, hi?"

"Oh don't give me that." Kris laughed. "Come on, get
something to eat!" He set his plate aside and hopped down from
the counter, but his blanket trailed after him and knocked the
plate to the floor. "Shit. Balls." He staggered sideways.

It was at that time I noticed a shot glass on the counter.
"Kris. What's that?" I pointed to it.

"What? 'What is this?' You've never seen a shot, a shot glass
before?" He snatched it up. At some point during its journey to
his mouth it had refilled with clear liquid. "Vodka. Great stuff.
Not a worry in the world when you're drinking."

"Drinking? Why are you drinking vodka in the morning?
What are you doing? Why are you drunk at breakfast?"

"I am not *drunk*, good sir. I am mere– merely *tipsy* at
worst." Kris leaned forward with each emphasized word. My
first instinct was to catch him, but he maintained his balance.

"Really? Why don't you just sit down?" I pulled a chair over
to him from the table.

"I never sit in chairs in my house!" He tried to lift himself
back up to the counter, but he slipped and couldn't quite
coordinate the feat. "Fuck it, dammit." He waved out his arm in
a wide ark and gravity disappeared from the room.

For a second I didn't realize what had happened. The
moment I did I grabbed the chair for support, but both myself
and it merely started floating upwards, slowly drifting towards
a wall.

"Ah! Kris! Stop it!"

"Hang on, hang on."

He positioned himself over the counter and gravity resumed. He plopped right down back into his cross-legged position while I fell less gracefully to the floor with the chair, toppling forwards over it.

"And you say *I'm* drunk." Kris laughed aloud.

It was a strange laugh, but really it was only strange because it was of the sort I almost never heard. It was a laugh of someone who had just gone skydiving or composed a symphony.

I pushed myself up from the floor. "Tipsy, drunk, whichever; you're crazy."

"Everyone's crazy. It's just a matter of degrees."

"And you were sitting in a chair just yesterday."

"Huh?"

"Out on the patio, you were sitting in a chair. You just said you never do."

"Ethan! Oh, Ethan, Ethan. That was *outside* my house. Clearly!" He laughed and took another shot. "So? Food? Yes?" He created another plate of pasta as he erased the mess from the floor at the same time. "I highly rec-recommend my spaghetti. I've always been told it's to kill for." He held his plate forward, holding the fork down with his thumb.

"Oh sure, 'cause making it just entails snapping your fingers."

"Hey, hey now. It's good regardless. And there's details that go into this. Fine details, I mean."

"Whatever. I'll try some when you're not drunk, how about that?"

Kris just rolled his eyes and shoved a forkful of the spaghetti in his mouth.

I walked over to the table where the pizza box still was. It hadn't floated far during the gravity drop. I pulled out a slice and sat down to eat.

"Not gonna freshen that up? The pizza?" Kris asked.

I looked at the pizza and shrugged. We ate in silence. After I finished the first slice, I made up a glass of soda. Kris kept watching me, but he looked away every time I looked up at him.

"You really don't approve?" Kris suddenly asked.

"Huh?"

"Of vodka?"

"I don't really care. Whatever. It's just... nevermind."

"What? What?"

I sighed. "I've never dealt with drunk people before."

"Well, you know, when I told you I drink–"

"You've actually never mentioned drinking before."

"Gah!" Kris jerked forward. A meatball rolled off his plate and fell to the floor. "Don't interrupt me!"

I shook my head and picked up another slice of pizza.

"See, see look. I drink a lot. Because my parents, they were immigrants. To London. Wait..." He created a piece of paper and squinted at it. "Yeah, annex date. Ireland wasn't... yeah, immigrants." He tossed the page to the floor and looked back at me. "So, half my family's Irish. The other half's Russian. You see? So I drink vodka. All the time!" Kris grinned widely. Add some face paint and he could have been a clown.

I picked up the paper; it read: *26/3/1899*. "Sounds more like you're just playing up the stereotypes."

"Uh! Don't put me in a box!" He tossed his plate aside and jumped off the countertop again.

I ignored him and looked out a window. I didn't really want to bother with Kris anymore, but suddenly he was at the table beside me, spinning a chair around so he could sit on it backwards.

"Lookie here. This." He was holding a clear vial with light blue liquid in it.

I was silent a moment, then gave in. "What is it?"

"Warp extract."

"Huh?"

His shoulders fell. "Okay, that's just what it's called. Basically though, basically, it cures everything." He pulled off the stopper and drank it all in two gulps. "I'll be sober in... I don't remember. Soon. Like a minute."

"Okay, I'll humor you." I dropped the pizza crust into the box.

Kris grabbed it and started eating it.

I didn't bother to comment on that. Instead I said, "I'm gonna go take a walk."

"I'll come too." Kris stood up immediately, tossing the blanket to the floor.

"That's not–" I sighed. "Fine."

We left the kitchen and when I opened the front door I was surprised to see that it led directly out to the beach. There wasn't even a slab a cement to denote a transition. Kris walked right out and kicked up some sand. After taking off my shoes and socks I followed.

"So, where are we now?" I asked.

"Outside, duh."

"That's not what I meant and you know it."

"Do I?"

"Okay, you walk that way, I'll walk this way. I don't even want to try talking to you right now." I turned and walked off.

"No, wait! Come on, I was only kidding." Kris ran up next to me. "We're on a flat biome plane in space. They're created to have only a specific environment."

"Why?"

"I dunno. Why ever the warper who made it wanted it for."

I blinked. "What?"

"Sorry." He was quieter now. "They're like exercises. There's a whole bunch clustered together here. They were left after being made."

"So the ground is just flat? There's nothing under us?"

"Just space. The whole thing's a hundred meters thick though."

"And the edges?"

"Eh, the water and air just stop. They don't flow off or anything. It's like a can of tuna fish, but no can. And no tuna. Just the disk... of beach. Or whatever the biome in question is."

"Hmm." I walked towards the water, letting it lap over my feet. It was pleasantly warm.

"Want to go swimming?" Kris asked as he stood next to me.

"Not particularly."

"Meh. You probably wouldn't have wanted to go skinny-dipping anyways."

"Not with you."

"Oh! I'm hurt." He looked at me and smiled.

I purposefully kept my face blank. "Come on." I kept walking.

After we had gone a short distance more Kris asked, "You know the best part about this beach?"

"What?"

"No stupid animals anywhere. Nothing to sting you or stab you or bite you." There was suddenly a flat rock in his hand. He threw it out over the water, but it hit a wave and disappeared.

"No coral reefs either then. I've always wanted to go snorkeling at one of those."

"We could just make a reef."

"It's not the same."

"How?"

I stopped walking. "It wouldn't be natural. You know. We'd never be able to make it as great as the original."

"Are you kidding me? We can make it a thousand times *better!*"

"But I don't even know what a coral reef should really look like. If I made one it'd probably look stupid."

"No it wouldn't. Didn't I mention this? Auto-making? The power fills in the details if you let it."

"Yeah you mentioned it, but how does that work?"

"Well, take this tree for example." Kris snapped his fingers and an oak tree appeared in the sand a short distance from us. "I didn't consciously think about how each of those branches or how all of those leaves would look. I just thought 'oak tree.' The power did the rest."

"No, I mean, how does *it* know? How does the *power* know what an oak tree is?"

"It's not literally, literally *knowing*. But I dunno. No one really knows the exact reasons why or how that explain warping. Not even Radcliff. Maybe warpers from the Eras before did, but we don't. But why does it matter? It works, it's awesome, and it's *ours.*"

I wasn't satisfied.

"What if you tried to make something that you didn't know?" I asked.

"What do you mean?"

I thought a moment. "A cortal. Make a cortal."

"A what?"

"Exactly." I smirked.

"Oh! Oh, I get it. This is a test then?"

"Yeah. So make it, or try to at least."

"Alright." Kris shrugged his shoulders and turned to the empty sands behind us. He closed his eyes and snapped his fingers.

Nothing happened.

He opened his eyes. "Huh."

"There. So what's that mean?" I asked.

"I dunno."

"Maybe Radcliff will have an idea."

"That's not fair." Kris crossed his arms. "I know how to use warping for legit stuff, not experiments."

"Yeah, I've seen that."

"Okay, I'll show you. Watch this." He held out a hand, fingers stretched out, and pulled up a great torrent of water from the ocean.

It flowed through the air like a spiraling river. At the same time rocks jutted out from the sand around us. They arced up and back down, creating a grotto. Grass carpeted out from the center; long vines of green shot up, and shimmering leaves sprouted that were the size of CDs and glistened with every color. Then the water fell down on us, filling the cylindrical grotto, not spilling out between the rocks. I found myself floating but still able to breathe. Everything was tinted blue, and the iridescent leaves swayed on the vines around us.

"And how's that?" Kris asked, his voice loud and almost directly in my ear, carried by the water. He swam towards me.

I gazed at the sunlight streaming through the water. I looked at him. "It would be awesome, except now I'm completely soaked."

"Oh, details, details. Come on! Enjoy it! Isn't it amazing? I kinda think I even out did myself. I hadn't expected it to turn out so well." He did a backwards somersault in the water.

It was beautiful; I just didn't want to admit it. Instead I swam away from him and reached out of the water through an opening in the rocks.

"Careful. It's tricky," he said.

"I can manage." I let myself sink down and pushed off the ground, propelling myself out. I put more force into it than necessary and fell forward on my face. I rolled over and saw Kris was laughing, but I couldn't hear him.

He stuck his head out from the water. "I did warn you."

"I know, I know." I stood up, preparing to wipe sand off myself, but found that I was completely dry so there was little to brush away.

"And you're even dry. Just look at that." Kris had rolled over in the water and was looking at me upside down.

"*Okay*, okay. Fine. You win. That was awesome, and you did it all very well." I crossed my arms and looked away to the ocean.

"Just what I wanted to hear." His head dunked back into the water and he swam up to the top. After climbing out onto one of the arches Kris jumped off and drifted slowly down to the ground as if he were in low gravity. He flipped in the air once before landing safely in the sand.

"Now you're just showing off," I said.

"Maybe, maybe not."

"Anyways." I paused. "Now that you're apparently sober, can we just go see Radcliff already?"

Kris didn't respond immediately. First he snapped his fingers, removing the oak tree and the water grotto from existence. "Yeah. I guess so. But I think going to see Alicia would be better."

"The recluse in the Grand Library?"

"Don't call her a recluse." He crossed his arms.

"You're the one who said it first."

"Did I?"

"Yeah."

"Oh."

"Anyways, I think I'd rather just see Radcliff first."

Kris sighed. "Fine, fine. I guess I did promise. I'll drop you off then." A white shirt appeared in his hands, and he pulled it on. It was a dressy button-up shirt, the kind you'd wear with a suit, but the sleeves were ripped off.

"Classy," I said.

"Better believe it." He held out his hand. "Let's go."

"Wait, I don't have my shoes. I need to go–"

"Here." Kris held up my shoes and socks that had just appeared in his hands.

Right. Warping.

"Thanks." I took them and he teleported us away.

Chapter 5
We Are Gathered Here Today

Teleporting had always been such a weird thing. I hadn't really liked it then, and I still don't like it now. When it happened you would be standing still and surrounded by blurring colors and flashing lights, all the while a soft *whooshing* would filled your ears. Nothing would be distinct, everything ethereal. Then it would be over, always over so quickly.

When we reappeared Kris and I were floating in space above a planet. It was unlike anything I had expected. There weren't continents and oceans; there were twelve huge arms of land, all spiraling in the same direction and all originating from the point directly below us, the planet alternating between land and water. Five and a half of the arms were green with plants, two were various shades of tan, another mostly white, and the last three were all brown. Orbiting the planet were countless yellow glowing crystals like a field of shimmering sequins garnishing the atmosphere.

"You can see he's not finished yet," Kris said. "He's making each arm different from each other. I think he's working on the rainforest now."

"Wow. How long has he been working on this?"

"Um, a while now. I guess like sixteen years or so."

"And what are all those crystals all around it?"

"They're in storage."

We descended, the planet rushing towards us. Soon it was all that I could see as we passed through the atmosphere. At the origin of the spiral arms I could see some sort of structure. We landed in front of it and something about the ground seemed strange. Small trickles of warp energy were leaking up from deep below, but no source could be distinctly discerned.

They were like wisps of a veil drifting before a fan. The structure before us looked like a huge Greek temple: pillars, pediments, and all. The only oddity was the freestanding towers near each corner of the temple. They looked very similar to obelisks, and at the top of each was a floating crystal that glowed yellow-amber and had to be at least the size of a refrigerator. Above the double doors was a large symbol: three circles forming a triangle and one circle in the center that was connected to each of the other three by a single line.

"What's this?" I asked.

"It's called the Archives."

"Okay, but what is it?"

"It keeps all the archives. There's also rooms inside like bedrooms and kitchens and things, so you could live here if you *really* wanted to."

"And what's that symbol?" I pointed to it. "With the four circles?"

"That's the warper symbol. Us. Our thing. You know. And we know it's ours, because the thing's warp locked and has been around longer than anyone knows. No one could've changed it."

I sat down and started putting on my socks and shoes. "Warp locked?"

"Yeah, it's just a level one lock though. If something's warp locked that means it can't be changed by warping it at all. You could still blow it up with dynamite or whatever, well, normally. The Archives are indestructible, because of how they were made, aside from the warp lock, that is. Anyways, warp locked stuff stays immune to warping unless the person who locked it unlocks it."

"And if you die before unlocking something?"

"Forever locked then."

"I see."

"There's also a level two lock. Covers more. You lock an area and inside that locked area no warping can be done at all."

"And you can just make locks whenever you want to?"

"Precisely." It wasn't Kris who said this. The new voice came from behind us.

It was Radcliff. I was as sure of this as if he had shaken my hand and told me himself. He was Black, his head bald, and he stood like a brick wall with his arms crossed. He wore simple clothing: loose gray shirt and pants, both smudged with dirt. I imagined him shaking the dirt from his clothing, the fragments falling into the ocean of a planet below, each one forming an entire continent. The image seemed to suit him.

"Hello, Kris. I see you found the newest warper."

"Yeah. I did. I told you I would. See, this is Ethan. He's from that one Earth near the Dark Zone, so I got him as quick as I could. But you should see what he did to his planet! He didn't even know it! It freezes at night and–"

"Kris. Calm down."

Kris shut his mouth immediately.

I stood up, looking between the two of them, unsure of what to say.

"Ethan, I am Radcliff Farth. I hold the meditative warping, and I am currently constructing this planet, Cosmos, for the Archives. It is both a safe haven and a reserve bastion of warp energy." He extended his hand to me.

"Uh, hi." I shook his hand.

Radcliff smiled. "Come inside, where we can relax." He walked towards the Archives.

"Well, then. I'll just, um, see you later." Kris took a step backwards.

"So you're gonna just leave?"

"Yeah." He nodded. "Pretty much."

"How am I supposed to leave when we're done? I can't teleport yet."

"Just call me."

"Call you?"

"Yeah, here." He handed me a cell phone he hadn't been holding a second ago. "Later." He disappeared.

I sighed and looked back at the Archives. Radcliff was nowhere in sight. I hurried to the building. It had to have been at least twelve stories tall. I walked up the stone steps, feeling far too small. Apprehension started to creep under my skin and was threatening to get the better of me, but I ignored the feeling and walked through the arched opening.

Inside was a short hallway, the stone walls painted like dark mahogany and lit by amber colored spheres hanging from the ceiling. It led out to a huge spherical room. Balconies on every floor formed the sphere with their growing then shrinking diameters. Curving stairs against the circular walls lead up to the other floors. In the center of it all was a huge amber crystal configuration floating in space. It was ovoid at the center, the length of perhaps three cars. Protruding from it were countless tubes, at the end of each was a sphere, and extending from each sphere were two more spheres also connected by tubes. The whole thing glowed just enough to fill the room with soft light.

"Beautiful, isn't it?" Radcliff was standing at the second floor balcony.

"What is it?"

"I'm not really sure. Could just be decorative lighting."

"Oh."

"I see Kris disappeared on us."

"Yeah, he did."

"He'll come around in time. Come on up. I'll show you the Archives. That is what you are here for, isn't it?"

"Huh?"

"Didn't you come to see the Archives?"

"Oh. Oh, no, not for this place. Kris didn't even mention it was here."

"Didn't he?" Radcliff paused. "Then why did you come?"

"Well, to see you." I started climbing the curving stairway to where Radcliff stood. "Mostly to learn warping. Then I can get back and fix my Earth."

"Fix it? What has happened to it?"

"I guess I changed it all after getting hit in a car wreck. Nothing's the same, but the biggest problem is that the whole planet freezes every night now."

"An accidental warp because of trauma is understandable, especially with your power."

"Yeah, that's the other thing. Kris said my power is different, but all he did was mention something about mental hoops and say you have a better way to explain it. And several things have been like that. He'll mention something and then say you can explain it better."

"That's probably because he just doesn't try."

I was silent a moment. "Or doesn't think he can."

"And which would you say is worse?"

"Between those two?" I weighed them. "Not trying."

Radcliff smiled and nodded. "Let's go sit down."

He led me into a lounge of sorts. The walls were no longer painted and were simply gray stone. Green carpet covered the floor and a half sphere of crystal in the ceiling filled the room with yellow light. There was a low table near the center of the room, and several couches and armchairs circled it.

"Would you like anything to drink?" Radcliff asked as we sat.

"Just some water."

Radcliff closed his eyes for a moment. A blue colored glass cup with water and ice appeared before me and a tea cup on a saucer appeared before him.

"I'm curious. Where exactly are you from?" he asked.

"Utah. In the United States."

"We're a bit close then, metaphorically. I'm originally from a Canada. Alberta, specifically." Radcliff took a sip of tea. "Now. The matter of learning warping. Is that all you wish to do right now?"

"Yeah, I mean, that's all I need to know so I can put my planet back."

"I see. First off, 'learning warping' is a bit of a misnomer. It's like learning to talk or walk. You are guided more so than taught, and you learn more through experience than lessons. But this can help." He created a thin, black booklet and handed it to me.

"What is this? A 'Welcome to Warping' pamphlet?" I started flipping through it, expecting to quickly get a glance at its contents, but the pages didn't stop coming. I held the book open with my thumb, letting the pages automatically flip past, but an impossible number were contained within the thin binding. I stopped, book still only halfway through, and looked up at Radcliff.

He was smiling. "Clever isn't it? I still don't even know how the original creator folded the pages in with warp energy like that."

I shut the book and it thumped as if it were hundreds of pages long. "Wow. Shit. How long is it?" The cover was blank aside from "MANUAL" in white letters.

"About 2100 pages. It's an extremely useful reference. It's a constant of sorts, more of an idea than an object. A group effort to answer questions and collect information, like an encyclopedia. It was spearheaded by a warper generations ago, before this Age had the Archives in use. Anyone can edit it, and anytime you create a copy you'll get the most recently updated version. It's not necessary to learning, but I would definitely recommend it as a supplement."

"So this is 'Wikipedia, the Book?' "

"Excuse me?"

"You've never heard of Wikipedia?"

"Can't say I have. This will happen frequently though. Given the fact we are all from different Earths, misalignments are common."

"Huh. So what about the Archives? Do they supersede this?"

"No. The Archives serve a different purpose, which I will show you shortly. First though, I want to know what you already know about warping as a whole."

"Well. I know there's different types of warping for each warper. And Kris just told me about warp locks. There's six of us, and we can do anything. And apparently we don't really know why warping is a thing." I hesitated. "And things are a bit... weird."

"Indeed. You'll find many new things you'd never have imagined before."

That wasn't exactly what I had meant, but I didn't know how to clarify it.

"As for the powers," Radcliff continued, "each is different and I will start with yours. It is known as possibility warping. Essentially you create what is not there by finding it possible to be there, or change something by finding it possible to be changed. Imagine an image on a computer. It's just comprised of pixels, little squares of color, and that is true for every picture. Every picture is just pixels. If you change the pixels, you change the picture. Every possible picture is right there in the pixels. Or consider a music CD. The groves on it determine what the music will sound like. Every song just comes down to the groves. If you changed the groves, you would change the song. The potential for any song is there, but only one in particular is currently present.

44

"Extrapolate those examples to the universe. Everything is just the warp energy and molecules, atoms. They could be anything, they have that potential, but currently they are only one thing. You just have to realize this and you can do anything.

"In a way this makes your power both the easiest and most difficult. There is no middle action for you as there is in the other powers, but your power can be much more difficult to control, specifically in the way it can 'go off' without you entirely intending for it to do so."

I turned over his explanation in my mind a few times. "Sounds, daunting."

Radcliff smiled. "I suppose so. It simply takes the most mental control. Let me tell you of Kris's power and my own. That will give you some context. For myself, I must draw up the warp energy by meditating. After collecting the energy I can retain it for a very limited time before using it. As an example, if I desired to create a new planet the same size as most Earths I would have to meditate for approximately twenty seconds. As for Kris, he has the highest capacity out of any warper to retain warp energy within himself."

"I know a bit about his power already. He's shown me the Reality Converter."

"Yes. So long as he has enough warp energy stored within him, he can create or change whatever he wants instantly. However, the Reality Converter is his only means of replenishing his energy. On the other hand, since he draws warp energy from the Converter, as long as it is plugged in Kris can continually draw up energy until the warp energy in the immediate area runs out."

"It can run out?"

"Just in an area. Warp energy flows through the entire universe, but some places have more of it than others. If any warper is in a place that completely lacks warp energy, then that warper would be powerless unless they had warp energy stored within themself. Not all warpers can do so though. Like yourself."

"So I can only warp if there's warp energy around me?"

"Yes."

"That's good to know."

Radcliff nodded. "You should always avoid draining an area of warp energy though. If that happens, Nókrutar have the potential to start appearing."

"What's that?"

"The Nókrutar. It translates literally into 'agencies of the darkening,' or just Dark Agencies. It's one of the few First Era words the Warper Born still remember. You see, alongside warp energy there is also dusk energy. Warp energy is expansive and creative, but chaotic, whereas dusk energy is constrictive and limiting, but stabilizing. In general you will never have to worry about dusk energy. It's just an underlying mechanic of the universe. However, if there is a suffice amount of dusk energy within an area that has little to no warp energy, Nókrutar will congeal and rise up. And once they rise, they won't go away unless they are destroyed."

"So just avoid that. Okay. What else do I need to know to warp?"

"If you do only want the barebones information to be a warper, then you must know to also avoid warpers who are in their Ego Stage."

I remembered my glass of water and picked it up, but didn't drink from it. "Do you mean Erika and Jett?"

Radcliff leaned back. "Kris has mentioned them to you?"

"Yeah." I wiped my thumb across the glass surface, collecting condensation. "He said that Jett's 'god-moding.' "

"Slang." Radcliff drummed his fingers on his armrest. "Jett Cavallaro is currently going through his Ego Stage, and I believe Erika Hall is soon to follow, if she hasn't already crossed over to that Stage. There are five Stages that we go through: Initiation, Indulgence, Learning, Ego, and Wisdom. There are some records which suggest a sixth Stage, that of Greatness, but that's a philosophical debate for much later."

"So... is Jett in his Ego Stage, because he's killing people? Or is he killing people, because he's in the Stage?"

"A subtle difference, don't you think?"

"So? That's still really important. And we *have to* go through these Stages? I don't understand."

Radcliff tapped the tips of his fingers together. "It's better thought of as a pattern. You are currently in the Initiation Stage: you are feeling out the edges of this new object. Settling in basically, though there is still some room for erratic behavior during the process. After you have mastered your power, you will use it for fun. For pleasure. Then you will grow bored of novelty and seek to understand the world at large, to devour knowledge. Sometimes about some topic in specific, sometimes about everything. Then you will seek control, to put your knowledge to practical use and wield it like divine authority. After all that, if you survive, you will simply *be*."

"Survive?"

"The highest rate of mortality is in the Initiation Stage, followed by the Ego Stage."

"But how can you be so sure the Stages will be followed?"

"Simple. I have seen them happen time and time again. The likelihood you will follow them far outweighs the likelihood you won't. But the strangest part is that when you do the things that have already been said, at that point in time when you *do* do them, the actions will be exactly what you want to do. At the point you pass through each Stage you will likely be aware you are in the Stage, but you will also know that you are doing exactly what you want to do. The Stages are inevitable, but different for everyone."

"Isn't this determinism?"

"Ah." Radcliff leaned forward. "Good thought, but no. If it were anything, it would be closest to compatibilism. But try to think of it more in terms of a natural process, such as growing up or getting the flu. Though you won't actually get that again, or any sickness. We also age much slower as I'm sure you've noticed. I am 434, but I hardly look a day over 30."

"Yeah. Kris mentioned the aging, but not the sickness immunity."

Radcliff nodded. "Anyways, it is a natural process. A series of events which are similar enough to chart but not similar enough to know exactly what shape they will take. It will really only be a problem if you worry about it and thus make it a problem." He chuckled. "It will make your head hurt if you think about it too much."

"But what about Jett?"

"What about him?"

"Well, he..." I hesitated. "If he's committing genocide then, I mean, what do we do?"

"Nothing."

"What?"

"Nothing. We do nothing. We do not get involved in the affairs of warpers going through their Ego Stage."

"Why?"

Radcliff was silent a moment. "It is a very poor idea."

"But *why*?"

"Listen. You're new. You don't understand. I'm trying to explain everything in order, but you're jumping around. Believe me when I tell you that I know a warper in their Ego Stage is not to be trifled with. Once a warper leaves the Learning Stage, that warper will start to think that they know what is best. The warper will proceed to conduct whatever plans or tasks they see fit with great self-assured vigor to change the world to match their views. Such a warper will usually have a sharp white-black moral view on life. Right, wrong. Useful, not useful. For, or against. But they can also be incredibly unpredictable. Their own preconceptions are what drive them."

"So Jett's committing genocide, because he thinks it's right?"

"Yes."

"And who's he trying to kill?"

"The Rurrians."

"Who are they?"

"Just a certain group of Humans. Not truly important."

"Kris said kinda the same thing. He said they weren't real." I crossed my arms. "He also said Peter wasn't real."

"Peter? Who's Peter?"

"My boyfriend."

"Oh." Radcliff was silent a moment. "Tell me about him."

"Well, we've been dating for almost a year now and he's really great but... he got changed a bit too when my Earth changed. It's really unsettling. He's never changed before, never. And, what if... No." I shook my head. "I'm gonna fix everything as soon as I learn warping. He's probably freaking out right now too since I literally disappeared right in front of him."

"So your plan is to go back and fix your planet?"

"Yeah."

"And tell me exactly, what needs to be fixed?"

"Everything, really. It's all different. The continents are different, cars look different, my house is different, the world freezes every night, and who knows what else. But especially the freezing. That's all wrong." I paused. "And there's these really weird trees now too."

"Why do you need to fix it though?"

"Why wouldn't I? It can't stay like that. It's not supposed to be like that. Besides, it's probably making things a lot harder for everyone there."

"Perhaps. But you know that there is no set state for anything in the universe, excluding us warpers of course. Everything is in a constant flow, always changing."

"But it's not right. It's not supposed to be freezing on my home."

"I merely wanted to point out that 'fix' might not have been the best word. Besides, if the change was so complete, then you assuredly created adaptive techniques as well that everyone lives by. Did anyone mention the world was different?"

"No, but they never do. Things have happened before. Just crazy stuff. Things always changed. My friends always thought I was so weird. They never understood how I always got things confused and mixed up. Like when New York and Paris got switched. No one listened to me. Sometimes I thought I was crazy. Seeing things, remembering things completely wrong. But I'm not.

"Back then I would always think about books or movies where someone was insane and they went to the hospital in a straightjacket and how everything turned out so badly for him. I didn't want that to happen to me. I started hiding." I still hadn't taken a drink from my water, its condensation slipping over my fingers. I set it down and wiped the water onto my pants. "There were so many times I was so afraid that someone would find out, you know? But it really wasn't me all that time. It was my power. I was the only sane person."

Radcliff simply nodded.

"But Peter really helped, when he showed up. I was able to forget it all and stop worrying for once in my life."

For several moments we sat in silence, then Radcliff leaned forward again.

"Does Kris know about Peter?" he asked.

"Yeah... yeah, he does. But you know what? That didn't even stop him. Do you know what he did last night? He wanted me to go to bed with him! Sorry, I know that's probably more than you want to hear about, but I just don't understand him. You know he drinks enough vodka in the morning to get *drunk*? Like, like I don't even know what to do when I'm around him. He's just so... *out* there."

"Yes, I know. I've known him since he was eighteen. I think he'll be leaving the Indulgence Stage soon though. He's the only one still behind, but he seems to be showing the signs."

"What signs?"

"Indications of progression. It could still be a while yet, but I think perhaps his growth will not be so stunted anymore." Radcliff stood. "I should show you why this building is called the Archives."

"Will it help me learn warping?"

"It will help you understand."

We left the lounge and he led me down a hallway deeper into the building. We walked in silence for almost a minute, then I asked, "Which Stage are you in?"

"Myself?" Radcliff chuckled. "I've already passed through my Ego Stage a while ago. That would imply I am in my Wisdom Stage. I suppose I am, but there are still many times when I don't feel wise at all."

"And what exactly is the Wisdom Stage?"

"I do not know how to define it. It's difficult to put your finger on. I know what others before me have written in their poetic terms. It's being. Being for yourself but also for others. A delicate blend of experience brought about by the many years. Knowing your purpose. That's probably the best way to put it: Knowing your purpose."

"What's your purpose then?"

"To guide new warpers."

"Really?"

"Yes."

"Seems a little, I dunno, like 'wise man on the mountain.' "

Radcliff laughed. A quality of it was similar to Kris's laugh, the same joy. "I chose that purpose for myself, though in reality I suppose it was influenced by external sources. To a small degree at least."

I smiled. "Probably." But then something occurred to me. I waited a minute before asking, trying to think of the best way to say it. "Um, Radcliff. What did you do, before?"

"Before?" He looked at me. "Are you referring to my Ego Stage?"

"Yeah. What'd you do? What'd you believe?"

"I'll tell you after this."

He opened a set of double doors, and we entered the strangest room I'd ever seen. It stretched from the floor of the building to the roof and from one side to the other, but was rather narrow. It reminded me of the gap that would be created if you removed a slice of bread from the middle of a loaf. The wall through which we had come was filled with balconies and stairways all leading down to the ground floor. The wall opposite had six iron doors, all evenly spaced across it.

"Come on down," Radcliff said. "I'll show you your door."

"My door? My door to what?"

"The archives of the Archives." Radcliff led me down to the ground floor and to the second door from the left. "Behind each door is a section of the Archives where records from warpers have been left behind. However, each warper can only open the door to the records room of their own predecessors. This one is yours."

"Predecessors meaning the warpers who had my power before me?"

"Yes."

"Kris mentioned this. That the power goes to someone else when the warper dies. But what records are in here?"

"Look and see."

I stepped up to the door. "How? There's no handle."

"Just touch it with the intention of opening it."

"Okay." I reached up and pushed on the door. It swung inwards freely. "Oh."

"Were you expecting something else?" Radcliff smiled.

I shrugged. "I guess not."

Inside was a long room that would have been mistaken for a hallway if it weren't for the rows of shelves that reached all the way to the ceiling many meters above. Every shelf I could see on the left of the room was filled with books; on the right side only the bottom two had any.

"This is *insane*," I said.

"Indeed. They're probably mostly just journals or notes or personal reference material. And certainly not every warper bothered to or was able to leave a record. Case and point, these Archives had been lost and only recently rediscovered about 800 years ago, drifting aimlessly in space. There's so much ancient information here. Found, but still lost."

My head was craned back so far that my neck started to hurt. I rubbed it as I looked over at him. "What?"

"Look in one of them." He pointed at the first shelf on the left.

I took a book at random and opened it. Inside was a written language I didn't recognize. It was unlike anything I had ever seen. "What is it?"

"An ancient language once used by ancient warpers. But at the same point in each room, the books on the shelves all change to another language we don't know either. An instant language change happens like that three times in these records."

"Three different languages?"

"Well, three different languages we don't know. The most recent shift is to English."

"Why?"

"The Archives must have been lost multiple times. 800 years ago, or two generations ago—the generation before mine—the warper with Jett's power found the Archives again."

I was silent a minute, trying to visualize what he had just said. I wasn't successful. "Generations?"

Radcliff chuckled. "A bit confusing I know. The warpers alive at any given point in time can usually be referred to as the 'current generation,' though that description is certainly lacking. There can be a fair amount of overlap between who is new and old to the group, and that's the norm. Take right now for example. The 'current generation' refers to all of us, but technically it only applies to Kris, Alicia, Jett, and Erika. I am from a previous generation, and you are from the next generation. This directly relates to the history I must tell you and what I believed in my Ego Stage. First, did you know all four of them are the same age?"

"They're all 117?"

"Yes."

"How'd that happen?"

"If you look to the right, on the second shelf, you'll see the only two books that are in English here."

I waited for him to continue, but he didn't, so I picked up the two books. One was written by Gen Porth, the other by Tavin Bellic.

"When I went through my Ego Stage," Radcliff started, "I believed myself to be the greatest warper in all of existence. And what I did... I'm not proud of it. I regret it with my every fiber. You need to understand that. But to prove I was the greatest warper, I sought to kill every other warper from my generation. It took nearly twelve years, but eventually I killed all of them." He closed his eyes. "If I think on it too long I can still hear the ones who begged to live. And Gen Porth, whose record you're holding, was actually the first I killed."

I dropped both of the books and took a step back. "Then you killed Tavin too?"

"No. Tavin did not come until later. Remember, this was all in the distant past. I am well over my Ego Stage; you have no need to be afraid of me."

"I, I'm not. I'm just... you, I never would have ever, ever guessed."

"You understand I'm telling you because I'm not hiding it."

"Yeah, I get it. Just finish."

He took a deep breath. "After killing everyone from my generation, I sought out the next warper who would be born. Eventually, almost nineteen years after killing Gen Porth, I found his successor. She didn't know what warping was at all. She knew even less than you. I had her, and, and was about to kill her, but I realized that I should save her until I had collected all of the successors. Then I could kill them all at the same time and make my continued slaying more efficient.

"I took her away to a biome plane with a level two warp lock on it, so she would never learn to use her power and escape. Eventually I had them all together, and I killed them all." He paused. "They never knew. Never knew why. Never knew what was happening or who they were. Nothing. Then for almost nineteen years I rested, knowing that *I* was the greatest. After that rest I went out and killed all the successors

53

again. This cycle continued until I finally left my Ego Stage. Then the current generation came, including Kris.

"I loathed myself afterwards and wanted to redeem myself in some way for what I had done. I took the five of them in and taught them everything I knew. I did for them what I didn't do for all the others."

"Hang on a minute. You said five... but that didn't include me." I looked down at the two books on the floor.

"Yes. Tavin Bellic was your most recent predecessor. He died almost nineteen years ago."

"How?"

"You should ask Kris. They were in a relationship at the time."

"Kris?"

Radcliff held up a hand. "Don't mistake me though. I mean nothing of foul play."

"That's not what I meant."

"Understood. Tavin's death was out of everyone's control, but let me tell you that Kris has *not* fully recovered from it."

"And you want *me* to ask him about it? Excuse me, but I don't think you have any idea how he'll probably react to being asked about that."

"And you do?"

I opened my mouth. I was about to tell him I certainly did know exactly how Kris would respond. "No."

"I have known him longer than you, and it is something you both will need to discuss. Sooner rather than later."

"I'm not sure when that'll happen. But, you killed them all because they were warpers, even though they didn't even know it?"

"Yes. Pre-emptive measures. It's what I thought was the best thing to do back then. In all reality it was even worse than what Jett is doing now."

"This is crazy. Just, crazy. Is everyone here completely fucked up?" I whispered.

"No. No more so than anyone else given such power. I think you're going to need some time to think through all of this before we are able to have complete discourse again. Before I send you off though, just remember, you've entered a world that is already in motion. And I'm afraid we're just getting to the roughest parts." He closed his eyes and in the next moment I found myself standing outside the Archives.

Chapter 6
Die Trying

At first I couldn't move, couldn't react, but then I fell to my knees and punched the ground. A ring of stone spikes shot up around me, jutting away as if to protect. I leaned back, sitting on my legs, and stayed there for a while.

I wondered absently if Radcliff was watching me. As far as I knew he was still in the Archives. The building had no windows, so I doubted it. I pulled out the cell phone Kris had given me and flipped it open. It only had a single button with the letter K on it. I pressed it and listened to the ringing.

"So how'd it go?" Kris's voice was as clear as if he were standing next to me.

"How do you think?"

"Uh, I dunno. But considering the spikes, I assume badly?"

"What? How'd you–?"

"Turn around."

Now I realized it. His voice was coming from both the phone and behind me. I looked over my shoulder at him and chucked the phone aside. "Why didn't you tell me?"

"Tell you what?"

"Tell me that Radcliff killed so many people?"

"Oh. Well..." Kris scratched the back of his head. "Because that was way before. Before any of us were born. And no one likes bringing it up."

I stood, my legs aching from sitting on them. "Whatever. I don't care. Just teach me how to teleport, and I'm going home."

"What?" He stepped forward but didn't cross the line of spikes. "You can't leave."

"I will right after I can teleport."

"But, but, there's so much I want to show you. All the

planets warpers have made. Artwork made from stars and black holes. The, the Reisler Network. Please, Ethan?"

I took a deep breath and looked away from him. "No."

Kris didn't respond for at least a minute. Before saying anything he waved his hand and the spikes disappeared.

"Ethan."

I looked at him and he was suddenly hugging me.

"Please don't go," he whispered.

My arms hung at my sides. I didn't know how to respond. I almost wanted to push him off, but I didn't. Instead I asked, "Who was Tavin?"

Kris pulled away. "He told you about him too?"

"Nothing specific. He told me to ask you."

"Figures." Kris crossed his arms. "He died, and that was that. Now, please, come back to my house. At least 'til tomorrow."

"How did he die?"

"I don't want to talk about him, okay? I really, really don't. Just come back with me."

"Why are you so difficult? I mean, *dammit*, Kris. You're over a hundred years old."

"Over a hundred." He gave a sort of half smile and laughed, but it was forced and empty. "It feels so much longer than that sometimes."

"You know, whatever. That's not important to me. All I want to know is how to teleport. Will you teach me or not?"

Kris looked at the ground. "No. I won't."

"Fine." I turned and walked away from him.

"I'll come back tomorrow," Kris called after me. "There's plenty of rooms you can stay in in the Archives. Once you come around I'll show you everything you've missed!"

I ignored him, and I didn't go to the Archives either. I march right passed it, towards a cluster of trees. I didn't need the Archives or Kris. I could make a little house right here until I learned how to teleport on my own. Before passing the first tree I looked back; Kris was gone.

I didn't care. I knew I didn't care. I told myself I didn't care. I kept walking. The trees grew thicker and soon I was in a proper forest. But it was so silent. Not a bird or deer or squirrel or even insects. I realized it was because Radcliff hadn't made any animals yet. I stopped walking and covered my ears for a moment. It was a trick, a self-made illusion, by making myself think I had blocked out all sound the forest started to look almost homely. I could forget I was on a different planet and imagine I was still on Earth. My Earth before I changed everything.

I continued walking and found a fallen tree to sit on. All I really needed to figure out right now was how to teleport; the rest I could figure out later. I created a piece of paper and a pen, and I wrote down everything I already knew how to do.

make small objects
warp extract?
make food
make bed

It was a short list. I scratched my head with the end of the pen, trying to think of anything else I knew specifically. "Small objects" covered a lot of things though, and moving on from there I assumed the main thing I would need to work on was the scale of things. Then I remembered warp locks, but I didn't know how to actually make those yet, so I wrote it down in parenthesis. Oh, and the manual.

I created a copy of it in my hands and opened the cover. The first page listed several dozen people who had worked on it: Radcliff Farth was the second most recent and Alicia Middelian the first. I opened it from the back and looked through the index for teleporting. Page 394. I flipped to it and found a lengthy explanation twenty-four pages long detailing the process and the theorized mechanics behind it. I groaned. This was not what I wanted.

I started skimming through the essay but couldn't concentrate properly, and in the end I wasn't able to make use of any of the information within. I set everything aside and stood up, deciding to just wing it: I was going to teleport to the tree across the way. I closed my eyes and focused, visualizing myself appearing next to the tree. Drawing up a good amount of warp energy, I tried to make this image a reality. It didn't work. It was the same as when I tried to warp myself clean: I simply couldn't "bend" the warp energy back onto myself.

I slumped back onto the fallen tree. How did they do it if you can't warp yourself? I made myself some water as I thought, wondering what the trick was. I remembered a dinner my family had had several years ago at a restaurant with preforming magicians. The only trick I distinctly remembered was when he had produced our menus out of an empty felt bag. I smiled a little and then breakfast this morning popped into my mind, when Kris had produced the paper with the annexation date of Ireland.

It seemed feasible: warp into existence a piece of paper that had the information you wanted written on it. Like a cheat sheet. I hesitated though; it seemed too easy. Maybe it only worked with things you had known but had forgotten? I could still try. I held out my hand, palm up, and focused. The paper appeared, but there was no writing on it.

"Damn. Useless cheat sheet." I dropped it. It slid through the air, arched upwards, flipped over, and landed on the grass. Something was written on the other side.

Afraid the wind might suddenly rise, I jumped up and grabbed it. The words on the paper were a standard typed print. *You must move not yourself but everything else. That is the trick.*

I raised my eyebrows. Move everything else? It almost sounded like a riddle, but I couldn't help feeling that the words were literal. I remember the first time Kris had taken me off my planet; how we flew through space so quickly, but it felt like we weren't moving at all.

But how could I do that? Surely the entirely of the universe was too huge to move? What would it even be moving *in*? I flipped the page over, double checking for anything else. There was nothing.

What the hell. I closed my eyes and thought of how I would visualize this. The universe was too big for me to imagine it all, let alone to move it and still visualize it properly. I tried a smaller scale instead. I opened one eye to double checking my surroundings, closed it again, and visualized the forest moving without me. There was a small jolt and I found myself several paces away from where I had been standing.

It did work. I actually did it. It was similar to the first time I had teleported, going from my house to the beach. I tried a new image. I visualized the forest, this planet, stars, my planet, my yard; all the while knowing that they were moving and I was not. I drew the energy to me, up from the depths of reality, and focused. Focused. The path home, imagined as a representation: forest, stars, yard. Another jolt struck me as lights flashed before my closed eyes.

I landed in the grass and fell forwards, but I saw my house for a moment as I fell. Each blade of grass was incredibly brittle, snapping like a field of pencil lead beneath me. Then I felt the cold.

I gasped, the thick white haze of my breath billowing before me. I pushed myself up, already shivering badly. It was night; the new freezing night I had created. I stagger to the door and tried to turn the doorknob, but my hands were already numb. And it stuck. My hand stuck to the door knob.

"F-f-f-f-f–" I couldn't even finish the word. I'd never felt anything as cold as this before. I couldn't pull my hand away, couldn't even rip it away, my arm wasn't responding. I tried to ram the door, but my shoulder only hit the metal with a soft *thump*. I couldn't blink, couldn't move my lips. Shit, shit, shit, I was freezing alive. Couldn't breathe, my throat was frozen shut. Don't die. Don't die.

Do something. Warp something. Just ignore the frigged air for a moment. The porch light turned on. Had I done that? Wasn't sure. Just focus. Need warmth. Make warmth. Making warmth. A shimmering dome appeared over the house and instantly the air around me became warm, blazing warm. But it wasn't fast enough. The door opened, pulling me forward. I hit the floor and passed out.

*　　*　　*

The first thing I was aware of was pain across my whole body. It was as if my skin had been pulled taut and there wasn't enough to go around. I twitched my hand and the pain flared stronger. I tried my hardest to keep still.

There were also voices. Or a voice. I didn't want to open my eyes and find out.

"...people get caught ... amount recover..."

"But I just..." Mumbling. They weren't in the room with me.

I cracked an eye ever so slightly. The room was completely unfamiliar at first, but I realized it was the living room in my family's new house. A fire was burning across from the couch I was lying on. Slowly I raised my head, my neck protesting every millimeter I moved. I was under a blanket. The stretching in my neck became too much to handle and I let myself fall back onto the pillow. Could I make morphine?

I found my arms were both wrapped in white bandages that covered them completely. The fingers on my left hand were individually wrapped, but my right was completed encased like a mitten. I focused on creating a shot of morphine and it appeared resting on my stomach quickly enough. I had no idea where to even inject myself. I warped a page of paper floating in the air with the answer.

This new cheat sheet read: *Intravenous injection is the best, but you should not do so. Drink warp extract.* It fell from the air after I had read it.

The pain was building in my skin like lines of fire. I produced a vial of warp extract in my left hand and lifted it to my lips in an agonizing arc. The morphine shot rolled off my stomach and fell to the floor. At last I drank the extract, and the taste was better than I had expected. Rather sweet, almost like watered down honey. I dropped the empty vial. My vision blurred and I closed my eyes, suddenly extremely tired.

A few minutes or maybe longer passed. I really have no idea how long it was.

"Where'd this come from?"

It was my father, and he had picked up the shot of morphine.

"No idea. Don't worry about it." I sat up and stretched my arms. They didn't hurt at all.

He jumped back. "Ethan, you're awake. You shouldn't move. We have a doctor coming."

"No, I'm fine." I started unraveling the bandages on my right arm. "Perfectly fine." And it was true. It felt amazing as if nothing had happened. I smiled.

"But... that's impossible." He was staring at my arm.

"Nope, apparently not." I stood up as I finished with the bandages. "Where's Mom? I thought I heard her."

"Upstairs, but wait, hold there. This is absolutely

impossible." He grasped one of my arms and looked at my skin closely. "You had frostbite all over you."

"Ethan!" My mother had just rounded the corner into the living room. "You shouldn't be standing!"

"Mom, Dad, I'm fine. Really. You can tell the doctor he doesn't need to come."

"But how? I saw your arms myself," my mother said.

"This isn't important right now. I'm *fine*." I reached down into the warp energy, imagining that they believed it.

"Right, good then, healthy as a horse it seems," my father said. "But where have you been? You've been gone for over a day."

"Peter said you simply *disappeared*," my mother said.

"Where is Peter?"

"Home now. His parents posted bail," my father said.

"*Bail*? What?"

"Naturally. His story of you just disappearing into thin air held no water at all. And he would have the financial gain if you died, considering your engagement and all."

I opened my mouth and closed it a few times. Just how much had I actually changed? That wasn't even how engagements worked. "En-engaged, you said?"

My mother exchanged glances with my father before speaking. "Of course. It's been almost six months now."

"Okay, I really can't deal with this right now." I pressed a hand to the side of my head. "I just need to talk to Peter. I'll deal with everything else later."

"But you won't be able to until morning. We were in such a rush to get home after your disappearance we didn't even bother picking up our insulated car from the office," my mother said.

"Besides, what you really need to do is tell us where you've been," my father said. "Disappearing, just to show up on the porch at midnight! We need–"

"Damn it, I don't care! It'll be too hard to explain. I just need to know where Peter lives," I said.

"He's not far from here, about a twelve minute drive," my mother said.

"I'll draw you a map." My father left the room.

I blinked, confused, then realized I had accidently warped

them. It was suddenly like being back at my cousin's house when we were both young. She had her playhouse and the toy family that came within. They would all be saying one thing until I grabbed one family member from her and made it say something else. This was the strangest break from reality I had ever felt before.

My mother simply stood before me, smiling.

"Stop it," I said.

"Okay, darling." Her smile disappeared, and her face became emotionless.

I couldn't stand it anymore. I left the living room, looking for my father. He was leaning over a counter in the kitchen, his pen scratching lines onto a piece of paper.

"Dad?"

"Almost finished."

I waited, not really knowing what to do. Outside the window I could see the ocean and several of the strange cone-shaped trees. The Moon was low on the horizon.

"Here you go, son." He handed the map to me.

It looked like it had been drawn by a robot: perfectly straight lines, every road labeled, far more information than necessary. The fastest route was highlighted and Peter's house was circled.

"How are you going to get there?"

"I'm gonna drive." I folded the map into my pocket and left out the garage door.

I made myself a copy of the key to the non-insulated car and hopped in. The air shield still surrounded the house, but after a few tries I was able to move it to the car. The night was completely empty; not a vehicle nor animal nor whisper of movement anywhere. I wondered how difficult it would be to change the planet back.

I reached Peter's house without really noticing the time it took. I parked the car in the driveway and walked up to the front door, but I hesitated. I didn't want to wake the whole house; I only wanted to talk to Peter. I could make a cell phone and call him, but then again, I could just warp him awake, couldn't I? I considered it, then did so. I focused on Peter, visualizing him waking up and wanting to come down stairs to the door. Quietly. Waking no one else.

A *sik-clack* came from the door as the bolt was unlocked. Peter opened it, wearing just a pair of sweatpants, rubbing an eye with his fist, and gasped.

"Ethan!"

I didn't say anything. I just grabbed him in a hug, holding him tightly.

It took him a moment before he hugged me back. "Where've you been?"

"I don't even know. Not where I should've been."

"Huh?"

"Never mind." I just squeezed him tighter.

"Why isn't it cold out here?"

"That's part of the reason I was gone. Let's go in."

"Yeah, come in." He stepped back and closed the door after me.

The inner door of the airlock was still open, and I realized I might have been a bit too direct in my commands.

"You know, it was the weirdest thing." Peter was walking down the hallway, headed towards the stairs. "I just woke up and thought that I needed to go open the door. I don't even know why, but then you were there!"

"Shhh, I don't want to wake your parents."

"Why?"

"Because I don't know how I'm even going to explain everything to you, let alone them too."

"Is it really that big of a deal?"

"Yeah. Yeah, it is."

He stopped and folded his arms. "I guess this has something to do with you disappearing like a snapshot?"

I nodded.

"How did that even happen? Cameras and mirrors? You know I got arrested for it right? And I was the one who called the cops."

"I know, I know, just come on. I'll try to explain it all upstairs."

Peter only turned on his desk lamp once we reached his bedroom. It cast high shadows on the opposite wall. We spoke in hushed tones.

"So what happened?" Peter sat down on his bed.

"Well..." I took off my shoes and climbed on the bed behind

him, leaning my head on his shoulder. "I don't think there's any way really to say this other than I have superpowers."

Peter laughed. "Yeah, good one. Now, what happened?"

"No, really. Superpowers. Um, reality warping specifically."

"What? You were just asking me about that before you disappeared. Is that code for something?"

"No, it isn't. Watch."

I sat up, held out my hands, and concentrated. A stuffed alligator plushy appeared in my hands.

"Whoa. Whoa!" Peter jumped out of bed. "That's amazing! Make something else."

"Like what?"

"Uh, I dunno. Can you make money?"

"Really, Peter?"

"Yeah, come on. If you can make anything, why not?"

I sighed. A few moments of concentration and a stack of hundred dollar bills appeared in my hands.

"Fucking-*A*! I really hope this isn't a dream. Sure doesn't feel like a dream, but still." He picked up the stack and looked through it. "So you can make anything you want? How was that so hard to explain?"

"Peter, how are you not getting this? This isn't about what I can make. It's about the fact that I can make things out of *nothing*."

"Yeah. I get it." He nodded. "A superpower."

I squinted my eyes, staring at him. I knew he didn't get it. I could tell by the way he was smiling, how he kept glancing down at the stack of bills in his hand.

"No, this is more than that. This is way more. This is like space stuff and planets. We can make *planets* and even change gravity."

"We? Like, do you mean me?"

"No. There's five other warpers out there, and I'm the sixth one. There's only six warpers in the whole universe and somehow *I* got to be one. That's like, impossible odds."

"There's only seven billion people on the planet. Six out of seven billion is like winning the lottery, I think."

"Peter. You do *not* get it at all. There's more Earths out there than just this one. I dunno how many there are, but there's at least a few. The odds are way worse than that."

"Alright, alright, so you're incredibly lucky. But this is really good. Why are you freaking out?"

"Because I can't control it yet. But as soon as I figure it out I'm gonna fix the planet."

"Fix it from what?" Peter sat back down on the bed next to me.

"The freezing nights, first off. That's gotta stop. And, um, we're not actually engaged yet."

He looked me in the eyes. "But, we are. We are engaged. Don't you remember?"

"No, listen, this engagement happened the same time the whole planet changed. When the nights started freezing."

"But the planet's always frozen over at night. That's how the atmosphere works."

"No! That's just it. Everyone can't remember it, because I warped everything wrong. On my birthday when I got into that car crash. You remember that at least, right?"

"Yeah, it was just a fender-bender, but you were getting in your car when it happened. You got knocked to the ground and hit your head."

"A fender–?" I sighed. "Okay, no. Come here."

"What?" He scooched closer to me.

I placed my hands on the sides of his face. "I'm gonna try to make you remember. That should be the easiest. Just, uh, relax I guess." I focused on his mind, but I wasn't sure exactly what I was doing. I hesitated. This wouldn't be like making some object, this was my boyfriend. This was me trying to make him remember, trying to change his brain. I proceeded carefully, speaking slowly. "Think. Just, think. Try to remember the things that have changed. All those times before when something happened but nothing was remembered, because no one saw it but me. Right now. Remember the world as it was but also remember right now. Remember both, so you can see the difference."

Peter gasped and slapped my hands away. "Fuck!"

"Peter?"

"Fuck!" He clenched his hands about his head and pressed his elbows together in front of his face. "We, we, we went to two different high schools! Met two different ways! All those nights when the air was warm at the same nights when they're frozen!

I remember two lives!" He staggered away from the bed but couldn't keep his balance and collapsed against the wall, sliding to the floor.

"Peter! It's okay!" I jumped up after him and wrapped my arms around him, trying to hold him steady. He was shaking violently.

"It's *not* okay." He struggled against me, but I held him tight.

"Peter? Peter, what's happening?" The voice came from outside his bedroom door. It was his mother.

"No! No, you're making this too complicated. Go away," I said.

There was silence beyond the door, followed by receding footsteps.

"Ethan! You can just *do* that. You could do anything. What have you already done? How would I even know?"

"Peter, *stop*. Just trust me, okay. Stop."

He suddenly became calm and stopped trying to squirm away. "Of course I trust you. I've never doubted you."

My stomach went cold as my heart started pounding. It was the same thing I felt whenever I was suddenly concerned. But concerned isn't a strong enough word. It was the same thing I felt when I realized I had just downloaded a virus by mistake or sent a private message to the wrong person.

"Peter. Peter, what about the memories of two lives?"

"No big deal. They're both true."

My eyes went wide. "Go back. Go back!"

He suddenly knocked my arms aside and crawled backwards away from me until he ran into the bed. He took several deep breaths and swallowed before speaking again. "You just changed me. Again. You just fucking changed me again!"

"I didn't mean to! I still don't know how to control it completely. I *promise*."

"I felt it." Peter touched his cheeks. "I felt it. I trusted you so completely, felt like I always had. I believed it. For that minute I believed exactly what you wanted me to. Like retconning." He fell silent.

"...Peter?"

"No. How do I know? How do I know? How do I know?"

"Peter, look. I'm gonna fix everything, okay?"

"I'm gonna die."

"You won't die! I promise. I can *make* you not die."

"No no no no, if you make me forget, forget, no." Tears started falling down his cheeks. "You know it. Losing yourself. It's so easy to lose yourself. If I can't remember, then I'm nothing. You know it. Memories. I have no memories but what you give me. If you take this away, if you make me forget, I'm already gone. I'm gone. When I woke up just twenty minutes ago, he's gone. Dead. I'll be dead again. Molded. Just molded."

"Peter, please. Stop, *please.*"

"I have two lives and only one of them is real. Just three minutes ago I thought the other one was real. Just three minutes ago."

I was on the verge of crying too. I crawled over to him slowly and pressed my hand against his chest. "Don't worry, don't worry. Peter, please, don't worry." I focused on him and made him forget. Forget everything I just gave you. Forget it all. Don't be broken.

His tears stopped immediately, and for a minute we were silent.

"E...than."

"Peter. Peter, I'm *so* sorry. I'm so, so sorry."

"What...? What, happened?"

"Nothing, nothing. Don't worry about it."

"I remember... forgetting. Did I forget something?"

"No. It's fine, it's going to be just fine." I made him forget forgetting. "Peter, please, I'm so sorry."

"For, what?"

"Everything."

Chapter 7
Last Testament of a Killed Cat

About a week passed after that night at Peter's house before I came into contact with another warper again. I suppose I had been waiting for it; I'd known better than to think I could distance myself from these warpers completely. The week leading up to the meeting had been rather productive though.

I had made myself a house out on the ocean 120 kilometers from my family's house. It was small and stood above the water on several tall pillars. I spent my days practicing warping, slowly being able to create and destroy larger and larger objects. I used the cheat sheets to guide my learning rather than the manual. I eventually got a map of my corner of the galaxy and found another Earth that was devoid of Human life only about twelve light years away. I used it for most of my larger practice. The excursions also led me to refine my teleportation skills.

It was on the Moon of this other Earth that they found me. Kris and a woman I'd never met before appeared a few dozen meters away. I had been fine-tuning my weather control on the planet below.

Neither of them approached me immediately, and I felt somewhat annoyed that I should be pulled from my work; I had made quite a good deal of progress today controlling the upper levels of the atmosphere.

I watched them. Kris had stopped the pair of them from coming over immediately, and they were talking though I couldn't hear what they were saying. I considered extending my air bubble to encompass theirs, but that would be too obvious. At last the woman turned away from Kris and headed towards me.

"Ethan, hello," she said as soon as our two bubbles merged. "Who are you?"

"Just right into it then? I'm Alicia Middelian. Kris mentioned me before." She extended her hand.

"Yeah, I remember." We shook hands. "You're the recluse in the library somewhere."

Alicia smiled. "Recluse, maybe, but I prefer to think of it as 'devoted.' You've been something of a recluse yourself though, from what I've heard." She put her hands in her pockets.

She had a narrow chin and surprisingly high cheekbones, which I assumed was the Hispanic and Elf mixing in her, and her hair was cut short. But her pair of glasses drew my attention the most. They had no temples: the part that would go around the sides of her face and behind her ears, which were pointed as Kris had said. At first I thought the glasses were simply floating by some warping trick, then I realized the bridge of the glasses was pierced through the bridge of her nose. They were literally attached to her face.

I blinked in surprise. "I... I guess I have been."

"Kris has been worried." She nodded her head in his direction.

He looked like he was skulking: head down, arms crossed. He looked away as soon as I glanced over at him.

"I don't understand him," I said.

"I wouldn't expect you to," Alicia said, "considering how long you've known him. Now, I'm perfectly fine with standing on the Moon, but perhaps we could go to your place? Be a bit more comfortable I should think."

"Is Kris coming?"

"Would that change your mind one way or the other?"

I thought a moment. "I guess not."

"Then we'll go." She raised her arm and quickly waved twice for Kris to come over.

He approached us but was shuffling his feet, knocking clouds of dust up behind him.

"Ay dios mio. Come on!" Alicia called out.

Kris didn't respond. Once he reached us he just said, "Hey."

" 'Hey?' *Hey?* That's all you have to say?" She hit him on the back of the head.

"Ah! What?" He rubbed the back of his head reflexively.

Alicia muttered something then turned back to me. "Let's go. You'll have to 'port us since you're the only one who knows where you're staying."

I smirked. "I don't like teleporting actually. I'll just make a doorway." I waved my hand and a door in a freestanding frame appeared a meter away. I opened it. "After you."

Alicia looked confused, but she went ahead and walked through it and Kris followed.

"How did you–?" Alicia started to ask.

"The few times I have teleported I've always found it hard to do." Once inside my house's entry hall I closed the door and let it disappear. "Now the cheat sheets I've been reading have always said that the most direct route is the best for warping. I remembered some short videos I'd watched about wormholes and dimensional stuff, and after some experimenting I was able to make my first doorway. Works perfectly."

"That's incredible." A notepad and pen appeared in Alicia's hands. "Bring it back; I need to see this."

"Sure. Here." I created the doorway again.

"It is true that the more specific your warp then the less energy you need." Alicia walked around the open doorway. "I've never seen anything like this though, nor have I read any records of something similar. Fascinating. Just a general distortion on the opposite side." She scribbled something down and walked through it. "Give me a few minutes."

Kris sighed exceptionally loud. He had walked over to one of the windows and looked out over the ocean.

"You don't approve?" I walked next to him. "You see, I can learn things on my own."

"That's not it. It's just Alicia. She's been like this ever since she started booking it. No fun like the good old days." He crossed his arms.

"I heard that!" Alicia called out through the doorway.

"The parties?" I asked.

"Yeah." Kris grinned a moment, but it faded. "Before everything went to hell. Before Jett and Erika left and before..." He fell silent and kept staring out the window.

"Before what?"

Kris just shook his head.

Alicia was standing behind us and she cleared her throat.

"Well, um, I'm going to have to look into this doorway business more later. In the meantime, Kris, I think it would be best if you took care of that errand now, yes?"

"Sure." Kris turned to me and gave a sort of joke salute with three fingers. "Later." He disappeared.

I waited a moment.

"Is he really that angry at me?"

"Not exactly 'angry,' but yes. He's never really been one for subtly. Maybe that will change." She glanced out at the water. "So where are we?"

"120 kilometers from the coast."

She nodded and waited a moment, then asked, "Where is your family?"

"Why?"

"Just curious. Wondering how involved you still are with them."

I hesitated. "I don't really want to be around them right now. They just seem so hollow now. And I can't really explain any of this to them."

Alicia nodded. "Not surprising. Humans and other self-aware beings are better off being left in the dark."

"Others?"

"Of course. We can make any sort of creature or race we want."

"Oh, right." And with that, any possible conversation topic to continue into preemptively vacated my mind. What was I to say now?

"You also mentioned 'cheat sheets?' " She raised a single brow.

Ah ha! I asked what should I say and created a paper in my hands. "Yeah, I saw Kris do it once. He made a piece of paper that told him when his Ireland was annexed." I glanced down and quickly read the cheat sheet. *Moose.* So apparently they didn't do social interactions.

"Ah, yes, I'm familiar with that, but they're usually referred to as 'fact sheets.' " Alicia suddenly grabbed the paper from me before I could react. "Useful for common knowledge, but somewhat limited. What did you ask it?"

"Why do they just say 'moose' if they don't have an answer?"

She shrugged. "It's something more interesting to say than nothing? Doesn't really matter."

"It seems weird."

"Your house is so open and airy. I rather like it."

"Oh, thanks."

"Also, Kris mentioned your planet is different? Something about the atmosphere?"

"Yeah. It freezes at night."

"Is there a way to go outside?"

"There's the back patio."

"Perfect. Show me."

I led her outside. She created a gyroscope hanging by a thread and stuck the thread in the air, so it was attached to nothing. Next Alicia created a small cylindrical device and stuck it in the air as well, then she started writing in her notebook again.

I waited as she ignored me and wrote in silence. Now what? Normally you should offer a guest a drink, right? Does that apply to warpers? Radcliff had offered me something to drink in the Archives.

"So, something to drink?" I asked.

"Sure, sure." Alicia's eyes never left her notepad.

"I'll be right back."

I walked into the kitchen and could still she her on the patio via the half wall and the glass doors. I pulled out two cups from a cabinet but didn't know what to serve her. I guess I should have asked. I brought the empty cups out.

"What would you like?" I asked.

"Oh, I already made myself some coffee." Alicia sipped from a blue mug in her hand. "Always excellent." She smiled.

"Uh, okay." I set the extra cup on the patio table.

She looked down at her notebook then back up at me as if realizing something. "Did you leave to get those cups?"

"Yeah."

"Why?"

"They were in the kitchen."

"You keep things in your kitchen?"

"Doesn't everyone?"

"No, no. You can just make whatever you need. No reason to leave things lying around."

"So you all do that? I thought that was just another of Kris's oddities." I shook my head. "But I like my house to feel lived in. Not empty."

"His furniture *is* eccentric, but kitchenware is always unnecessary. Suit yourself though, I suppose." Alicia tore out a page from her notebook and forced it into my hand. "These are my calculations. They explain what you need to do."

The page in my hand had line after line of complex formulas with more variables and symbols than actual numbers. A few numbers were circled. "What is this?"

"Atmospheric measurements and the changes you'll need to make in order for this planet's atmosphere to match a standard Earth atmosphere."

"I can't understand a single thing on here. But that's a three there." I pointed. "And I think this is a Greek letter."

Alicia sighed and snatched the page back out of my hand. "Wasted. All of it's wasted. I'll set your planet back. Just give me a minute." She stuck the coffee mug in the air.

"Whoa! No, no! I want to do it."

"Oh I don't have time for this nonsense. I'll just go ahead and reset it for you."

"*No.* I'll do it. It's my planet."

Alicia hesitated a moment before lowering her arms. "Fine. But when you give up, you can come ask me for help and I won't give you a hard time about it. Or at least, not a lot." She smiled, then detached one of the lenses from her pieced glasses and wiped it on a cloth she produced.

I was having mixed feelings about her, but that wasn't surprising considering the other warpers I had met.

"You don't know about Nókrutar yet, do you?" She was looking up at the roof, shading her eyes from the sun.

I looked up at the roof too. "I do. Radcliff told me a little about them.

"Did he mention they always attack warpers violently once they notice you? And considering you're fairly close to a Dark Zone–" She was suddenly silent.

I looked over at her but she was gone. "The hell...?" I checked over the railing even though I hadn't heard a splash.

"There, much better."

I spun round. "Where'd you go?"

"Slipstream. Sorry, my warping power is the most different. I can move around warp energy as much as I like, but I can't warp anything larger than a text book without first going into a slipstream. You'll be safe now though." Alicia pointed up at the roof.

Floating a meter above the shingles was a large yellow-white crystal that looked similar to the ones floating at the corners of the Archives.

"Man, there's so much stuff I don't know yet about all this warping stuff."

"Naturally," Alicia said, "and that's why I'm here. I guess we did get a bit sidetracked, didn't we, what with your doors and atmospheres and crystals, oh my." She laughed heartily for a moment or two then stopped abruptly. "Let's get back on track. Quick, let me see your hand."

"Huh?"

"Your hand. Quickly, dear."

I held out my left hand. "What do you–?"

She tapped the palm of my hand with a finger and burning seared over my skin.

"Ah!" I jerked my hand away, clutching it.

"Don't worry, it'll only hurt for a moment more. I'm actually the only warper who can warp other warpers, but that there is the extent of my abilities."

I looked down at my hand. A white ring was glowing on my skin, fit perfectly into the valley of my palm. "What is it?"

"A palm ring. It's a tracking sort of thing. Everyone has one, and so long as it's active I can know where you are and how your vitals are doing."

"You're tracking me now?"

"I do it to everyone. Helps keep people safe. But you can turn it off, so it's really up to you."

I looked back down at it and willed the ring to be off. The ring faded.

"See? Perfect work. Now, about Kris."

"What about Kris?"

"It's a tad complicated." She tapped a finger to her chin then continued. "You don't know about the power-matching phenomena yet, do you?"

I stared at her blankly. "No?"

"Of course, of course. Now. There's this strange little quirk to who becomes a warper. We know that when a warper dies, the very next Human to be conceived inherits the warping power. Oddly enough though, each of the six powers is a 'counterpart' of sorts to another. For example, you and Kris. Your powers are counterparts. Now I don't mean opposites; it's not like that. The two powers just *go* together... same as the two warpers do. You see what I'm saying?"

I suddenly felt like I needed to do something with my hands. I needed to put them somewhere other than hanging from my sides. I wanted to put them in my pockets, behind my back, and across my chest all at the same time.

"Ethan?"

"Uh, yeah. Um..." I took a deep breath. "You're saying I'm *destined* for Kris, or something?"

Alicia's eyes grew wide. "Yes! But no." She drummed her fingers on the railing. "Basically, you're going to find that you've never been more compatible with anyone else as you are with Kris. Essentially."

I finally settled on crossing my arms. "Well, I guess that idea explains things." Like that first night at Kris's house. "I really don't like this. What about Peter?"

"Peter?"

"My *current* boyfriend."

She mouthed the word "oh" but didn't actually voice it. "Hmm. Troubling. I'm very sorry to say, but, no warper can ever truly be happy with a non-warper. I've been with several myself, and it only works in the short term."

"Why?"

"Have you spoken with this Peter since you've become a warper?"

I hesitated. "Yeah."

"Did it go well?"

I didn't answer.

"Right... that's what I mean," Alicia said.

"We'll see."

"Fine, fine. Now, I'm telling you this, because I want Kris to be happy, but I also don't want you getting scared off again."

"That's not what happened. I didn't get sca–"

"Not important. Anyways, Kris has been more down this

week than he's been in a long time. He's also been as anxious as a badgermole on a boat. He doesn't want anything to happen to you. Just give him a chance, hm?"

"You know it's not that I don't believe you, it's that I'm already spoken for."

Alicia stepped closer to me and put a hand on my shoulder. "But don't you see? It's like being in love with a puppet. Worse yet, a puppet you control."

"Peter is *not* a puppet." I knocked her hand away from me.

She sighed. "Okay, but you'll see. Can you at least promise me that you'll give Kris a chance?"

"Why would I do that? I just met you."

"True, true. Then let me rephrase that: Will you at least promise me that you'll give us all a chance?"

I was silent a moment. "Fine. But I doubt I'll be seeing any of you very often."

"You might be surprised." She picked her mug of coffee back out of the air where she had left it. "In any case, it was nice to meet you, Ethan, but I need be going. Important date at the Restaurant."

"Alright. Later, I guess."

Alicia hesitated. "And, you do know what the Restaurant is, correct?"

"No."

"Ah! Then I'll have to show you! Lovely place, really." She took my hand before I could react and teleported us.

Chapter 8
To Mourn the Loss

My back porch vanished around us, and we both hurled through the familiar light show. Just before it ended everything went black and we arrived.

We were in some sort of fast food restaurant, like the kind you'd find next to a corner store. Dingy was the first word that came to mind. The square gridded ceiling, hanging lights with dull yellow bulbs, small tables, chairs that would wobble just by looking at them, the windows black as if maybe they had been painted over, and a robot behind the counter. The robot was built in the shape of a Human but was un-bashfully non-Human: whole body metallic, eyes glowing white, and an oval speaker where a mouth should be.

"What is this? I have not seen this many people here since that last five-way birthday party," said the robot in a voice that wasn't monotone, but the attempt at inflection was almost as bad.

"Oh, come on, Bot. You should be happy to see us. Especially the newest warper here." Alicia grinned and poked my shoulder.

"Oh yes, overloaded with the emotion." Bot's arms crossed with a *clank*.

"Bot?" I asked. "That's your name?"

"Yes."

Alicia grinned. "I'll let you two get to know each other." She walked away.

I looked after her and saw that Kris was here along with a young girl I'd never seen before who looked about fourteen years old. I suddenly felt trapped, to use the old cliché, between a rock and a hard place.

"You *can* leave my presence. I won't be disappointed, I can assure you," said Bot.

"Um..." I looked between Bot and Kris again, then left without saying anything more.

Alicia had joined Kris's and the mystery girl's table.

"Bot scare you off?" Kris asked.

"No." I sat down.

The girl laughed, then started coughing, half a French fry still in her hand.

"Are you okay, dear?" Alicia asked.

"Yes–" she coughed. "Mom. I'm fine. Just," cough, "went down the wrong pipe." She recovered. "Don't you know that so long as you're coughing you're not choking?"

"Yes, yes. I know. I just wanted to make sure." A plate of grilled salmon appeared before Alicia.

The girl leaned forward to talk to me. "You see what she does to me? See what I gotta put up with?" She smiled.

"Oh hush," Alicia said.

"You look so confused. Again." Kris grinned and leaned back in his chair. Less than half a cheeseburger sat before him.

"Well I wonder why. I get taken to a restaurant of some sort with a smarmy robot, and you have a *daughter*?" I turned to Alicia.

"Yes. You're surprised? Also, I don't think 'smarmy' is the word you mean," Alicia said.

"Why didn't you tell him about me, Kris?" The girl punched him playfully.

"I was getting to it, but he ran away. Also, smarmy sounds like the right word to describe Bot to me." Kris raised his voice, obviously on purpose.

Bot gave no indication of even having heard Kris.

" 'Smarmy' means something more like an insincere flatterer. Common mistake," Alicia said. "Also, this is Raine, my daughter."

Raine tipped her chair forward, extending her hand to me. "And you're Ethan. Kris has been complaining about you all week."

"Don't tell him that!" Kris leaned in front of Raine to block her from my vision. "Don't listen to this brat."

"Rude." Raine jumped off her chair and came around the

table, bypassing Kris completely. "You have to show me your house on the ocean. Kris really liked it."

"Raine!" Kris said behind her.

"Uh, okay." I said. "Later sometime, I guess."

Raine's voice had a strange affect to her persona. It made her sound older.

"Okay, okay, Raine, you can talk to him later." Kris got out of his chair. "Right now I need to talk to him."

"Then talk to him." Raine grinned.

"I mean *alone*."

"And I don't get any say in this?" I asked.

Raine laughed.

"Well yeah, but this is really important, okay?" Kris looked right into my eyes.

I glanced over at Alicia for a moment and sighed. "Okay, fine. What is it?"

"Come over here." Kris walked away to a table at the other end of the Restaurant.

I glanced back at the other two.

"Don't look at me. I'm just eating lunch here." Alicia hid a smile by eating another bite of salmon.

"Don't look at me either." Raine sat back down, grinning widely.

"Dammit," I muttered very quietly to myself. I considered just making a doorway out of here, but I had just promised Alicia that I'd give them all a chance. This was obviously all a ploy to get me to talk to Kris, but I supposed it was at least well intentioned. I reached the new table and sat down. The chair was off balance.

"Okay, before you say anything, I wanted to say that I'm sorry for how things got off. I don't think we really got the best impression of each other, and I'd like to start fresh." Kris extended his hand to me. "Can we do that?"

I was silent a moment. "This was all Alicia's idea, wasn't it?"

He opened his mouth, closed it, then let his hand fall to his lap. "Yeah. But so? I still mean it."

"Okay, see, I think I understand what's going on from what Alicia told me, but I don't really have a problem with you. It's Peter. I've *told* you."

"I know." Kris looked away. "I know. But, can't we at least be friends?"

That caught me off guard. There was obviously no reason why we couldn't be, but it seemed obvious that "friends" still wasn't his end goal. I thought about calling him out, though I wasn't sure.

"Fine. Friends." I offered my hand to him.

He closed his eyes and shook my hand. Then we sat in silence.

I ventured something first. "So... where are we?"

"The Restaurant, didn't Alicia tell you?"

"Yeah, but I mean, where is it? Why are the windows black?"

"They aren't black. It's the Void that's black."

"The Void?"

"Yeah. Big, black, and empty. What'd you think 'Void' meant?"

"I know what a void is. That's not what I'm asking. I want to know where we are. Where is the Void? In space?"

"Nowhere. Well, for all intents and purposes, nowhere. There's theories and stuff like it's outside the Universe or in a membrane-like thingy between realities, but it's all just fluff. Impossible to really know or test it."

"Why would someone put a restaurant in this Void?"

"Oi. Hey, Bot! How about a history lesson?"

"I am not your textbook. Tell him yourself." Bot didn't move.

Kris sighed. "Geez. Okay, so, the Restaurant's always been here, or at least as long as anyone knows. There's almost no warp energy in the Void, but a little bit naturally trickles up here. We can make food here with the free ambient energy."

"But everywhere has free ambient energy."

"It's different though, can't you feel it? It's more pure. It doesn't matter which warping power you have, you can use the energy here directly without any of the normal intermediaries."

"Oh. So that's why the Restaurant is here?"

"Yeah. I already said this." He chuckled and leaned back in his chair.

"You didn't explain it that well. That's why I didn't get it."

"Sorry," Kris said.

I glanced up at the ceiling. "So does Bot know if the Restaurant has always been here?"

"Nah."

"Then why's Bot here?"

"Bot must've been put here by some warper long ago. Someone's gotta run the place."

"But if we're the ones making the food, what does Bot do?"

"I dunno." Kris shrugged.

I glanced at Bot, and I wondered how that lack of knowledge didn't bother Kris.

"So... what do you want to talk about now?" he asked.

"I have no idea."

"Well pick something."

"Why do I have to?"

"Because I said so first. Obviously." Kris leaned forward.

"Pssh." I thought a moment and my Earth came to mind. "Did you ever do anything to your home after you became a warper?"

"Nah. I just left."

"Why?"

"Nothing there for me. And here, here I have everything I could ever want. The choice was obvious. At least for me."

"Really? But, how could you just leave your whole life behind?"

"Well, I mean, I guess I didn't completely drop it like cold turkey. But, like I said, there wasn't really much to hold on to." He was silent a moment. "I gotta show you something."

"What?"

"I told you about the parties. You gotta see this picture." He held out his hand and a photo appeared in it. "It's of the good old days."

I took it. It showed a dark room with six people posed together. There were streaks of light from the ceiling and fog around their feet. For a jarring moment I thought Peter was in the photo. Then I realized it was actually Kris with red hair. He was wearing black jeans and a black jacket with the hood up and no shirt on underneath. Next I recognized Alicia and Radcliff and my jaw dropped. Alicia's hair was green and spiked up in a mohawk with a silver hoop pierced through the bridge of her nose. Radcliff was there too, but he was the more conventionally dressed in a button up shirt and jacket held over his shoulder. There was another couple to the other side who I assumed was Jett and Erika. Jett was wearing a fedora and purposely pulling down the brim to cover one eye, and Erika had a copper robotic bird on her shoulder. And the last person, he had to be Tavin. He had his arm around the back of Kris's neck and was kissing his cheek, his other hand raised in a peace sign.

"Wow," I whispered.

"Yeah. This was one of the rare ones when even Radcliff was there."

"You look really different with your hair dyed red."

"No, it's dyed black now. My hair's naturally red. I just wanted something different."

"Oh." That was really odd. "And this is Tavin?" I pointed to him in the photo.

"Well, yeah. It's the only group photo I have." He pulled it out of my hands. "Sorry."

"For what?"

Kris stared down at the photograph. "That he's kissing me in it."

"Why would you need to apologize for that?"

He hesitated. "I dunno." He dropped it onto the table.

I touched the corner and spun it round so I could see the image properly again. "It's a really good picture."

Kris just shrugged. "I don't even know why I showed it to you." He snapped his fingers and it disappeared. He stood up, his chair screeched across the floor.

Alicia and Raine both looked up at us.

"Where are you going?" I asked.

"Nowhere." He disappeared.

"Kris. Dammit." Alicia stood. "I'll follow him. I can't believe he's doing this. Stay with Raine. Someone always has to be with her." She disappeared.

"Did he really just–? I can't believe this." I leaned forward, propping my head up with an arm.

Bot was still standing behind the counter motionless, and Raine tapped her knife against her plate.

"He's just sad." Raine walked over to me. "You know, I wish I could say he wasn't always like this, but I've really only know him well these last sixteen years or so. I can't really remember how he was before Tavin died."

I looked at her. "How old are you?"

"Twenty-seven."

"Wha–?" I started laughing. "Oh come on. How old are you really?"

"Twenty-seven, really. I'm a Warper Born, born of two warpers, so I age only half as quickly."

"Alicia and...?" For a second I thought Raine was referring to Alicia and Kris, but then I remembered the pairings Alicia had mentioned before. "Radcliff?"

Raine nodded. "Yep, that's them."

My gaze drifted as I considered them as a couple. Why had I never seen them together? Of course I'd only seen each of them once, but still.

"Alicia tells me that Kris took Tavin's death really badly and has never been quite the same afterwards," Raine said.

"Sure, but that's no reason for him to keep disappearing like that." I walked to one of the black windows. "And he's just so, I don't even know. Fast paced. Even if I didn't have Peter to think about, I'd still want him to slow down." I sighed and started pacing and passed the front glass door. It had a sticker which read: Watch your step. "Can I open this?"

"I guess. It's not locked." Raine had followed me.

"We won't get sucked out or something, will we?"

"It's a Void, not a vacuum." Raine smiled.

"Is there a difference?"

"They're called different things, aren't they?" She shrugged.

"Alright." I pulled the door open and a quick whoosh of cold air breezed into the Restaurant. It blew right in my face, making me close my eyes, and I let the door close. It was accompanied by the jingle of a bell.

"That was weird," I said.

"A little. Thanks for doing that though. I wanted to know what the Void was like too."

"Why didn't you just look then?"

"No one's ever opened the door before all the times I've been here. And *you're* the warper."

"You can't warp? Even though your parents are warpers?"

"No, I can't. It gets really frustrating. Hanging out with

warpers all the time and they always forget I can't do the same stuff they can." She crossed her arms. "They could remember if they actually tried to. My mom's recently been trying to teach me how though."

"Teach you warping? But you just said you can't."

"I know, but my mom wants me to try anyways. She's explained what the warp energy feels like, but I've never felt anything close to it. Don't get me wrong, I'd be absolutely ecstatic if I could learn it, but there's just not–"

"Wait, wait." I waved my hand at her. "What's that?" I pointed into the Void.

There was a small white dot of something far off, or I assumed it was far off due its size. It seemed to be coming towards the Restaurant.

Raine cupped her hands to the glass of the door and gasped. "It's *Jett*. Jett's coming here!" She turned to me, panic in her eyes.

"A-are you sure? I though he was... busy."

"I'm not a kid, I know he's killing people. We need to go! Get me outta here." She pulled on my arm.

"Okay, okay. Hang on a sec. Let me– let me focus."

I turned around, ready to make a doorway and I saw Bot, still just standing there, like nothing was happening. The doorway appeared, blocking my view, and we hurried through. Inside my house I shut the door and let it disappear.

"That was close. That was way too close," Raine said.

"This is the whole 'avoid Stage 4 warpers,' right?"

She nodded. "But more so, for me. He... he wants me dead. Specifically."

"*What*? Why?"

"Because I'm not a warper and I know warpers exist. He wants all non-warpers that know, descendants or otherwise, destroyed. There's probably underlying grudges against my father at work too. Alicia explained it all to me."

"Not just the Rurrians? He wants to kill Warper Born too?"

"Yes. And there's two planets, Riktor and Ven, that are exclusively filled with the Warper Born and their descendants. Warpers made those planets long ago and they've always protected them, but now Jett could threaten that." She paused. "It's a good thing he's attacking the Rurrians first."

I shook my head. "I don't like this."

"Me either. But we need to get in touch with my mom. Let her know where we are and that Jett's at the Restaurant."

"How do we do that?"

"Use the palm ring."

I looked at my left palm, and the white circle lit up. "Oh. How?"

"I dunno. I know you can talk to Alicia through it somehow. Just hold it up to your head and think about wanting to talk to her, I guess."

I shrugged and I raised my hand. "Hello?"

Nothing happened for a moment and I started to feel rather ridiculous. Then I heard her voice in my ear. "Ah, Ethan, great timing. I've got Kris. He went to his house, but we're coming back now."

"No, stop. Jett's at the Restaurant."

"*What*? Where are you? Where's Raine!"

"It's fine. She's safe. She's with me, at my house."

"Thank the powers." And the connection ended.

Kris and Alicia appeared next to me, and Alicia instantly grabbed Raine in an embrace.

"Oh Raine! Are you okay? Were you scared? Everything's okay now."

"*Mom*. I know, I'm fine. Let me go." She pulled away.

"Don't leave this room, Raine." Alicia looked at me. "Thank you so much for getting her out of there. What did Jett say?"

"Nothing. He was out walking in the Void. We left before he got there."

"Good. Don't get involved with him, whatever you do."

"You're fine?" Kris asked.

"Yeah. Nothing even happened."

"I'm sorry."

"What for this time?"

"For, you know... I just needed a moment. Alone."

"You could've just said that."

He looked away and didn't reply.

"We need to get back to the Library." Alicia took Raine's hand. "Let you two have some time. See you both later." They disappeared.

I waited a moment in the silence. "So now what, Kris?"

"I dunno. What do you wanna do?"

"That's not what I'm asking. I mean are you okay now?"

"I'm always okay." He crossed his arms. "Your house needs more decoration."

"This is only a temporary place. I don't care too much what it looks like."

"Oh, good. Here." He reached up and started creating a light orange linen draped across the ceiling of the entry hall that cut across the house from front door to the porch door, his hands mirroring the dips as he moved them over above his head. In the roof he created several skylights and the light filtered through the linens, giving everything a slight amber hue. "There."

I looked up at them. "Why?"

"Why not?"

I shook my head. "They're nice, Kris."

"You like them?"

"Yeah. But right now I'd really like to work on my planet some more."

Kris sighed. "Hmm. Why don't you take a break? I can show you what a Single Action Puzzle is."

"What is it?"

"They're worlds that are set up like a game, and you can reset them. The game is to achieve whatever the goal is by making the smallest single change you can. Like one time I was able to avert a World War III by changing one diplomat's food from hot spice to mild spice. It was really clever." He grinned.

"That sounds a little, taxing. I'd rather not go solve random puzzles now while I have my own to fix."

"We don't have to. There's tons of other things. Or we could just *go* somewhere. Go and see what we find."

I thought a moment. "Like where?"

"I dunno. Let's find out." He grabbed my wrist and teleported us.

We ended up standing in ankle deep water in an oasis surrounded by desert. Half a dozen tents were set up, and a woman completely swathed in fabric and a head wrap screamed and fell backwards, trying to crawl away.

"Oh. Sorry!" Kris called out to her.

"Great. My feet are soaked now."

"I know. This is really disappointing." He turned around in a circle. "Normally this works so much better."

"Are we still on my planet?"

The woman had gotten to her feet and ran to the cluster of tents. A few others had appeared and approached her, pointing at us and raising their voices.

"No, I jumped us to a random Earth between six thousand and six million light years away. Let's go to the nearest city. That'll be better."

"Yeah, I think we need to get out of here."

He teleported us again, and we ended up on a flatpacked earthen road in a corner of a city. The buildings were made with dusty tan bricks and weren't very tall. Not many people were a round and donkey tethered to a cart was standing nearby. The sun was high in the sky, and I instantly felt too hot.

"Oh, this is an old version of Earth then." Kris warped our shoes dry.

"What is this? Mesopotamia?"

"Hell if I know. It could be an early Earth, or it could just be completely different. Radcliff explains the different types of Earths in this 'normality bell curve' or something like that. Most are really similar, and the really weird ones are far and few between. I would call it more of a 'how-likely-you'll-find-something-boring' bell curve."

"Sounds like you."

"What's that mean?"

"Just that it sounds like you."

"Whatever. Hey, we're already here. Let's have some fun anyways."

"I thought you just said this was boring?"

"That's why we make fun." He started ticking off on his fingers. "We could go find whatever their local deities are and pretend to be them, or make some alien saucers and simulate an alien invasion, or make it night time and create a zombie mob, or make two giant robots and duel each other. Or, or! Given the lack of tech here, we could just make some endless spray paint cans and claim they're magic!"

I blinked and waited for him to start laughing. "Did I miss the joke?"

"No. Here, here, just think of your favorite action story set in a desert, and we'll re-enact a scene or two from it."

"Hang on, hang on. Let's take the giant robot dual you mentioned first."

"Good choice. They're really fun." Kris nodded quickly.

"No, no. Wait. What about all the people around?"

Kris tilted his head to the side. "What about them?"

"Won't hundreds or thousands of them get crushed or blown up while we're just fighting for fun?"

"Sure, I guess. There's nothing really to protect them."

"And you don't see that as a problem?"

"No. Why? We can just fix it."

"*Fix it*? Fix what? Their death?"

"Yeah. Easy. Watch." Kris pointed at the nearest pedestrian: a tall man wearing a white robe. He was walking by but eyeing our clothing. "Dead." He fell to the ground.

I stared at him. A few others nearby stopped and were looking at us.

"But now, alive." Kris snapped his fingers and the man was walking again as if he had never even fallen down.

I realized I was holding my breath. "Kris. W-what?"

He looked at me. "It's no big deal. You can see for yourself." He snapped his fingers again and the man felt to the ground.

"Alive. Dead. Alive. Dead. Alive." Each time he snapped his fingers, and each time the man either fell or walked, completely oblivious that anything was happening to him.

"Kris, stop!" I grabbed his arm and turned him away from the man.

"But, Ethan, nothing's wrong. He didn't even feel any pain. And look, he's totally fine."

"But he was dead!"

"He's not real!" Kris pushed me away, and the Reality Converter appeared in his hands. "Can't you see? It doesn't matter what happens to these people." He walked to the nearest building and went inside.

I looked around quickly. More people were gathering nearby, talking in quick voices and pointing at me. "Forget!" I waved my hand at them and ran after Kris.

I pushed open the building's ill-fitted door and inside looked like someone's home. Kris had set the Reality Converter on a rough wood table and was busying himself with plugging it in. He had clamped it to the table, stuck a small wire into a loaf of bread, and now was looking for a third thing. A woman was couched over a cooking pot that hung above a fire, frozen.

"Kris, what are you doing now?"

"I'm going to show you what I'm talking about." He took the cable with a spiked end and wedged it next to an exposed brick in the wall.

He held his hands over the silver sphere. I could feel the warp energy flowing past me and into him. Kris raised a hand and the whole front of the house became transparent and we could see the street. A father outside gasped as his young son laughed and pointed. Then they both fell to the ground. Everyone out on the street fell to the ground. Even the donkey tied to the cart fell to the ground. The woman slumped over and hit the floor.

Kris lowered his hand, but continued replenishing his warp energy as if he had not just refilled it. "They're all dead now. Everyone on this planet just died."

"Dead?" I asked. "You mean you just killed an entire planet! What the fuck! What the *fuck* was that for?"

"To show you this." Kris raised his hand again and the street changed. The donkey was standing, people were walking, the child was still laughing. The wall returned opaque.

The woman got up off the ground and gasped. She started yelling in some other language, but Kris froze her again.

"You see," Kris said, "these people aren't real. They can't truly die and they can't truly live. With us around they're meaningless, because they can be changed so completely."

He was still drawing up warp energy, and my ears started ringing. I massaged my left temple. "No, no. That was genocide. You just killed billions of people!"

"I brought them back. That was *not* genocide. I didn't just kill them to kill them. I was making a damn point!"

"If that's not genocide, then I'd hate to know what Jett's doing."

"He's committing genocide, because he's trying to kill specific people, and he sure as hell isn't going to be bringing them back once he's done it." His hand was still over the Reality Converter.

"Everyone on a planet isn't specific enough? Well tell me, what about Tavin? Did Tavin go around killing random people just because he could? Did he?" My mouth was going dry.

"No! No! He never did and never would! I did this to make a *point*! Don't bring Tavin into this! You don't know him and you never will, because you're not him!" He raised the Converter, ripping its connections apart and making it disappear. "Dammit, fuck!" He groaned and leaned forward, his fingers almost touching his ears. The room was getting darker.

"What's happening?" I glanced around quickly; the shadows in the corners were expanding and my lungs started to feel constricted as the ringing in my ears grew.

"I drained too much. I wasn't paying attention. God, *dammit*."

The burning fire when out and hardly any light continued to filter in through the cracks in the wooden door. Two deep blue eyes opened in the darkened recess behind a large wicker basket. A Nókrutar rose up from the shadows, sliding from behind the basket, a humanoid silhouette, rough around the edges and wavering like it wasn't fully physical. Its eyes were its only feature, and it started into me, never blinking. More eyes opened as they formed out from cracks, down from the weaved roof, or from the dark ashes of the fire pit.

"What do we do?" My voice broke as I spun around, trying to count them, but I kept losing track. They were all reaching out for us, their eyes like fire: streaming off to the sides and trailing after them when they moved.

"Run. We just run!"

Kris barreled into me, his arms around my chest, and for a sickening moment we floated in the air even as it felt like we were slowly being stretched. Finally we broke free and teleported away. I hit the ground hard and Kris landed on me. I groaned as countless points of pain jabbed into my back.

We had landed on a pebbled beach with small waves rising and sinking between the spaces of the rocks. It was overcast, and a slight mist was drifting from the sky. Kris rolled off me and sat up quickly.

"I'm sorry. I'm so sorry."

I just groaned again as I slowly sat up and rubbed my back.

"Warp extract?" He held out a vial to me.

I took the extract but didn't say anything. I remained silent even after I drank it.

Kris sat with his knees pulled up to his chest, spinning a small rock on the ground next to him.

The pain slowly faded out, and I sighed in relief. "You... you are so fucking crazy."

"Thanks," he said softly.

I used his shoulder for support as I stood and looked around. There were no trees in sight, and inland was just empty steppes with dark grass and a small shrub here or there. "This is a really dreary place."

"I'm sorry."

"What?"

"I'm sorry. That was really stupid, and..." He hugged his knees closer to his chest and shivered slightly.

I licked my lips and hesitantly patted his shoulder. "It's not your fault. Just, just don't do that again."

"I won't."

I ran a hand through my hair. "That was the scariest thing I've ever seen."

"Yeah."

I walked away a few paces, still waiting for my heart to slow down. Small droplets of water had collected on my eyelashes, and I wiped them away.

"I won't let them hurt you." Kris stood up. "No matter what I swear I'll never let the Dark Agencies hurt you."

"Thanks, but... well, I don't think I'll see them that often. You know, not if..." I looked away. I didn't want to blame him. "I need to go."

Kris just looked down at the ground and didn't say anything. I created a doorway and disappeared through it.

Chapter 9
In Silent Shadows Moving

A few days later I was at home, putting together the final pieces of my plan to fix my planet. I focused on it solely, even ignoring my hunger as the sun started to set. I had made a miniature copy of my Earth in my work room off the entry hall, and I used it to measure the proportionate energy that would be necessary. It was going to be the biggest thing I'd ever intentionally warped, so I had to get it as specific and "cheap" as possible. It was either that or wait until I had honed my skills further, and I didn't want to wait. I just wanted to have it over with.

Finally, around 11pm, I gave in for a break and went to the kitchen. I made myself a huge banana and chocolate ice cream sundae with six scoops. I ate in the silence of my house, watching the frost patterns slowly form on the outside of my triple-paned kitchen windows.

I had barely finished a single scoop when I couldn't stand the dessert any longer. I tossed my spoon aside and paced around the kitchen. I was still hungry, but there wasn't anything I could possibly stomach right now. All I wanted was to fix the world.

I went back to the spare room and looked at my notes. I was sure I knew what to do; I was sure that I had found the best solution. There was really no point delaying, because I would never be any more ready that I was right then. But there was still a lingering doubt. I ignored it, went out to the back porch, and rose up into the sky.

I left the atmosphere and stood on the nothingness above the planet. Oceans, continents, and clouds stretched out beneath me, just like in the model. I looked up to the stars and prepared myself. I focused back on the planet and reached out as far as I could stretch, pulling warp energy from as much space as I possibly could. I went to my limit and pushed a little further. I was afraid of draining the energy from the immediate area. Once I was sure I could reach no more, I pulled it forward. I could feel the warp energy flowing towards me, through me, invisible tendrils that stretched into the entire atmosphere and beyond, even moving the planet slightly, tugging on its orbit around the sun. The air changed, slowly at first, then faster as the energy started to pour over everything. Heat returned to the night sky.

The second the change was finished I snapped back into myself, back together, back from far reaches. Like a rubber band I went limp, but I didn't collapse. There was nothing on which to collapse. I just started drifting, no longer standing straight. My mind was foggy, and I felt I could just sleep here, comfortably suspended above my planet. Perhaps I did.

Eventually I returned to normal awareness. I was still above the planet, but a different side was facing me now. How long was I asleep? I jerk forward and yanked my head around, looking behind me, and I pulled a muscle in my neck.

"*Ah*, ah." I slowly turned my head back, one eye closed in pain.

I drank some warp extract and was about to make a doorway back home, but then I thought of the warp locks. If I warp locked the atmosphere I would know for certain the fix would be permanent. I tried and after a few close attempts I had it set. My planet's atmosphere was fixed, and it would stay unchanged as I had ordained it. I smiled faintly to myself.

I returned to my house and closed the doorway as I glanced at a clock. I'd been gone for less than three hours. I felt better.

"Ethan!"

I jumped and suddenly was hugged from behind. I knew it was Kris, and I pried his arms from me.

"Kris, what are you doing?" I turned to face him.

"Look, look, I really, *really* am sorry. I really didn't mean for anything to happen back on that planet, and I know it was bad enough that I killed so many people, but, but the Agencies too." He was swaying slightly. "Please say you believe me."

"Are you drunk again?"

"No, no. Well I guess. A bit. That's not the point. I just came to tell you how sorry I am, but then you weren't here, so I was really confused. Then, then I saw the door you made just now, and I knew it was, knew it was you and that you were okay."

"Why don't you just sit down?" I made a chair behind him and eased him into it. "I'll make you some warp extract, so you can actually talk to me."

"No, no! I want to be drunk! *Fuck*, I am drunk, aren't I? Ugh..." Kris leaned forward, clutching the sides of his head.

"How did you even teleport here?"

"It's not so hard."

"Okay, so you wanted to apologize. Fine, it's okay. But if you aren't going to have some warp extract then you should probably lie down or something."

He looked up at me. "You real– really forgive me?"

"Yeah. Now are you going to lie down or what?"

Kris laughed a moment, then burped.

I took a step back. "You're not gonna throw up, are you?"

"...no?" Kris stood up, keeping one hand on the chair as he wobbled. "I hope."

The house suddenly trembled slightly with an incredibly low *krrr*, like the sound of far distant thunder. Kris fell to his side, sprawled out on the floor and propped himself up by one arm.

"The hell was that?" I asked.

"Sounded like... but we're not at... was, did–?" He pulled himself up and staggered to the back porch doors. "Did Alicia put a, uh..."

I ran to him and grabbed his shoulders before he fell over again. Just in time too, because another *krrr* vibrated through the house.

"Did Alicia do what?" I asked.

"Put something, put something outside?"

"Uh, there was this crystal thing she put above the roof."

Krrr.

Kris pulled forward. He managed to push the backdoors open, and he stumbled out onto the porch. I followed and at first all I noticed was the pleasant temperature of the night air. It made me feel accomplished. Then I noticed what the crystal above my house was doing.

It was glowing brighter than normal, with a layer of yellow-white energy around it that kept growing brighter until it shot off in a ball of light. *Krrr*. The ball didn't travel far before it hit something in the air and flashed out.

"Fuck!" Kris ran back into the house, almost falling forward.

"What the hell is it doing?"

"Get in! Get in!" A vial of warp extract was in Kris's hand, and he downed it immediately.

"What's going on?" I pulled the doors shut and noticed something that was clearly not good. The stars were winking in and out again—like something was blocking them momentarily—and it was dozens of them being blocked. My ears started ringing. For a second everything froze, and I had a really good guess what was happening.

"It's them," I whispered. "Nókrutar."

"I know, I know." Kris ran back to me and grabbed my hands, holding them in fists against my chest. He started speaking very rapidly. "They're here right now but this is your house and we have a crystal so we can fight them and kill them, are you *ready* for this?"

I blinked twice. "Don't we run?"

"No. Not this time. Here." He created two thin visors, handed one to me, and donned the other over his eyes.

"What is this?" The ringing was steadily growing.

"Helps you see them in low light!" He ran back out on the porch and formed a silvery, transparent dome to encase the area.

With the visor on, I looked up. Everything was tinged blue and several blobs of darkness—each the size of a car—were highlighted against the sky as they flew around in circles above the house. I was confused. I had thought it was Nókrutar, but these didn't look anything like them. The crystal was holding them off; anytime one flew down to attack, the crystal blasted a chunk of it into nothingness. Kris held out his arms and spheres of white light consolidated around his hands, growing quickly. Once they were larger than a basketball he fired both of them up and they curved after their targets and struck, disintegrating parts of the blobs like the crystal's fire was doing.

The dark masses immediately took notice of Kris and swooped down towards the porch. A blast from the crystal cut one in half, and Kris shot another before the five blobbed attackers collided with the dome. For a moment they covered they shield, oozing over it like tar. I was frozen. I just stared up at them, not even shaking, my mouth going dry.

Krrr. The explosion ripped a hole in the dark mass, and Kris fired another twin sphere of light, widening the rend. They pulled up and flew away in an undulating manner like oil through water. The crystal fired again as the darkened shapes circled around and started to return for another attack. The blobs were smaller now and started breaking apart, forming into the humanoid silhouettes I'd seen before.

"Help me!" Kris screamed.

I suddenly regained awareness of my legs and ran to his side. "What do I do?"

"Just draw up the warp energy but don't shape it, just shoot it!"

"Uh. Right. Okay. Sure." I held up my arms like I was about to stop a tank from rolling over me.

The Nókrutar charged. *Krrr.* One disintegrated. Kris kept firing the pure warp energy at them, but seven individual Agencies still remained and slammed into the dome. Actual cracks started to form through its glistening surface.

"Holy shit!" I shot the warp energy forward as unformed as a mere notion towards a thought. It seared through my fingers but did not burn. The two spheres of light hit one of the things square in the chest and it split in two, each half fading from existence.

Only four were left and they broke off again, flying away for another pass. The crystal picked off another as they retreated and a second as they came back. I threw another shot, destroying one, and with a final roar Kris destroyed the last Nókrutar.

He stood panting and my lungs felt constricted.

Kris stepped hesitantly to the side, like he was about to fall over, but he was able to direct himself into a deck chair. He started half-laughing. "We did it."

I didn't say anything; I just slid back against the wall until I was sitting on the floor. The crystal over our heads had dimmed back to its normal state, and Kris let the dome faded away.

"So... yeah..." Kris leaned back, face up to the sky, and pulled off the visor. A light green cocktail appeared in his hand and he drank it all.

I took a deep breath. "Why... why?"

"What is it?" The cocktail refilled, but he only sipped it this time.

"Why did they come back? How did they find us?"

"They weren't the same ones from before."

I was silent a moment. "Radcliff did a horrible job explaining these things."

"What did he say?"

"*Nothing* about this. He just talked about dusk energy and how I'd probably never run into the Agencies."

Kris grunted. "Well, yeah, this isn't normal." He paused. "They're real fuckers. They're semi-corporal and completely bloodthirsty. And you can't erase them either. Well, you can, but it takes way more warp energy that it would to just blow them up, because they have, like, a resistance to being warped."

"I don't understand. I can't believe there were more Nókrutar so soon. I didn't even drain that much energy when I fixed my planet. I specifically pulled energy from as far as I could to avoid this very thing. Even when I locked it I–"

"Don't fret. It's okay." Kris looked at me. "Come over here. The floor can't be that comfortable."

I just looked at him for a few moments. I still hadn't taken off the visor, and its blue tint brought out the whites of his eyes and accenting his green irises. Suddenly the image blurred as the visor zoom in on his eyes. "Wow." I blinked several times and took off the visor.

"What?"

"I didn't know these things could zoom in."

Kris laughed. "They sure do. What were you so focused on, hm?" He grinned.

"The zit on your nose." I sat down in a chair next to him.

"What?" A small mirror appeared in Kris's hand as he searched his face.

I laughed a moment. "Just kidding. You don't got one."

"You think you're so funny, don't you?" He waved a finger at me and finished his drink.

"Maybe I do think I'm funny."

"Well I think you're cute."

"Huh?"

"I think you're cute." He just had this small smile on his face, like a last sliver of sunlight slipping between window blinds.

I looked away. His smile faded.

I could feel a dreg of nervousness and guilt moving up my spine. "You know it's because of the situation... not because of you."

Kris didn't say anything at first; he just refilled his drink and downed it. "Yeah. I know."

It was silent now in the dark of night. Neither of us had turned on the porch light. Only the water lapping against the support pillars made any noise.

"Why don't you have a cocktail?" Kris asked.

"I don't really know what cocktails even are."

"They can be anything. That's what makes them so great." He leaned forward and offered a newly created one to me.

I took it. "So, what exactly is this one?"

"Mostly vodka with lime schnapps and a splash of rum. It's one of my favorites."

I sipped it and coughed. "Geez, that... that's really something."

Kris laughed. "Never had alcohol before?"

"Only in a few mixed drinks."

"We'll fix that soon enough."

"Right..." I set the glass down on the floor by my chair. "Gonna teach me how to dance and throw parties too?"

"It's on the list." Kris looked back up at the sky. "You know... I really am sorry–"

"I said it was fine."

"I know, but I want to make sure you really understood how–"

"Kris, just drop it. You don't have to keep beating yourself up about it."

"I'm not. I'm trying to tell you what the difference is, now that I'm more, uh, level headed."

"Difference?"

"Yeah, the difference between Humans. Listen. There's some planets in the universe that know about us. It's not really a big deal, but Jett sees them as a threat."

"The Rurrians know what we can do?"

"Pretty much."

"How?"

"I dunno. Maybe some warper told them a long time ago, or maybe they're just that smart. Either way, that doesn't matter. What matters is that, yes, Jett is trying to commit genocide, but it's specifically on the planets that know about us. And he doesn't want to bring them back. Not even without knowledge of us. It's different."

"Let's just talk about something else."

Kris leaned back again, crossing his arms. We were both silent until Kris suddenly said, "Hey, wait a minute." He stood up. "Wasn't you planet supposed to be frozen at night?"

"Yeah. But I fixed it."

"When?"

"That's what I was doing just before I got back. I was just saying a minute ago that I was trying to be careful about draining the warp energy when I did it."

"Did you—?" He paused and looked up. "You warp locked the atmosphere."

"Yes. I was also literally just then telling you about that part too."

"Okay, two things: good work and that explains the attack." He turned to go into the house, picking up my unfinished drink as he went.

"What is it?"

"Come on, I'll show you. How big is your kitchen table? I need to make a map."

"It's a good size." I closed the doors to the porch behind me. "But why don't we go in my office type work room."

"Your what?"

"That's where I have all my notes and maps of the surrounding space and stuff."

Kris laughed. "Sure. Show me this office-type-room then."

From the entry hall I opened a door that was across from the kitchen. Inside Kris looked at several of the maps on the walls before pausing on the miniature planet floating in the center of the room.

"What's this?" He asked.

"My Earth. This is how I figured out how to fix the atmosphere."

"Hmm." He squinted at one of the continents. "You have been busy this week then, haven't you?"

"I guess."

"Did I mention you made a really nice house too?"

"Raine did for you, and you're the one who put up the drapes in the entry hall."

"Oh, right, she did. And I know, but everything else is still very inviting. I mean, do you like architecture?"

"As much as the next guy, I guess. Why?"

"Oh. Just wondering. Not important." Kris floated my miniature planet to the side of the room and made a map on the table. He rolled it out flat and stretched it upwards into three dimensions, paper planets, moons, and stars floating in air. "Now look here." He pointed to the planet in the center. "This is your Earth."

"And this is the planet where I was practicing weather control." I pointed near the base of the diorama.

"Yeah. Now this is pretty zoomed in, but over here..." Kris traced his finger halfway up to one of the corners and pointed at a black sphere about a quarter the size of the Sun. "This black thing."

"What about it?"

"It's a Dark Zone about six light years from here. Very dangerous. It's where a ton of the Dark Agencies are all trapped. There's these giant crystal clusters made of defense crystals like the one above this house that surround the Dark Zone. It's like a, um, spider web. Only it makes a sphere and it's in space and it's not as organized."

"And I assume the Dark Agencies are all trapped in it?"

"It's not the only Dark Zone in the universe. There's actually kind of a lot. Radcliff told us the theory goes that some warpers a long time ago were able to herd most of the Dark Agencies together and trap them in various places."

"Then how did any attack us just now?"

"There's still more in the universe. There's always more

Agencies out there. But this could mean there's a containment breach. You see, the Agencies only mass up into blobs like that when there's a lot and they've been near each other long enough. Also, they tend to gravitate to places with lots of warp energy and especially warp locks. They probably came here because of the warp lock, and if we hadn't've had that crystal over the roof we would've had to run. If you *ever* seen them all massed up and you're not in a defendable place, just run."

"I know. Like that first time."

"But what I mean is that if there's like five or less of the regular Agencies and you're not taken by surprise, you can usually kill them just by making a shield and smashing them all. But the big blobs of them will crush a single warper."

"Alright. So there was an abnormal amount just now, and there's a Dark Zone right next door. When's the last time it got checked?"

"That's the thing. No one goes around checking Dark Zones. We don't even know if we know all the locations of them. The kicker though is that as far as I know, no one from my generation has really been over in this corner of the universe, so I bet no one's checked it in well over a century or two."

"So you're saying we need to go check it, aren't you?"

"Yeah."

"Why?"

"Well, I assume you want to keep your planet safe, right?"

"Yeah. I do. That's why I warp locked it."

"Okay, but you see, that'll just draw them right here if there is a breach. And once Dark Agencies occupy a planet, it's not a pretty picture. Everything kind of... stops."

Peter flashed into my mind. "What?"

"Yeah. They like, drain the life out of things. Slowly. Now that's normal things. If there's no warp lock or warpers to draw their attention, then Dark Agencies just linger. They ignore everything else, but they still affect everything."

"So what do we do? Just go fly by the Dark Zone and check for a breach?"

"Basically. But we'll have to be really, really careful." He extended his hand to me. "We'll 'port in about a Moon from the perimeter and check with binoculars first."

"Do you do this often?"

"Not with Dark Agencies, but I've been in war games before. You know, I mean, you do get bored over the decades."

"I think you're taking the 'game' part too literally." I took his hand.

"No, no. We have to do this. I hate dealing with the Agencies, but we have to now. For you." We disappeared from my house.

Chapter 10
Don't Know You Don't Know

We reappeared in space.

"So when you say 'a Moon,' what does that mean?" I asked.

"About 380,000 klicks. The standard distance of the Moon from Earth."

"And a klick?"

"Kilometer."

"Oh. Pretty far then."

"Not really."

Before us was a massive, circular web of blue-purple light. It was brighter than a full Moon, and it looked three times larger than Jupiter had looked when we were on Io. Beyond the lines of light nothing could be seem; all the odd shapes made from negative space were black. It made the entire thing seem flat, like it was just hung a short distance from me and I could reach out and touch it.

"We're really too close," Kris said.

"We are?"

"Yeah. Yeah." He shook his head and grabbed my hand. "I'm moving us back three more Moons."

We teleported and the Dark Zone looked much smaller now.

"So what exactly are we looking for?" I asked.

Kris was looking through a newly created pair of binoculars. "This is bad."

"What is it?"

"Have a look." He handed the binoculars to me.

They tinted the world blue like the visors, and they magnified my view far greater than any binoculars I had ever used before. They were more like a telescope. I could see the clusters of crystals that created each point where the beams of light connected. The spaces between weren't black any more, and planets inside the Dark Zone revealed themselves: a gigantic one like a gas giant and two smaller rocky planets.

"There's *planets* in there." I said.

"Yeah. I mention they can take over planets. You see the breach?"

"No. Where?"

"Upper left."

I looked again. There was an empty space much larger than any other and in it were three black crystal clusters. Hundreds of highlighted Nókrutar swirled around and outside the opening, some even larger than a crystal cluster.

"Shit," I said.

"Yeah. There's a fuck ton of them, but it's really good we found this now. I'm calling Alicia."

I lowered the binoculars. "With the palm thing?"

"Yep." Kris lifted his left hand, the white circle glowing on its palm, and held it to the side of his head. "Alicia?" He paused. "Hey, listen. Get Radcliff and come to my point ASAP. We've got a breach in the Dark Zone near Ethan's Earth." Pause. "Ethan's here, so don't worry about that."

"About what?" I asked.

"Hang on," he said to me, then focused on Alicia again. "No, yeah, Alicia, we're safe right now." Pause. "Okay, see you in six." The circle disappeared from Kris's palm as he lowered his hand. "Alright, so. Alicia and Radcliff are coming and I'm gonna help them close the gap. You're gonna stay here with Raine and watch how we do it." He created a platform beneath us and a table to the side.

"Raine's coming too?"

"Yeah, but she's waiting with you."

"Why can't I help?"

"Because you don't know how. No offense." He raised his hands to chest level.

"No, I get it."

"Good. In the meantime, you should learn how to make the defense crystals."

"Like the one on my roof?"

"Yep." Kris stretched out his hands and created one the size of a refrigerator floating in space a few meters away from us.

"They're not hard to make and don't need to be bigger than this. Just be sure to make them use ambient warp energy to attack Dark Agencies only. You have to be a bit specific with them."

"Okay... sure." I reached down, pulling up the energy and focusing on what I wanted. It wouldn't form at first, not the way I intended it too. I could shape it as a crystal, but I could feel that it wouldn't work as an automatic defense. I just couldn't find the possibility; I was groping in the dark. I let the energy go, unsuccessfully used.

"The trick is to not use the energy, but to contain it."

I recognized Radcliff's voice and turned around. He stood near the table, along with Alicia and Raine.

"Oh. I'll try that," I said.

Radcliff nodded once.

I turned back to the empty space between us and the Dark Zone. I pulled the warp energy back to me and pushed it forward, not yet formed. I shaped it and set an outer layer, then the crystal took its own and almost built itself, like tipping something just enough until it starts to fall over. It was unlike anything else I had yet created.

"Wow." I turned back to the others, but they were already gathered around the table. Kris was still watching me though. Our eyes met; he smiled and looked away.

"...since it was found so early this shouldn't be too difficult," Radcliff was saying. "We'll make a pyramid shape to trap the escaping Nókrutar and force them back into the Dark Zone before reforming the downed clusters." He created a three-dimensional diagram floating above the table. It showed the Dark Zone the size of a basketball with a three sided pyramid protruding from near the top. "Are you going to be okay, Kris?"

"*Yes*. I'll be fine." He crossed his arms. "We need to do this."

"Good," Radcliff said.

"By my estimate we'll need at least 180 crystals," Alicia said, "sixty for each side of the pyramid."

"Agreed. We have more than enough orbiting Cosmos. Alicia and Kris, go get two hundred just to be safe. Ethan, let's talk."

Alicia and Kris disappeared.

"Uh, if this is about last time..." I started.

"No," Radcliff said. "There will be time for that later. Now we must stay focused on the present. Just listen to what I need you to do to help."

"I thought I was just going to stay with Raine?"

She had sat down on the edge of the platform, legs swinging off into space, watching the Dark Zone.

"You are, but during a situation like this warp energy goes very quickly, especially around Nókrutar. With this many present they stifle you and make it harder to warp, which forces you to use more energy. The crystals drawing away warp energy only compound this problem. I'm going to need you to channel warp energy to us the whole time we're down there."

"So, what, just make it move to you?"

"Yes, it's quite easy. Just direct it to move."

"Anything else?"

"Take this earpiece, so we can remain in contact. Also, I am glad to see you improving in your warping skills." He patted my shoulder. "It's good to see you learning from Kris and that he has taken on some more responsibility."

"Thanks, but uh, I actually learned a lot on my own. No offense to Kris though."

"Perhaps. But even the vacuum of space is not completely empty."

"Huh?"

Radcliff didn't say anything more. Kris and Alicia re-appeared; behind them floated dozens and dozens of crystals glowing blue-white. The sudden light from them stunned my eyes.

"We're ready to go," Alicia said.

"Everyone knows their part?" Radcliff asked.

"I think so," I said.

"Here." Kris handed me an extra pair of binoculars. "For Raine to use."

I took them. "You're shaking," I said quietly.

"No I'm not." He turned quickly and followed Radcliff and Alicia away from the platform, most of the crystals floating after them.

I handed the extra binoculars to Raine and watched them go. "So, how much do you know about this sort of thing?"

"Not too much," she said. "I've only seen them seal a breach once before. It's not often this happens. I actually can't even see Nókrutar, so it's only because of these binoculars outlining them that I can actually follow what's happening."

"What do you mean you can't see them?"

"Only warpers can see Nókrutar. They're invisible to everyone else."

"Man. So I guess you don't know how breaches happen in the first place?"

She shrugged. "I've been told that Nókrutar get persistent sometimes. Or they just get lucky. But you need to focus now, they just arrived."

"Right, right."

Through the binoculars I could see the others already moving into place, using the walls of crystals as a barrier between them and the cloud of Nókrutar. They formed the pyramid and halted.

"Ethan, we're about to move in." It was Radcliff over the earpiece. "Start directing warp energy to us."

"Will do." I set the binoculars down and reached out towards them.

I assumed this would be much the same as when I formed the crystal. I pulled the energy around me and just gave it a push forward. I didn't think about making anything, I only thought about movement. It started to flow forward, and I imagined the receivers, trying to direct it further. Suddenly there was a drain in the energy. Something pulled the energy away, forming it into something else. I opened my eyes, expecting to see another warper.

"Was that on purpose?" Raine asked.

Floating out in space before us were three stone busts: Kris, Alicia, and Radcliff. All three were frozen in a moment of laugher.

"No. Did I do that?"

"Yeah, you did."

"Are you having a problem, Ethan?" Radcliff asked. "The energy stopped."

"Sorry, sorry. Just a, uh, misdirection I guess. Hang on."

I closed my eyes again and refocused my efforts, drawing more energy from behind us and pushing it all towards the others.

"What's Kris doing?" Raine asked.

"Huh?" I opened an eye.

"They were moving in like planed just fine and had all the Nókrutar back in the Dark Zone, but Kris just sent all his crystals into the Zone. I think... yeah, he's pushing the Nókrutar back even further, trying to scatter them or something. What's he thinking?"

"Is it bad?"

"*Yes* it's bad. He could get cut off if he goes in there." Raine stood up. "It's a containment mission, not a destruction one. If he doesn't get out he won't last."

"What do we do?" I had dropped the warp energy.

"I can't do anything."

"Ethan! We need you to keep the warp energy coming!" Radcliff said.

"What about *Kris*?" I asked Radcliff

"Don't worry, he's going to be fine. We'll get him out just as soon as we seal the hole."

"How long will *that* take?"

"Six, twelve minutes. Not long. We have to merge enough crystals into clusters to reactivate this section."

"Six to twelve minutes, that's what Radcliff said. Can Kris make it?" I asked Raine.

"I dunno."

I looked through the binoculars again. Radcliff and Alicia couldn't do anything while they were occupied with the crystals, that was obvious. And Kris was just floating in the Dark Zone, hundreds of Nókrutar swirling round before him. Only the crystals were keeping him safe, but they were no longer firing.

"Dammit, I'm gonna get him."

"*What*? No, don't!" Raine tried to grab me, but I had already flown off and away from the platform.

I pulled one of the extra crystals along with me for an idea I just had. I held it a good distance away and used the warp energy to splinter and smash it. A burst of warp energy surged out from it, sweeping over me like a wave.

"*Ethan*! Ethan, what are you *doing*?" Radcliff yelled through the earpiece.

"I'm saving Kris! And I got all the warp energy you'll need."

I flew towards the Dark Zone, pulling a dozen crystals behind me.

"No! I know what he's about to do!" Radcliff yelled across the earpieces. "Alicia, stop him!"

"I can't do more than one loop at a time, you know that! Not unless I release the first," she said.

I was halfway there.

"Fine. Abandon this and get Kris. I'll stop Ethan," Radcliff said.

The crystals near the breach were released and started drifting on their own accord. Alicia went into the Dark Zone, and I suddenly found myself in a glass sphere. I nearly ran into the wall.

"What the *hell*? I was trying to help!"

"I know exactly what you were about to do." Radcliff was instantly standing outside the sphere. "You were about to bring those crystals to us and detonate them to give us warp energy while you went in to save Kris."

"Uh, yeah... how'd you know?"

"Because that's exactly what I would have done if I were in your place and didn't know two key facts. First, it is true that detonating a crystal gives a quick boost of warp energy, but doing that so close to a Dark Zone would have likely caused a chain reaction, overloading the nearby crystals and causing them to explode. That would have cascaded and led to the entire protective web exploding right in our faces, not only resulting in possible fatalities but also releasing countless Nókrutar into the universe."

I was too stunned to say anything. Radcliff removed the glass sphere and walked to me.

"Secondly, Kris was not in any serious danger for the moment. Alicia put him and the surrounding Nókrutar into a time loop, thus preventing any of them from doing anything until after we had sealed the breach. Then we would have been able to walk right into the time looped area and pull him out, just like Alicia has already done."

Alicia showed up with Kris in tow. She had her arms crossed and he was looking down at his feet, not saying anything.

Radcliff sighed. "We'll return to the platform first. It's too dangerous this close and we need to be with Raine." And we were there, even before he had finished saying her name. "Now, this was very disappointing. Kris, Ethan. You two are the only other warpers we can rely on right now. We don't have any room for mistakes or breaking the plan. I'll talk to you both separately after we're finished here. At least since the crystals are where they need to be Alicia and I can finish the job. So both of you, just stay *here*. Got it?"

"Yeah... I got it." Kris still hadn't looked up.

"Yes. I, I'm sorry. I didn't know," I said.

"We know," Radcliff said before he and Alicia disappeared.

An awkward tension hung in the air, and it would have been a bit better if Raine hadn't been there too. I really felt like I should say something, but no words came to mind.

Kris walked over to the table and slammed his palms against the wood. "Dammit!" He knocked the table over. The diagram of the Dark Zone remained hanging in the air.

"Kris? Why did you go in? What were you thinking?" Raine asked softly.

"Thinking? I guess I wasn't thinking." He kicked a leg of the table. "I know that's exactly what Radcliff is gonna say when he gets back." Kris deepened in voice in a mock impression of Radcliff. " 'I thought you were over this. I thought I could count on you. You need to think things through.' Blah blah blah." He picked up the binoculars I had left on the platform and threw them out into space. They arced at first, but once they soared out of the air bubble they started gliding in a straight line, spinning slowly away.

"He only wants to make sure you don't get hurt," she said.

"Yeah, yeah." Kris turned to me, and for a moment I thought he was about to say something. He didn't. Instead he turned away, a new pair of binoculars in his hands, watching the progress of the breach being sealed.

"Kris?" I ask.

He didn't say anything.

"Kris."

"*What*? I don't even know why he's mad at you. You didn't even do anything."

"He almost blew up the crystal grid while trying to save you when you were time looped," Raine said.

The binoculars disappeared from Kris's hands as he stared at me for just a moment. "You did?"

"I– I didn't know that'd happen." I shook my head.

Kris hugged me. He didn't say anything; he just hugged me.

I was so surprised I almost fell backwards. "Uh... you're welcome. I didn't actually do anything though."

"I was afraid you hated me," Kris whispered.

"No. I don't. You're just crazy, that's all." Over his shoulder I could see Raine smiling, but she looked away back at the Dark Zone.

Kris released me from the hug. "I would've been fine though. Even if Alicia hadn't time looped me."

"What even is this time loop thing?"

"Well basically she just stops time from moving like normal inside a small area. Things kinda progress without progressing."

"I don't understand."

"Neither do I really."

I forced a laugh. "Well then..." I walked over to Raine. "How are they doing?"

"They're nearly done," she said.

"Hey, what are those?" Kris pointed to the stone busts floating a short distance from the platform. He pulled his own bust towards him. "This is me, isn't it?"

"Yeah, I kinda made them by accident," I said.

Kris laughed. "Did you? Well I know your power. It's easy to get unexpected results. Like I remember back when..." He trailed off.

I waited for him to continue, but I realized he was probably about to say something about Tavin. Everyone remained silent then until Raine changed the focus.

"They've finished," she said.

A moment later both Radcliff and Alicia appeared on the platform.

"We're good to go," Radcliff said. "Kris, Ethan, will you both accompany me back to the Archives?"

Kris crossed his arms and didn't say a thing, which was unhelpful because I was waiting for his lead.

"Please?" Radcliff asked.

"Come on, Kris. This is no time to be difficult," Alicia said.

"Whatever. Fine," Kris said.

"Good. And Ethan?" Radcliff turned to me.

I nodded. "Let's go."

Chapter 11
This is the Mark

We three appeared in the familiar mahogany entry room, the circular one with the giant amber light fixture floating above.

"Kris, if you could go to the main common room I would like to speak with Ethan first."

"Why can't you talk to us as the same time?" Kris asked.

"Because I have different things to say. Now off with you."

Kris seemed to hesitate, but he did turn to go. However, I noticed that I suddenly had something in my left pocket.

"This way, if you will." Radcliff headed off in the opposite direction, waving for me to follow.

As we ascended a flight of stairs, I quickly checked to see what I had been given. It was a small microphone with a note attached to it: "Shh. Let me know what he says. If he's too harsh on you, you don't deserve it and I'll get on him about it when he talks to me."

I stuffed both back into my pocket and tried to think of something I could say that could give Kris a confirmation without alerting Radcliff, but nothing came to mind. Instead I just tapped the mic twice and hoped he would guess my meaning.

Once we were on the correct floor, we returned to the same lounge room from my last visit. Redcliff motioned for me to sit and then began.

"First, I didn't bring you here to yell at you for any mistakes."

"Then what—?"

Radcliff head up a hand. "Just listen. You're a very new warper; there's still many things you haven't yet learned. That means when we're in a very tense moment, as we were just a few minutes ago, I need you to do everything I tell you to do. If you had been there, up close and personal with the Nókrutar, then I wouldn't need to be telling you just how dangerous they are. I'm going to tell Kris much the same and give him a real earful for rushing in to *attack* them. But, Kris, you'll have to wait your turn to hear all that." Radcliff held out his hand. "The microphone, please."

At first I couldn't believe he was actually referring to the microphone in my pocket, but it quickly became obvious that he was. I handed it over. "Uh... sorry."

"I know you didn't make it, but Kris," Radcliff spoke to the microphone now, "honestly, how did you expect me to not notice that little burst of warp energy used to create this?" The microphone disappeared from his hand, and Radcliff focused on me again. "I wish you had a better role model to guide you through such an important Stage as Initiation."

"What's wrong with Kris?" I folded my arms. "I mean, he means well, doesn't he?"

"Doing the wrong thing for the right reason is still doing the wrong thing. You know as well as I do how reckless he is. He still hasn't grown up and refuses to take much of anything seriously." Radcliff sighed and rubbed his forehead. "But Kris isn't why I need to talk to you. He's a part of it, yes, but only in relation to your education. The fact you didn't even know one of the more basic principles of the defense crystals concerns me.

"I had originally thought that Kris could be given more-or-less free reign of your education, but I see that isn't the case. Especially considering the time that has already passed."

"But Kris and I haven't really even been around each other for most of the last week. If not for that–"

"That absence was not out of either of your hands though. If Kris had been able to keep his emotional states in better control, he would have been able to return to you much sooner and resolve the conflict. The fact he needed Alicia as a mediary is no excuse either. If that was necessary he should have gone to her sooner."

"Okay, hang on. You can't blame it *all* on him. He was staying away from me, because he thought I was mad at him. And I was. So it was my fault too."

Radcliff was silent for several seconds. "Very well. I'll take that into consideration, but I want you to take this into consideration: My primary goal is to make sure we warpers are as united as possible, but I'm certainly not going to be around forever. You and Kris must both learn, so you can eventually teach others." He stood up. "I will go speak with Kris now."

"That's it?"

"Yes. Like I said, I'm not here to chew you out. I merely need you to understand the gravity of the situation." Radcliff started to leave the room.

"Wait. I wanted to ask about Raine."

Radcliff stopped at the door and turned around. "What about her?"

"She told me a little while ago that Jett wants to, you know, kill her."

"That is the theory, yes."

"Theory?"

"Given Jett's actions and stated intentions it seems to be a possibility, and Alicia is not willing to take the chance."

"So then... what are we going to do?"

"Nothing."

"*Nothing*? Are you serious?"

"Aside from avoidance, of course."

"But– but she's your *daughter*."

"I am well aware of that, thank you."

"I mean, how can you do nothing? Doesn't he also want to kill billions of people on other planets? The Rurrians?"

"Yes, but *believe* me, a warper who is in their Ego Stage is the most dangerous thing in the universe. Attempting to oppose them would likely only lead to more violence and unnecessary death."

"But... all those people."

"Who can be remade. Remember that. No damage is permanent except damage to a warper. That is why the rules of avoidance are absolute. No exceptions."

"So nothing matters except us? That's what you're saying?"

"Of course. Nothing else is as real as we are."

I furrowed my eyebrows. "I don't believe that."

"It's not up for debate, I'm afraid." Radcliff turned again.

"And your daughter?" I asked quickly. "Can *she* be remade?"

Radcliff hesitated at the doorway but did not turn to me again. "She's being kept safe."

"Really?" I stood up. "But she's not a warper; she can be changed. Is she not real?"

Radcliff remained silent.

"*Is* she?"

"She's different," Radcliff whispered so softly I almost didn't hear him.

"Yeah? Well I got my boyfriend back on my Earth, and I think he's different too, but that won't save him from anything. If Jett or anyone threatened him I wouldn't follow any stupid rule of *avoidance*. And for some reason I don't think you would either if it came to your daughter. If she died, what would you do? Just remake her?"

Radcliff sighed and walked back. He stood toe-to-toe with me. "No. I would never be able to remake my daughter. I couldn't betray her like that, but, but that is simply from *my* perspective. From a universal perspective, she isn't– is not, actually real." He closed his eyes. "Only we are." He paused. "Besides, she's a Warper Born. She was born with a natural warp lock. That makes her as real as she'll ever be." He left the room much more swiftly than I had ever seen him walk before, and he shut the door behind.

Did he truly believe that? Even about his own daughter? I sank down into the couch as some abstract flame of defiance waned in me for a moment before regaining strength.

I knew Radcliff couldn't be right, he simply couldn't, but not a single rebuttal came to my mind nor argument that could highlight my belief. I simply didn't have anything going for my argument, not logistically anyways. I knew there had to be something though, and I would figure it out. Both Radcliff and I knew deep in our gut that the people we loved were undoubtedly real, even if we couldn't pin it down to an empirical reason. Changeable maybe, but certainly no less real. I crossed my arms. If Warper Born are born warp locked then they were already miles ahead of regular Humans. A twinge of frustration rose up that Raine should have that advantage over Peter.

There was nothing I could do about it at the moment though, so I simply promised myself that I would solve the problem soon enough. In the meantime I stood and started pacing the room. Radcliff hadn't said anything about what to do after the little talk, but I got the feeling that it would probably be best to wait until he finished talking to Kris.

After three minutes had passed I grew tired of pacing and sat down again. I created a copy of the manual and looked through it more thoroughly since I had been putting that off. I flipped the pages absently, not really reading any part in particular. The contents were on a number of things I was already familiar with: defense crystals, Nókrutar, teleporting, some general rules of thumb on energy management, warp locks. It seemed like I knew all the basics, so I didn't understand what Radcliff was all upset about.

The more interesting part though was the last two-thirds of the book. That section contained hundreds of maps of different parts of the universe, with places of interest highlighted along with co-ordinates to allow instant teleportation. The Archives and Grand Library were listed, along with the Tallest Cliff in the Universe, the Art Quadrant, Prabble, recommended race circuits, an alphabetical list of Earths A through 83,906,012 with an asterisk mentioning those are only the catalogued ones, Dark Zones to avoid, and more. The last page before the index had a special section about the Void, which basically only included a short paragraph about the Restaurant its "mysterious origin and purpose."

Apparently my own Earth was Earth-312,960. I assumed that was either an arbitrary number or it indicated my Earth was relatively old. Either way, I decided I should give my Earth an actual name and see about getting it updated in the manual. Would that be enough to get my name in the "contributing authors" list?

I closed the book and realized I had probably only killed about twelve minutes. Hopefully Kris and Radcliff's meeting wouldn't last too much longer. I was getting rather tired. It was well past midnight back home, even if it was only about 6pm here according to a wall clock. It seemed strange. Obviously everything would be at all sorts of different times, but I hadn't really thought about it until now. I would have to ask Kris how he dealt with the constant time changes.

In the meantime, I debated whether or not I wanted to

make a cup of coffee. Maybe I'd just go home. I could leave a note or something. Radcliff wouldn't really have any reason to get upset; he had already gotten to talk to me. What the hell, I thought. I stood up and made a doorway home.

However, literally a second afterwards, Kris burst the hallway door open. We both stopped, equally confused.

"Kris?"

"Ethan?" He pointed at my doorway home. "Did–? How–?"

"Did you just come to tell me not to leave?"

"No, I came to get you so we could leave."

Radcliff came into view from the hallway. "Kris, I haven't even finished. Why are you standing here like a–?" He saw the doorway. "What? What is this? Did you have a microphone too?"

"No," Kris said.

"I didn't even know you guys were coming," I said. "I was just about to go home 'cause I'm tired. It's probably like three in the morning for me."

Radcliff looked between the two of us. "You're saying this was just a coincidence?"

"I guess," I said.

"No. Clearly, Ethan and I are on the same wavelength." Kris walked over and took my hand. "Let's go. Radcliff is getting on my nerves even more than usual."

"Is that so?" Radcliff crossed his arms.

"Yes. Totally." He looked at me. "Let's go."

"I mean, I was going anyways." I slipped my hand out of Kris's grasp and glanced at Radcliff.

He sighed. "Fine. But, Kris, I do intend to finish our conversation later. Perhaps when your disposition is less cagey."

"Me? Cagey? Please. You're the one who always has to get the last word."

"What?" Radcliff looked confused. "I simply cannot wait until the day when I can have a fully formed conversation with you."

"Oh yeah? Well you just think you're like, like the master crafter of conversations, don't you? And we're just a bunch of stupid lines you gotta measure and make a pattern out of, right? Well we're not, and I certainly aren't either."

Radcliff rubbed his forehead. "Just go, just go then. This is literally causing me pain."

"And that's 'cause you're such a pain in the ass, right?"

This obviously was going nowhere and I was tired of being caught in the middle of it. "Kris, if you just wanna argue with him all night, fine, but I'm going to bed." I walked into my house.

"No, wait, I'm coming too." Kris jumped in after me and slammed the doorway.

I let the door disappear. "If you acted like that all the time you'd be unbearable."

"Acted like what?"

"Like a complete moron." I turned to my bedroom.

"Wait, wait, come on. He started it. He thinks he's so high and mighty, but he doesn't really know anything more than anyone else."

"Kris, I *don't* care, okay? Honestly, I just want to sleep." I flicked my bedroom light on and took off my shoes.

"But he was lecturing me like he always does." He followed me into my room. "Though he was blaming most of tonight on you, so I couldn't let him do that, 'cause like I said in the note I gave you, none of this was your fault. I still can't believe he realized I had warped that mic into your pocket. He shouldn't've noticed a warp that small, unless he was actually *sensing* for it. Maybe he just guessed what I'd do." He looked around. "You don't have much in here."

I was silent a moment as I contemplated opening the floor beneath his feet so he'd fall into the ocean. That'd be both funny and far more effective than dropping hints. A small smile crossed my lips, but I decided against it. "Well I bet there's more in this room than there is in your whole house."

Kris opened his mouth to say something but closed it right after. He looked up at the ceiling.

"What?" I asked.

"Nothing."

"Are you even tired right now?"

"Not really." He made a watch and glanced at it. "It's about an hour 'til midnight for me."

"Then we're not off by too much. Look, you can stay here if you like, but just don't be loud. I'm going to sleep." I pulled off my shirt then glanced back at him. "Of course that means I want you to leave the room."

"Yeah, I know, but you're the one stripping. I'm just enjoying." He chuckled.

"Go, get out. I'm not stripping." I pushed him out of my room and shut the door. "You can make the living room into a bedroom if you like."

"So tell me," he asked through the door, "what do you sleep in? Underwear? Nothing?"

I could just imagine him standing out there grinning like a buffoon. "Wouldn't you like to know."

"That's why I'm asking."

"Well I'm not telling."

"Don't be lame."

"I'm pretty sure that having privacy isn't a component of being lame."

"Okay, I'm sorry." He laughed a moment. "I'll just see you in the morning then?"

"*Goodnight.*"

"Okay, okay." His voice dropped, followed a few moments after by footsteps fading away from my door.

I just shook my head and went to bed.

Chapter 12
Justify Yourself

I woke up around noon. If there's one thing I really enjoy the most about being a warper it's the complete and totally unnecessity of having a schedule. The ability to make any food I want instantaneously is a close second.

I dressed and left my room. The house was very quiet, and I wondered if Kris had even stayed the night at all. The wall separating the living room from the entry hall was no longer a half-wall, but the door stood slightly ajar. I pushed it open a bit and peeked inside. Most of the furniture was gone from the living room to make space for a large bed in the center of the room. Kris lay atop it on his back, still asleep, with the sheets strewn over him and one leg dangling over the side of the bed. His mouth was open and it looked like he was preparing to sing, but it mostly just made him look a little ridiculous. I pulled the door shut quietly and went to the dining room.

I made myself a large omelet with cheddar, Swiss, provolone, and Colby cheese, red and green peppers, a few onions, bacon bits, spinach, sausage, and ham. I also made hash browns on the side just for good measure.

As I ate I considered my current house and what I would eventually like to live in. I didn't want something austere or overly flashy, but I certainly wanted it to be unique. The ability to ignore normal architecture methods only added to the possibilities. I doubted I could make anything as extreme as the Penrose stairs, but I knew I could get away with a lot less support. I had already done so with my current house. I also considered whether I truly needed to include a kitchen or not, and I hadn't yet come to a conclusion as I weighed the matter.

I continued my musings through breakfast, making a few

miniatures of ideas I had. I was nearly finished with my omelet when the living room door opened and Kris walked out. He was wearing sweatpants and had the blanket draped over himself again, letting it trail after him on the floor.

"Good morning. Even though it's not really morning anymore." I smirked.

He mumbled something and sat down. A vial of warp extract and a box of "Crunchy Hexagons" appeared on the table in front of him.

"What's that?" I asked.

Kris didn't respond until after he had finished the warp extract. "Crunchy Hexagons."

"I can see that. Is it cereal?"

"Yeah." He poured some into a bowl and started eating.

"Did you make that up?"

"No. It's actually a legit cereal from my planet."

I hesitated a moment. "Really?"

"Yeah." Kris nodded quickly. He looked much more awake. "I could take you sometime and you can see for yourself."

"How will I know that you didn't just add them yourself?"

"Would I really go through so much effort just to prank you?" He smiled.

"Not like it's *that* much effort. What does it even taste like?"

"Try some." He offered me the box.

I made a bowl and spoon of my own and poured out a small amount. The hexagon pieces came in red, blue, and yellow, and they each had a slightly different sugary taste: apple, berry, and honey respectively. As I chewed I noticed a small circular scrape on the back of my right hand and wondered absently when that had happened.

"It's not quite my thing. I still can't believe it's actually called 'Crunchy Hexagons,' " I said.

"Why not?"

"Because that's just such a ridiculous name."

Kris pointed at me. "But *memorable*."

"Uh, yeah, sure. Memorable like all other bad food is."

"You're just jealous you didn't come up with such a brilliantly simple brand of cereal yourself."

"Yeah, exactly. That's exactly it." I waved a hand over my empty dishes and made them disappear.

"So what are these?" Kris picked up a house model I had made, one that looked like an upside-down capital L.

"Just some stuff I was working on. Nothing really. I'm thinking about making a better house."

"Gonna make this a hobby?"

"Making houses?"

"Yeah."

"I don't think so. I just thought I'd try my hand at it since I can. Once I have a cool house I'll be set."

He just kinda nodded and ate another spoon of cereal.

"Did you sleep well?" I asked.

"Yeah, I guess. I didn't get to sleep for a while though. I went to this giant rave party up in these mountains, but I didn't stay very long. When I came back I went swimming, then slept around three in the morning or something."

"You went swimming in the ocean?"

"No, I added a pool. Hope you don't mind."

"A pool? Where?"

"Out back. It's connected to the porch and that small room behind the kitchen that just has a few plants in it. It looks really awesome too, if I say so myself."

"Really?" I stood up. "Let me see."

We walked out to the back porch, Kris still trailing his blanket, and just as he had said there was a pool attached to the patio hanging over the ocean. Its bowl was completely clear, revealing pipes that supplied the pool with a continuous source of water. The edge of the pool was a waterfall that cascaded down into the waves.

"You see, it's completely self-cleaning, because it keeps getting fresh water from a filtration pump beneath the water there." Kris pointed to the nearest support pillar. "And the best part is that it's always warm."

"Is this glass?" I tested the transparent material with a single foot. It wasn't completely solid, instead the clear material yielded to my weight a small bit.

"It's a transparent plastic covered by a soft shell. No sharp edges and no hard surfaces. Not easy to hurt yourself on."

I walked out onto the plastic fully. "This is really weird." It was sort of like standing on a very firm mattress.

"Yeah, I'm awesome." Kris flicked his bangs to the side.

"Okay, you don't get to go that far, mister."

Kris laughed. "Eh, fine. So do you want to go swimming?"

"Not right now." I stepped back onto the porch.

"Then what do you wanna do today?"

"I dunno. I was kinda thinking of working on my planet some more."

"But you were doing that yesterday."

"So? It's not done yet."

"But you can't be working every day, *especially* since you're a warper. We're supposed to be out having fun."

"Really?" I stared at him, trying to make my face look as skeptical as possible.

Kris chuckled. "Really."

"Well if I have over 600 years to live as a warper, I'm sure there'll be plenty of time to have fun."

Kris shrugged. "Oh, that reminds me, you didn't change everything back yet."

"I know. I just said it isn't done yet."

"Yeah, yeah, but you didn't change the biggest problem: the sun." He point up. "It's still a cold blue star."

"But... everything's warm again."

"Yeah." His eyes grew wide. "You really did something. Over compensated the atmosphere or something. The atmosphere is 'normal' again, but the whole set up is still completely different."

"But, then, how do I fix it?"

"Do you really need to fix it if the end result is the same?"

"I, dunno."

"It's really tangled now. I would just leave it maybe."

I put my hand on my hips and looked up at the sky. "That's really concerning."

"Anyways, if we're gonna do something we should get going. Hang on." Kris hung his blanket up in the air in front of him. A few moments later he erased the blanket and was wearing a whole new outfit. Black boots and black leather pants with thin chains looping up the side of each pant leg, and a midriff black jacket with straps going all down the sleeves over a black t-shirt sporting the warper symbol.

I was startled, but I started laughing. "What? What did you just do? What is that?"

"I just warped away my sweatpants and created some going out clothes. And what is what?"

"What you're wearing. They're so unique."

"I just said they're going out clothes. They're not the most creative ones I've ever made, but I think they're good for today."

"Alright." I was still smiling. "You just look like something out of an anime or video game."

"Thanks. So come on, let's go do stuff."

"Like what?"

"Ugh! You always ask 'what,' but you're missing the point." Kris grabbed my hand. "You just have to *go*."

He teleported us away, and we appeared out in space overlooking a galaxy.

"Your home," Kris said.

"The Milky Way?"

"*A* Milky Way."

"Whatever." I glanced over the slowly rotating arms of blue, purple, and yellow. "Where's the Archives in there?"

"Oh no, no, no. The Archives are far off from this corner of the universe. In the Kalakos galaxy."

Kris wasn't looking at me, instead he was spinning around slowly. For a second I thought he was imitating the galaxy below, but then I saw his eyes darting in all directions.

"Are you looking for something?" I asked.

"Not exactly."

"Then what are you doing?"

"Looking."

"Isn't that what I just asked?"

"No." Kris laughed. "Pick somewhere."

"What do you mean?"

"Pick a direction to go."

I glanced to my sides, but all I could see were stars in the blackness. "How am I supposed to pick? It all looks the same."

"What? You're kidding right? Just look around. There's so much."

I looked again, remaining silent for a minute as I tried to see what he saw. "I don't get it."

"You'll learn to see it. I forgot I couldn't before too. Just pick a direction then."

"What can't I see?"

Kris looked at me and opened his mouth, but he hesitated. "See the... well, see everything." He looked back up into space. "See the life. See the possibilities. See the, the, um..." Reaching out the full length of his arm, Kris closed his hand as if grabbing something. "That." He pulled his arm back, hand still closed.

"What? What is it?"

Kris opening his hand. Nothing was in it. "Let's just go. You'll get it."

We started flying away, but the galaxy didn't seem to move at all.

"How fast are we going?" I asked.

"As close to the speed of light as we can get."

"*That* fast?"

"This is hardly fast at all. Still will take us forever to get anywhere. I'm just thinking for a moment about what we should do, but I didn't want to be standing still." He paused. "We need to go somewhere really awesome."

"Like where?"

"I got it!" His eyes lit up. "How about the edge of the universe?"

"The edge? Of the universe?"

"Is there an echo?" He laughed.

"No. That just sounds insane. What's it even like?"

"You'll see. It's definitely not a brick wall."

"I remember some things about it from high school and stuff I've read online. Like we're in a bubble and all that, but the edge might be unstable."

"I wouldn't call it unstable." He teleported us. "We're here."

At first all I saw were dim stars in the distance, then I almost jumped back in surprise. Directly in front of me was my own reflection, but it was dim as if being reflected by glass. I looked around, but there was no indication of an ending to the strange reflection. I couldn't tell where it ended and the real stars began.

"That's so weird," I whispered.

"I told you. But look at this." Kris stepped forward and poked the edge of the universe with a finger. It rippled like water, distorting our reflections.

"Wow." I reached up as well. It was incredibly smooth and a bit cold.

"Thought you'd like it."

As I held my hand to it, a small space grew between my palm and the reflection. "It's moving."

"Of course it is. Expansion and all that."

"What's beyond it? Like, can we go past it?" I reached further forward, touching it again but didn't stop. My hand broke the surface. I gasped and didn't feel anything beyond the reflective veil.

"I dunno what's beyond. No one does. But you *kind of* can go through it."

I pulled my hand out; it looked just fine. "What do you mean?"

"If you go through it you end up on the other side of the universe."

I blinked. "How?"

Kris just shrugged.

"Is it safe?"

"Yeah. I've done it a few times before."

"And you just walk through?"

"Yeah, it's totally legit. Here." Kris walked right through the edge of the universe, leaving me standing in the emptiness of space.

I waited a minute, expect him to walk back out, but he didn't.

"Kris?" I asked quietly at first, but then my voice rose. "Kris?"

Nothing.

I assumed he was waiting for me to come through. I looked behind me, back into the universe, trying to imagine that across the whole expanse of space Kris was standing at the other edge. I closed my eyes and walked through the veil.

Beyond the end of the universe I was tumbling, no direction at all, head over feet, somersaulting through a pressing, fog? It felt too dense for air, too light for water. But was I really moving? I felt myself pass through another veil and it was over.

I ended up seated on a green hill of grass. Everything was too bright to be real. A tree nearby was weeping white leaves, and the sky was like polished gold, blinding me. The grass rose up around me, stretching out, a sparkling emerald meadow slowly rising into far off mountains with frosted pink peaks on the horizon.

"Kris?" I realized my voice was far too quiet to be heard.

Behind me everything was reflected and dimmed. I stood up and thought about running back through the veil, but then I saw Kris reflected over my shoulder stepping out from behind the tree.

I turned. "Where are we?"

"At the other end."

"But then all this...? What is it?"

Kris suddenly laughed. "I made it!" He flopped onto his back, eyes squinted as he looked up into the golden sky.

I walked to him. "Why make all of this? And how did you make it so quickly?"

"This isn't as big as it looks. Only about twelve meters across. It's an illusion."

I stared at the mountains. How could they be so close? I started walking towards them, and the ground inclined so quickly that I nearly fell. The blades of grass became microscopic, the trees like twigs then toothpicks, a small trickle of a river followed between my feet. Once close enough I could touch the tips of the mountains themselves and run my hand over the sky just behind them.

"You look colossal from here," Kris said.

"And the whole thing looks so wrong from this end. I'm feeling claustrophobic."

"I can fix that." Kris raised an arm and golden shell of sky disappeared. Stars took its place as if night had instantly fallen.

"So you just made all this to mess with me?"

"Not to mess with you. I just wanted to make something for you."

"Oh. Well, thanks." I looked around again. "It's nice."

Kris half smiled and walked to me. The tree, the grass, the mountains, everything disappeared and we were left standing in space.

"Let's go to the nearest planet and see what's happening," Kris said.

"Just so long as you aren't gonna kill everyone again."

Kris forced a chuckle and scratched the back of his head. "I promise."

"Good, but I'll take us there. I don't like the teleporting." I created a doorway and opened it.

"That's fine."

Kris walked through and I followed. We ended up in the back alley of some downtown.

"I'm really gonna have to learn how to make these doorways myself," Kris said. "It is a pretty clever thing you thought of."

"I'm surprised no one else thought of it."

"Me too."

We walked out onto the main sidewalk. Skyscrapers towered over us, taller than any buildings I had seen before, with transparent roadways in the sky and cars racing along them at incredible speeds. People in business suits walked by, not all of them Human. There were aliens that were only about 130 centimeters tall with brown skin and round heads and no neck. They also had two pairs of arms, one large set at the normal shoulder position and a smaller set beneath them.

"Whoa. Aliens," I said.

Kris bumped me with an elbow. "Don't be rude."

"I wasn't." I rubbed my side. "Where are we?"

"Well..." A paper appeared in Kris's hand. "This is 'Julius' and I've never been here before. Apparently not anything really of note though. Oh well." He tossed the paper behind him.

"But it's an Earth with normal Humans and an alien race?"

"You never know. These 'Humans' might not be normal either. I remember this one planet I came to randomly. None of the guys had external balls."

"You're kidding."

"No, no, really. It was a non-Human race that looked like Humans, but they had their balls on the inside. So there was this guy I hooked up with, and you can imagine our surprise once we got to the bedroom. Oi. I didn't much freak out, 'cause I know to expect weird things, but that guy, oh man, he freaked the *fuck* out. He thought I had some giant cancer or something hanging out. Pretty funny now that I look back on it."

"So what happened?"

"I gave him balls, made him think they were normal, and

we got down to business. Afterwards I put him back how he had been and made him remember me not having balls."

As I listened I speculated when exactly this had taken place. I assumed probably recently, while he was looking for me, but I wanted to know for sure. "Um, can I ask a personal question?"

He just gave me this look, almost squinting at me. "I was just telling you about a hookup I had. Of course you can ask me a personal question. You can ask me anything."

"Okay, well I was just wondering, when exactly did this hookup happen?"

"Uh..." Kris looked up at the sky. "I guess about, um, close to thirty years ago?"

"But wasn't Tavin still...?"

"Alive? Yeah. He was."

"Then–? Did, or, I mean, what–?"

"What did Tavin think about that?"

"Yeah. That."

Kris laughed but stopped quickly, like the sound had been cut in half. "Warpers don't have exactly the most stable relationships, but that's mostly just because we live for so long. I mean, look at Radcliff and Alicia. They haven't been 'together' in over twelve years, but I know they still love each other to death. Same thing with Jett and Erika. They're both kind of insane right now, but deep down they still love each other."

"So it's on-again, off-again?"

"Exactly." Kris came upon a small withered looking brown mushroom with amber-ish bubbles of puss on its cap growing up through a crack in the sidewalk. He kicked it loose as we kept walking.

"That doesn't sound very reassuring," I said.

"It's better than the alternative."

"What?"

"Someone you can control."

I didn't reply. I knew he was referring to Peter, and I knew he was right. No, no, wait. How could I give up hope so quickly? There had to be something, some way.

"Why not just *not* control them? Ever think of that?" I asked.

"Oh, sure, sure. That's like saying don't eat any of the

dessert that has no fat and no calories but still tastes fantastic."

"But that's not the same thing."

"It's close enough. They're both things we can make, and they're both things that we can control. There's no reason not to."

"What about the person's feelings? What about their thoughts or desires? Don't they have a right to be who they want to be?"

"But they're not real." A few seconds passed. "Especially if they're a copy. You know, the warp energy is kind of weird sometimes. Sometimes it makes answers to problems you aren't even aware of yet."

"What are you talking about?"

"Just something I was thinking about." Kris turned to face the street. "Let's go driving." A red sports car that was very flat and low to the ground appeared in a parking meter space. A few passersby gasped and stopped.

"Pretty sick isn't it?" Kris asked them. "It's a modified Lamborghini."

"How did you do that?" One of the aliens asked, his voice husky. "Is this a street show?"

Kris turned back to me. "Come on, I'll make you one too and we can race."

"What about them?" I asked softly, nodding my head slightly to the pedestrians.

Kris looked at them and back at me. "What about them what?"

"Aren't you gonna make them forget?"

"Why bother?"

"Aren't we like a secret?"

"Not really. Why would we? We literally have the whole universe. Who cares if a few people see us warping, no one else will believe it." Kris leaned on the car.

"But isn't the whole thing with the Rurrians all about them knowing we exist?"

"Yeah, but that's just because Jett cares about it."

"Uh... let's just not perpetuate things." I made the people watching us forget and they continued on down the sidewalk.

"N-e-ways. Racing. I'll make you a car."

"I'm pretty sure racing in a city is a bad idea."

"Not with the right fail-safes." Kris grinned.

"I'd still rather not do it."

"Well I suppose you are still a newbie."

"And what's that mean?"

"I mean you don't have a hundred years driving experience. Come on, get in. I'll show you how it's done." Kris got into the driver's seat.

I opened the passenger door and leaned down to continue talking to him. "Sure, you've been driving longer, but what makes you think I'd want to ride with you?"

"Oh, come on. Don't you trust me?"

"Don't play that card. Honestly, I have no idea when it comes to this."

"You'll see. This'll be awesome. You can be my wingman. Just make anything that's about to hit us disappear. I'll take care of the ramps."

"Ramps! Oh no. No, I don't think so." I closed the door.

It popped back open. "I was just kidding. Stop being lame," Kris said.

"Knowing you, you weren't kidding."

Kris gave a dramatic sigh. "Okay, maybe, but it's really perfectly safe, I promise."

I deliberated for a few moments. "Fine, fine. But if you do anything insane, I'm leaving right then."

"Deal."

I got in the car. Almost the second I closed the door Kris zipped us into traffic and down the road. Several cars blared their horns at us.

I gripped my seat; I hadn't even had time to put my seatbelt on. "Whoa! See! See! That's what I was talking about!"

Kris laughed. "Really? That wasn't anything." He ran a red light as an SUV swerved to avoid him. More horns.

"Stop! Stop!" I yelled. "You're gonna get us killed!"

"No I'm not. I told you–" He turned the car suddenly to avoid a line at a light, skidding onto another road, scraping the side of a sedan, costing him the driver side mirror and most of the paint. "–safety features. Man, I really wonder how you get up to those clear roads in the sky."

Less than a block ahead of us a limo was turning out onto

the street. "Oh shit!" I raised up my hands as if to block it, but the vehicle disappeared mere moments before Kris drove through the same space.

"Good one," Kris said.

"*You* didn't do that?"

"Nope."

"But I did that by *accident*! What if I *hadn't* made it disappear?"

"We'd've been fine. Don't worry."

"Sorry if I'm still skeptical, but I don't want to die today!"

"Don't worry about it. No one's gonna die today."

Kris's eyes were fixed on the road, but a perpetual grin brightened his face.

"That's odd," he said.

"What? What's odd?"

"There's already a cop on us."

I felt my stomach clench for a moment, an automatic response. But then I wondered. "What does that mean?"

"That this one got lucky to see us so quickly. Or maybe they've got really good social order here or something."

"No, I mean, since we're warpers. Do we just teleport out?"

"We could." Kris hadn't slowed the car. "But it's usually more fun to mess with them."

"Mess with them?"

"Oh yeah." He glanced over at me. "Watch." Kris flicked on the hazard lights, slowed down, and turned into the next parking lot.

"What are you gonna do?"

"Just watch, just watch. I am gonna give him this license though." Kris handed it to me to see.

It had Kris's picture on the license, but the name said "Narzok ki Rorr" and the address was in a city I'd never heard of before.

"I don't get it," I said.

"That's the cop's name, address, date of birth, everything."

"Okay, that's smart, I'll give you that, but there is no way this is gonna go well." I gave the license back to him.

"If we don't warp him of course this won't go well. But that makes everything so much more fun." He was still grinning.

I just shook my head and watched the cop through the

mirror as he exit his car and approach us. He was one of the four armed aliens and he had a hand on his holstered gun as he tapped on the window.

Kris rolled it down. "Yes, officer, can I help you?"

"First, I want you to know I've called backup and they're on their way. Second, you'd better give me a really good reason not to arrest you right now. Do you know how fast you were going?"

"Of course, officer. I was pushing ninety, but that's only because I couldn't get enough space to break triple digits. He's my license."

Officer ki Rorr took the license. "You don't even have a license plate on..." He trailed off.

"Yeah, funny story. You see, that's 'cause I ordered a custom plate, but it hasn't come in yet. It was gonna say 'kiss my ass,' but because of space constraints I had to take the vowels out. So now it's just gonna say 'kssmss,' which I think is actually twelve times funnier."

"This isn't a real license."

"But of course it is, officer."

Officer ki Rorr undid the strap to his gun. "I need you to get out of the car right now. Keep your hands visible."

"Oh, geez," Kris checked the car's clock, "less than three minutes. Ah well, but I certainly have seen better."

Without turning the key, without revving the engine, the car was on and speeding away from the cop. I was thrust back against my seat as we drove up a ramp that had just appeared and sailed through empty air towards the road over a line of cars. For the span of a breath it seemed we would hang in air forever, perpetually aloft. Then we slammed down onto the road, car jerking to both sides, finding traction. Kris was laughing and gave a loud whoop of joy as we sped away, racing through another intersection. It ended. From the corner of my eye I saw a truck mere centimeters away, just like before; it was the one that had hit me and I was in my car and Peter, Peter I'm not coming home.

I close my eyes, screaming as the car spun round and round like a top. We were falling through the air; we must have been launched several meters off the ground.

"Ethan! Ethan!" Kris was fighting back his laugher. "It's okay. We're fine."

We were still falling. I stopped screaming and opened a single eye. Above us was the clear open sky and below was an endless sea of pink. The car was still spinning but not as quickly anymore as we plummeted towards the mass of color.

"What's happening? What's happening?" I clutched the handle on the door, ridged in my seat.

"We're just falling. We're fine, don't worry. I told you there were safety features. If there was ever a change of speed greater than a certain amount, we'd immediately be teleported above Fluffy World."

"*Fluffy World*? Fluff–! The, fuck! Kris! We almost died!"

"No. No, we didn't. We're completely fine, Ethan. Calm down. Look, it's just a mass of fluff below us that slowly gets thicker. When you fall into it, it stops you safely."

"But why are we still falling? Why not just make the car start flying, or teleport out, or, or something?"

"Because this is more relaxing. Just calm down, okay?"

I clenched my teeth and took a few deep breaths. "Dammit, Kris."

"What's the matter, Ethan? Why are you getting so upset?"

"When are we gonna stop falling?"

"Not long. A few minutes more."

I noticed a few tendrils around the car and realized that we must have already entered the actual limit of the "planet." I glanced at Kris. "How often do you do this?"

"Crazy driving?"

"Yeah. And also end up here."

"Not as much as I used to."

"Then why are you doing it again now?"

"I have someone to do it with."

I didn't respond. The pink fluff was all around us, collecting on the car like a cotton candy machine. It didn't make any noise, and we didn't seem to be slowing down yet.

"Well, I don't think I'll be riding with you again."

"That's fine. We can race if you have your own car." He chuckled.

"Yeah. Sure." I crossed my arms.

The pink strands of fluff covered the windows now and they shrouded the interior a dim pink. I could feel the car slowing.

"Who made this planet?" I asked.

"Dunno. No one knows. Just another thing lost."

"Because of the different languages?"

"Yep. Alicia and Erika used to work on them before. The different Eras' languages. But that stopped a while ago. When Erika locked herself away. Neither of them figured it out.

There was a ripping sound outside, like a shirt being torn, and a small jolt. We stopped.

"Here we are." But Kris didn't move. He kept sitting, watching me.

It was very dark now; I could hardly make out his face. "Now what?"

"Nothing. We could leave. Or stay a while."

I opened the door and pushed, but the tangled fluff resisted me. I leaned more weight onto the door and it only moved a few centimeters. Kris snapped his fingers. The fluff encasing the side of the car disappeared, and the door swung open as I tumbled out onto the ground. Kris laughed.

"Thanks. Thanks a lot." I tried to stand but stumbled and fell to one knee. The compacted fluff was unstable like a giant cotton ball and just as soft.

Kris climbed out on top of the car and sat on the roof, looking down at me. "Need a hand?"

"No." I sat down to keep myself from falling.

High above us was a teensy oval of blue at the end of the pink tunnel with only diffused light reaching us so far down.

"Are you upset?" Kris asked.

"About what?"

"Me crashing?"

I was silent a moment. "No. I wasn't upset about that."

"Then what?"

"Nothing. I just freaked out. That's it." I lied back in the fluff and sank into it slightly. It was quite comfortable.

Kris jumped off the car and lied down near me. We both remained silent for a long time.

"It's all just too much sometimes," I said.

"What is?" Kris rolled on his side and propped his head up with an arm.

"Being a warper. Everything that *means*. Like, look." I created a donut in my open hand. "I just made a donut out of nothing. Literally nothing. Like, fuck. Warping. Just... *fuck*."

Kris laughed. "Technically you made it out of warp energy."

"That's not what I mean." I erased the donut and crossed my arms.

"I know. I'm sorry. Just vocalize it. That can help."

"Vocalize what?"

He scooched a little closer to me. "What you're feeling. If something's bothering you. You know, anything really."

I sighed and looked up at the tunnel. "I'm scared."

"Scared? Of what?"

"The ways things aren't different."

Kris remained silent, waiting for me.

"I... I can literally do anything now, but there's still things that aren't good. There are still things I *can't* affect. All this power only points all the stronger to the things I... the things that can't be different."

Kris titled his head to the side. "Like what?"

I thought a moment. "Things I don't know, I guess. And things that've already happened."

"Oh." He hesitated. "Yeah... those things."

We both didn't want to speak after that. Instead Kris crawled over and plopped down right next to me. He took my hand in his and kissed the back of my fingers. "It'll be okay," he whispered.

I looked at him. "Thank you for this, this part," I finally said.

"This part?"

"Showing me Fluffy World."

He smiled faintly. "I'm glad you like it."

I didn't reply.

"Does this make up for the car ride?" Kris asked.

I breathed in. I breathed out. "Yeah. We'll call it even."

Intermission I

"...and now we're passing through an asteroid field." Kris looked over at me, making sure to catch my eye. "Of *liquid.*"

He was probably enjoying playing the tour guide too much, but his antics had a certain endearing quality to them.

"What do you mean, liquid?" I asked.

"It's some gas that's a liquid when in space. Can't remember which one it is though."

I scanned the area through the cockpit window of our small spaceship. "I don't see anything."

"Yeah... that's the problem with these fields in general. Not much at all in them, contrary to popular belief. We'll fly past a few in a minute or so."

"Pssh, not impressed." I leaned back in the chair and put my hands behind my head, my left elbow carefully blocking my smile from Kris.

"Oh please. Not everything can be as great as floating glass mountains." He reached his hand up and warped the cockpit's front window, stretching it out to allow him to see straight up. "Look! There's a few."

I could just barely make out two faint globs far above us. "So what's so awesome about them?"

"Okay, okay, they aren't that awesome on their own. But just wait 'til we get further into the field and there's more of them."

"What? Is it gonna look like a giant space-sprinkler?"

Kris just looked at me, his eyelids low.

I snickered but tried to stifle it with a hand.

"Anyways," Kris said. "I'll show you, just watch."

All the stars around us blurred for a split second as we

teleported. In front of us I could make out some array of globs, but they were too dark to truly see.

"This is really fascinating, Kris. Truly. You've enriched my life with this."

"Hey, knock it off." Kris pushed me lightly. "I'm not done yet."

He snapped his fingers but nothing happened.

I waited a few moments and said, "What are you doing, Kris? Nothing's happening."

He held up his hand. "Wait for it. Wait for it."

A minute passed then the globs of liquid were illuminated. He had created a miniature sun one light minute beneath us, and now the swirling clandesence sparked before us. Hundreds of the large globs were rotating around each other, with countless smaller drops scattered everywhere like a mobile of diamonds.

"This particular bit is going to all join together eventually," Kris said, "so this is a limited time experience here."

"Okay, this does look pretty cool, but I do want to point out that you had to make a sun just to make it look cool."

Kris sighed. "You just love to play hard to get, don't you?"

"Ha. I wouldn't call it that."

"Whatever, I got something for you now." Kris shook a finger at me. "We're gonna go to the temple of doom!"

"What?"

"Okay, that's not literally what it's called, but it's fantastic." He grabbed my wrist. "I'll show you."

We teleported out of the spaceship and appeared in a rectangular room with walls of dusty tan bricks and a smooth floor and ceiling the same color. There were seven cylindrical pods attached diagonally to the floor and one of the walls, and a black screen was set into the wall opposite them.

"Here! This. Now this is the Hall of Hostile Hosts. It's in the first planet of the Vechian solar system, and I mean literally the first planet. It's a huge maze all inside the core of it. Basically, you get into one of the pods and it makes a body that's just like yours inside the maze, then you gotta try to beat it. Think 'Indiana Jones' meets 'platformer' meets 'Rubik's Cube' meets 'laser tag,' and all in real life! How fucking awesome does that sound?"

"Okay, I'm intrigued. But, hang on, it *makes* a body?"

"Yeah. So when you get impaled or set on fire and die, it's not for reals. The pods only work with warpers though, so we're the only ones who can play."

"Impaled?"

"Yep. But don't worry, you can set the pain levels, so you only get 10% of the pain or however much you want. Got it?"

"Yeah, sure. Okay."

"Good. Now I'm gonna boot everything up. Be just a tick."

He went to two of the pods and turned them on. I followed him and glanced inside. They looked pretty comfortable, but I was more interested in knowing how exactly I would be controlling the body it made inside the maze. I wandered over to the screen next. It remained blank until I was standing right in front of it, then words lit up in white text.

Hall of Hostile Hosts
created by
Mitch Roberts
35/06/1111
in loving memory of
R-T

"Cool isn't it?" Kris asked from behind me. "It detects what language you're most comfortable with and depicts the message in it."

"Who's Mitch Roberts?"

"Obviously a warper from the past. Now, the whole thing's running through a system check. It'll be just another minute."

"Why does it take so long to turn on?"

"Hey, we're activating a whole planet. That's not exactly an instantaneous process. Also it's gotta check through everything to make sure it's running smooth and none of the traps have jammed up or anything."

"There's traps in the maze?"

"Loads of 'em."

"Any monsters?"

"Only on the higher difficulty settings. We'll probably just play on Normal this go through. But oh man, Nightmare mode, oooh man. There's this *thing*. I've never been able to see it all, because I've never survived that far, but it basically eats whole rooms and lives in the walls. Or behind the walls. Not completely sure. Oh it's *so* scary though. I love it!"

I blinked. "Um, is it still there? Like, even if it's Normal mode?"

Kris shrugged. "I guess."

"Well... okay, then."

"*Final check finishing now,*" a genderless computer voice said. "*It is now safe to enter the pods.*"

"Come on, come on." Kris pulled me towards the pods. "You're gonna love this."

"How does it work?" I asked.

"Just hop in." Kris touched the pod and the cover slid open. "It's all automatic. See you inside." He climbed into the pod next to mine.

I hesitated a moment before climbing in. I reclined against the blue padded body mold and the lid slid shut. For several moments the pod was dead silent as a display appeared on the glass in front of my face, showing my vital signs.

"*Welcome. Body has been scanned and a game proxy is being constructed. Consciousness will be relayed into proxy momentarily. Please, relax.*"

The greeting certainly could have been better; it didn't make me feel more relaxed, but a sudden drowsiness washed over me. My head lolled, my eyelids fell, and when I opened my eyes again the drowsiness was gone. However, I was not in the same room.

Through the glass I saw a much smaller room with a vertical storage locker. The pod slid open with a quiet *sssshw*, and cool air drifted over my body. I realized I was naked and I sat up instantly. No other pods were in the room; I was alone. As I stood my body felt a bit stiff and, more oddly, slightly off. I looked down at my hands and noticed my finger nails were shorter. Then it hit me. The proxy. I was literally in a proxy body. I worried what the default pain setting was since I hadn't changed it.

The next logical thing to do was to look inside the locker, which was exactly what I did. Inside was a pair of briefs, sport shorts, a sport t-shirt, socks, running shoes, and elbow, knee, and wrist guards. I took everything and dressed quickly.

Outside the room was a short hallway in which Kris was waiting for me.

"Rookie mistake," he said.

"Huh?"

"The guards. You don't need them if your pain setting is low enough." He wasn't wearing his.

"Where was the pain setting? I didn't know I'd actually be *in* this other body."

"I said this, I said it makes a body. You change the setting in the pod. You just say what you want it to be before you transfer."

"So what's the default then?"

"30%."

"Oh."

"Don't worry, it's really not that bad." He patted my arm.

"Great. So now what?"

"We go to the starting point. Once we get there and hit the ready button we'll be off." He pointed down the hallway and we started walking. "We'll just be racing against the clock since we're the only ones in right now."

"What exactly should I expect in here?" I asked.

"It'll be more fun if I don't tell you." Kris grinned.

"Goddammit, Kris."

He just laughed.

We reached a door that said "Ready" on it and passed through into a sort of holding room. There was another door on the opposite wall that said "Start." In the middle of the room on a pedestal was a green button.

"Would you like to do the honors?" Kris asked.

"Okay."

I pressed it and a buzzer rang out as the "Start" door slid up. A timer set to one hour, zero minutes, and zero seconds flashed alive and began counting down.

Kris slapped me on the back. "Let's go! Let's go! Trial by fire!" And took off sprinting.

I ran after him down a long hallway lit by torches on one side. "It's just hallway."

"We'll hit a room in a moment. It's random every time."

After a short distance the hallway turned and we entered the first room. Kris took three steps in and looked everywhere:

up, down, both sides, and all around in-between. It looked like just an empty square room to me. The only things in it were four pillars placed evenly in the four quadrants of the room.

"Okay, no visible pressure plates or openings in the walls or trip wires. Of course, it is just the first room." He treaded lightly to the center.

"So what do we do here?"

"Find the hidden passage. Could be anywhere and there's probably multiple ones." He dashed to the left wall and started sliding his hand over it up and down, looking for a switch or loose stone. "Help me look."

"Sure. Just randomly feel up the wall then?" I pressed my hand against the wall on the right of the entrance.

Kris laughed. "If you wanna call it that."

I passed my hands over the bricks, but all I found was dust. Kris darted away from his wall after he'd checked it halfway and started kicking the bases of the pillars. There was a loud click and something slid away.

"Sweet! A slide."

I turned around just in time to see Kris hop down an opening in the ground. I ran over and looked. Just as he said there was a slide that led to uncertain depths. What the hell, I wasn't in my actual body. I jumped in after him.

I could hear Kris's laugher echoing from below me as we slid rapidly down the chute. It was a short ride, and I landed in what I first thought was the outside. I looked around and realized that was not the case.

It was a huge open area; in fact it seemed impossibly big. Cavern walls loomed around us and enclosed the hollow space, but they were over three thousand kilometers from the center. Everywhere around us were floating cubes, each the size of a large building and arranged in a perfect three dimensional grid. Between the many cubes were empty spaces that stretched across the whole cavern with bridges here and there connecting the cubes. Many pockets of blinding luminescents crawled slowly across the distant walls, casting odd angles of light everywhere. We had been deposited onto a small ledge on the side of a cube.

"Whoa," I said.

"Oh yes, and we can actually enjoy the view for a second

instead of shitting our pants because we landed in flying vermin territory."

"What territory?"

"Flying vermin. Vermin is the general term for the monsters in here. This place is really bad if you haven't found a weapon yet."

"There's *weapons* in this maze?"

"On the harder modes with the vermin. Come on. We should keep going. If we're lucky we'll find a checkpoint too." He started jogging across the ledge.

"So I assume you respawn at checkpoints if you die?"

"Yep. It's not always that helpful though, because sometimes you'll get a random checkpoint somewhere but then go a little further and find a dead end. Then whenever you get respawned there you have to backtrack."

"You can't choose your respawn?"

"Nope, it's just the last one activated."

We turned a corner and saw a thin bridge leading across to another cube.

"Look there." Kris pointed to a ladder on the cube across the gap. "The way out of this area is usually on top of a cube. We just have to cross this bridge. Easy." He ran up to it and started walking across slowly with his arms held out like a balance beam.

"And I see why this is worse with flyers," I said.

"Yep. For now though, just don't look down." He was already a fair distance across the bridge.

"There is no way I can get across like that. I do not have that kind of balance." I sat down on the bridge and started scooting sideways across it.

"Don't have that kind of balance? Aw man, what are you gonna do later then?"

"Are there more balance tests?"

"Not here. And I wouldn't exactly call them 'tests.' "

From his tone of voice I assumed he was smiling. "Then what do you–? Oh. Oh, I see what you did there. I have absolutely no idea how that would really involve *balance* though." I was about halfway across now.

"I don't know what you think I'm implying. I'm just referring to general balance needs, like changing a light with a swivel chair or walking across a roof in the rain." He reached the other cube and looked back at me.

"Yeah, sure. Sure you were."

Kris laughed. "Come on then! Hurry up!"

"I'm almost there."

Once I reached the other side we ascended the ladder and ran across the dark top of the cube. As Kris had expected there was an opening in the floor, and we descended down a flight of stairs into another torch lit hallway. We jogged down it a short way when an opening appeared in the wall next to us.

"And that's a checkpoint. Come on, no time for doddling."

"You're the one pointing out the scenery," I said.

"No I'm not." Kris continued without me.

I just shook my head and followed. Not too far down there was a faint click.

"Look out!" Kris yelled.

Shink. I fell to the ground, but it was worse than that. My waist tingled with pain as my upper body hit the floor separate from my legs. I had been cut in half.

"Oh fuck," I said more out of shock than pain. It felt perhaps as bad as if a circle had been cut around my waist with a knife.

Kris dropped to the floor next to me. "Ethan! This is costing us time!"

"Time...?"

My vision faded and I woke up inside the original pod. My hands instantly went to feel my waist, but I was perfectly fine.

"Good effort. Would you like to try again?"

"Shit." I still had my fingers on my waist.

"Sorry, non-understood answer. Would you like to try again?"

"Yes, I would."

"Respawning. Please, relax."

My vision faded again, and I was in the checkpoint. I climbed out, redressed quickly, and met Kris outside.

"Nixed the body armor this time?" Kris observed.

"Yeah. That was a cheap shot though."

Kris just nodded, and we took off again down the hallway. There was no click this time; the trap didn't go off at all. If that was to reduce the difficulty to just to give us a false sense of security, I wasn't sure. However, something else started bothering me a lot more than the lack of traps as we continued.

"Wait, Kris. I thought we were inside one of those floating cubes? How is this hallway so long?"

"Oh that. Yeah. Wibbly-wobbly, spacey-wacey. Pretty much impossible to keep track of where exactly you are relative to anything else here. We're just *inside*. It's part of the point. It is a maze after all."

"That's really bizarre."

"I really like it."

Soon we came upon another room with a huge laser turret in the center of it. There was a rectangular reinforced door in the wall the turret was point at, and side passages in both the walls left and right of it.

"A laser room! Yes!" Kris hopped up onto the platform and opened a panel on the turret. "I have a hypothesis that this is how you might be able to destroy the room-eating-behind-the-wall-monster-vermin, but, like I said, never gotten far enough before."

"Why is it here if we're not on the harder modes?"

"Because we can cut through the blast door there if we find the missing pieces to the laser. Or, if we really wanted, we could ignore this sub-challenge and take that back path." He pointed to one of the side passages.

"I assume the way through the blast door is faster?" I stepped up onto the platform.

"Lots faster. You're getting the swing of this place."

"Where are the missing pieces?"

"Other hall. It'll branch out and go to other areas. It looks like we need a driver board and a focus orb." He stood up. "I hate getting focus orbs."

"Why?"

"Because they're glass. If you drop it, it shatters and you gotta go all the way back and get another. If there even *is* another."

"Oh."

"Come on, let's go find our sub-challenges."

We headed down the hallway with a sign that said "Collecting" above it. It came to a fork, and we took the left route. At the end of the hallway was a door that led out into a desert. The sun was high above us, a cluster of cacti nearby, and a tumble weed blew past us. The door we had just come from was on a small shed that looked like not even a couch could fit inside it without being tilted partway.

"Why are we in a desert?" I asked.

"Because it's a bunker bust. Man, bunkers..." Kris started poking at the cacti.

"A what?"

"We gotta go down into a bunker and get the item out. Since there won't be vermin, it'll be rigged to self-destruct probably. It'll probably also be the focus orb in there, and we'll have to climb out on a ladder some twelve to sixteen stories because the elevators will of course be offline." Finally he hit something important on the cacti. There was a *clack* and a whirring of gears as a hatched flipped open from the sand.

"I feel like I'm getting way too many spoilers from you doing this."

"Really?" He glanced at me. "You couldn't just guess that those things would happen?"

I shrugged.

We climbed down a ladder into a small lobby with an elevator. Before we took it, Kris checked the room for alternate entrances. There were none. We entered the small moving room and descended. A bell dinged and the doors slid open.

It was dark. Outside the elevator looked like a sort of waiting room. It had rows of seats along both walls and two rows back to back in the center of the room. Only one light was working near the back of the room, and it flickered erratically. There were glass help windows along the far wall with doors at that end of the room as well.

"Something tells me there would be horrible, scary monsters here if this was a harder mode," I said.

"Yep. Or maybe they're still here? And they're simply intangible, because they're not turned on? Wouldn't that be interesting?"

"No, because there'd be no way to tell."

"Details, details."

We walked past the rows of chairs, and I tried a door upon reaching it. It was unlocked and creaked as I pulled it open. The corridor was dim, the light bulbs barely producing enough light to illuminate the floor. There seemed to be something standing in the middle of the hallway, and I squinted into the gloom. *Pzzat.* It was an automatic turret, and its muzzle flash lit the area like lightning. A small black circle zipped at me, its silhouette outlined in dull gray. I woke up inside the pod again.

"W-what! What was that?" I said.

"Good effort. Would you like to try again?"

"No, no, wait. What happened?"

"Game mode: 'Game Over,' equaled one. Would you like to try again?"

"Wow, so informative. Yeah, get me back in."

"Respawning. Please, relax."

I woke up inside the same checkpoint and groaned. I dressed as quickly as I could and ran down the hallway. I would have to get all the way back to the laser room, then back to the bunker desert, then back down into the bunker. I heard a faint click. I was running too fast, my mind tripped over itself trying to think of how to avoid the trap. I fell down to my knees, attempting to duck under the sliding blade, but was too slow. It decapitated me. The last thing I saw before waking up inside the pod again was the ground as my head rolled over it and was stopped by my nose.

"Goddammit!" I yelled after opening my eyes again.

"Good effort. Would you like to try again?"

"Yes, yes. Hurry up!"

"Respawning. Please, relax."

Respawned and redressed I proceeded down the hallway again, this time ready for the trap, but it didn't activate. I sighed. Through the laser room and back to the desert, I found the hatch to the bunker had closed. I didn't know how Kris had opened it, so I started poking at the cacti as he had done in hopes that I could find the trigger. I was at it for less than a minute when a rumbling ran through the ground that almost made me lose my balance. I tensed up, worried I might have set off a trap.

Nothing happened. I waited, and nothing else implied any sort of imminent threat was approaching. I continued prodding the cacti but still wondered what that tremor had been. A short while passed and suddenly the hatch flung open. I was just about to congratulate myself, but Kris came scrambling out.

"Fine timing!" He yelled as he dash to his feet, almost stumbling forward in the loose footing of the sand. "Move! Move! We have to get out!"

"Wait, wha–?"

"No time to explain!" He pushed me towards the door.

"Okay, okay. You don't need to–"

"Yes I do."

I was just about to protest again, but I noticed the sand a few meters beyond the hatch had started sinking downwards as if we were inside a giant hour glass.

"What is–?" I started to ask.

A jet of flame shot out from the center of the indent like a giant Roman candle. Kris didn't need to push me again; I was already running. He was right ahead of me. The sand was still draining away, even faster now. Kris rammed through the door. I just barely reached it as the surface gave way under me and I fell forward. I clutched at the door frame, and Kris pulled me in. Behind us the pillar of flame was expanding, seconds from the door. Kris kicked it shut and not even a moment later the wood cracked, groaned, and all was silent. Thin lines of smoke slipped out through the cracks in the door.

I remained laying on the ground, trying to catch my breath.

Kris helped me stand. "See why I wasn't excited about a bunker bust?" he asked.

"Yeah. Yeah, I think so." I ran the back of my hand over my forehead. "Wow."

"At least I got the part. Turns out it was the driver board there." He lifted his shirt and took it out from the waistline of his shorts. "What took you so long?"

"The respawn was far away."

He shrugged. "You didn't miss much."

"What was that turret that killed me in there?"

"Antimatter. Most destructive thing in the universe, well, after a warper of course. They're a pretty rare obstacle. I'll show you how to shield against antimatter later, but it's completely unneeded in real life. Hell, I only know how to do it, *because* of this game."

"Isn't there antimatter in the universe?"

"Yeah, but in such small amounts you're almost guaranteed to never see it unless you go looking for it."

We returned to the fork in the hallway, and Kris left the driver board leaning against a wall. Down the other branch we did not find a door, instead the hallway slowly changed into the rough unrefined walls and floor of a natural cave.

"Why is this a cave?" I asked.

"I... I'm not sure." Kris clicked his tongue twice. "I won't know for sure 'til we get all the way in, but I don't really recognize this so far."

His statement wasn't reassuring.

The floor became less solid and more gravelly as we continued into the cave system. Our footsteps crunched with each step, and the air grew extremely humid. The cave started to grow dim as well. There were no more torches, but as we proceeded we found that growing on the ceiling and part way down the walls was a strange plant. It was a tangle of thin vines and tendrils, and budding from the vines were small blue orbs that glowed with bioluminescence.

"This is rather pretty," Kris said.

"Yeah. But, I don't understand *why*. I mean, what's the point of these caves? What's the catch?"

"Why does there have to be a catch?"

"Because isn't this supposed to be another obstacle in the maze? Another challenge?"

"Maybe there's normally vermin in here."

"Like the bunker?"

"Yeah. Basically."

The cave remained linear as we proceeded, though it did grow larger. The tunnel widened as the ceiling pulled further and further from us. The light did not diminish too much though as the glowing plants were becoming incrementally larger: the vines thicker, the orbs greater in diameter. There was a sharp turn to the right and the tunnel abruptly opened up into an expansive cavern bathed in pale blue light. We were partway up the wall of this cavern, and the vines covered everything within. The ceiling, the walls, the floor. Great clusters hung down from above like living stalactites with water dripping slowly down them. Some of the clusters even reached the floor and looked like strange, tangled support columns. Growing from the floor above the settled mist that clung to the lows of the cavern were huge leaves, bigger than either myself or Kris. At the center of the cavern was an immense spiraling knot of vines rising up in the mock form of a giant tree trunk. The glowing orbs were everywhere, including huge meter wide orbs in the mist that gave the haze an ethereal quality.

"Definitely have never seen this before," Kris said.

"So what do we do? Where do we find the focus orb?"

"I have a hunch."

Kris reached up to a blue orb that was growing low down the wall of the cavern and plucked it from its vine. The vine twitched and writhed away from him, and he jumped back in surprise. The vine bumped more vines and they started twitching as well, and a few other orbs were loosed from their stems. The whole cascade dropped a dozen glowing orbs around us that smashed open on impact as rustling filled the air. The vines soon slowed and stopped. By happy luck, Kris had plucked an orb from a less densely populated spot.

"I think," Kris said slowly, "we need one of these." He held up the orb.

"Hang on, what the hell just happened?"

"They don't like being touched?" He shrugged.

"Great."

"But look, feel this." He handed me the glowing orb he had taken.

It was incredibly smooth for something that had apparently been grown. "But it's not glass. I thought the focus orb would be glass?"

"I thought so too. They've always been glass in the past." He nudged a broken orb on the ground. Glowing juice oozed out of it as the shell crackled beneath his foot.

"Well let's head back then." I nodded my head in the direction we had come.

"Wait. We don't have the orb yet."

"I though you said this was it?"

"Yeah, but not that one. It's too small."

"Then where...?" I glanced out at the spiral tree of vines. The orbs there were larger. "Uh... hmm."

Kris patted my back. "Yep. Those ones. They look about the right size. But don't worry. I'm just as green here as you are. It'll be fun." He grinned.

"Aw hell. Alright, let's go then." I tossed the orb behind me, and we carefully descended into the cavern.

As we reached the floor, Kris stepped on a vine and it jerked away violently, knocking him to the floor as his footing was lost. It hit several more vines and another ripple of fading rustling passed through them.

Once it grew silent again Kris looked at me and said, "Don't step on them." He stood and brushed off his shorts.

"But you're the one who just did that."

"*Lies*. Lies, lies." He stepped carefully over the vine.

"Kris, seriously. Sometimes..." I shook my head

"Seriously sometimes what?" He grinned.

I hesitated before answering, placing my step delicately. "I think you do these things on purpose sometimes."

"What? Never."

"Really? Okay, that's true. But only if by 'never' you mean 'always.' "

Kris laughed but stopped walking abruptly.

I was about to put my foot down, but he was still standing where I was going. I started to fall forward and I grabbed his shoulder. He leaned forward in surprise but was able to support me.

"Why did you stop?" I asked.

"We're about to enter the mist."

I looked over his shoulder. A few more centimeters and it would be impossible to see where we were stepping.

"What do we do?"

"Be as delicate as possible and probably be ready to run." He raised a foot and held it out, fanning it back and forth a few times in an attempt to clear the mist. The gesture did very little, and he simply placed his foot down. "Ah, see. Nothing to it."

"Sure. One step down, who knows how many hundreds or so to go."

"Don't be such a downer." Kris pressed on.

I continued behind him, watching where he placed his feet in the mist.

"Now, worst case scenario," he started to say, "we run to the glob of vines there and we each grab an orb and run back. That'll double our chances of making it."

"That's what I love the most about your plans: so much detail."

"Hey, simpler is usually better."

I had lost track of where Kris had been stepping as the mist thickened. It was almost a meter high, and with each step I placed my foot down ever more slowly. If a vine was just lightly brushed it would twitch only a little and I'd have a chance to recover. The false touches and twitching vines were growing far too common though. My hands were starting to shake and I was afraid I would lose precise moments of my feet next.

"This is going to be so hard coming back carrying an orb. Oh *man*, is this gonna be hard," I said.

"Don't think about it. Just like when you're up high you don't look down." As soon as Kris said that, he mis-stepped and a vine writhed away from him.

I lunged forward, trying to catch him before he fell and hit more vines. But as my hands grabbed him I leaned too far forward to support him. We both fell to the ground. I felt at least four vines beneath me. Each one started writhing, but they weren't strong enough to lift me.

"Run! Run now!" Kris pushed himself to his feet as the vines started knocking against his back and calves. He ran two paces before more writhing vines brought him down again.

I tried a different approached. I rolled to the side as quick as I could, away from the vines that had already felt me and onto others that had not yet started moving. It gave me a second to scramble to my feet and run forward. My running became more like hopping as I tried to avoid as many vines as I could, but I still got tripped up repeatedly. I was even knocked into the huge glowing orbs on the ground every now and then. They crunched beneath me, and soon the glowing goo was splattered across my whole body. Even if I did reach the spiral tree without a concussion, I had no idea how I'd get back without breaking the focus orb.

A number of meters to my right, Kris wasn't doing much better. I had made it a bit further than him, but I noticed something that would be a very bad development for us. Kris was drawing near one of the clusters of vines that grew from the ceiling that had tangled with the vines on the ground. The vines were thrashing all around him now, and the movement was spreading. It had reached the base of the vine column and started working its way up, vines shaking vines.

"Look out!" I yelled to him.

He didn't seem to be paying attention and neither was I. Looking back at him had cost me my lead against the vines. The bundle beneath me snapped upwards, tipping me back. I landed inside a huge orb, its warm ooze drenching over my shoulders, down my shirt, sticking to my arms and hair. I had been so glad in that moment that I hadn't been in my real body.

I pushed myself up, peeling away from the broken orb, and slopped away. The ooze made me heavier, and I had much more difficulty making progress. Around that time a number of glowing orbs started falling from the ceiling like bombs. I covered my head with my arms as they splattered around me, making the ground slick. One of them hit me directly, knocking me to the ground. My shoulders and arms stung, and I wonder how bad it would have been if my pain hadn't been reduced.

I got up again and was getting so close to the spiral tree. My clothes were completely soaked with the ooze, almost like I had come out of a pool after swimming in them. Before I reached the base of the tree I was crawling. The vines couldn't lift my whole body, but my progress was exceedingly slow. My legs continually lost their friction against the battering vines. I keep one arm across my face so it wouldn't be smacked directly. Finally, finally my fingers touched the vines that turned upwards.

These were far harder to the touch, almost like wood, and I feared for a moment that the one I had touched would whip forward and knock me into the air, flying backwards, but it didn't move. I pulled myself up onto the small ledge created by the thick vine and was able to rest. I wiped the glowing ooze from my face and looked out over the cavern. The vines were still shaking all around the spiral tree, but they seemed to be slowing. I didn't see Kris anywhere.

"K-Kris." I called out. "Kris!"

I turned around and studied the vine I was sitting on. The vines that comprised the spiral tree must have been much older than any of the others. They had grown stiff and remained thankfully still. I scanned the mist for Kris again.

"Kris? Are you there?"

I ran a hand through my hair, slicking it back and rubbing away more of the glowing blue goo. I flicked it from my hand. He must have either been battered to blacking out or battered to death. I bit my lip. If you were knocked out did that force you to respawn? I didn't think there was much of anything I could do now, so I looked up the spiral tree for a focus orb.

I spied a good looking orb a short distance above me and I climbed up. The way the vines grew made almost a giant staircase up the side of the spiral tree. The orb was about the size of a basketball; I plucked it from its stem, and the tree remained still. I breathed a sigh of relief and slowly crawled back down.

I paused on the lowest vine, considering my options. The orb I was carrying didn't feel stronger than any of the other ones. I could try picking my way across the ground again, but one wrong move and I'd have to go back and start again. I wondered what the other focus orb challenges were like.

I decided to survey the entirety of my surroundings before proceeding. I worked my way counterclockwise around the base of the spiral tree, but everything around me looked much the same as the way I had come. However, as I neared my original position I noticed something. The sound of softly trickling water.

I squinted into the mist, trying to find anything that would hint at the location of the sound or what exactly it was. I couldn't see anything definitive, but I had an idea of its location from the noise. I set my orb aside, grabbed another, and chucked it into the mist. It smashed against a vine that flick upwards and triggered others around it. Their twitching subsided, and I tried another orb. This one landed with a splash. Perfect.

I climbed as low as I could on the tree and reached a foot into the mist. Sure enough, there was flowing water. I dropped down but slipped on a few pebbles and fell to my knees. The water wasn't very deep, only barely over my ankles once I stood, and there wasn't a single vine in it. I slogged through the stream and followed it by sense of touch and sound alone. I projected from the initial direction of the stream that it was headed in the general direction of the opening in the wall to the tunnel. Upon reached the wall of the cavern I was only several dozen meters from the opening. I climb up the incline to be free of the mist, then it was a simple matter of picking my way over the vines.

"Ethan!" It was Kris standing at the mouth of the tunnel.

"Hey. What happened?"

"Clobbered by one of the orbs, I think." He pointed at his head. "Looks like you did really well though."

"Yeah. We should've looked around first. There was a stream I followed."

"That figures. But, we're missing the most important part here."

I clambered up the ridge into the tunnel with him. "What?"

"You look like a blue firefly." He laughed and wiped a bit of the goo from my ear.

"Yeah, well I like to look at it this way: I didn't get killed by a plant." I smiled.

"Oh shut up." He punched my shoulder lightly. "Let's get that orb back."

We returned to the laser room, my footprints glowing behind us, and Kris installed the components. He shut the panel and turned to me. "Would you like to crack that door open?"

"Sure. How?"

"Here. Just sit right here, hit the green button, and aim the laser. Easy."

"Alrighty." I sat down and pressed the button. The turret started humming, and a red dot appeared on the metal blast door accompanied by smoke and a small flame. I started cutting a circle in it.

"We might be really close to the end now. We'll see in just a sec," Kris said.

I finished the hole and shut the laser down. Kris motioned for me to follow him. We gave the door a moment to lose the greatest of its heat, then we pushed on the circle I had cut. It budged forward, slid relatively easily inward, and a few seconds later it was free. It hit the floor with a deep *thum*. In the next room was a raised pedestal with a trophy cup atop it, and a screen displaying the countdown. Four seconds left. Three.

"Oh. Damn," Kris said. Two.

One.

My vision went white, and I woke up inside the pod again.

"You did not win this time. Thank you for playing." The door slid open.

"We were so fucking close," Kris said from his own pod.

I leaned forward and looked over at him. "That really didn't feel like a whole hour."

"Not at all. Ugh! So close!"

"Wanna go again?"

Kris grinned. "Hell yeah, but this time we'll race each other since you know what you're doing now."

"First to the finish?" I asked.

He nodded with a smirked.

"You're on." I leaned back, and we began again.

Chapter 13
Steps to Take

"No. You *can't* move in with me." I was home again, and Kris was not listening.

"But I'm over here often enough anyways," he said.

"Yeah, but you know what, I think you're over here too often. I can't be hanging out with you all the time."

"And why not?"

"I don't want to be around you that much. Okay? I can't be. And sometimes I just want to be alone."

Kris crossed his arms. "Is this still about Peter?"

"That's not the point, Kris. I just don't want you to live with me."

"If that's not the point then *why?*" He was looking straight into my eyes, and I knew he wasn't asking just be to be difficult.

"I don't know. I don't know how to explain it. I just don't want to live with you."

"Ever?"

"Not right now, and that's it. That's it," I repeated slowly.

Kris looked away. I was trying to think of something else to say, some other way to arrange the words into an explanation. Before I could think of the right thing Kris disappeared.

"What?" I called out into the emptiness where he had stood. "Oh, sure, sure, great. Just great. Go disappear then! Goddammit." I left the living room and marched into the kitchen.

I wished above anything else that Kris wouldn't be so erratic, but then amended that wish to second place. What I really wished for above anything else was that things didn't have to be so complicated.

159

I yanked open the refrigerator, not really looking for anything in particular, but apparently I had seen the eggs first and thought of them. Three whole cartons of eggs appeared in the air nearby and few in random directions. Two hit the walls and one smashed on the floor.

"*Goddammit!*" I slammed the refrigerator closed and kicked the carton on the floor.

It smeared yellow and clear across the floor. The impacts on the walls were dribbling down. I reached out, imagining the egg wiped clean from my house, but instead the mess slid across the wall like a dead bug smeared by wiper blades. I was too frustrated; I couldn't focus. I wanted to go someplace else, and the first place that hit my mind was the Restaurant.

I made a doorway and stepped through. To my relief the Restaurant was empty, aside from Bot of course. I sat down at the counter.

Bot remained silent until I sighed.

"What would you like?" asked Bot.

"I don't know. A lot of things."

"The law of averages wins again."

"What?"

"That was the best way it could be stated such that you would understand the meaning quickly. I do know that 'law of averages' is inaccurate terminology in this context."

"Whoa, hold on. I am completely lost now."

"Oh. I had been momentarily hopeful that you were actually attempting to call out my misused words, but instead I have been ahead of you this entire conversation. Disappointing. What would you like?"

"Look, I'm really not in the mood for this, whatever you're talking about. Just give me a milkshake or something."

"One standard mil– wait. You are really going to do this to me? I am not interested in your current frustration. Go to some standard Earth bar if you want to drink and cry."

"What? *What?* That's not fair. I haven't even told you anything that's happened yet! Actually, you don't even know if anything has happened at all."

"On the contrary. I can tell your heartbeat and respiratory levels are not at baseline. The fact you looked around the Restaurant and were relieved upon finding it empty puts standard exercise or extraneous activity outside the realm of high probability. In addition, the fact this is your sixth time coming to the Restaurant puts you in the time range of beginning to think of me as less of an acquaintance and more of a 'comrade-in-arms' due to any number of factors which would take even longer to list. Furthermore, the fact I always remain here makes you inclined to think of myself as a neutral party, thus far more likely to tell me about your grievances. Now that I have demonstrated only a number of items I calculated in the first few seconds of your arrival, you will not again doubt my abilities or think that I am on *your* level."

Every word Bot spoke was quick and even, a continuous steam that sounded all the stranger for the fact that Bot's voice was almost Human. I fidgeted slightly, suddenly quite uncomfortable. I imagined it would've been better if Bot's voice had been completely robotic instead.

Bot stopped waiting for a reply. "One standard milkshake."

It appeared in front of me: vanilla with chocolate swirls along the inside of the glass, topped with whipped cream, and garnished with rainbow sprinkles and a cherry.

I didn't touch it.

"If you wish to leave, I will not hold it against you," said Bot. "In fact I will not even bring up this incident again the next time you venture in here, or any other time in the future. So go. Slink away."

I was about to stand and leave, but then Bot spoke those last two words. I looked him straight in his glowing robotic eyes. "No."

There was an actual detectable pause before Bot replied. "Interesting."

"What?"

"Your response, of course."

"What, did you expect me to just leave?"

"Yes."

"Really?"

"Yes. Your ears are still working. I remember having similar conversations with every warper I have ever met. Very few did not leave afterwards."

"So you did this with Kris too?"

"Has the definition of 'every' changed?"

"No." I hesitated. "What did Kris do?"

"I will not reveal that information about him or any other warper."

"Why not?"

"Why do you think? It is private, and there is absolutely no true reason why you would need to know. If you are so desperate to know, ask Kris yourself."

"What would I even ask him? 'Hey, did you have a weird conversation with Bot at any point in the past hundred years where Bot told you to leave?' Yeah, sure. He'll know exactly what I'm talking about."

Bot laughed. It was a genuine laugh without a hint of mockery that made me jump in my seat. I had never expected Bot to even be able to laugh like that.

"Yes, that is exactly what you should ask Kris. Yes, he will exactly know. Or will not. Unless, of course, you do not wish to speak with him because Kris is your current frustration."

"Yeah, but you already made it perfectly clear that you don't want to hear about my 'current frustration' at all."

"I will hear it now."

"What?"

"I will, however, *not* hear it if you continue to make me repeat myself."

"Sorry... I was just, surprised."

"Doubtless. Give me the short version."

I thought a second. "Well, um, basically Kris just won't lay off."

"Oh how I wish you Humans were better at consolidating your words without sacrificing content, even with your inherent disadvantages. Explain further."

"Well what else am I supposed to say? You don't want to hear all the details, so how am I supposed to explain everything?" I was thinking about leaving right then. Peter was suddenly in the forefront of my mind, and I wanted to see him.

"You misunderstand. I want you to prove to me, without unnecessary words, that your current predicament is actually significant rather than petty drama."

"No, that's it, I've had it." I stood up. "If you're just gonna be condescending all day, then I don't even want to talk to you. It's no wonder no one else talks to you either. Keep your milkshake. I'm gonna go see Peter and sort out this mess myself."

"Peter?"

"Yeah, my boyfriend. Back from before this whole mess happened." I walked away from the counter and made a doorway.

"Wait. A non-warper you are still affiliated with?"

"Yeah, and I'm not gonna wait around to hear you talk bad about him too. How he's not real or whatever the hell else."

"That is not what I was going to say. Quite the contrary, actually."

"Yeah right."

"I understand your skepticism. But if you leave now, I will merely inquire the next time you return."

I paused, hand on the door knob. A smirk crossed my mouth as I thought of something. I looked back at Bot. "Prove to *me* in as few words as possible why you'd care to know about Peter."

"So now you wish to be clever? Very well. Continued interest in non-warpers for anything other than short-term enjoyment is a rare trait in warpers, even in a warper that is hardly a month old."

"So? Being left handed is rare too."

"Indeed."

I waited. "That's it?"

"Yes."

"Well I'm not convinced." I crossed my arms.

"That is all I am going to say."

"Then I'm leaving."

"Very well."

"But, aren't you–?"

"Yes. But my existence does not depend on knowing everything I wish to know. I can wait. Your life has centuries yet."

He was right, I *was* just about to ask him if he was curious. A slight shiver ran down my spine. I left through the doorway, ignoring Bot, and entered into my parents' house.

My father was in the living room, patching a hole in the popcorn ceiling. He did not notice me, because I did not allow him to. I left the house through the front door, making it insubstantial temporarily, and started walking in the direction of Peter's house.

I don't know why I came to my parents' house first instead of going straight to my destination in the first place. I suppose I wanted some time to think—time to gather my thoughts and decide what I was even going to do when I arrived.

I had already fixed everything on my planet. Moved my city back to Utah, just the same as before, but I kept the bigger house and my parents' ownership of Rebaxis Medical International. Continents, cities, and prevalent technology were all back to normal. All the airlocks, the extreme insulation, the artic proof cars, the permanent wintery fashions, the cold adapted plants and animals, the frozen/unfrozen water cycles of the rivers and lakes were all gone, erased from existence. And most importantly of all: the memories.

I had wiped every scrap of knowledge of the icy disorder from the mind of every living thing still on my planet. Three weeks of time gone. I even moved the planet backwards in its orbit, set the calendars back, reversed everyone's aging. Three weeks that never even happened. To everyone on this planet it was still only a week after my birthday, instead of a month. Even to Peter's mind.

I had reset him too. There was no way around it. I still hadn't warp locked him though. It seemed to be impossible. No, correction, it seemed to be impractical. I had only visited him a few times since that initial night, and I never again tried to explain what was going on. I just have to wait, I kept telling myself, wait until I can find the right way to make him understand without forcing him or breaking him.

The sun was still wonky, and the atmosphere was still overcompensated, but those were minor details could I ignore for the moment. Perhaps later I would tweak them back to the way they had been before, but right now I was happy with it just being good enough.

I was growing tired of walking. His house was still over twenty kilometers away; I knew I would never have walked the whole way. I made a doorway and appeared a few blocks from his house.

Now the sinking feeling in my stomach was growing

stronger. I was that much closer to him and I still didn't know what we could even do when I got there. I wouldn't let myself stop to think about it though, because I knew I would more than likely not go at all if I stopped moving forward. The last time I had felt such apprehension before seeing Peter was back when we had first met, during the beginning of senior year in high school.

He went to a different school, and it was our mutual friend Catharine who had set everything in motion at a Halloween party when she practically threw us together at the snack table and sat back to watch her work, like a chemist playing with elements. Though I suppose it was fitting: she was dressed as a mad scientist. We talked, we laughed, we exchanged numbers and social networking. Within a day we were talking all the time; within a week had gone on our first date.

I remember it vividly.

"You know, I really didn't understand that one spy-chick's reasoning for trusting Clint," Peter said.

I was driving us home, late at night, after that first date at the movies, a thin rain falling over the world outside the car. "The one played by Hatty Cadwalder?" I asked.

"Yeah, her. I can't remember what her character's name was."

"Melena."

"That's right. But it didn't make any sense why she would just hand over the evidence to him just because he promised to use it as fake bait. Even though it turned out he wasn't lying, it seems like there was no way they could have kept the files actually safe during the plan."

"How else were they gonna get in the base of operations?"

"I dunno. I mean, I'm more happy with who I saw the movie with than the movie itself."

I smiled, unable to stop myself. I looked away, out the side window. "Me too."

" 'You too' about the movie? Or the other part?" Peter glanced over at me with a grin.

My smile wasn't going away, so I just looked at him and said, "The other part."

"Cool." He nodded once, watching me.

I couldn't see him that well in the dim light, only when we

passed under a street lamp did his face glow with amber-yellow light that swept over him for a second before flitting away. He must have seen the same thing: a darkening world with sparks of light rushing past. The sparks caught his eyes. I had to, but didn't want to, look away; eyes back on the road.

"I wish we weren't so close," I half whispered.

"Huh?"

"I mean so close to your house." A stoplight, finally. I looked at him again. "I don't want to drop you off."

"We could stop somewhere."

"Wouldn't you get in trouble if you're late?"

"No. My parents are probably already in bed."

"Okay."

"And you?"

I thought a moment. If I did get in trouble, it wouldn't be too much. "No, I'm good. But where can we go? It's late."

"We don't really have to go anywhere." Peter was silent a moment. "We could just stop at the park outside my neighborhood. The parking lot's always open, and I never see anyone there. You won't have to drive anywhere extra."

"I don't mind driving with you though."

"Thanks."

We arrived on the street, and Peter showed me where to turn. Once the engine was silent there was only the most subtle tapping of rain, a kind you almost had to strain to hear. The park itself was dark and motionless, a single lamp shinning over a tennis court without a net. There was a lamp post near the playground, but it was out. I could only see the swings and monkey bars, because they were next to the parking lot.

"This place has seen better days, hasn't it?" I forced a chuckle.

"Yeah, it's an old neighborhood."

I wished it would stop raining. "Stupid weather."

"What?"

"It'd be nice to walk around instead. Instead of just sitting here. I guess. Not if you didn't want to, I mean, but it's raining. So, I mean... yeah." Damn it, words, why do you do this to me?

Peter laughed softly. "I get it. It would be nice if it wasn't raining."

"Yeah."

We were silent again as I bit my lip, trying to think of something more I could say. "So, the ending of the movie was good."

"It was pretty decent," he said. "But flying the helicopter through the mall was a bit over the top, I think."

"There was enough room though. I guess it could work."

"I dunno. I just thought it was kinda silly."

I was watching the nearby tree line now, their branches shuffling in the wind. "I'd like to try flying a helicopter someday."

"I've been in one once," Peter said.

"When?"

"It was one of those helicopter tours over the Grand Canyon. My grandparents live in Williams, Arizona, and we drive out to see them during the holidays. But I got motion sickness from it, so I didn't think it was that great."

"I've never been to the Grand Canyon. Not yet. Even though we're so close to it. My parents have talked about it before, but they're always so busy at their office jobs. You know."

Peter shrugged. "It's a kinda over hyped. You know it's only about six hundred meters deep now? Lots of it has eroded and all." He raised his hand and pressed the back of it against his window, taping the backs of his fingernails on the glass.

"Yeah, I've heard some stuff about that."

There was another pause of silence, then I added, "You know, I also don't understand how they *drove* to Paris in just a few hours. They were in Washington DC. That's literally impossible."

"It's only like a six hour drive or so."

"What? No, no it's across..." I remembered the two cities were still in the wrong place. I slumped in my seat and muttered faintly.

"What's the matter?" Peter leaned towards me a few centimeters.

"Even in the movies it's different. There's no proof I can point to."

Peter tilted his head. "What are you talking about?"

I pressed my teeth together and debated if I wanted to get into this now. The internalization just made me more frustrated, and I turned to him suddenly, looking him dead in the eyes. "How long has Paris been in New York State?"

"Huh? Is this a trick question?"

"No. How long has it been there?"

"I dunno. I have no idea when it was founded, but it's been at least three hundred years I guess."

"No. It's not right." I crossed my arms and turned away from him, looking out the driver's side window.

"Ethan, why are you getting so upset?"

Because these things won't stop happening. Because no one ever listens. Because things won't just stay the same for once. I remain silent.

"Ethan, come on. Talk to me."

I was silent a moment longer. "Have you even been so alone, but never able to explain it? So alone even when you're surrounded by people you know?"

Peter opened his mouth part way but hesitated. "I... I don't think so. You're not alone. I don't understand."

I sighed. "Just forget about it."

He sat bewildered for a moment and huffed. Then he reached out to me. "Let me see your hand."

"My hand?"

"Yeah. Let me see it."

"Why?"

"Just let me see it."

I held out my hand. "Okay, what is it?"

Peter took it in both of his own hands, thumbs brushing over my skin. The lightness of his thumbs as they slid over my palm was surprising, almost like soft tickling. It sent a shiver up my spine. He turned on the overhead light to see better.

"I'm trying to read your palm."

"You know how to palm read?"

"Not actually." Peter gently pulled my hand a bit closer to him. "I've just read a few websites about it. Do you know what this line is?" He pointed at a curved line near the base of my thumb.

"No."

"Good. It's the relationship line. Look. See all these lines crossing it? They're all people who care about you. You're not alone."

168

I leaned forward slightly, moving closer to him. "But..."

He didn't let me finish; he leaned forward and kissed me. The first time we kissed.

I was standing outside Peter's house now, refocused on the present. I had kept his family's new house when I changed everything back, just moved it to where the old one had been. I licked my lips and approached the door, ringing the doorbell. Almost a minute passed before the door opened.

"Ethan!" It was Peter. He wrapped his arms around me in a tight hug. We kissed again. There was no way to know how many times it had been now.

"Hey."

"What are you doing here? I thought you were just starting your first week at that college in London."

That was the story everyone believed: I got accepted into a fancy academy in London and had already left, but I only planned to spend one year there to "broaden my horizons." After that I would return to the States next summer and go to college here. That would be more than enough time for me to get the warper situation settled before returning.

"I'm skipping class today and decided to fly into town to see you."

Peter laughed. "Man, that sounds so unreal. Like, I dunno, from a movie or something. How'd I get so lucky with you?" He leaned forward and kissed me again.

"Who knows. Let's go in. I just wanna... chill. You're parents aren't home are they?"

"Dad's on a trip, but my mom's here. I think she's already working on dinner. She got this new recipe–"

I closed my eyes. "She's at your grandparents', visiting." I made it true. I felt the warp energy flow out: to her, to the van, down to Arizona.

"–so she won't be back for another three days. How long are you going to be in town?"

I cringed on the inside. I hated to do that to Peter's own mother, but all I really wanted was to be alone with him. Maybe I could make a nice apartment for him? And some form of income, so he– I stopped my train of thought. "I dunno. Maybe just for the day."

"Aw, really? We should call up a few people then, see if

anyone's free to hang out. We do have a whole house to ourselves." He stretched out his arms, grinning.

"Maybe later, but right now let's just..." I stepped forward, resting my forehead on his shoulder. "I'm just tired."

Peter rubbed my back. "I get it. Come on."

He pulled me over to the couch, and we sat together. I pulled up my legs to my chest and leaned on him. He put his arm around my neck and let everything be quiet for a while. I didn't want to think about anything. I just wanted to feel Peter next to me.

"I love you, Peter," I whispered.

"I love you too, babe."

"I..." I couldn't think of anything to say or anyway to say it. Suddenly I started to feel that I might cry.

"Ethan, what is it?" Peter rubbed my shoulder.

"I just, I love you so much. So much. You been one of the most permanent things I've ever known, and I don't want to lose you."

"What are you talking about? Come on, tell me what's wrong."

"Nothing, nothing." I shook my head and made him forget I had said anything. Now I really wanted to cry. I held my breath.

"So, if we did have some friends come over we could just move the flower vases to the dining room, then we won't have to worry about... Ethan? Ethan, are you crying?"

"No." My voice broke. "I'm not."

"Whoa, babe, what is it?" He reached up and stroked my cheek again.

"I can't tell you."

"Why not?"

"Because every time I've tried before you either don't get it, or you do get it." I was crying now. It was pointless to make him forget again until after I had stopped.

"Huh? What are you talking about? Is this about me not having chosen a college yet? Come on, don't cry. I, I'm going to pick something."

"No, no. Stop being stupid." I sniffed and wiped a few tears away. "I'll tell you after I've stopped crying. Just, just hold me."

"Okay, Ethan, okay. I'm here for you." He squeezed me.

170

"Thank you."

About twelve minutes passed before I finally stopped crying. I cleared my eyes with the heel of my palm and took several deep breaths.

"So what is it? Why are you–"

I stopped him. I promised myself it would be the last time I would make him forget, last time I would change him. It would be an impossible promise to keep, but I had to warp him at least a little right now when things were so precarious. I had an idea though.

"Listen, Peter. You're not gonna remember this. Not exactly. I'm gonna put this so deep in your mind that you'll know it, but you won't know you know it." I hesitated. "I love you, I really do. But I don't know what to do. Something so impossible is separating us, and I'm afraid we'll never truly be together again." I sniffed and rubbed a last tear from my face. "But I don't know yet, but I'm gonna find out. And when I do, we'll be together. I promise."

Peter looked at me, not quite blankly, but as if he were sleepwalking. His green eyes didn't move, didn't even blink, but something deep in them gave me the confirmation I needed to know the words had reached him. The knowledge went far into his mind, into an inner kernel where it would be safe. I linked my arms behind his neck and kissed him.

He was back now. He kissed me, and we stayed together for a number of minutes that neither of us kept track of. We were lying down on the couch now. I was next to Peter but also slightly on top of him. I brushed a strand of hair away from his eyes.

"We should just have a few people come over, if anyone," I whispered.

"Just our closest friends?"

"Yeah."

"So Catharine for sure," he said. "And how about Allie and Zack too?"

"Yeah." I nodded. "It'd be good to see them again."

Peter laughed quietly. "You say that like you haven't seen them in months."

"Well... you know what I mean."

"You're gonna have to let me up, so I can go get my phone."

"I know." I didn't move.

"We can cuddle more when I get back." He smiled.

I thought about warping his phone here, but I held back. "Okay." I got up.

After Peter left the room I slumped back into the cushions and listened to his footsteps ascending the stairs. I sighed. The effort of actually pulling together a party suddenly seemed far too tiresome to even consider; even a small get-together seemed too much. I could have just warped all three of them here and started the gathering right off in the middle when everything was already happening, already flowing. But I wouldn't let myself. I pressed my hands to my face and pulled them down, stretching my cheeks and mouth. What was I even doing here? What was I even doing at all?

"So, Allie does have that summer job at the deli," Peter said as he walked back into the living room, looking down at the screen of his phone. "I dunno what her work schedule's like."

"I think I changed my mind."

"Huh?" He looked up at me.

"I don't really want to see anyone tonight. Really I just came to visit because I wanted to be with you."

"Aww." Peter flopped down on the couch next to me and lied down with his head in my lap. "But Cat's gonna be really upset when she finds out you were back in town and didn't see her."

"I know. I'll see her next time."

"Are you sure?" He held up his phone.

"Yeah. I am."

"Alright." He reached down to the floor and dropped his cell phone on the carpet. "So what do you want to do instead?"

I was silent, thinking of nothing really in particular as I started to run my fingers through his hair.

"Something's bothering you," Peter said.

I forced a single syllable of laughter. "Yeah. I can't reach down to kiss you when you're on my lap."

"Oh? Really? Is that is?" He tilted his head on my lap.

I just nodded.

Peter's eyes sank and so did the rest of his face. "We wish," he mumbled. He got up and kissed me.

*   *   *

A few hours later we were both lying in Peter's bed, my hair still damp from our after-sex shower. The sun had set, and not a single light was on in the house. A few slits of dim orange were thrown across the ceiling from a streetlamp outside. Crickets were chirping.

Neither of us were asleep, but neither of us spoke either. I turned my head to Peter. The covers came up to his waist, and I gazed at his chest. The memory of Kris shirtless in the morning drifted to the front of my mind. I pushed it away.

I turned to my side and rested my hand on Peter's chest.

He made an indistinct sound—just barely an, "Mm"—to show he was still awake. He had always had a tendency to fall asleep quickly, but that had never bothered me. It usually didn't take me long to fall asleep either.

I didn't say anything; I just absently traced spirals across his chest and stomach. Peter took my hand in his own, lifted it to his lips, and kissed my fingers. A car drove past, and its lights momentarily light up the room as they flashed across the window.

"Ethan?"

"Yeah?"

"If you could have one wish, what would it be?"

"Why are you asking?"

"Just wondering. It was something I was reading online the other day."

I didn't reply immediately. "To stay with you."

"What? But you're already with me."

"I don't want it to change."

"Why would it change?"

"Because. It could."

He was still holding my hand. "It's not gonna change: I must be the lover."

I was suddenly aware of how warm it was in the room and how warm it must still be outside. I smiled. "The AC isn't on."

"Yeah. We don't have that anymore."

"What'd you say?"

"Just trying to make a joke." Peter reached out and pulled me closer. "Come here."

I moved to my side and he held me, his chest pressed to my back.

173

Peter took in a breath to say something, but he hesitated. "When are you leaving?"

"I dunno." I paused. "Tomorrow morning I guess."

"After breakfast?"

"Yeah."

"Okay."

We didn't talk again. Later, perhaps half an hour or more, I could tell Peter had fallen asleep. His breathing was slower, and his arm was draped over my shoulder instead of holding me. I still couldn't sleep, even though I had been looking forward to this: lying with him again, knowing I would wake up with Peter by my side. I was still unhappy.

Very carefully I extract myself from Peter's arms and left the bed. There was just enough light to allow me to gather up my clothes and look back at Peter once more. I set his schedule for the next half day: he would wake up at eleven and remember driving me to the airport very early in the morning, returning home, and going back to sleep. And that would be all. I closed my eyes and imagined a time when I would never have to warp Peter again.

Chapter 14
Running Into Cobwebs

A few days later I was touring the universe again, but this time I was alone with only the manual to guide me. I had just left a whole stack of wide cylindrical planes that had every biome imaginable, including a good number of biomes that were simply impossible for most Earths to sustain.

The manual described such planes as "exercises of fabrication" that were recommended for fine tuning practice of creating and modifying planetary ecology from the ground-up. They reminded me more of Hollywood movie sets.

I touched down on a few Earths as I passed them. One was currently locked in something of a World War that had been ignited by allegations of orbital bombing when one super power's faulty satellites just happened to crash into another super power's capital and three most economically important cities. I turned the clock back on that Earth, erasing the war, repairing the cities, and I made it impossible for the satellites to fall from the skies.

Another Earth I passed was being devastated by a hypercane. I erased that storm as well, repaired the damage, and cooled the oceans. I felt such great exuberance in my actions. Here I was, flying across the universe and fixing problems I came across. I finally felt I had some control over the world. That I could actually make a difference myself. I stood in the middle of the former hypercane Earth's New York City and laughed aloud, too happy to care what looks the passersby gave me.

I amused myself by flying through a sun, skirting the edges of a black hole, and reforming the shape of a nebula to make a giant cosmic sail boat. I took lunch above the exploding heart of a galaxy, the string of solar detonations having started decades ago.

Several hours later I was flying through a solar system with six hundred planets and only six orbital paths around the sun. Each planet was encased in a metal shell and connected via colossal bridges to its four neighbors, except the planets on the outer orbit that were only connect to three. The sun itself was completely surrounded by an absorption grid that distributed the light and heat among the planets. The whole solar system was invisible to the rest of the universe, because it didn't give off any light. It was here as I walked along the outside of one of the planetary bridges that I noticed in the manual I was rather close to the Nekkar galaxy. The galaxy with the people who know about warpers.

I stopped in my tracks and read the small entry on them. Ever since they "woke up" to the reality of the universe, they have collectively referred to themselves as the Rurrians in homage to a golem named Rur in a mythological story of theirs. An ancient king commissioned a magician to fashion a great weapon for the royal army. The magician created Rur, the first golem to fight the nation's wars. But Rur turned against the magician, striking the self-proclaimed master down and fled the world. The Rurrians also had renamed their planet to Rur, no longer accepting the imposed name "Earth."

The Rurrians.

I had a sudden desire to go see them myself. For a moment I pondered how good of an idea it was, but in the end I trusted my powers to keep me safe. However, when I tried to create a doorway to the coordinates listed in the manual, I found I was unable to plant the pathway there and set the connected door at all. It was as if my power stretch out like a long cord but simply could not stay straight as I reached it out to the planet. It was a level two warp lock, and it extended far past the surface. In the end, the closest I could plant my doorway was about a light hour away from the planet.

I stood at the edge of the warp lock, wondering why it was here. The manual hadn't said there were any warp locks around. Aside from that, I wondered about the best way to proceed. There was no way I could maintain my air supply once I entered the lock without some other source besides my powers. I decided to make a spacecraft. A light and highly maneuverable craft of some sort, but what would be the best way to go about that? I created a cheat sheet.

A sphere shaped craft that can create thrust fluxes from any point of its hull would be the most ideal. Make it no bigger than six meters in diameter with no external lights, and you will be, for practical purposes, invisible. External cameras with internal view screens and thought-controlled motion would also be ideal. Make sure it has near-light speed capabilities; you are a ways away.

I loved my cheat sheets. At least, I did when they worked.

I created the spacecraft as specified, giving it a non-reflective black exterior with a single sliding door to enter. Inside was a chair mounted up to be in the center of the sphere, surrounded by monitors. I strapped myself in and flew off towards Earth-6012, now known as Rur.

Less than an hour passed, because of time dilation, before I was able to see a small speck that was Rur on the screens. I decelerated my craft and moved in cautiously. The planet slowly grew on the monitor. It occurred to me that I should probably give this spaceship a name. I drummed my fingers on the armrest, thinking of a few names I knew from movies. Maybe something related to photons? Just then a number of red circles began blinking on one of the monitors over to the right.

"Warning: Incoming Missiles. Engage Auto-Pilot or Take Evasive Action," a computerize voice said in a calm manner, its words filling the entire cockpit. The sudden voice made me jump in my seat; I hadn't realized there would be an onboard computer, and in hindsight I should have realized that there wasn't.

"Whoa, whoa, wait. What's going on? Who's shooting at me?"

A dozen blinking red squares appeared from the same direction.

"Rurrian Automated Defense Stations. Long Range Scanners Also Detect an Inbound Squadron of Unmanned Ship-to-Ship Fighters. First Missile Impact in 47.5 Seconds."

"Oh shit. What do I do? Get me out of here!" Reflexively I reached out, trying to grasp the warp energy, trying to find it, but it was impossible. It was as if I were pressing up against glass, unable to reach just beyond it.

"Do You Wish to Engage Auto-Pilot?"

"Yes, *Yes*. Do it! Get me out."

"Permission Accepted. Craft Control Now Diverted to Rurrian Command. Please Have a Pleasant Day." My ship decelerated to a stop, no longer approaching the planet. It was still quite far off. The blinking circles and squares disappeared from the monitor.

"Wait, *what*? No, no! Disengage auto-pilot. I want manual control. Stop!" The skin on the back of my neck tightened, and I felt my face flush.

"–actually got something." The monitor directly in front of me switched over to a man sitting at a control station in a room with a few other people. He wore a headset that only covered one ear and a loose tie over an un-ironed button up shirt. He had a pin on his breast pocket that depicted the Rurrian emblem: three triangles, two connected into a sideways square above the third which jutted out to the right. It was somewhat reminiscent of a key.

He turned to look at someone behind him. "That, that's him. Just pulled him up on screen." The man turned back to me. "Who are you? A warper? You're actually a warper?"

For a second I sat stunned, unable to think of what to say. "Uh... no. No, not at all." I swallowed. "What's a warper?"

The man looked confused. "But you...? No. Hang on." He covered his mic and looked over his shoulder.

Another man came on screen and took the headset. He wore a uniform that was clearly military in nature and it also had the Rurrian emblem on it. "Goddamn desk boys." He adjusted the headset and addressed me. "I am Colonel Roderick O'Neil. Who are you and what are you doing here?"

"Uh, uh, but wait, why did you take over my ship? *How* did you take over my ship?" I kept pressing buttons on my armrest, but nothing was happening. I discovered I still had manual control of my exterior cameras, and I zoomed in on the planet. I could just barely make out an orbiting space station between Rur and myself.

"No. You see, you're going to answer my questions. You're either a warper, or you know a warper, because your sorry excuse for a spaceship doesn't even have the proper onboard computers to fly, let alone take off. Whoever made it left out half the basics. Now, who are you?"

"I'm just an alien from another planet. You know, 'I come in peace,' and all that." I smiled. "Really."

"Ha! Like I'd believe that! Jett's bombarding the other side of the planet with a whole fleet of ships, and you just happen to show up in a warper's ship at the same time? Not likely."

"Well, truth is stranger than–"

"Shut up." O'Neil pulled off the headset and turned to someone else who had just run up to him. She was close enough that I could just make out what she said.

"Sir, his fleet's being routed, but several of his ships have broken off and are flying around the planet right now. They seem to be heading towards us."

"I knew it. Have the scans found anything on his ship?" O'Neil put on the headset again and turned back to me. "What do you have on your ship? A supernova?" He turned away and yelled across the room, "Where are those interdiction cruisers! I want this son-of-a-bitch out of our system!"

"All of them from our current generation of ships have been destroyed, sir," someone called out from across the room.

"No! Wait! Okay, I am a warper, but I swear, I'm not with Jett or helping him at all. I was just curious, and I wanted to see your planet. I've only been a warper for like a month and half! Please! Please believe me."

Colonel O'Neil was silent. On the left side of the planet I saw six small streaks of light that must have been Jett's ships arcing around and zooming towards the space station. Dozens of smaller flecks of light fired off from them.

"It doesn't matter what I believe anymore." My view of the control room and the people in it cut off.

I watched the fire of missiles engulf the space station. At first the explosions were held back by a blue shimmering shield, but it started to crack and fade. The rest of the missiles hit the station directly. As this was happening, something very large and seemingly flat was slowly rotating around the side of Rur, also coming from the left of the planet. A huge curved rectangle the size of an ocean was floating in low orbit above the atmosphere like armor.

The attack on the station was not without repercussion. The planet armor launched a salvo of missiles and they were about to impact Jett's ships. Not far behind them, a whole armada of new lights were curving around the left of the planet. They were the remnants of the Rurrian fleet.

The destroyed space station was spinning slowly and falling away in three main pieces. My ship shut down with the station's destruction, and I started floating in my chair. Only the monitors remained on by some quirk. I hit more buttons at random, sweat starting to rise on the small of my back. If what O'Neil had said was true, then I had no way of turning the ship on without warping it.

I got out of my chair and looked down at its base, searching for any sort of override or fail-safe that could help me. There was literally nothing but a metal support; there wasn't even wiring. I glanced up and noticed one of Jett's ships was no longer attacking. It had turned away from the planet and was flying straight at me.

Jett's ship was an elongated octahedron with four wings, one at each of the four middle corners, and at the end of each wing was a rounded cylinder. For a moment it looked as though it would ram right into me and dash me against the front of it. Instead the tip opened like a flower: four sections pulling away on hinges. With swift precision it swallowed my ship and closed around me.

Everything was dark. I dropped to the floor as the larger ship's artificial gravity started affecting my own ship. There was a thud as some large arm or couplings connected with the hull of my sphere. Vibrations from the huge spaceship started pulsing into my own, up the chair, and into my hands. They were increasing, and I assumed we were accelerating away from the planet.

"Brace yourself, Ethan." A male voice filtered in through my speakers. "The Reality Generator on that space station is gonna blow any second now. It's going to send a huge wave of disrupted warp energy out, and when it hits you'll probably throw up."

The lights came on in the docking bay, all pure white glistening off shiny metal and polished edges. Everything in sight was either white, silver, or light green glowing from computer consoles and buttons. My ship was being held tilted sideways and forward slightly by the docking arm. Through a screen I saw the main doors to the rest of the ship and a single person standing in front of them.

He was Latino and a bit bulkier than I was. He wore black pants and a thick white jacket with silver fur trim on the collar that looked much like an aviator jacket. His brown hair was short enough to be a buzz cut, accompanied by a thin chinstrap beard. It had to be Jett. I felt goose bumps rising over my arms and neck.

He looked down at a wrist controller on his left arm. "Here it comes."

A second before the wave hit I could sense it rushing at us like a tsunami, but it was like a tsunami that knew it was a tsunami and wanted to ensure everyone else knew it as well. It slammed into me, over me, through me. It pushed me back, hundreds of colors popping in my eyes, my ears pressing in from a sound that was not sound but was more like being under hundreds of meters of water. But it was warp energy. Ragged and raging warp energy stampeding past me. I grabbed hold of it.

Somehow, though I hardly had any focus on what I was doing, I grabbed hold of it. Nothing besides the knowledge that I wanted to be anywhere but here filled my mind. In the short second of the blast I was able to escape. I teleported out of my ship, away from Jett, through bumping colors and rushing, half-shaped forms. I ended sprawled out on the uneven ground of a forest.

For the longest time I was unable to sit up, hardly even able to focus my sight on my surroundings. A crushing migraine kept any thoughts from forming like repeatedly slamming your fists on a table while someone tried to set up a house of cards. I rolled to my side, clutching my head.

I did feel like I would throw up. As the migraine started to subside the pain slid down my body instead of fading completely. My chest contracted; my stomach felt like a hot rod had stewed up all my organs. I held my breath and squeezed my eyelids tight, focusing solely on keeping my mouth clamped shut.

Eventually, it all passed.

A faint pain still lingered through my body, but I was able to sit up and eventually stand. I staggered over to a tree and leaned on it. It was dark. Where was I? I conjured up a cheat sheet.

Currently on a ghost moon orbiting Earth-U13 approximately 23.1 light years from Rur.

I was safe then. I sat down, my back against the tree, and made a vial of warp extract. I chugged it greedily and sighed as I felt it working through me, erasing the queasiness that remained. The horizon blazed orange like the sun had just set, and I made a lantern bright enough to illuminate the surrounding forest. The chirping and whining of insects filled the air, but I didn't hear a single sound that would signify any larger animals such as birds. It was surprisingly tranquil. It was then that a full realization of hunger hit me. I decided to eat here and made a club sandwich.

As I ate I pondered these new developments. The manual had said absolutely nothing about a militarized planet or space stations. I asked a cheat sheet when the small section on the Rurrians had last been updated. *Moose.* I would have to ask someone else.

A flash of light from above grabbed my attention, and I looked to the sky. The horizon was still orange, like eternal twilight. There were stars and a faint purple nebula close enough to be seen, but nothing else. I was about to wave it off as a shooting star when I heard his voice again.

"How in the name of all the warpers that have come before us did you teleport out of a level two warp lock?" Jett's voice was flat as if suppressing a complete and total desire to scream.

My eyes snapped down to him. I didn't move for a second, but I knew I had to run. He must have known as well. Before I could even drop my half eaten sandwich Jett slammed his hand against the tree next to him, dissolving it to nothingness, and set a level two warp lock around me.

"Escape again."

I felt the warp energy cut away, the glass walls slamming down around me again. I scampered to my feet and turned to run, but a sudden stab of pain leaped from my back. He had shot me with some sort of dart, and I fell to my knees, my vision almost instantly blurring.

The last thing I heard before toppling to my side and slipping into oblivion was: "Why didn't you do it again?"

*   *   *

When I arose from the darkness I found myself lying on the most comfortable bed I had ever laid on in my entire life. Even to this day I have not felt a bed so soft, but I suppose part of that comfort had come from the drugs still wearing off. Regardless, I opened my eyes and listened before I moved at all.

I heard a very soft ticking that for a moment I feared was a bomb, but I realized it was only a clock on the wall. Aside from this rhythmic pattern I heard nothing else. I sat up.

The predominate color of the room was white. That coupled with the green glow of the switch by the door granted me the sinking realization that I was back on Jett's ship. Worse still, the whole room was level two warp locked.

I was alone. I jumped off the bed and ran straight for the door. It didn't open as I approached, and nothing I did to the control panel seemed to have an effect. It simply didn't respond to me. I turned around and surveyed the room.

There were several pieces of fancy silver furniture with black trim: a curved couch around a holographic fire, a circular table with two high backed chairs, the oval bed, and a hanging chandelier. No vents or other doors, aside from one that led to a bathroom. There was a window looking out into space, but when I reached it I found it wasn't a window at all; it was merely a screen showing the outside. As I looked down at the planet we were orbiting I realized I could actually be anywhere and maybe not in space at all. Not like that it really mattered if I couldn't even get out of this room.

I glanced around again. There had to be air vents, or crawl spaces, or a maintenance shaft, or something. Didn't all spaceships have those things? I started feeling around the walls of the room, looking for anything at all, but I found nothing. The room was clearly intended for permanent guests.

As I paced around the bed trying to think of what to do, a chime came from the door and it slid open. A man in a slick white tuxedo with white gloves and a white bowtie wheeled a small silver trolley into the room with two covered plates. Jett walked in behind him holding a loaf of bread, which he set in the center of the table.

"Good morning, Ethan," Jett said. "How did you sleep?"

"I don't think getting drugged counts as sleeping."

"Perhaps you'd like to consider it an open relationship with death?" Jett grinned and chuckled to himself.

The waiter set the plates onto the table and removed their covers, poured two glasses of red wine, and left the room silently.

"Please join me." Jett sat down.

I hesitated. I could almost literally feel the eggshells crinkling under my feet.

"I feel like... that's a bad idea," I said.

"Oh? Why?"

"Aren't I a prisoner?"

Jett looked away then down at his arm. He pulled back his sleeve to display the wrist controller he wore. It had one larger rectangle with a display screen against the back of his forearm, and twelve much thinner rectangles linked around to form the rest of the instrument.

"You know, when dealing with the Rurrians I'm almost constantly working within a warp lock. That's why I have this. It's saved my life more than once. I can control my ship remotely, keep in communication with my troops, and have a weapon when I need it. I have four explosive flechettes, four drugged flechettes, and four regular flechettes in here. The fact you're still alive proves I have no ill will towards you."

He picked up his fork and knife and cut into the food before him. It was duck. He raised a sliver of meat to his mouth and chewed silently.

"That... doesn't answer my question, really."

"You will be free to go after we have talked a while. Please, sit." He gestured towards the chair opposite him with his fork.

I bit my lip. "Talk about what?"

"I won't discuss the main points of the conversation until you at least sit down."

I remained standing, but he simply continued his meal. Almost a minute passed before I finally sat. The plate of food before me held roast duck drizzled with cranberry sauce, accompanied by loaded whipped potatoes garnished with scallions, and a fanned out half circle of roasted and honeyed asparagus. It looked and smelled incredible, but my stomach felt too tense to handle even a single bite.

"This is quite nice, really," Jett said. "It's been such a long time since I've talked to another warper. I'd almost forgotten that I'm not the only one."

"Well... everyone is, you know, freaked out by you."

He turned his eyes up towards me, looking out from under his eyebrows. "Yes. Just like when you and Raine ran from the Restaurant."

"How'd you know that was me there?"

"Bot told me you were the new warper." He turned his head up at me. "What happened to Tavin?"

"He died."

"Obviously." Jett rolled his eyes. "What happened though?"

"I dunno. No one's told me that."

"Hmm." He stabbed a piece of asparagus with his fork and held it up to consideration. "Are you uncomfortable right now?"

"What?"

"I asked: Are you uncomfortable right now?"

"Uh, can I not answer that?"

A grin touched the corner of Jett's lips. "You just did. Why are you so uncomfortable, Ethan?"

I crossed my arms "Well why do you think? You attacked me and I'm trapped here and I have no idea what you're gonna do."

"Attacked you? I saved you. The Rurrians were about to kill you."

"What about that dart you shot me with?"

Jett waved his hand. "It's called a 'flechette.' And it seems so odd you would come to Rur, especially given the warp lock you had to fly through. Didn't it concern you?"

"The dart, Jett. I want to know why you shot me."

Jett's eyes narrowed. He stood and leaned forward. "*Don't test me.*"

I scooted my chair back and remembered a line from a movie I had seen somewhat recently. "If I'm a prisoner, then I'm not going to answer any questions."

Jett hesitated and sat back down. "You're not a prisoner."

"You just said I can't leave until we've talked."

"That doesn't make you a prisoner. The choice is up to you."

"Not really a choice though, is it?" I crossed my arms.

He glanced at his wrist controller. "I guess not."

"Then I'm not answering any questions."

"Goddammit! Don't you understand what's at stake?"

"How does this relate–?

Jett slammed his fist on the table, and I jumped in my seat. "The Rurrians are a threat to us. That's why I'm killing them. Didn't you even wonder why they have a warp lock around their planet?"

"Only after the fact."

"It's Reality Generators: artificial means of making level two warp locks. And very extensive locks by combining the power of multiple Generators. They have the power to fight us, and that is unacceptable. For over two decades I've been hammering away at them. They had their entire solar system colonized before I came along. They were even reaching out into neighboring systems. But now that I have them down to their last planet they've suddenly acquired an impossible amount of resources. No matter how many ships or space stations I destroy, there's always more when I return. I had thought maybe a warper was helping them, but everyone was accounted for, aside from Tavin. I thought it was him thwarting me, but only later did I learn he had perished. But even if they *did* have a warper, the whole place is warp locked!

"But now, you've shown up." He inclined his head, looking at me out of the corner of his eye. "A random little warper randomly flying to Rur, that randomly accepts their pathetic override malware, because of his equally pathetic excuse for a spaceship. One who I happen to save *not* randomly, because I intercepted the transmissions," he started speaking very slowly, lingering on each word, "then he's *somehow* able to teleport out of a level two warp lock."

I sat there, staring at him. I knew he wanted me to say something, but I had no clue what.

"It reminds me," Jett continued, "a little of a time when Kris created a car without a drive shaft. The engine simply turned the wheels directly. That's one of the problems with just automatically making things. You leave holes. Holes that the warp energy covers over. That's why I never make any spaceships. I only copy my flagship. Nor do I make any missiles. I copy the original that was actually made by technicians with all the correct specifications. But of course all this is just me waiting for you to finally speak up and explain what you *did*." Jett shoved the table to the side, wine glasses falling over and silverware clattering to the floor. "Why did I shoot you? Because I have to know how you teleported out of a level two warp lock!" But even as he screamed, his voice wavered.

"I– I– I don't know."

He stalked forward and leaned into my face as I tried to back into the chair. "How, did, you, do it?"

"I really don't know. I really don't. There was just that blast of warp energy, and I just, kinda, grabbed it."

Jett eyes narrowed and he rubbed the side of his jaw, tracing the line of his beard. He turned away and walked to the window, standing in silence.

I sat there, watching him. I glanced over to the knife on the table near my plate and considered an attack. Jett wasn't that much bigger than me, but that flechette launcher on his wrist would be too much of a problem. An attack probably wasn't a good idea.

"Do you know what this new piece of information means?" He remained by the window and glanced back at me.

I just shook my head.

"If it is true, that the raw warp energy from an exploding Reality Generator can be used in a warp lock, then I'd never have to leave Rur to create more ships." A smile slowly spread over his face. "I can finally end this."

Oh shit. Did I really give him just the weapon he was looking for, completely by accident too?

"End it?" I asked.

"Yes. To finally be able to kill every last Rurrian on their last planet. They have too many defenses, too many ships. They don't even need people to pilot them, because they've got golems doing most of the footwork. On top of that they have working graviton technology, so I can't even throw a sun at them. They'll just bounce it away with their interdiction cruisers. But now, if all I have to do is destroy one Reality

Generator, and I'd have access to warping..." He paused. "Dammit."

I remained silent, waiting.

Jett walked back to the table and picked up his knocked over glass of wine. He held it up and considered the small amount of wine that remained within it. "Why did I have to be stuck with *my* version of warping? You could make a hundred ships in three seconds if you wanted you, but for me three seconds would be hardly enough to make a dozen." He drank the remnant wine in a single gulp.

I ventured a question. "Why's that?"

"You don't know how my power works?"

"No."

"Do you know *anything*?" He threw his arms up and let them drop again. "Radcliff is slipping."

"It's mostly been Kris–"

"Kris is an idiot. I always liked Tavin better."

"Why?"

"To which statement?"

"Huh?"

"Are you asking why Kris is an idiot, or why I liked Tavin better?"

"Uh, both."

"Kris is an idiot, because his only concern has always been partying. Tavin at least had an idea of the bigger picture. He and I, we actually talked about things. How things could be better. 'Cause you know, those marked by greatness always show it. Whenever I talked to Kris, even right up until I left, it was always just, 'try this drink, this song is awesome, what are the plans tonight?' " Jett wobbled back and forth on his heels and held out his wine glass with two hands, trying to give some comic impersonation of Kris. It just came off as really odd.

He must have noticed the weird look I was giving him, because Jett stopped immediately and frowned. "But, I was talking about my warping power. I, unfortunately, must destroy before I can create, though I suppose it is somewhat poetic. I disintegrate objects, converting them into pure warp energy that I can store and use later. I can also harvest the 'thunder' of this disintegration. Warp energy crashes into the void left by this action, and I gain part of that energy as well.

The end result is a double energy value of any object I disintegrate. However, I can't store this energy for very long, and the more energy I have, the less time I have to use it. So I'd be lucky to get a dozen ships off at all in three seconds.

"You, however, have the best warping power there is, at least in my opinion. You don't have to collect or store or mold the warp energy at all. You just *use* it. If I had you working with me, well, we could squash those usurpers like the cockroaches they are."

I kept silent. I had a strong suspicion that Jett would be unhappy if I refused.

He watched me, waiting, then asked, "You don't want to, do you?"

"I think I'd rather work with people who haven't shot me with a dart before."

Jett nodded very slowly. "I didn't think you would. Not yet at least. You don't understand what's at stake. But fortunately, you don't have to agree to be on the front lines to be useful to me."

He walked towards me again. This was it, I knew it: fight or flight, but flight wasn't an option. I grabbed the knife from the table and jumped away, keeping my chair between us to block any flechettes. I held the knife out, directing the serrated edge at Jett.

"Don't think I'm gonna to make this easy for you," I said.

Jett rolled his eyes. "I didn't really expect you to cooperate." He pulled back his sleeve and pressed a button on his wrist controller.

A bolt of electricity surged through my hand, the charge coming from the knife. I yelled and dropped the knife as Jett ran forward and shoved me to the floor, knocking the wind from me. I was sprawled out, and Jett knelt down. He took my left arm and clamping something metallic and cold around my wrist. It secured itself into my skin with spikes, and I screamed in pain.

"Yes, you feel that? I have your attention now, don't I? Huh?" Jett leaned over me and grabbed my jaw, forcing me to look straight at him. I could only make out his blurred face through the tears in my eyes. "This is the price you pay. I knew you weren't with me, so you're against me, but I'm not going to let you get away with it. You're gonna go run back to all the other warpers, and you're going to get me an audience with them. You're gonna let me tell them what fools they are for their self-blinding to this crisis! Do you *hear* me?" He shook me and pushed my head back as he released me from his grip. The back of my skull knocked against the floor.

I pulled my arm up against my chest and looked at the device. It was about six centimeters wide, gray metal, with a black screen above my forearm. A few streams of blood trickled out from under the device, and I could feel the warm trails sliding towards my elbow.

Jett walked away again to the window. "The device around your wrist will only activate once all the warpers are with you, myself excluded of course." His voice had become calm again, his words unrushed. "The trick though is that you only have one week, counting today. If it isn't activated within six more days it will explode, and probably kill you. Also it's warp locked. The only way you could save yourself without getting the audience is if you cut off your arm, but I wouldn't recommend doing that. Getting everyone to listen to me would be so much easier." Jett walked back to me and squatted down. "Now, my little courier, do you have any questions? Do you need any clarifications?"

I sat up, still holding my arm to my chest. "What the hell do you want me to ask you?"

"Nothing really. I just want to make sure you completely understand the severity of your circumstances."

"Fuck you."

Jett chuckled. "Save it for Kris. Has he broken you in yet? I know he and Tavin used to be like rabbits."

I swung my arm out at him blindly, trying to strike his face, but Jett blocked it easily by raising his arm so quickly I hardly even saw it move. He just shook his head. I felt the warp lock disappear, but before I could do a thing Jett rammed his palm into my forehead and forced me into a teleport. It was the worse sensation of falling I had ever felt as I soared backwards through the rushing colors and finally crashed onto the ground in front of the Archives.

Chapter 15
Fail-Deadly

"I told you, I told you, we all told you! *Don't* get involved with Jett. It was so simple. Don't get involved with him; he's in his Ego Stage. How did you even get involved with him?" Radcliff was storming back and forth in one of the lounges in the Archives as I sat on a couch and watched him.

He had called Alicia through his palm ring and she was contacting Kris. We were expecting them to arrive any minute. I kept finding myself touching the smooth metal of the manacle around my wrist, and I jerked my hand away every time I realized it. It felt so strange. Not physically—physically it still hurt—but mentally. Mentally I felt like I was marked; like I had failed something, and now I was facing an imminent doom that couldn't be avoided. Despite my power to change almost anything in the universe, I felt hopelessly trapped: locked onto a path I couldn't deviate from. My fingers were on the metal again, and I pulled them away.

Kris burst through the door and ran to me. For a moment it looked like he was about to dive on top of me, but he checked himself and stopped in front of me. "Are you okay? Let me see it." He took my left hand and pulled my arm towards him.

"Hey! Don't pull my arm from its socket."

"Sorry." He let go.

I sighed. "It's okay. Just, sit down or something, then you can see it."

Kris dropped down next to me, leaving no room between us. Our eyes meet for a moment as he took my arm again in his hands, but I didn't say anything.

Alicia walked into the room with Raine. "So tell me, what's the exact situation we're dealing with here?" Alicia asked.

"You can see the thing yourself." Radcliff pointed to me. "He ran into Jett and got that manacle stuck to his arm."

"By *accident*," I added.

"Yeah," Kris said hastily.

I glanced at Raine. She was standing next to Alicia, and she gave me a pained look like she really wanted to help even though she knew she couldn't.

"Regardless," Radcliff continued, "Jett now demands an audience with us. Otherwise that device will explode and kill Ethan."

"Then why are we here?" Alicia asked.

"What do you mean, 'why are we here?' We're here to help Ethan!" Kris said.

"Sure, sure, that's obvious for you, but why call me here as well?" Alicia turned to Radcliff. "You're not actually thinking of giving Jett the audience he wants, are you?"

"I certainly don't want to," he said.

"But what choice do we have?" Kris yelled. "We can't get it off otherwise, it's warp locked!"

"Kris, please don't yell. We certainly don't need that right now," Radcliff said. "Just calm down and think about the situation. If we grant Jett his request we will not only have to interact with him, but we will be forced us to interact with Erika as well."

"Is that really so bad?" I asked.

"By definition it's bad, yes," Alicia said. "She made a prison for herself, and she's in her Ego Stage. If she is as self-destructive as that, just imagine what kind of threat she could pose to us."

"That is, basically, correct," Radcliff said. "Jett and Erika were a couple before Jett entered his Ego Stage about twenty-one years ago. She didn't take it well at all, especially once Jett started his campaign against the Rurrians. Long story short, she swore she would never do what Jett was doing, and she started building a huge palace as a prison for herself. We haven't talk to her since, and she most likely is in her Ego Stage now."

"Exactly. Two warpers in their Ego Stage, both of them we would have to talk to," Alicia said. "I won't have any part in it, and neither should any of you." She pointed around the room.

"But being self-destructive doesn't automatically mean you're a threat to others," I said.

"Of course it does," she said.

"But what about Ethan? We have to help him," Kris said.

"It's his own fault for getting into this mess." Alicia didn't look at Kris or myself as she spoke.

Kris jumped up from the couch. "And so you're just gonna let him *die*? The Alicia I know would never do that!"

"That's not what I'm saying. We do have other options we can consider. That manacle is only on his arm, his wrist no less. We could easily cut it off and–"

"Hell fucking no!" Kris yelled.

"Jett *already* said not to do that," I said.

"*Mom.*"

We all glanced at Raine.

Alicia tugged on Raine's arm, then continued speaking. "That's not what I mean, any of you. Radcliff, you know what I'm talking about, back me up here. A surgical amputation would be easy and painless, and, most importantly, reversible. We can make the best doctors in the whole universe. A simple cut and paste is nothing. And even if they did somehow fail against all odds to reattach your arm, they could simply outfit you with a completely seamless cybernetic arm. There's nothing that could go wrong."

"Alicia." Radcliff said her name quietly—quickly—before Kris was able to yell anything else. "I think you are overlooking two very important things. First, you are suggesting that Ethan sacrifices his arm for us, whom he has known for less than two months, simply so we do not have to face our fears."

"It's for our own safety that I–"

"No." He raised his hand. "Please don't interrupt."

Alicia closed her mouth, but I could tell from the way she stood, leaning forward slightly and as tall as she could make herself, that she was just bristling to speak again.

"Secondly, and perhaps a more convincing argument, we don't know that a surgical removal will work." He pressed his hands flat together, the tips of his middle fingers touching his chin. "As Ethan just said, Jett did mention amputation as a possible course of action and very clearly said he did not recommend it. Given the methodical and callous nature of

Jett's actions as Ethan has described to me, I can't help but believe he isn't bluffing. Anything could potentially set off that bomb, even something as simple as a heart monitor."

The room was silent. I shifted on the couch, pulling my arms closer, pressing them to me. I wished I was with Peter. Kris sat down next to me again. I didn't know if he had noticed my movement or if he was just tired of standing, but I was grateful for his presence next to me either way.

"Easy solution," Alicia started. "Open a small portal to someplace far away, have him stick his arm through it, and shut the portal. Arm comes off, bomb is gone, nothing could go wrong." She waited a moment to hear if anyone had a response. "It's fail proof."

"Far from it," Radcliff said. "I can already think of a way to prevent that. Have two sensors at both ends of the manacle broadcasting signals to each other. The moment half the manacle goes through a portal the sensors will begin to detect two signals from each other and detonate the bomb."

"The signal wouldn't travel that fast."

"You and I both know we can make signals travel that fast."

Alicia furrowed her eyebrows. "So then, what do we do?"

"I think, I mean, shouldn't Ethan decide?" Raine asked. "He is the one who's in the most danger."

Everyone looked at me, and I glanced down at the manacle. "I dunno. I mean, shit, I don't wanna die."

"You're not gonna die." Kris put his arms over my shoulders. "You're *not*."

"No, he won't," Radcliff said. "The decision isn't up to anyone. There is *no* decision to make. It's clear to me that we can't afford to risk Ethan's life. We will go to Erika and we will hear whatever Jett has to say, but that is all. We will take no further action. But, if Jett does not hold up his end of the bargain then I will go to him myself and ensure that he releases the manacle."

"Radcliff. You ca–" Alicia started to say.

He turned to her. "Yes, I can. And I will."

"But what about Raine? We can't take Raine to Erika. What if Erika–"

"I have already considered that."

Alicia waited, as if expecting more, then blurted out, "*And?*"

"Nothing more. She will be safest with us."

"How dare you risk our child!" Alicia slapped Radcliff across the face and grabbed Raine's hand, practically dragging Raine out the room after her.

Radcliff rubbed his cheek.

"Uh... sorry," I whispered.

"For what?" Radcliff asked.

"For, well, *this*."

He signed. "It will be alright. I'll go explain to her that it is *highly* unlikely this is a trap just for Raine. If it was it would have been far easier for the bomb to just explode once Raine was close enough to it. I'll be back. Get ready to go: we'll leave as soon as we return." He left the room and closed the door after him.

It was just Kris and myself now, and I was quite aware of his arm still around my shoulders. I wanted to end the silence, so I said the first thing that came to my mind. "I don't think I ever want to play chess against Radcliff."

Kris chuckled. "You don't."

"You've done it?"

"Well, no. I've only played checkers against him. Never have beat him."

I smiled, but looked down at the manacle again. "I feel like such an idiot."

"No, no, it's okay. You're still learning. I feel bad for not being there."

"But that was my fault. I didn't want you there."

"No, it's my fault that I upset you."

"Are we really gonna do this? Keep fighting over blame? This is stupid."

"Heh." Kris gave a weak grin. "I guess it is."

"But thanks anyways... for being here. Even though I kinda pushed you away."

"It's fine, I..." Without any forewarning or even a hint to his intention, Kris kissed me. He just leaned forward and kissed me once. He waited, still centimeters from my face.

I blinked several times, my mind balking. If I had thought I felt like an idiot before, I *really* felt like an idiot now. Kris kissed me again, this time leaning completely into the kiss. He put his other arm around me, and I started to kiss him back. It was only for a moment before I stopped myself and pushed him away, the manacle bumping against his arm.

"No. I, I'm sorry... I..."

He retracted his arms from me and leaned away, his eyes closed.

"Kris," I whispered.

"What?" He didn't look at me.

"I'm sorry. Really. But Peter–"

"Don't talk to me about him. Don't mention him. He doesn't deserve you. He can't appreciate you."

"But he–"

"*No.*" Kris stood up and stepped a pace away from me. "Why? *Why?* Why did you have you have a boyfriend before this? Huh? Why did *you* have to be the next person in line? Why you? Why did Tavin have to die? Huh? Why!" He yelled it up to the roof before looked down at me again. "Can you answer it? *Can you?*"

"Whoa, wait a minute. No. You just wanted to make out with me, and now you want to yell at me?" I stood up to face him evenly. "How is that fair to me?"

"Fair? Of course it's not fair! Nothing's fair. But you're a warper now and you're my counterpart. You shouldn't have someone else!"

"Oh, I'm just supposed to just do whenever you want? Just because our powers go together? What a goddamn pickup line." I crossed my arms.

"I know you're attracted to me. I don't need matching powers to tell me that. I can see it in how you look at me sometimes. So why not? What's the problem?"

"Problem? I'll tell you: because this isn't about me liking you, and it's not about our powers either. Peter and I have something more–"

"You and him have something more than what you and I have? *Really?* You really haven't seen it yet?"

"Now what are you talking about?"

"I've gone and I've watched him. I didn't realize it in the beginning, but I knew there was something familiar about him when I first saw him. It's the same thing. I have the exact same thing, you just haven't seen it yet."

"You've been *spying* on him?"

"Don't get off track. It was bugging me. I had to be sure. I know what Peter really is and that the relationship will always be one sided, always be dead. Believe me, I know. A warper and a non-warper can never work ever. Period."

"And how would you know?"

Kris furrowed his eyebrows and glared at me. "I know it. But I don't want to have to wait around for you to realize it before you finally give him up."

"I won't give him up. I'll never leave him."

"Bullshit."

"We'll see."

"You're impossible." Kris turned away, as if he were about to leave, but then he faced me again. "You know what the worst part is? In the end you *will* give him up, that's guaranteed, but when that happens you'll come back to me, and you know what I'll do? I'll accept you. I'll accept you, because you're all I've got. And the worst part is that we still have to get there and still have to go through all this crap."

"No. The worst part is that you think this is all set in stone."

"Dammit, Ethan, it's all about the initial conditions. If you fall off a building you can argue all you want, but it doesn't matter. As soon as you fell you were set to hit the ground no matter how long it took to happen. I'm leaving for a bit." He disappeared.

I was shocked, then yelled, "What! You have to be here right now!"

A moment of silence passed.

The door squeaked open and Radcliff entered. "Now what happened?"

I turned to him instantly. "Were you listening?"

"No, I wasn't. I did hear yelling though, so I refrained from entering and instead walked down the hallway and returned. Where did he go?"

"I dunno. He just left"

"What were you both fighting about?"

"I dunno." I threw my arms up in the air. "We were talking, then he kissed me. I stopped him, but then he–"

"Alright stop. Stop right there." Radcliff held up a hand. "Why is it always with such bad timing that things like this happen? Listen, you just stay *here*. Alicia and Raine will be back in a few minutes. I'll go talk to Kris."

"Will he listen to you?"

"I'm not going to give him the option."

"How are you even gonna find him? When he disappears like that I never see him again until he comes back on his own time."

"If his palm ring isn't on then I'll go a few places I know. He's still rather predictable."

Alicia and Raine suddenly popped into the room. Raine was grinning ear-to-ear, looking more pleased than a pyro in a match factory. Alicia's face looked oddly blank, though the downward curve of her eyebrows seemed to hint at some displeasure.

"Perfect timing. Alicia, is Kris's palm ring on?"

Alicia glanced down at her left hand. "No, as usual."

"Right then, plan B. Take Ethan to Erika's palace, and I'll go looking for Kris. The Restaurant, his house, Prabble. You know the list."

"Wait, he's *gone*? Are you kidding me?" Alicia leaned forward.

"Temporarily. Do you really think Kris would make himself completely scarce considering the current situation? He knows his presence is mandatory if he wants to keep Ethan from being blown up."

He was talking to Alicia but in a strange way I felt as if he were talking to me, and in the pause afterwards he was waiting for me to answer. For a sickening moment I considered the possibility that Kris wouldn't help save me.

"No, I see your point," Alicia said.

"Good." Radcliff hugged her, then knelt down and hugged his daughter. "I'll see you all in just a bit." He disappeared.

"Well," Alicia held out her hand to me, "let's get this over with."

"Alicia, I am sorry about all this. Sorry that Raine—"

"You can apologize about it later," Alicia said.

"But it really is all going to be just fine. Don't worry," Raine said.

"I wish I felt the same way," I mumbled.

Chapter 16
Save Me

The three of us appeared floating in space. Not far away was what looked like a dusky-brown and extremely rocky planet, but upon a second look I realized it was a huge, roughly spherical building. It seemed reminiscent of ancient feudal Japanese fortresses with thatched, curving roofs and columns of wood, but the entirety of the structure was clearly a unique design.

Some of the pillars curved to round out the sides of the sphere or to create spheres within the structure. The top half of the fortress was two separate asymmetric wings that were connected to each other by a series of bridges on several different levels. From the alignment of the exterior windows it seemed that no single floor cut across the whole building without disruption, either splitting off into two floors or ending at a gap in the building. At the top of the fortress was a connected garden supported by the two wings with different sized trees completing the spherical shape.

"This is it? It looks incredible," I said.

"Yes." Alicia looked over to me. "Tavin helped Erika design this fortress. It was the last thing he made, as far as I know."

"It was?"

"I think so. Hasn't Kris told you anything about him?"

"No."

"Oh." Alicia disappeared and reappeared with a platform and a set of couches. "In the meantime we might as well get comfortable while we wait."

"Mom, could you make me some stuffing? Like from Equinox Night?" Raine asked.

Alicia seemed surprised for a moment. "You're hungry?"

"Not completely, but I must be the child and I really want to eat some stuffing. To taste it, you know?"

Alicia shifted from one foot to the other, then knelt down and brushed a strand of hair behind Raine's ear. "Yes, I'll make you some."

She did so, and Raine accepted the dish happily.

As we waited in silence, I felt like I should say something. I knew Alicia wasn't happy to be here, especially not with Raine present too, but I couldn't think of anything that would be any good. Luckily Alicia spoke first.

"Tell me what happened between you and Jett. All I know is that you ran into him and got that manacle stuck on you."

It took about twelve or sixteen minutes to tell her the details, and several times she stopped me to ask for clarifications. Raine didn't say anything the whole time; she just watched attentively.

"And that's about it, because then Jett blasted me to the Archives. And now we've almost got everyone together."

"I see."

"But I still don't understand why this is so bad. Just talking to him now, I mean. We're all going to be together, and he's not actually here."

"It's a matter of principle, really." Alicia leaned back on the couch and laced her fingers together. "We do not involve ourselves in Stage 4 warpers. They're too dangerous. Too unpredictable. That Stage is the worst thing we have to go through, because we become a threat to everything and everyone."

"And the Ego Stage is always that bad?"

"Of course. Look at Jett. You know he doesn't just want to kill the Rurrians. He wants to kill the Warper Born as well, which includes Raine."

"I know. She told me back when we almost ran into Jett at the Restaurant."

Alicia glanced over at Raine before looking back at me. "I don't like to think about it. The bigger problem right now is our forced interaction with Erika, who is almost positively in her Ego Stage as well."

"When was the last time anyone talked to her?"

Alicia was silent a moment, thinking. "I know I haven't talk to her since shortly after Jett went into his Ego Stage, before she started making this fortress. I assume Tavin was probably the last to talk to her."

"So she's been alone for at least *nineteen* years?"

Alicia waved her hand. "Not *alone* alone. I'm sure she has countless servants and her usual robot pets at her disposal in there. Besides, not interacting with her is for our own safety. If she is in her Ego Stage, as she likely is, even trying to talk to her could be deadly for anyone involved."

"And this place is her prison? How does it keep her in?"

"It has a special shell around it, like a force field. The shell is warp locked, and so long as Erika wishes to leave the shell is impregnable to her. Anyone can walk through it except for her. You also can't teleport in or out, because you can't teleport through warp locks. It's a perfect prison really."

I scratched the side of my head. "That seems a bit... extreme."

"I wouldn't expect you to understand it. You're hardly even in Stage 1."

"The Initiation Stage."

"Yes. At least you've got a good memory."

"That's always been one of my strong points." I shrugged.

"What's the first thing I ever said to you?" Raine asked.

"Uh..." I thought a few moments. "That was in the Restaurant. You said, 'You see what she does to me? See what I have to put up with?' " I smiled, remembering that day at the Restaurant.

"Wow, you're good," Raine said.

"That was really what you said?" Alicia asked.

"Sounds right. That was with the French fry and you thinking I was choking."

"Well, that is impressive."

"It's not really anything special," I said. "Especially not compared to reality warping."

"It is what it is," Raine said.

"Anyways, I *am* intrigued by Jett's report of the Rurrians," Alicia said. "They've always had Reality Generators, but they shouldn't possibly have the ability to rebuild so much protection in so little time. Not without a warper at least."

"That's what Jett was wondering."

"It's probably what he's going to accuse us of when we talk to him. Or, perhaps it is a trap of some sort. Perhaps he wants us to think he is ineffectual to lull us into a false sense of security."

"By risking his life?" I asked.

"What do you mean?"

"I mean, if he's pretending to be bad at fighting the Rurrians, then wouldn't he be putting himself at risk every time he does it?"

"Maybe not, but he is in his Ego Stage. Something like that could possibly be expected. Or, perhaps he staged the whole attack the moment he saw that you were arriving. Or maybe he is working with the Rurrians to kill us. Or, or maybe he already killed all the Rurrians and has replaced them with these unnaturally strong imposters to trick us."

I glanced over at Raine and she looked as confused as I was.

"But... why?" I asked.

"It could be any reason," Alicia said. "How am I to know?"

I shrugged.

For several minutes afterwards, we all sat in silence.

"Also, there was something else I was wondering," I said. "Jett mentioned a little bit about the Rurrians taking over my ship. He said they could because it wasn't complete. He mentioned that the warp energy can cover over gaps in the things you create. Do you know what exactly he means? Or how they did it?"

"Oh, that's a common problem all warpers run into: the balance between what you have to specify yourself and how much the power can create for you."

"You've mentioned that before."

"Have I? Well, like I said, it is common. Especially for more complex things like spaceships. When you are too abstract about what you want to create there are strange holes in the final design. Usually whatever you created will still work perfectly fine, but the holes create unusual vulnerabilities or sometimes advantages. Given the Rurrians reported knowledge of us, I suppose it isn't too unlikely to conjecture that they could exploit such holes, such as your incident."

"Hmm. Also, the manual didn't say anything about them having Reality Generators."

"No one's updated their little blurb in millennia, probably. At least not in this millennia."

"Why not?"

"They're not important." Alicia shook her head. "Obviously."

"Oh." I remained silent for a little while after that, but something else appeared on my mind. "One other thing, have you ever had duck before?"

"Duck?"

"Yeah. Jett tried to serve some to me, but I didn't end up eating any of it. I've seen it before in restaurants but never had it before."

"It's not too bad," Alicia said. "It's not my favorite though. I greatly prefer sea food over any other meats. For example there's this most fantastic fish called *salmon*, which is an absolute delicacy on my home planet. So much so that they're almost extinct. You have to try it some time."

"Um..." I hesitated a moment. "Actually, I've had salmon be–"

"Am I late?"

Kris. I turned my head to see him as soon as I heard him. He was standing a few meters out from the platform, hands in his pockets.

"Well, speaking about ducks," Raine said.

"What? Ducks?" Kris asked.

"Yeah, because you *ducked* out on us." She bit her tongue, holding in her laugher.

I smiled, but Alicia didn't.

Kris laughed. "That was really lame, Raine."

Raine stopped holding her breath and laughed as well. "So? You still laughed."

"True." He walked onto the platform and turned to me. "Sorry, Ethan."

"For which part?" I asked.

"Which part? What are you talking about?"

"Do you really want me to list them all now?"

"List them? You actually have a whole list of things you're upset about?"

I started ticking points off on my fingers. "Not taking things seriously, continuously railing off about Peter, but mostly you always running away."

He crossed his arms. "I do take things seriously, and usually if I'm talking about Peter it's because you brought him up. But for running away... I, I am sorry about that. I just needed a minute."

I sucked on my cheek, considering what he said.

Alicia cleared her throat and stood up. "I'll tell Radcliff you're here." She contacted him through the palm ring.

Kris turned away and walked to the edge of the platform, looking out at the fortress. I watched as he walked way, then I glanced over at Raine. She nodded her head vigorously. I mouthed the word "what?" and she pointed at Kris. Obviously I should go talk to him, but what the hell would I say? I stood up and went to him.

He didn't say anything at first even though he was aware of my presence next to him.

"Thanks for coming back," I said.

"Did you doubt I would?"

I hesitated. "I guess not."

He turned his head to me. "Someone told me I need to make sure you understand that I do want to be with you, but I won't keep fighting with you if you're not ready. I'm just going to give you your space. However much you need."

"Who told you this?"

"Not important." He wasn't looking at me anymore; his eyes were fixed on the fortress.

"So this is about Peter?"

"I'm not going to say anything else."

"Fine, we have more important things to do anyways." I held out my left arm. "Like getting this off me."

"Yeah. We do."

I turned around, and Radcliff had already arrived. He, Alicia, and Raine were standing together away from Kris and myself, politely ignoring our conversation. I felt a little embarrassed, but I walked up to them anyways.

"So, you found Kris then?" I asked.

"Actually no," Radcliff said. "I still hadn't found him when Alicia told me he had returned. But now we need to focus on the task at hand." He raised an arm, close his eyes, and the platform began gliding towards the fortress. It was slow at first, but the speed increased as our destination loomed higher.

"And we'll see if this is a trap or not." Alicia crossed her arms.

"Don't worry," Radcliff said.

I looked at Kris. He still stood at the edge of the platform, the first who would arrive. I wished he would turn his head, look back at me and smile. Something. I realized my heart was beating faster the closer we drew. A *thud-thud thud-thud* that grew with the rising fortress. If only Kris would say something stupid or do something to break this feeling of a shadow looming over me. But he remained still.

Alicia stood determined, like a feline watching its prey. Raine seemed discomforted like myself. We happened to glance at each other at the same time, and we held each other's gaze for a few seconds. She wanted something to look to as much as I did, and for a striking moment I remember she was older than me.

Both her eyes and mine fell to Radcliff. He was moving us forward; he surely knew what to do. I wondered if he had been one of the few to stand strong against Bot's accusations. Hadn't fled when Bot gave an excuse and an exit to run to. I wanted to believe Radcliff had not run. I truly wanted to. I found my hand was on the manacle again, and I pulled it away.

The platform gently docked at a staircase that ended at the edge of the fortress and dropped off into space. Up the stairs was a small courtyard and a large set of double doors. They were painted red, and the tops of the doors curved like the top of a teardrop. Kris stepped off the platform first.

Radcliff was next to leave the platform. "Let's go."

We crossed the courtyard, our footsteps echoing off the surrounding walls. Radcliff reached up and knocked. The wood sounded far too thick as if the doors were actually a wall, and a sensation of being trapped washed over me.

The doors clicked as they loosened themselves from the frame. They both slid backwards, stopped, and were lifted up and to the sides. A single man stood at the entrance, older with white and thinning hair: a stereotypical butler.

"Ah, warpers, I presume?" he asked.

"We are. We're here to see Erika," Radcliff said.

"Yes, yes. I think perhaps that I remember you." He pointed to Kris.

"Yeah, I was here before."

Alicia snapped her head to Kris. *"When?"*

"Back when Tavin and Erika were making it. Geez."

"It was some time ago. Pity none of you have been around since then. Not good for the mistress's health, I should think. Alas. This way, if you please." With a gracious flowing of his hand and wrist the butler invited us in.

We passed through a long corridor that was ornate in its simplicity. The ceiling was high above us, and we walked on a black marble path in the center of the room. Orange columns lined both sides of the path with red drapes hung and flowing between them. As we walked down the corridor I noticed Alicia holding Raine's hand, not letting her daughter move more than half a meter away from her.

We came to a room that I could only imagine was close to the center, if not the center, of the fortress. A large circular elevator was in the middle of the room with an intricate metal frame around it.

"This lift will take you directly to the antechamber of the mistress's private quarters."

"How do we know it isn't a trap?" Alicia asked.

The butler laughed. "Ah, I suppose you don't, but if it would make you feel any better I would be willing to ride it up with you."

"That doesn't make me feel any better, thank you very much." She was walking around the elevator, examining its structure.

"I am sorry, ma'am, but that is the best I can do," the butler said.

"Alicia, you know as well as I do that she wouldn't need us to be in this elevator to trap us," Radcliff said.

"No, but it would be far more elegant."

"Well, I remember how Erika used to be, and I know she wouldn't want to kill us even if she was god-moding right now." Kris pulled aside the metal screen and entered the elevator.

"Wait," I said. "Why don't we just make a doorway up there? I mean, then we don't have to worry about the elevator at all." I paused and added, "If it's such a big deal."

Everyone was silent, waiting for someone else to say something.

"I, for one, certainly did not expect you would make this so difficult," the butler said. "Perhaps there is some truth to the mistress's words after all. But never mind. If making an alternative route would truly put your minds so at ease, then by all means. We want nothing more than for guests to be comfortable."

I created the doorway. "Come on. I want to get this thing off me."

The antechamber far above was designed much the same as the rest of the fortress I had seen so far, but the lighting was a bit dimmer, the ceiling not as high. It felt more personal and homey. The others came through the doorway, and I let it dissolve.

"So who wants to knock on the doors?" Kris pointed to the only set of doors in the room.

"I will do it." Radcliff stepped forward, but before his hand had even hit the wood twice they both opened inward at the same time.

Beyond the doors was a long rectangular room with a number of book cases, dozens of tables, and two fireplaces halfway down the room facing each other which were the only sources of light. A few small robots with two digitigrade legs and no other limbs scampered across the floor, hiding behind table legs. We walked into the room slowly, and the homey feeling vanished.

The walls were covered in scribbled words and letters I didn't recognize, some of them were matched up to English, French, or some other language I assumed was Sanskrit. The tables were covered with stacks of open books and piles of papers. Some stacks were even taller than myself, and I wondered how they hadn't fallen over yet. A few of the small robots were also upon the tables, hiding behind piles of books as we passed them. I learned later that these were copies of every book Erika's predecessors had left behind. Strange metal scraps and clockwork mechanisms also covered a number of tables. They looked like deconstructed machines or appliances that had never been put back together. A few of the items among the scrap heaps seemed like newly fabricated devices, but none looked properly finished. The floor was littered with leafs of paper, bolts, screws, and scatterings of jellybeans.

"God..." Kris whispered.

"Erika?" Radcliff called out.

There were a few doors in the room and another set of double doors across from where we had entered. Our walking had slowed to a stop before we even crossed half the room.

"This isn't..." Alicia picked up a notebook and flipped through it, scanning a few of the pages. "Is it?" Her eyes shot up to the walls, flicking between the different clusters of scrawlings.

"What is it?" Radcliff asked.

Alicia walked to the wall and reached up to trace the lines of a word written there. "It is. This is the ancient warper language from the Third Era. Erika and I had worked on translating it decades ago." Alicia flipped through a few more pages. "She never stopped."

"Did she solve it?" Radcliff picked up another notebook and scanned a few pages of it.

"It doesn't look like it."

I glanced over to Kris. He wasn't distracted by any of the things in the room, instead he was watching the doors. He saw me looking at him, and he quickly glanced away.

"It looks like she's done an absurd amount of organizing though. If I'm not mistaken, I think this notebook is just a list of every unique word from the language in a sort of alphabetical order," Alicia said.

"How did she know what order the alphabet went in?" Radcliff asked.

"I don't think she did. I think this is a completely arbitrary alphabetization."

"What would be the point in that?"

Alicia was silent a moment. "I don't think there really was one."

"That's, troubling. Do you think—?"

"Put those down! Put my books down right *now*!" It was a scream, almost like a scream of pain. It came from the far end of the room, and Erika was there, running at us. Three bipedal robots smaller than any others scampered behind her.

Kris stepped out of the way as she ran past him. Erika snatched the notebooks from Radcliff's and Alicia's hands. Radcliff let his go easily, but Alicia held onto hers a bit too long and several of the pages tore once Erika finally yanked it from her hands.

"Look what you did!" Erika clutched the books to her chest. The small robots caught up to her and hid behind her legs.

"*Me?*" Alicia asked.

"Yes, you! Why are you even here? Why are *all of you* even here? No one comes here, not even Tavin! And he was the last one who ever came. Where is he? I want an explanation!" She kept snapping her head back and forth at our group as if the answer was a small bug flitting between us. She was shorter than everyone in the room besides Raine, and her hair fell in matted tangles behind her as if she had not bathed in weeks. Her hooded sweater and mini shorts looked equally dirty.

"Erika, calm down. We'll expla–" Radcliff started.

"No! Don't you talk to me! Where's Tavin? And who is–" She pointed at me but was suddenly silent. Her hand dropped to her side. "Tavin's dead, isn't he?"

I glanced at Kris. His eyes were tightly shut, his teeth pressed together. It was the most pained face I'd even seen him wear.

"Yeah," I whispered, turning to Erika. "Tavin isn't here anymore."

She stared at me and blinked a few times; I thought perhaps she was holding back tears. She dropped the two notebooks and hugged Kris.

"I'm sorry, Kris."

He was surprised, but his arms were pinned to his side so he couldn't do anything. He wrinkled his nose at her smell.

The hug was short, and she faced Radcliff and Alicia again. "Why are you here? You didn't even bother to tell me Tavin had died." She pointed at me but continued staring at them. "What do you want? Tell me why I shouldn't punt you both into the nearest black hole."

"*Don't* you threaten us," Alicia said.

Radcliff raised a hand instantly, holding her back. "We need your help."

"Oh. Sure. Of course. Isn't that it exactly then?" Erika walked a few paces away from us, picking up jellybeans from the floor she passed. "Why do you need me? I thought no one wanted me?" She grabbed a chair and hopped onto it, crouching on the seat instead of sitting. The three robots hopped around the chair's legs, attempting to reach Erika.

"Listen." Radcliff stepped forward. "I understand why you're upset. I really do. But this isn't about us, this is about Ethan. Jett's put a bomb on him and—"

"Jett?" She jumped up, now standing on the chair. "What's he been doing? Tell me what he's been up to."

"Killin' bitches," Kris said absently.

"That's a crude way of putting it," Radcliff said. "What he means is that Jett's trying to—"

"Commit genocide," Alicia cut in. "Specifically against the Warper Born. Like Raine."

Erika sank down in the chair, sitting this time. She ate a few of the jellybeans she had picked up. "My poor Jett..."

"Poor Jett? *Poor Jett*? He wants to kill Raine!" Alicia yelled.

"Yes." Erika scooped up the three robots, cradling them in her arms. " 'Poor Jett,' because he got caught up in the trap of the Ego Stage. 'Poor Jett,' because he wasn't able to predict what he would do and prevent himself from doing it. He has brought down your anger and hatred on himself because he did nothing. 'Poor Jett,' because he is not me and didn't trap himself in a prison where he would also gain your anger and hatred."

"I do *not* hate you. You have no proof," Alicia said.

"You fear me."

Alicia narrowed her eyes but didn't respond.

"Fear. Hate. How different are those two emotions, really? Always so closely linked." Erika stood up on the chair again and walked onto a nearby table, carefully placing her bare feet between the piles of books and papers. "So why is he trying to kill the Warper Born?"

"He isn't actually doing that," I said. "Right now he's trying to kill the Rurrians."

Erika stopped where she was, poised in mid-step. "The Rurrians?"

"Yeah, the people with the Reality Generators and—"

"I know who they are. Taking their name from Rur, who, like them, decided to live his life for himself without masters of any kind. They've known about us for as long as we can remember knowing them." She finally placed her foot on the table and leaned down, releasing the robots before scooping up a handful of jellybeans from a bowl hidden among the papers. "Why are you all here again?"

"To save Ethan," Kris said.

"Ethan." Erika looked at me. "That's your name?"

"Yeah."

"Hmm. I like that name. I don't know if I like you yet though. Why do you need to be saved?"

"Because Jett stuck this on my wrist." I held up my arm, showing her the manacle. "It's gonna blow up if I don't get everyone together to talk to Jett."

"Oh, of course. You have all avoided him, the wolf, just as much as you have avoided me, the mouse. All of you are pathetic. I won't help."

"Oh yes you will." Kris grabbed the edge of the table she was standing on, threatening to tip it over. "You're gonna help, because I don't want Ethan to die."

"Yes. You have to help us," Radcliff said.

Erika crouched down, eye level with Kris. "I don't have to do anything. Why should I help?"

"Because he'll die if you don't," Kris said.

"Why should I care about Ethan?"

"Not Ethan. Jett."

Erika pulled her head back, surprised. "What?"

"If Ethan dies because you don't help I swear to you I'll kill Jett myself."

"And I'll gladly help Kris," Alicia said.

"You would?" Kris looked back at her.

"Of course. If he's dead, he can't kill Raine."

"That's enough." Radcliff pulled Kris away from the table. "No one is going to kill anyone. And I mean *no one*. Ethan isn't going to die, and neither is Jett. I need everyone to calm down. Just take a few deep breaths."

Erika laughed. "You know, I probably would have helped you, Radcliff, but I don't think I wanna help you if it helps them."

"Goddammit! Don't you understand!" Kris pulled away, but Radcliff grabbed him again before he reached Erika.

"The best way for me to calm down is to leave. I didn't want anything to do with Erika anyways." Alicia looked at me. "This is, of course, all your fault." She walked out of the room, pulling Raine along behind her.

"See? How am I to help you if you can't even help yourselves?" Erika asked.

Alicia slammed the doors as she left the room. She had literally warped the mechanical doors into hinged doors so she could slam them shut.

Erika started rolling a pencil back and forth on the table. "You just get so used to having your own way..."

"Why, why, why," Redcliff muttered to himself. "Kris, please go talk to Alicia and convince her to come back. Please."

Kris sighed. "I'll go try. I can't promise anything." He left.

"Now," Radcliff turned to Erika, "all we have to do is sit here and listen to what Jett wants to–"

"How did Jett get that thing on your arm anyways?" Erika asked me.

"Uh, I kinda ran into him."

"And?"

"Well, he wanted me to help him kill the Rurrians and I refused. Because of that he put this manacle on me and said I had to get everyone together. He wants to talk to everyone since he hasn't gotten to for a long time. He wants to explain the problem with the Rurrians."

"He's having a problem? With the Rurrians?" She smirked and jumped down from the table. "That seems odd. What problem?"

"Something about them being able to rebuild too quickly."

She walked over to a wall and looked up at her writings. The three robots were stranded on the high table, and I reached out to them. As soon as they saw my hand they scattered and hid in the piles of papers.

Erika mumbled something.

"What was that?" Radcliff asked.

"I do miss Jett," she said quietly. "But why has he never come to me? I haven't left here. Surely he knows where I am."

"How would he know?" I asked.

Erika turned around, studying me. "How old are you?"

"Eighteen."

"And how many months?"

"About one and a half."

Erika snatched up a piece of paper and pencil. After a few moments she looked up. "He died only a few weeks after we finished this fortress. Didn't he?" She was looking at Radcliff.

"Yes," he said.

"He must never have told Jett. He promised to tell Jett where I was."

"He never mentioned such a duty."

"Of course not. You would have tried to stop him."

Radcliff remained silent.

"So will you help us? Will you help me? You don't even have to really do anything. Just listen to what Jett wants to tell us." I held out my arm, displaying the manacle. "I really don't wanna die."

She turned away, picked up a jellybean from the floor, and ate it. "What were the exact orders he gave you?"

"I just have to get everyone together to listen to what he has to say."

"About the Rurrians."

"Yeah."

"I think I know what he's playing at."

"What do you mean?" Radcliff asked.

"He wants us all together. You said the Rurrians were rebuilding too fast? If he has everyone together then he will know what we are or are not doing. He will know if we are actually helping the Rurrians or not."

"He did mention that he had first thought someone was helping them," I said. "But why do you think that's his exact plan?"

"Because I know him. Very well." Erika smiled. "It seems like what he would do. Not much of a subtle ploy though. I think it seems a bit desperate of him. He could be genuinely scared. Come here." She walked down the room, away from the door, following the writing on the walls. She stopped and pointed at a single word.

"I'm almost certain this word here is 'Rurrian.' Maybe plural." She picked up a book from the closest table and checked a page. She tossed it aside and picked up another book. "This one. Over half this book seems to be about this word." She pointed to the same word inside. "This warper was very concerned with them as well. But I don't know what exactly the

213

concern is. Concern to help or to hinder? I just haven't been able to figure it out. This language. Any of the three languages. This Third one is the one I've worked on the most, but I just can't *get it*." She dropped the book on the table and turned back to the wall. "I've been trying for so long. It seems like it's all I've been doing my whole life. Even in my dreams I'm trying to crack it, but I just can't." She pressed her hand against the wall, slowly sliding it to the side, smearing the words. "I just *can't*." She sobbed and knocked her forehead against the wall. She leaned back and did it again. *Thud.*

"Stop." Radcliff caught her before she knocked her head into the wall a third time, his hand against her forehead. He pulled Erika away and put his arms around her, hugging her as she continued crying. "It's going to be fine. You don't need to worry about that language. Everything will be okay. I'm sorry. I'm sorry you've had to go through this."

For several minutes Radcliff held Erika, calming her as she cried. I couldn't do anything and stood there awkwardly, waiting until she stopped crying and until something could happen. I looked down at one of the copies of the ancient journals. Below a block of the strange writing was a drawing of what looked like a sea of square tiles flowing and rolling with the whole plain fragmenting and diverging at the end. The drawing resonated with me strangely. It seemed to be the rough sketches of a beautiful work of art.

"Okay," she said.

I turned around. She and Radcliff were standing apart, and she was still rubbing one eye but otherwise seemed collected.

"Chin up, and we'll drown a little slower," Erika said.

"What?" Radcliff asked.

"I'll help you."

Chapter 17
Sheep Turned Wolf

Radcliff had gone out to the antechamber to help convince
Alicia to return. In the meantime I was left with Erika in her
work hall. She had gathered the three robots back to her, one
perched on each of her shoulders and one atop her head. She
milled about, picking up books or papers from one place and
setting them somewhere else. I assumed she was organizing
them, but I couldn't shake the feeling that she was just
shuffling them around.

She turned to me. "Why are you staring at me?"

"Oh. Oh, sorry." I looked away. I could feel a heat rising in
my cheeks.

"I didn't say you have to stop. I just wanted to know why
you were."

"Uh, not really any reason. Just, looking."

Erika rolled her eyes. "As you say." She turned back to her
papers.

"You're, um, Japanese, right?"

She turned to me, put her hands together, and bowed. She
said something I could not understand. As a note, she was
speaking Japanese.

"Wh-what?"

"I said 'how could you guess?' " She didn't look amused.

"Sorry. Your eyes and hair. I was just wondering."

"Right." She stepped forward and studied me a moment.
"You though... you though. Partly Eastern European, I can tell.
Probably German or Dutch, or maybe even Igden, depending on
your planet. But the rest..."

"Native American."

"Oh?" She sounded genuinely surprised. "Which tribe?"

"Odawa. Mother's side."

She said something else I didn't understand.

"Why do you keep doing that?"

"You don't even know your own language of heritage?"

"No. No one ever taught it to me."

"Oh. No matter. You'll learn plenty of languages eventually."

"Why's that?"

"Because you can now. You'll learn the top six by necessity: English, Mandarin, Bógdee, Spanish, Russian, and French. Well, and also because of boredom. Eventually. I personally know 163 different languages and dialects."

"That many?"

"Indeed." Her eyes brightened. "It's my personal obsession, philology and linguistics." She smiled. "It's so fascinating and so important too. Have you ever wondered why so many planets are so similar?"

"So similar?"

Erika sighed. "No, you haven't then. If it were possible to trace back the copying of planets we might have a clue to our origin, but alas, not many have thought to preserve the past."

At that she drew out a silver tuning fork from her pocket and struck it against the table. It vibrated, the ringing grew, pierced my ears, and for a mere fraction of a second the vibrations distorted the air as a new bowl of jellybeans appeared from nowhere.

"What in the world was that?" I asked.

"What was what?" Erika looked up, a single eyebrow raised.

"That. What you just did. That fork." I pointed at the instrument in her hand.

"Oh, this. This is the Ad Infinitum Fork. It's how I warp. My power is vibration warping." She scooped up a handful of jellybeans and dumped them all into her mouth at the same time.

"So you just hit the Fork and warp?"

"It's a bit more delicate than that," she said as she chewed. "I have to control the vibrations and amplify them for larger warps. It takes a fair amount of finesse, and it took a long time before I could do it well at all. Not like when I first found it." She smiled.

"What happened?"

"I was in a doctor's office, getting a yearly checkup. He was almost finished when I noticed the Fork on the counter and asked about it. He was a bit confused at first, wondering why it had been left out, but he brought it over to me and showed me how it worked. He struck it on the palm of his hand and held it up to my ear. 'We can test your hearing with it,' he said. I asked to try it and he smiled and said of course and I took it in my small hands. I was about thirteen back when this happened. So I hit it, and you'll never guess what the warp energy did."

I waited a moment. "What?"

"The whole building and every nonliving entity in it turned bright red. The same shade bright red. It was very taxing on the eyes."

"Geez. Then what happened? What did everyone do?"

"I don't really remember. I remember there was a lot of screaming and commotion but not what happened after that. I don't even remember my dear mother ever talking about the incident afterwards." Erika shrugged her shoulders."

"Some really weird things happened in my childhood too, but no one noticed the changes."

"Premature incidents are a common thread."

The doors opened at the end of the room and Radcliff was returning with Kris, Alicia, and Raine. Erika mumbled something I was unable to perceive as she took another fistful of jellybeans. The three robots jumped into her sweater's hood that was hanging down Erika's back.

"How do we get this underway?" Alicia asked as the group reached us.

"I'm not really sure." I looked down at the manacle.

"Let me see it." Radcliff lifted my arm so he could better examine the device.

"He didn't tell you want to do?" Kris asked.

"No."

"I suspect it's something relatively simple." Radcliff cleared his throat. "Jett. Can you hear me? This is Radcliff, and we're all here."

Nothing happened.

"Now what?" Kris asked.

A small green light flicked on in the center of the manacle. A small disk detached from it and floated up towards the ceiling. It scanned a thin wave of green light over the room, beeping each time it passed over one of us. The disk split into seven pieces, one smaller disk from the center and six sections of the ring that had surrounded it. The sections of the ring drifted away and created a perimeter while the central disk projected a green, holographic Jett before us.

"That was a bit quicker than I had expected." Jett stood with his arms crossed, still wearing the same aviator-esk jacket. His eyes scanned over us, taking each of us into account, and lingering on Erika.

In her face she seemed to be suppressing a reaction: as if two conflicting pillars emotions fell at the same time and towards the same direction, thus tenuously supporting each other.

"And why is that, Jett?" Radcliff asked.

"Because of the way you all continuously ran from me before. But that is all in the past now, so listen up, because you're on my terms now." He held out a small device that was about the same size and shape as a pen. "With this I can release Ethan from that cuff, but that will happen if and only if my demand is met, which is simple: all of you will hear me out to my satisfaction. You will listen to everything I have to say, and you will heed the gravity of my words." His eyes narrowed.

"That's not fair," Kris said.

Jett jerked his head to him. "Isn't it?"

"No. 'To your satisfaction' could mean anything."

Jett walked over to him and jabbed a finger into his chest. The holographic hand passed right into Kris and he flinched. Jett laughed. As of the time of writing this I know that almost half a universe away Jett was standing in an empty white room on his flagship, surrounded by ghostly green holograms of us and a partial reconstruction of Erika's work room, his hand jabbing through Kris's immaterial chest as he laughed.

"I suppose that is true, but none of you have a choice." Jett held up the trigger device again. "I could detonate the bomb right now, if I wished, but I do not wish to so long as you cooperate. But you have my word that I will let Ethan go as soon as I don't need him as collateral."

Ch 17 – Sheep Turned Wolf

"*Collateral?*" Kris's voice rose again.

"Kris, stop," Radcliff said. "Listen, Jett, Kris has a point. Your terms are undefined, and not all of us think or act rationally while a threat of death is looming over us. You have to let Ethan go now."

"But I can't," Jett said to Radcliff. "How do I know you all won't just run away if I do? He's the only thing keeping you here." He pointed at me.

"Yes, I understand that you find it difficult to trust us right now, especially since we've never done anything besides flee from you ever since you entered your fourth Stage, but you have my word that we will hear you out. So please, let Ethan go."

Jett hesitated with a look on his face that seemed genuinely conflicted. But he raised his arm as if keeping the detonator away from Radcliff. "No! I can't trust you."

A beat of silence filled the room.

"Then begin." Radcliff crossed his arms. "We're listening."

Jett's eyes jumped to each of our faces, checking us. "Fine." He pulled a piece of paper from his pocket. "Now, listen: the Rurrians want to kill us."

"So?" Alicia asked. "There's no way they could possibly do that. And last I checked they weren't doing anything besides building Reality Generators."

"Well you're wrong. Last you checked was too long ago. They know about us, and they're not us, so they're a threat. I've been fighting them for over twenty years now, and I know what they want to do and what they can do. They have too much power now and I don't know how, but they've got it and they're using it. It's only because of my constant bombardments that I've been able to keep them in check. And that's the biggest problem!"

"What is?" Radcliff asked.

Jett pointed a finger at his own chest. "The fact that I've *only* been able to keep them in check. Don't you understand what that means?"

"That you're incompetent." Alicia gave a sly grin.

"No! It can only mean something or someone is helping them! And I'm going to find out in just a few minutes."

"What do you mean?" Radcliff asked.

"He means he's attacking them right now. Aren't you, Jett?" Erika spoke softly, looking at the floor.

"How...?" Jett trailed off. He walked up to her and his hand moved forward, as if to touch her cheek, but he stopped and let his arm fall back to his side. "You know me too well." He smiled faintly.

Erika still wouldn't look up at him.

"Erika... darling. Look at me."

"No. Stop. I *can't*." Erika turned away from him, her arms wrapped around her torso.

"What's wrong with you?" Jett's voice rose.

"Jett, this isn't what we came here for," Alicia snapped. "Is there anything else you want to tell us, or are you going to release us already?"

Jett spun around as if he was surprised that the rest of us were still here. "No! I'm not finished yet. Listen." He glanced back down at his paper. "It's true that my new fleet of ships are attacking them right now, and you're all staying right here until I get their report. I don't want any of you as my enemy, but if you're helping the Rurrians then that's what you'll be."

"Jett, stop," Radcliff said. "Ask yourself: Is that a logical course of action? To turn against us? Aren't you trying to kill the Rurrians, because they want to kill us?"

"Yes. They want to kill us, so we have to kill them first."

"But if we were helping them, you'd turn against us and kill us instead?"

"I'd have to."

"But then wouldn't you just be doing what you are trying to prevent?"

"No! I'd be saving us! Any warper who's stupid enough to help the Rurrians doesn't *deserve* to live as a warper. That person would be betraying themselves, and killing them would only be protecting us all."

"That's stupid as hell," Kris said.

"You're probably the one who's doing it!" Jett pointed at Kris.

"Really?" Kris raised his eyebrows.

"Is there anything else you want to tell us?" Radcliff asked. "Or do you just want to spend the rest of the time throwing accusations at us?"

"I know you're not convinced, but let me tell you what they plan on doing. I dug this out of one of the Rurrians I captured. Haven't you wondered why they were expanding? Why the Rurrians were rushing to every planet they could reach?"

"Have they been doing that?" Alicia asked.

"Yes! But you wouldn't know it. None of you would, because you're all just sticking your heads in the sand. They were expanding everywhere like an infestation when I first started fighting them. They don't want to just kill us, oh no, they want to *trap* us."

Alicia laughed. "You expect us to believe that? How could they trap us?"

"The Reality Generators! They want to fill the whole universe with Reality Generators. They want to kill us all and warp lock every planet that has Humans, so on rebirth the new warpers will be cut off from the warp energy forever. Then, when new warpers are discovered by their lack of aging, they'll be caught and the Rurrians will–"

"Kill them. Yeah, yeah. The power will just move on. They can't stop it," Alicia said.

"Wrong! They won't kill that new warper. No, they'll *imprison* the warper. They'll keep all new warpers locked away in the deepest vaults; locked away to live out their whole lives in bondage. Locked away as 'security,' because each warper trapped in a warp locked vault is a warper they won't have to worry about. If we don't kill them now, then our entire future, our entire linage, all my future lives will be lived out going insane from a lack of air!"

"We don't get reincarnated!" Erika suddenly screamed, her hands clutching the sides of her head.

"Yes we do!" Jett threw the paper at her, but it fluttered through her and landed on the floor.

"Jett. We all know that there is no evidence we are reincarnated," Radcliff said very softly, almost too softly to hear.

"There isn't really anything that says we don't," Kris said.

The room was silent again for a beat.

"Wait. Wait." I looked around the room. "Reincarnation? No one's mentioned reincarnation before."

"That's because it's not true." Alicia pulled a book out of

thin air. "From what I understand of the equations of energy and creation, they show a continuous flow of *new* energy. I'm not some hand-me-down soul."

"No, the equations show a loop. An infinite loop of stable energy transfer between the slipstream and here," Jett said.

"That's just the warp energy conversion process," Alicia said. "Our souls aren't made of warp energy. Our souls are a difference substance."

"Then why can only Humans become warpers?" Jett asked.

"Because we're the original species of the Universe," Alicia said.

For a moment my vision seemed to fade, and I could only hear my own breathing loud and heavy in my ears, then it dissipated and I blinked rapidly a few times.

"–is capacity," Jett continued. "It has to be, because Humans are the only ones who have the potential to hold the warp energy. We warpers are the only ones who have souls! And the souls are warp energy, which is continuously recycled!"

"Souls equaling warp energy is a conclusion you're jumping to without evidence. The equations show that the warp energy is converted down in the slipstream and then back into warp energy before the loop is complete. You don't know what you're talking about!"

"*Me*? I don't know what I'm talking about? Ha! I studied all these same things myself, or did you forget that I already finished learning? I'm way ahead of you, and I know what's really going on. The equations clearly show that the warp energy is converted into souls. *Our* souls. It's the only thing that fits."

"You can't just throw 'souls' into the incomplete parts of the equations and hope they work," Alicia said. "The First Era of warpers–"

"That's exactly what I'm referring to," Jett continued. "The First Era of warpers knew the complete equations, but we can't translate their language. I was working on the equations before I realized the danger the Rurrians possessed to us."

"I'm so lost right now," I said.

"Of course you are. You're still just in Stage 1," Alicia said.

"I'll explain it to you after this," Radcliff said.

"I've been working on it too! In case you all forgot." Erika climbed up onto a table and pointed at her scrawlings on the wall. "I'm almost finished! I know it! I just need more time. Then I'll crack this language."

"But you're working on the Third Era's language. We need the *First* Era," Alicia said.

"No! Wrong! I was working on the Third Era, but now I'm working on an All Era language."

"What? Are you insane?" Alicia asked.

"No! I am actually a genius. I'm doing much better at it than you ever were. I bet you've given up since I last saw you."

"I have *not* given up. Once I return to it *I* will solve the First Era's language, and I will prove that I have the right answer. However, right now I have other more important matters, like Raine."

"What's an All Era language?" Kris asked.

"A derivative of all three Eras," Erika said. "Once I create it I'll be able to translate any of them!"

"Is that possible?" I asked.

"Of course. By synthesizing all three languages into one, I'll create a new root language that can translate all three."

"Erika, that can't–" Radcliff started.

"I'm almost finished!" She screamed.

"Alright, alright." Radcliff raised his hands. "But that's not what we're discussing here. Jett, is there anything else, or will you let Ethan go now?"

"I knew it. I knew you'd just be rushing me! That you'd only want to pretend to listen to save Ethan." Jett held up the detonator. "I-I'll *show* you."

"Don't you dare, Jett. Don't, you, *dare*." Radcliff spoke quickly, firmly.

Jett hesitated. "I'll do it. I really will. Everyone just shut up and listen to me! I have the report from the battle." He looked down at his wrist controller and stood motionless for several seconds, then he looked back to us. "The Rurrians continued to hold off, but... none of you are helping them."

"You see? Our policy has been complete non-interaction. There was never a reason to suspect us in the first place," Radcliff said.

"How else could they have continued to hold on?"

"Maybe you really are just incompetent," Alicia said.

"No! It's completely *impossible* what they're doing. No matter how much I rebuild my fleet, they are able to rebuild their defenses just as quickly. My power isn't stro— no, *fast* enough."

"No one can build as quickly as warpers."

"Exactly! This means there are *other, warpers!*" Jett pointed at her with each word. "The Rurrians have somehow gained the ability to reality warp! It's just what I've been trying to tell you! They're a dire threat, and they want to trap us all!"

"No. No, that simply cannot be," Radcliff said. "They can't have reality warping, because there are *only* six warpers. There's no way you are correct. You must have overlooked something. Something is not right."

"But that's it! Don't you see now! Something isn't right at all!" Jett was shaking, and he dropped the detonator. "I thought it was one of you. I *knew* it was one of you! But... but it *isn't...*"

"And you're not lying." Erika crouched down and sat on a stack of books. "I know you're not lying. For a moment I thought you were trying to trick us. That you were behind the Rurrians' supposed strength. That you were using them as a ploy behind some greater design. But you're not."

"You all have to help me!" Jett yelled.

"Help you?" Alicia asked. "Why should we help you?"

"Because they're going to kill us! They have reality warping! We have to kill them now!"

"Jett, calm *down*," Radcliff said. "There is no way they could have reality warping. It is absolutely impossible."

"But it's happening right now. Right *now*," Jett said.

No one spoke or ventured an answer.

"Jett. Will you let Ethan go now?" Radcliff asked.

Jett was still shaking, breathing heavily. He looked like he might collapse. "F-fine. Okay. Fine." He picked up the detonator, flipped it open, and pressed a button.

The manacle *clinked*, and a sharp pain shot through my arm as the rods withdrew quickly from inside my wrist. I yelled out and it fell to the floor, followed by a flow of blood. I dropped to my knees and clenched my wrist, but the blood kept flowing from between my fingers.

Radcliff created a portal on the floor where the manacle

rested, and it fell through and into some other place far from here.

"Ethan!" Kris was instantly at my side. "What do we do?"

Radcliff crouched down at my other side. "Be calm. Ethan, this will be very simple, but you have to do exactly what I say."

"Sure, sure," I said through clenched teeth.

A pair of rubber gloves appeared on his hands. "Let go of your arm and let me help it."

"But the blood–" I started to say.

"Just let go. It will only take a moment."

I glanced at Kris, then held out my arm to Radcliff, the blood flowing freely.

He turned my arm over with one hand and held the other above the two puncture wounds. A stream of skin colored gel appeared below his hand and shot straight into the openings.

"What is it?" I asked.

"Bio foam. It'll seal the openings and replacing the missing cells." As soon as both wounds were filled, Radcliff placed a vial of warp extract into my right hand. "Drink this quickly."

No sooner than I finished the vial the globs of bio foam started fusing with my arm, healing the holes. It didn't hurt, but it felt like the two points of my arm were writhing with a living conglomerate of pins that were expanding into my flesh. The sensation faded and soon the only thing left was two pairs of pale circles on either side of my arm with steams of blood drying around them.

Radcliff stood. "We're leaving now."

"No! You can't leave! I knew you'd leave! That was why I had to have Ethan. But you *have* to see the danger now. You have to help me kill them!"

"No, Jett. We won't help you," Radcliff said.

"You'll only turn to the Warper Born after the Rurrians are finished off," Alicia added.

"The Warper Born...?" Jett shook his head. "No! No. The Rurrians are who we need to worry about! How do you think they'll act when *they* find out about the Warper Born? It'll be all out war."

"No it won't, because the Rurrians will never reach the Warper Born planets." Alicia tugged on Raine's arm. "We're leaving."

"You can't just leave! You can't just ignore this!" Jett ran in front of her as if he could stop her, but Alicia simply walked right through his holographic image.

Radcliff sighed. "I'm sorry Jett, but we are leaving. Turn this thing off and don't threaten any of us again."

"You can't! You can't ignore me! You have to help–"

Radcliff raised his hand and with a crushing of his first smashed each piece of the array at the same time with invisible might. Jett's image disappeared.

"I'm sorry, Erika," he said.

"I... I understand... why. But, how? How has this happened? How have we come to this? How?" She was staring down at the floor, her long hair hiding her face.

"I fear something much worse is happening to Jett besides merely going through his Ego Stage," Radcliff said.

"What?" she asked.

"I think... perhaps the most likely explanation, the one that doesn't introduce needless assumptions, is that Jett is experiencing psychological problems."

"What do you mean?" Erika looked up at him.

Alicia also stopped, hesitating at the door to hear what Radcliff would say.

"He could have developed a split personality of some sort. That would explain everything perfectly. He is creating the attack and the defense, thus he thinks he is at a stalemate." Radcliff folded his hands together. "My old mentor, long ago, back when I was still in my Learning Stage, told me that such an occurrence has happened before. And given our loss of records it could be that this is a rather common effect of the Ego Stage."

"Maybe," Erika said. "But..."

"Yes?" Radcliff asked.

"What about the Yorrlak standing stones?"

Radcliff took a deep breath.

But Alicia spoke first. "They only record a failure."

"What are the standing stones?" I asked.

Radcliff just looked at Kris.

Kris raised his hands. "I can't show him everything in a day!"

"They are a record, yes." Erika sat down on a chair. "A very important one, and not necessarily of a failure. I think they would help me finish working on the language, because of the writing on them. But we all know I can't bring copies here. Not while I can't leave, at least."

Radcliff massaged his temples. "Yes, we know. Now, Kris, Ethan, I want you to go with Alicia and wait for me to catch up, then we'll discuss everything that just happened. I'm going to talk with Erika first."

"Meet me at Fractal," Alicia said before disappearing with Raine.

"Fractal? How many things do I still not know?" I asked.

"Sorry. I'll show you now. Come on." Kris took my hand, teleported us outside, led me through the warp locked shell, and teleported us again.

Chapter 18
Fight the Tape

We reappeared atop a raised stone platform on a rugged planet of crystal. The whole surface was unpolished indigo stretching out as far as the eye could see like an ocean flash-frozen during the beginning of a storm.

"So this planet's a giant crystal?" I asked.

"Basically," Kris replied.

"Why?"

"Because this planet masks teleportation energy and makes it impossible to trace," Alicia said. She was standing with Raine on the surface of the planet itself, a meter away from the platform. "Now come on, we haven't got all day."

Kris hopped down onto the surface.

I paused a moment. "I don't think my doorways can be traced. They don't leave a trail of energy."

Alicia waved her hand in dismissal. "But we've always used teleportation, so it's easier."

I just shook my head and joined them on the planet's surface proper.

Alicia held out her hand; Kris took hers and took mine, then we teleported again. Everything was strangely blurred, mere suggestions of light and shape instead of the dynamic show I was familiar with. We arrived standing in a concrete hallway with hanging, off-white lights at even intervals.

"A bunker? What are we doing here?" Kris asked.

Alicia started down the hallway with swift steps, no longer holding Raine's hand. "To pick up Raine."

"What?" Kris started off after her. "But isn't she...?"

I hurried after all three of them.

"This is a doppelganger," Alicia said.

"Yep, just in case there was a ploy against Raine," the doppeler Raine said.

"Really? Really?" Kris asked. "Why didn't you tell us?"

"Had to make sure you wouldn't accidently give it away. This was Radcliff's idea. I never would have brought the real Raine anywhere near Erika," Alicia said.

"Okay, so, this isn't the real Raine?" I pointed to her. "This is just a copy?"

"Yep, just a copy." Raine nodded.

"That's, bizarre," I said.

"It's a perfectly sound safety precaution. It does wonders to protect non-warpers," Raine continued.

"Why non-warpers?"

"Because warpers can sense other warpers, of course," Alicia said.

"We can?" I asked.

"Haven't you noticed?" Kris asked.

"Obviously not," I said.

"Did you ever tell him, Kris?" Alicia asked.

"I thought it was obvious! But I mean, I *was* getting to it. Eventually."

Alicia just shook her head.

It was at this point that we reached the end of the hallway and stood before a metal door. This end of the hallway and the room beyond the metal door were covered by a level two warp lock. Alicia pressed her hand against a scanner plate and after a moment there was a loud *clank*, and the door slowly swung inward. Beyond it was a large cube room with cement walls, ceiling, and floor. In the center was a small house that looked like a billionaire's cottage retreat. We crossed the room and went inside. The real Raine was here, sprawled out on a couch watching TV. There was a plate on a table near her with the crust of a sandwich, and every light I could see was turned on.

She jumped up from the couch. "Hey mom; hey guys. Hey me." She smiled.

The doppelganger laughed. "Hello, stranger."

"This has got to be the weirdest thing I've ever seen, and that's really saying something," I said.

"It's just like twins," Kris said.

"But they're *not* twins."

"Indeed they're not. They're even closer." It was Radcliff. He had dispelled the warp lock and was standing in the doorway.

"So what was that all then?" Alicia crossed her arms. "What'd you talk to her about?"

"Just trying to introduce some personal hygiene back into her life." He sighed. "I'm not sure if she is in Stage 4 yet. She might be. If she isn't, then that's really not good at all."

"Who cares about her?" Alicia asked. "She's locked away, so it doesn't matter what she is or isn't doing. She's a non-variable. We're all safe."

"There's still Jett. Which is very troubling. Even more so than Erika," Radcliff said.

"What are you talking about? We don't have to worry about him anymore. You said yourself he's probably just developing a split personality," Alicia said.

"Yeah, and we got the thing off Ethan," Kris said.

"True," Radcliff said, "but consider: if he is developing another personality, there is a possibility that that side of him could drive the Rurrians to attack us directly. On the other hand, if what he's saying is true–"

"Impossible," Alicia said.

"Erika did make a good point when she mentioned Yorrlak," Radcliff continued. "If it is true that the Rurrians are able to rebuild at a speed that should be impossible for anyone except a warper, then we have a very serious problem."

"What *is* Yorrlak?" I asked.

"Alright, Alicia, if you could clean up here, I'm going to take Ethan and Kris to the standing stones," Radcliff said.

"I'm not going," Kris said.

"Why not?" Radcliff asked.

"I don't wanna go." He glanced at the floor, then over at me. "But I do want to talk to Ethan alone before you both go."

Radcliff signed. "Very well. You have already seen them. Go outside and talk. Return when you've finished."

"Come on." Kris grabbed my arm and tugged it gently in the direction of the door.

I follow him outside into the cement cube. "What is it?"

Kris shut the door behind us and just looked at me for a moment. "I really like you. You know that, right?"

"Uh..." I started. This wasn't quite what I was expecting.

"You don't have to answer that. You don't have to say anything. Just take this." He held out a cell phone to me. "Call me when you want to... to talk to me."

It was just like the phone he had given me before: it only had a single button on it.

"I don't understand," I said.

"It's like I said before, I'm just gonna have to wait for you. But think about what I said about Peter. You know."

"Kris..." I kept staring at the phone, not looking up at him. "I don't understand what you're trying to say."

"You will." He paused. "I'll just see you later." He disappeared.

I remained standing for a moment or two longer, then pocketed the phone and went back into the house.

"Where's Kris?" Radcliff asked as soon as I closed the door.

"He left."

"Where to?"

"I have no idea."

A brief silence filled the room. I noticed the doppelganger Raine was gone.

"Isn't that just typical of him," Alicia said. "Would you like me to go try and find him?"

"No," Radcliff said. "No, just let him be."

"Where's the other Raine?" I asked.

"She's already gone," Raine answered.

"Oh..." I thought a moment. "You mean like gone *gone*? Not existing anymore?"

"That is the definition we're getting at." Raine nodded.

"That seems so weird."

"I can't imagine why." Alicia stepped forward and took Raine's hand. "Now, we're back off to the Library. Will you be by anytime soon, Radcliff?"

Radcliff was silent a moment, drumming his fingers lightly on the back of an armchair beside him. "If by soon you mean the next couple of days, then I don't think so."

Alicia rolled her eyes. "Fine. Let's go Raine." They both disappeared.

I glanced at Radcliff. "That was, abrupt."

"Yes." His hands were pressed flat together as he tapped his index fingers against his lips. "Unfortunately."

I waited for him to continue, elaborate, or change the subject so we didn't have to keep standing in this silence. I didn't know what to say. Kris's own teleportation floated through my mind.

"Let's go. We're finished here." Radcliff held out his hand but retracted it. "Actually, let me make one of those doorways you found. I'm still getting the swing of them." A small grin crossed his mouth.

"Oh, okay. Sure." I laughed a moment; it was a bit forced. "To the standing stones?"

"Yes." Radcliff closed his eyes, and a doorway appeared just a moment later. He opened it. "After you."

I stepped through and out onto a circular dais floating in space, about thirty meters in diameter. It was all gray, smooth stone, and near the center were six tall stones with writing and pictures carved into them. Behind the stones was an impossibly tall five meter wide metal tower; I craned my neck, but it rose higher and higher into space, disappearing from view. There were four more metal extensions like it, each placed horizontally at even quarters around the edge of the dais, stretching beyond sight, attached lights blinking off into darkness. A number of orbs of light drifted lazily above the dais.

"It's something isn't it?" Radcliff asked.

"Yeah." I was looking straight up again at the metal tower far above. "How...?" My throat hurt to speak; I turned my head down. "How does it do that? Go so far? Shouldn't it break?"

"In normal gravity with normal materials, yes."

"I guess I should've thought of that. But why? How long are these things?"

"Light years. There's also one going down directly beneath the one that goes up. This place was meant to last and to be found. And it accomplished both of those tasks."

"Who found it?"

"Naomi Yorrlak, from several generations ago, before I was born. An interesting character. She had Erika's power." Radcliff walked towards the standing stones.

"So what's so important about these?" I followed him.

"We don't know exactly what they say. They were most likely carved in the Third Era since that is the language used.

Given the images on them though, the agreed interpretation is that they chronicle the events of a warper attempting to gift reality warping to others." He pointed up to the first stone and traced the images through the story.

The carvings were stark and somewhat simple, reminding me of Egyptian hieroglyphs I had seen in text books. First: a man standing upon a planet, the warper symbol marked on his forehead. Second: the man again, this time holding out another warper symbol to a smaller man. Third: both men standing on the planet, both with the warper symbol upon their brows, but the second man was still smaller. Fourth: a whole row of smaller men with warper symbols, all reaching up. Fifth: hands, an organized cluster of hands reaching up towards a dome above them with waves coming from their fingertips. Sixth: all the men were now lying on the ground, the symbol gone from their heads, and instead the symbol was on the heads of half-formed beings rising up from the bodies.

"But can you do that? Give warping to others?" I asked.

"It's never been done before. It seems incredibly unlikely."

"*Seems*? Seems unlikely?"

"Alicia has recently had some thought that she might be able to teach warping to Raine."

"Raine mentioned that the first time I met her."

Radcliff nodded. "Nothing's happened and Raine says she can't even feel the warp energy. Alicia still has high hopes though."

"But she said this was a failure." I pointed at the stones.

"Yes. However, she thinks she has a better chance with Raine since Raine is a Warper Born."

"And these aren't Warper Born in the pictures here?"

"No way to know."

I stood looking at the stones for a minute. "So did this actually happen? Or is it just a story?"

"Again, no way to know. Even with a translation, the information here might just be inaccurate."

"Hmm." I placed my hands on my hips. "Why would someone want to give a bunch of people warping anyways? It seems a bit pointless. I mean, we can already do basically anything. Unless someone wanted to... no, that's also stupid."

"What?"

"Oh, I was gonna say to make an army. But why would you need to do that?"

"Ah, very good. Good question. You're thinking through the logical steps. You tell me though, if you had an army of warpers you created, what would you do with them?"

"I dunno. There's nothing they could do I couldn't do."

"Think, what do armies do?"

I shook my head. "Conquer?"

"Yes. What could you conquer only with an army of warpers?"

I thought a moment. "Nothing. That's stupid. I could already do it myself or just make a regular army."

"Remember, there are limits to what an individual warper can do. We can, however, pool our power and accomplish greater feats. So, what would you need a collective to accomplish?"

"I dunno." I heisted. Something did come to mind, but I didn't want to say it. "I mean…"

"What?"

"You could kill other warpers. Sorry. That's all I could think of."

Radcliff nodded. "Don't worry. That was a different person; it doesn't hurt to talk about it. However I can tell you that you don't need an army of warpers to kill another warper."

"Then what else? I can't think of anything."

"Don't get flustered. That hinders your ability to think. You're not on a time limit. Now tell me, what does reality warping give us power over?"

"Reality, of course."

"Yes. That is what we push against when we use warp energy. In many ways you could say that reality is our only opposition. Only opponent. The only thing we have to affect to create what we want."

"So, an army to kill reality?"

Radcliff laughed. "That's a bit crude, but close." He pointed to the fifth standing stone. "What do you think that dome is? Over the hands?"

I thought a few moments. "A level two warp lock?"

"No. The universe. If you had an army of warpers you could possibly escape the universe."

"Escape the–?" I blinked a few times, trying to imagine it. "Escape to where?"

"Good question. We're trapped on the inside, and it's impossible to see out with our limited view. Maybe to other universes. Maybe to the afterlife. Maybe to something else entirely." Radcliff paused. "That's the funny thing: if someone left the universe and never came back, then it would be the exact same as if they had died, and we would know just as much."

"What would we know?"

"That they simply aren't *here* anymore. They no longer exist with us."

I walked a few paces away from him, away from the stones. I looked out into the vast darkness of space, trying to imagine a crack in it. A fissure through which to flee. Flight with no hope of knowing if it would be to a better place or worse. More dreadful still, non-existence. Not here. Raine's face popped into my mind, but it wasn't truly her.

I shook my head, my eyes shut tight. "That's a lot to imagine."

"Indeed. I try not to think about it too much. It's better to focus on the now. There ain't no elsewhere, or at least, no elsewhere that should concern us while we have things to do here."

I turned back to Radcliff. "What was that reincarnation stuff they were talking about?"

"Oh, that. That's a bit, complicated."

"It just occurred to me. I mean, if you left the universe, you couldn't even be reincarnated. It would be worse than death."

Radcliff chuckled. "I suppose that would be true. But reincarnation isn't a thing to worry about. A warper in the past had the idea, and it happened to be preserved by the Warper Born scholars of the Grand Library. The problem with the idea is that it's lazy. The question it attempts to answer is why the powers are always paired up: yours and Kris's, mine and Alicia's, and Erika's and Jett's. How do the warpers always end up being compatible?"

"So has Kris's and my powers always been a gay relationship?"

"No. They weren't back in my generation. There have been

pervious same-sex relationships though; however, it's not that common. It would require both new warpers to arrive at the same time and some measure of luck. Or it would require one warper to be bisexual or such, which would open up a possibility for a same-sex relationship if the other warper died. With Kris and Tavin, it had been the former: both previous warpers had died at the same time, and it just so happened that both the successors were gay.

"However, the simple solution to the power matching probably lies in the mere volume of people in the universe. Most well populated planets have six to twelve children born every second. Multiply that by the number of planets with Humans in the whole universe, and that's easily hundreds of thousands of births every second. Since the power moves on the moment of death to the very next Human conceived, it would have a huge pool to pick from in that mere fraction of a second. Therefore, the power picks a child who will fit."

"The power picks? Like actually chooses?"

"Maybe." Radcliff shrugged. "Not everyone likes the idea that a random selection *always* works, and not everyone likes the idea that energy could choose, or more specifically *think* in order to choose. But given the two generations of warpers I've lived with, I can't believe anyone is the same person. Like you for example: I cannot believe that you are the same person as Tavin."

"Uh, thanks?"

"You're welcome." Radcliff smiled.

"You know though, when Kris and I first met, he seemed to think I would just instantly jump into a relationship with him. But he said he didn't believe in the reincarnation idea."

"Don't worry. I'm sure it was just hormones and the matching powers that made him think you two would instantly be together."

"Hormones?" I laughed. "But he's 117."

"He is still biologically twenty-four. Makes perfect sense."

"I guess." I took a deep breath and blew it out. "Also, why did Erika say she couldn't bring copies of the stand stones to her?"

"Because they're warp locked."

"You can never make copies of something warp locked?

"Locked objects can still be copied, it's just a more roundabout procedure. You have to be able to see them, to see the details and know the shapes in order to create something new that is the exact same. It can't be done over a distance."

"That makes sense. So, what now?"

"What do you mean?"

"What do we do now? About Jett? Or Erika? Or, anything?"

"Nothing. There's nothing to do."

"Huh? Then why did you bring me here to show me the stones and tell me everything?"

"So you will know, and understand. But just because we've had this run in with Jett and Erika, that doesn't change our policy of non-involvement. They are far more likely to make it out of their Ego Stages alive if we leave them be."

"But you said Jett is a danger if he has a split personality, and the Rurrians are a danger if he doesn't."

"Yes, true. But here's the thing, even though there have been attempts to spread reality warping, there is no evidence that it ever has worked or ever will. Because of that, the likelihood that the Rurrians are truly a danger is immeasurably slim. And if Jett has developed a second personality then that would make him all the more difficult to interact with. We simply must stay away from him."

"But *why*? Can't we do anything?"

"We do not need to. Even if it turns out the Rurrians or Jett are a true threat to us, they will have to come to us to fight us. Come to our places of power. To Cosmos or to Ven, where the Grand Library is. They will have to fight us on our terms with our defenses. It would be an immensely safer fight."

"So just sit and wait? That's your plan?"

Radcliff sighed. "Listen, do you know why I started creating a whole planet from scratch about sixteen years ago?"

"No."

"I did so, because I realized it had come time where I could do nothing else for the warpers around me, for the warpers who had become my third family. I raised them from eighteen and taught them everything I knew. Taught them my mistakes and all I had learned. It was so good back then. Alicia and I were together, we had Raine. Kris and Tavin were together off building cities. Erika and Jett were together too. They were insatiable in their learning, and Jett the most. It's no surprise now that he entered his Ego Stage so quickly.

"But about sixteen years ago everything was on a plateau, heading for a cliff. Jett had left us, Erika had boxed herself away, and I started to see Alicia slipping towards her Ego Stage as well. She's almost there now. Tavin had died; Kris was distant and seemed stunted, never properly entered his Learning Stage after Tavin's death. They had grown up, I suppose you could say. I had given them all the knowledge I could, and now it rested on them to make it through.

"There's nothing more I can do, and more than two-thirds of my life is already spent. Sixteen years ago I knew that all I could do was sit and watch as they entered into their Ego Stages. All around the same time as well. I still don't know how many will make it out. The biggest problem is the direction everyone's Ego stage is taking.

"Jett's is targeted at the Rurrians, and if Alicia's extrapolations hold any water, he is also targeting the Warper Born. And that would be an aim to kill indirect family. Erika, if she is indeed in her Ego Stage, has it directed against herself. She's afraid of herself and will not trust her own actions. It's the purest of self-implosion. And Alicia, my Alicia, her Ego Stage is going to revolve around Raine and the desperate desire to protect her from everything, anything, even things Alicia merely imagines. It's mixing the dangers of the Ego Stage with the fierce protective instincts of a mother, and I fear that combination. There's no telling who she could turn against, or what she could destroy if anything should happen to Raine." He fell silent and turned away.

I licked my lips as my mind ran a ticker tape of blank, white thoughts. "Is it, is it really that bad?"

"I fear so."

"Is that why you wanted Kris to teach me all the things about being a warper? So you could teach him how to teach?"

Radcliff turned back to me, a dry smile on his lips. "Yes. Doesn't seem to have worked completely though."

"Has he always done that?"

"What?"

"Run away from everything?"

"No. Certainly not. He had always been so promising. Both

him and Tavin. But it seems like something broke in him when Tavin died. Something I had hoped... um, had hoped would come back."

"You mean, you had hoped I would bring back?"

Radcliff was silent a moment. "Yes. But it was so long ago I became a warper, I had forgotten what it's like. To suddenly be ripped from your family, friends, and loved ones, because you are instantly so different from them. I should have anticipated you would already be in a relationship."

"What do you think of it?"

"Of what?"

"Of me still dating Peter."

"I won't say."

"Why not?" I crossed my arms.

"Because I know where it will end, but I might deviate you if I say too much."

"Is this where Kris gets his fatalistic-ness from?"

Radcliff shook his head. "Perhaps. But it's not fatalistic. It's just cause and effect, and that is why I don't want to say anything more on the subject. This is something that can't exactly be taught. You have to experience it to know it. If I told you its essence then you would have a changed understanding and would not progress through the events normally."

"But wouldn't that be good?"

"What? Irregular progress?"

"No. Being forewarned. That wouldn't be 'irregular progress,' that would be enhanced progress."

"Not if you don't take the path at all. If you avoid going somewhere you need to, because you know what lies between you and the destination."

I titled my head to the side. "Do you know something I don't?"

Radcliff chuckled and patted my shoulder. "I've been through it all before, but don't worry. In the meantime we shall return as we were as if nothing had happened with Jett. I'm going back to my planet to continue my work on it. What are you going to do?"

"I dunno. I really don't know." I was silent a moment. "I just wish none of this had happened."

Chapter 19
In Deepest Currents Moving

The day after I entertained the idea of making a new house somewhere, doing something to take my mind off Jett. But I didn't. Instead I became increasingly lazy the rest of that week and into the next week as well. I returned home to my Earth and made everyone forget about my enrollment across seas. The new story was the same as Peter's: enjoying the rest of summer before leaving for college. I spent most of my time at his house.

I felt utterly alone.

I saw most of my old friends, including Catharine, but I predominantly spent time with Peter. We didn't talk quite as much as we used to. We mostly just lied around together, on the couch or on his bed, sometimes watching a movie or sometimes just dozing. Today we had had a late lunch and were sprawled out on his bed. Peter was on his stomach, arms crossed beneath his head. I lied atop him at a diagonal, watching the swaying shadows of a tree branch in a square of light on his wall. A playlist of light music was on shuffle on his computer.

Kris's words kept haunting the back of my mind. I wished the music was louder, so it could fill the silence better.

"I love you, Peter."

"I love you too, babe."

The music shuffled to a mellow track from a movie I knew we had seen together last year. I shifted my body around, so I could see him better and started trailing my fingers through his hair. It was so soft. It was always so soft.

"Whatcha thinking about?" Peter asked.

"Space."

240

"Space? What about space?"

"Stars, I guess. Nothing really."

"Hmm." He fell silent again.

I moved my hand down, treading my fingers under the collar of his shirt. "What about you?"

"Wendigo."

"What?"

"Wendigo. Something I was reading about online the other day. It's been popping up a lot in a lot of different things recently. It's a bit odd. It's a dark spirit of cannibalism."

"...Cannibalism? Why were you looking up cannibalism?"

"I wasn't. I stumbled across it and read a few sites about it."

"Oh."

Peter was silent a moment. "It's not always a spirit though. A person becomes it. In some stories a person can become one through indoctrination if..."

I waited. "If what?"

"Oh, never mind. It's not really that interesting."

He pulled away from me, out from under me, and rolled over. My fingers slipped away from the back of his neck, and now we were both on our sides looking at each other.

"Why are you moving?" I asked.

"Just getting more comfortable."

"Okay."

The music switched over again, this time to a song I'd never heard before. A faint smile pulled my lips. I remembered how Peter always had a knack for finding new things we both enjoyed. I expected him to point out the song now and tell me how he stumbled upon it. He didn't. He just reached out and took my left hand, stroking my palm with his thumb.

I tried to think of something to say. "Have you ever seen an asteroid field of water?"

"A what?" He glanced up at me.

"Oh, nothing. Just a stupid thought."

"Tell me anyways."

"There's not really anything to tell."

Peter sighed. "Fine." He lifted my arm and kissed my wrist. "Hey."

"What?"

"What's this? These marks on your arm?" He pointed to the two small, pale circles that had been caused by the manacle.

"Oh. Um…"

"And on your palm. There's a faint circle." He traced it with his finger.

"It's… well, dammit. I *wish* I could tell you."

"Why can't you?"

"You can't understand it." I added very quietly under my breath, "I've tried before."

"What are you talking about?"

"That I could kinda be described as a god, and I can do anything, and ever since it happened nothing's been the same. And every time I explain it well enough that you really understand, you snap."

"Whoa, what?" He laughed, but I could tell it as forced. "Is this a joke?"

"No. Forget it."

He did.

"So, do you want to do anything today besides lying around?" Peter asked. "I mean, I like doing anything with you, you know that, but I would like to do something a bit different tonight."

"Like what?"

"Like go out. To like, rediscover the romance. You know, if that doesn't sound too, uh, generic."

"Generic? No, it doesn't. That sounds nice."

"But 'generic' isn't really what I mean. I mean if it doesn't sound too… like, obvious, or overly official, or like… rehabilitory."

"Huh?"

"I mean, I feel like there's this, like, *rift* between us now. And I've only noticed it this summer, since your birthday really."

"No there isn't." I leaned forward and kissed him, but I remembered Kris.

He kissed me back for a moment or two, then pulled away. "That's not what I mean. Not a physical rift, I mean more like a mental one."

"There's *not* a rift between us." My eyes were closed tight; I don't want to lose him.

"You won't lose me. I love you." He rolled over atop of me and started making out with me. We continued for a while.

It wasn't until he reached down and started undoing my pants that I stopped him. "I thought you wanted to go out tonight."

"Well, yeah, but we don't have to if you don't want to," he said.

"No, no." I might have answered a bit too quickly. "I'd rather go out. Do you have anything in mind?"

"Hmm. Well, tonight is the third Friday of the month, so the Park Walk is going on. The art museum has free admission too. We could go see whatever the new exhibit is that's opening."

"Sure. That'd be great."

"Do you wanna invite Catharine or anyone else to come with us?"

"I don't think so. I think it'd be nice to just go with you."

"We'll do that then." Peter rolled out of bed and clicked off the music.

*   *   *

A few hours later we were strolling through Grace Park downtown, moving with the crowd of people, perusing the many stands and booths. Most were independent artists showcasing their work, all of it tagged for sale. One artist specialized in handcrafted clay turtles, each painted to tell a story: one had two hands entwined with a third arm reaching out between their fingers, and another had a great tsunami arcing across its shell. Another booth was brimming with over-packed shelves of tiny, living bonsais trees; just twenty dollars and you could take your own home today. A booth on the corner with battery powered fans was run by a mother selling hand-braided necklaces with glass beads, her two teenage daughters creating ones right now to demonstrate the process.

We picked up corndogs at a circle of several food venders, and we passed an artist doing portraits, just thirty dollars, discounted for couples.

"You want to get one?" Peter asked as he stopped in front of the booth.

The man behind the easel was currently sketching someone's son.

"Not really." I took another bite from my corndog. I hadn't gotten enough ketchup, so I remedied that problem.

"Why not? It'll be my treat."

"I don't want to have to sit there for an hour."

"It wouldn't even be twenty minutes, I bet. He's not painting a masterpiece."

"I just don't want to."

"Fine. Another time, I guess."

"Yeah, sure."

We continued on, hand-in-hand. The sun was getting low, split in half by a skyscraper downtown.

"What time does the museum close?" I asked.

"Tonight? I think ten."

"Then we should start heading over there."

We passed more stands and even a live magic show. For a few minutes I imagined myself taking on a career as the best magician in the world with my secret weapon: warping. Broadcasted all over TV, preforming three nights a week at some grand hotel in Las Vegas, million dollar contracts and a penthouse above the city. But it was an idle fantasy, worse yet, a hollow fantasy. A fantasy I could create in seconds flat. Did create.

Peter and I were in the living room at a window that stretched the entire wall, overlooking the busiest street of Las Vegas. I was wearing my fancy duds: pinstriped short sleeve jacket with white gloves and a neo top hat purposefully crushed and crinkled. I had just finished a show, dazzled thousands, and now I had returned to my Peter. He stood at the window, silhouetted by the flashing lights below. He reached down, poured two glasses of deep red wine and turned to offer a glass to me. The darkness tricked by eyes and for a moment I couldn't tell if it was Peter or Kris who stood there.

"You're the most beautiful thing in the world," he said.

I closed my eyes. We were back at the Park Walk.

Peter's hand suddenly tugged against mine. "Huh, what is it? Why'd you stop walking?"

My thoughts were now covered over as if by a large cloth. Behold this next trick as they disappear. The cloth fell flat and the musing was gone, only dread filling the empty space. "Nothing. Nothing... Let's go."

Peter watched me for several seconds, trying to find what was behind my eyes. Eventually he stopped as we continued to the museum.

We waited in a short line to be admitted, then strolled through the softly lit galleries. I didn't pay the artwork much attention. Every now and then Peter would comment on something, a painting or a small statuette of a cube with orthogonal etchings covering it, but these slowly dwindled as I failed to respond with much enthusiasm. He kept rubbing his shoulder against mine as if to remind me he was here, to bring me back from the distant place I was in.

We wandered through the new exhibit hall, and we were just about to leave when a painting suddenly caught my attention. I had walked by it, not caring, but then a sudden point of knowing and exclamation sprouted in my mind. I wheeled around and returned. There, on the wall for anyone and everyone to see, was a painting of a cone tree.

It was a landscape painting and the cone tree just happened to be in the forefront, but that didn't change anything. It was still one of the cone trees from before, when I had messed up my planet, from before I had put everything back in order. It was impossible. I *fixed* it. I erased everyone's memory of it. Yet here it was in a painting created a few weeks ago by the hand of some budding artist.

"What, in, the, *fuck*."

Peter doubled back to my side. "What is it?"

"This is impossible!" I grabbed the painting and pulled it off the wall with such force the nail ripped loose and fell to the floor.

"Whoa! What are you doing! Stop!" Peter grabbed my arm. "Are you out of your mind?"

"I... fuck. I don't know. This can't be. This just can't be."

"Hey, buddy, you better put that down right now. Security's already coming," some guy nearby said to me.

"No!" I spun around, pulling my arm from Peter, my back against the wall. "None of you get it. This is impossible!" I waved the painting before me as if they could understand.

A few security guards ran into the room, headed for me, but

as soon as I saw them I erased them. A woman next to where they had been gasped and screamed. I turned my attention back to the painting, looking for anything of help. My mind flitted between possible explanations, but none of them made any sense.

"Hold this." I shoved the painting into Peter's arms, and he looked like he had just been given a live grenade.

The plaque on the wall credited a certain Eli Bevan. I summoned him to this room.

"What is this? How did you paint this!" I demanded, pointing at the painting in Peter's hands.

"Holy–! How'd I–?" His eyes went wide. He whipped his head this way and that, trying to figure out where he was, his short rattail flipping back and forth as he did.

I glossed his mind over the details. "How did you paint this!"

"Dude, I just used a brush." He raised his hands chest level. "Nothing special. Just my talent and a brush."

"That's not what I mean! I mean, why this tree? How did you know to paint this tree?"

"I didn't. What is it? I just started painting and I just let it flow. I just let it flow."

I grabbed his shirt and started shaking him. "No! That's impossible!"

"Ethan! Please! You're really scaring me." Peter dropped the painting and grabbed me from behind, trapping me in a bear hug. He pulled me back, and we both stumbled to the floor. "Please. This isn't right." He was breathing heavy now, quickly, each exhale of breath brushing over my neck.

"You have no idea! This isn't right at all." I squirmed in his arms, trying to break free, but I couldn't get the proper leverage against him.

Bevan scrambled from the room. Most of the other visitors had already fled, but a few lingered in the corner of the room or looked on from afar down the hallway. At least two of them were on their cell phones, speaking quickly.

"Come on, we have to get *out of here*," Peter said. "We're gonna be in so much shit if we're still here when the cops get here."

"Don't worry about them. Only this painting's important

246

right now." I finally pulled free of his arms and crawled away from him, towards the painting.

He tried to grab my leg, but his fingers slipped on the fabric of my pants.

I got up on my knees, holding the painting up to the light again. What if... my mind jumped to Kris. What if he had done this to mess with me? To jar me out of my old life. Or just as some kind of joke. I summoned the phone he had given me and hit the "K" button. It rang twice.

"Ethan, hey."

"Kris, get over here right now! Did you do this?"

"Do this? What are you–?"

"Just get over here right now! I'm at this museum on my planet, near–"

"If you've got the phone," his voice grew louder, "I can find you."

I realized he was in the room now and spun around on the floor.

"Hey." He flipped the phone shut and let it disappear.

"This!" I held the painting up to him. "Did you do this?"

"Where the hell did he come from?" Peter stood up from the floor.

"Oh, hello, chico," Kris said. "Nice to see you clothed this time."

"Wha-*what*?" Peter asked.

"Don't play coy with me, I remember you. All boxers in the hallway that morning." Kris grinned.

"No, Kris, he doesn't remember. That's the point, *no one* should remember." I pushed myself up from the floor as well.

"Aww, what? But that was *priceless*. How could you make him forget that?"

"Because that was back when my planet was broken. I fixed it, and I made everyone forget. But this guy painted it! He painted one of those trees!" I pointed to it. "How did he even *do* that?"

Kris really looked at the painting now. "Oh, I remember those. That is weird."

"That's it? That's it! 'That's weird?' This shouldn't exist!"

"Yet it does. Hmm." Kris shrugged. "Actually, I think I remember Alicia talking about this. Something about residual memories or subconscious direction. Something along those lines."

"Okay, hang on. What the hell is going on?" Peter stepped in front of me and touched my arm. "Ethan?"

"Peter, I've tried to get you to–" It hit me. Just then. In that very moment as I stared at Peter with Kris in my vision just to the left. My lungs froze and my stomach heaved. I dropped the painting to my side and covered my mouth, falling back to my knees.

"Oh my god! Ethan!" Peter leaned down to me.

I couldn't hold it in. I heaved, corndog and soda goop splattering on the marble floor.

"God!" Peter jumped back.

"Holy shit, are you going to be okay?" Kris asked.

My whole body was shaking, and I gasped for air as I crawled back a meter or so away from the mess on the floor. I pointed up at both of them with an unsteady hand. "You're the fucking *same*."

"What?" Peter asked.

"Oh. Geez, what timing to realize." The corners of Kris's mouth pulled down in a look of discomfort.

I got up on wobbling feet and started punching Kris's arm. "When did you do this? When did you do this!

"Ethan, stop! I *never* did this." He raised his arms and backed away.

"You had to 've done this! Peter was never you before!" I could still taste bile in my mouth.

"I'm not anyone else," Peter said, but neither Kris nor I was paying attention to him.

"Listen, I never saw him or even your planet before that first time you changed it!" Kris said. "I never changed him, and I didn't make him."

"No. *No*." I hit my fists on his chest and tears were falling from my eyes. "I *didn't*. I couldn't've. No!"

Kris just squeezed his arms around me tight. "It's okay."

"No. No." It was all I could say.

"Come on. Let's get you home," Kris said.

"You– you're not taking him anywhere..." Peter said, but he had lost all the certainty in his voice.

"I'm sorry," Kris said.

"Who are you?" Peter asked.

Kris just shook his head and snapped his fingers. Peter began sleeping on his feet.

The museum was empty now, red and blue lights flashing far off down the hallway against a wall. Kris changed Peter's memories and teleported him home, sent the cops away, and restored the museum. Patrons were milling around the room again like nothing had happened, ignoring us.

He teleported us both to my house above the ocean and kissed my forehead. "It's going to be okay."

I pushed him away and wrapped my arms around my torso, looking at the floor. "I've been lying to myself this whole time."

"You haven't. You didn't know."

"And you did?"

"Only later for sure, when I watched him."

"Why? Why didn't you tell me?"

"Would you have believed me?"

I didn't speak. We both already knew the answer.

Chapter 20
Blowing Off the Dust

The next morning I awoke on my couch. I didn't remember
falling asleep. My head was on a pillow propped up by one of
the armrests, and Kris was asleep across from me: his head on
the other armrest and his legs on top of mine. I got up slowly,
trying to disturbing Kris as little as possible, but he opened one
eye and murmured something.

"Don't get up," I said softly. "I needed some time alone to
think. I'll be back later."

"Mm... I'll be here. If you need me."

"Okay."

I went to the far side of the Moon and sat, watching the
stars that were far brighter than anywhere on Earth. I couldn't
believe it. From a detached point of thought I knew what Peter
was, but as soon as I tried to merge that understand with an
understanding of the implications, my mind stopped. The two
ideas seemed to destroy each other on impact, like matter to
anti-matter.

My head hurt and I felt so afraid. If I could dis-notice Peter,
someone who had been so central to my life, what else have I
still not seen? I held my hands up and consolidated an orb of
warp energy between them.

"Why can you do everything besides what I really want?" I
muttered and shot the orb in front of me. It dashed against the
ground, the impact spitting up dust and bits of rock.

I rubbed my shoulders. I needed someone to talk to about
this. Kris had said that Alicia knew something about the
residual memories, maybe she knew something about this as
well. I created a copy of the manual and looked up the Grand
Library. I found the coordinates to Ven, one of the Warper Born

250

planets, and created a doorway. I stopped in awe as I beheld the Library for the first time.

"Huge" was a mild way of describing the thing. It sat on a wide gleaming archway nestled between two mountain peaks. It was built like a stepped pyramid with dozens of floors, each one slightly smaller than the floor beneath it. Many towers and spinnerets extended from the roofs of the floors, all clustered in groups of matching design themes, leading me to believe most had been additions by many others. The expanders did a good job as none of it looked too jarringly out of sync. The entrance was two great white doors that could have easily allowed four elephants to pass through side-by-side if they were open. Set within them were six smaller doors that could easily be opened by a single person.

Inside the ceiling was nearly six meters from the ground with a grid of columns supporting the roof. Most of this floor was partitioned off into personal studies and offices by bookcases, desks, and standing stretches of cloth. At least half of these sections were occupied, either by single people reading or writing, a pair working, or one person speaking to a small group of others. A young woman walked up to me.

"Good afternoon, can I assist you?" she asked.

"Uh, I'm just looking for someone."

"And who would that be? One of the scholars?"

"No, I'm looking for Alicia. Do you, know...?"

She looked me up and down, her eyebrows rising slightly. "Oh, are you finally the sixth one?"

"The sixth warper?"

She nodded.

"Yeah, I am."

"Hmm." She rubbed her cheek. "You're not quite what I expected. Just go up to the second floor, her house is there. You can't miss it."

"House?"

"Yes, she lives here." She smiled.

"I know. I just wasn't expecting a house in a library."

She laughed. "I've heard tales about new warpers, but you really shuffle those back into the deck. It's pretty easy to find, but I could show you, if you'd like. I've got a few minutes."

"Sure."

She smiled and led me down a pathway between all the furniture. "The ground floor here is more of a work space, and all the books are on the second floor and above. I'm Lena, by the way. Apprentice scholar."

"Scholar?"

"Yes. It's a very important job, well, more important if you become an adviser. That's what I'm trying to be. Every representative needs a personal scholar. Someone who can give extensive advice about all the decisions they'll make. It's a whole tiered system of reps, so they all want to have the most extensive knowledge to look good.

"Right now I'm working with a group of two other apprentices on a presentation about... well, I can't– I mean it's politics stuff. We have nine applicants and there's only one position for my city's representative, so they're thinning us out." She paused. "You know it's really cool that I'm getting to talk to you just like regular." She paused again, then poked my arm. "So... what's your name?"

"Huh?"

"Really? Were you not listening to me?"

"I... Sorry. I'm just, distracted right now."

"What about?"

I hesitated; I didn't want to go into the details with her. For a moment I planned to warp her to forget we were having a conversation, but then I remembered the Warper Born were locked. I felt guilty afterwards. "It's complicated."

We reached a massive spiraling staircase that was wide enough for a car. It was connected to the floor only by the first step and to the ceiling only by the last step, and I wondered for a moment why it wasn't automated.

Lena rubbed her cheek again. "I am sorry to hear that. We're here now though, just go straight up these stairs. I actually can't go up without my mentor, so I have to leave you here."

"Why not?"

"Apprentice." She shrugged with one shoulder. "You could kind of consider this the closest thing we have to a 'temple' on the planet."

"Oh." I looked up again. "And it's okay that Alicia and Raine just live here?"

"She's a warper. She can."

"Huh." I looked back at her. "Well, thanks for your help."

"My pleasure." She hesitated a moment, then turned away.

The guilt was still lingering. "Wait a sec."

"Yes?" Lena looked back at me over her shoulder.

"Can I do anything for you? You know, since I'm a warper." I opened my hands out.

Her eyes went wide as she turned around. "Really? Well, there, there is a certain tradition. A pendant of the warper symbol made out of pure gold that can't be bent. I'd really appreciate that."

"I can do that." I created it in my hand attached to a thin gold chain and handed it to her.

Rene's smile would not fade as she held the necklace up for a moment, then placed it around her neck. She didn't remove her hand from the pendant. "Thank you *so* much."

"It's was nothing. You know, warping."

She took a step back. "Well, I've really got to go now. Sorry to run off. Thank you so, so much again. Have a good visit with Alicia."

"Yeah, see ya."

She waved and walked away. I watched her for a few moments, then went up the stairs.

The second floor was much more like the Library I had expected, with bookshelves stretching dozens of meters up to the ceiling, balconies and ladders crisscrossing the front of each one. A short distance from the stairs was a two-story house. It was painted the same colors as the bright brown bookcases and the white floors, but the architectural design was completely different and made a jarring spectacle.

I knocked on the door and Raine answered.

"Hey, Ethan! I didn't think I'd be seeing you here for a while yet."

"Huh? What do you mean?"

She shrugged. "Oh, I dunno. I just thought it'd be a few years at least before you got around to visiting here. Come in."

I followed her inside.

"Hey, Mom," Raine called down the hallway. "Ethan's here."

The living room was a bit posh with exquisitely designed furniture and a few accompanying paintings. However, it was difficult to get the original feeling of the place since every flat surface had at least three books on it. There were stacks of books lining the walls, a mountain on the coffee table, and one propped open on an armchair. The couch was mostly free and there was enough room to move around, so the books created a close and comfortable atmosphere rather than a cluttered one.

"Good morning, Ethan." Alicia came around the corner of the hallway. "What brings you here today?"

"I need to talk to you."

"Oh? Your tone sounds serious."

I shrugged and nodded half-heartedly.

"Why don't we go outside? It's a bit of a mess in here." She walked towards the door.

"It's not that bad. I've seen a lot messier."

"Raine, will you be alright while we're out?"

"I must be the student, so I was actually getting ready to practice my meditating before Ethan arrived." Raine rolled a small purple ball between her hands.

"Meditating?" I asked.

"For warping. Eventually. If I get it."

"But you said you couldn't feel the warp energy."

She shrugged. "I don't really know. I just need to keep trying."

"She'll get it soon enough." Alicia opened the door. "If I'm not back once you're finished just come find us. We won't leave this floor."

Raine nodded. "See you later, Ethan." She waved and walked off down the hallway.

I raised a hand back and left the house. Alicia closed the door behind me.

"So what's wrong? It is about Kris again?" she asked.

"No. I mean, it kinda involves him, but it's not about him. It's about Peter."

Alicia started walking, and I followed her. "He's that non-warper, right? Your boyfriend from before you were realized?"

I nodded.

"What about him?"

I looked away from her, up at the towering bookcases. I didn't know where to start. My thoughts were still jumbled. I saw someone who I assumed was a Warper Born ascending a ladder. "I *made* him. I made him like a copy of Kris, even before I met him. How the fuck is that possible?"

"Truly? How bizarre!"

I glanced at her. "You didn't know?"

"Why in the universe would I have known?"

"Kris knew, but I guess he knew what he was looking for when he figured it out. And I think Radcliff knew. In hindsight I think he was hinting at it."

"Ethan." She placed a hand on my shoulder. "I'm terribly sorry to burst your bubble, but I don't have time to be studying your life."

"That's not what I meant. I'm glad you haven't though."

She nodded. "So what is the problem then?"

"Didn't you just hear what I said? I made Peter. Peter was never, never... *authentic*. It's like if you were on a boat tied to a dock, but it turned out the dock was floating too! There's nothing solid there anymore. Don't you understand?"

"Ethan, you're spouting all sorts of nonsense. Of course nothing is solid: nothing is real besides us. We are our own solidarity."

"That's not enough for me."

"Are you truly so voracious?" She stopped walking and crossed her arms. "That's unreasonable."

"Are you kidding me? Back before I became a warper these were always the questions: why are we here, is there anything else, what's the point of it all? And now that I'm here, going all over the universe, the questions are *still* unanswered."

"You were always a warper. You just didn't know it."

"Whatever, 'realized I'm a warper' then. But how is it that we still don't know?"

"Listen, we warpers are the pinnacle. If we don't know something then it is unknowable, and that should not concern us. There is nothing that should concern us."

"How are you okay with that? That's not even an answer. And things *do* concern us. Just look at the Dark Agencies!"

She frowned. "A minor annoyance. Now if this conversation is just going to consist of you shouting at me, then I have better things to do."

I closed my eyes a moment and took a deep breath. "I'm sorry, I just... I just thought you would have some answers."

"But I do have answers. Everything that is knowable is right here, and I've spent the last thirteen years in this Library absorbing every book it has. Do you know how many books that is? Over three *trillion*. This place has copies of every important non-fiction book from every recorded civilized planet out there. Everything is here. I *do* have answers."

"Wait. Wait. Sorry. Three trillion? In thirteen years? ...But, h-how?"

"Don't you know what my power is?"

"Oh." I remembered. "Time warping."

"Yes, and since you are so desperate for answers, let me give you a demonstration of one of the unique divergences in timespace I can create." Alicia waved her arm out in front of her. "I've just put us in a time loop. Look around us. Do you see the people milling about? That man sitting on a couch reading? Those three students chatting by the pillar? That woman slowly browsing the shelf above us? They will never stop doing what they are doing as long as the time loop is active. And because I am on the inside of the loop, we will return without a single second having passed once the loop is closed. Everything inside the loop simply progress without progression."

"We're outside of normal time right now?" I looked around, but nothing really looked any different.

"We are between two seconds. This is space without time. Upon leaving the time loop everything will resume. This is how I've absorbed three trillion books in thirteen years: it was about 47 years from my perspective." A devious grin slipped across her face.

"Then you're..."

"151."

"You're out of sync."

"Oh that's only a relative term. So what if I'm a bit older now compared to others? To me, my life is still just the same, and that's the important part."

"But it's like you're abandoning everyone."

"It is not."

I watched the talking students. Every half minute or so they would make a gesture similar to one they had made before, but not repeat it exactly.

"This is how you saved Kris that time with the Dark

Agencies, right?" I could remember him unmoving, Nókrutar swirling around him.

Alicia nodded. "Nothing can enter or leave a time loop besides myself, so it makes for very safe containment. Though it does depend on my location. If I am outside the loop, the inside is frozen. If I am inside the loop, the outside if frozen. Imagine a car driving down a road—the car is the physical world and the road is time—my time loop lifts the car from the road. The engine is still burning and the wheels are still turning, but it does not move. And no one 'lifted' this way can ever notice a difference."

"I'm so glad you're the only one who can mess with time."

"It would be complicated otherwise, wouldn't it? Not everyone would be as responsible as me." She smiled. "Now what was all this for again?"

The woman browsing the shelf slid her finger over the same three books yet again.

"Explaining why you have all the answers."

"Right! I'm glad you can see that now." Alicia paused a moment and dispelled the time loop. Continuation returned and the woman browsing the book shelves was finally able to move to the next one. "Is there anything else you want to ask?"

At this point I doubted she would have an answer, but I asked anyways. "How can people remember things that have been erased from their memory?"

"Just put it back in their memory."

"No, that's not what I mean." I turned to her. "You remember how my planet was all messed up? You didn't get to see them, but there were these trees with trunks shaped like cones and really long leaf-branch things. When I fixed my planet I erased everyone's memory of what had happened, but just yesterday I was in an art gallery on my planet and someone had painted a landscape that had one of those cone trees in it. How can that be possible at all?"

"Hmm. You're certain you were completely thorough in erasing all the memories and removing all the trees?"

"Yes."

"Then this is not completely unheard of. Radcliff's original generation knew something of it, but that was only from one book in the Archives from the generation before him and from what the Warper Born here remembered. There do at times seem to be traces left over, no matter how effective one is at making a change. It's just one of those things."

"But... how? How can they remember something erased?"

"Warp energy is just weird like that." Alicia spread her arms out wide. "That's the best answer I can give you."

I sighed even though I had been prepared to be disappointed this time.

"Don't worry, Ethan." She touched my shoulder. "Are you hungry? I can make some breakfast."

"Not really."

"Here. I'm going to make a quick snack, and this will demonstrate how I reality warp using the other timespace divergence I can create."

Without even waiting for a response Alicia took my hand. For a single second my vision was pressed flat and narrowed to a single vertical line as all the world around me was squeezed. The next moment I could hardly breathe. We were still standing in the Grand Library—or at least a place that looked like the Grand Library—but everything around us was blurred and darkened, like looking through tinted and lightly frosted glass, and oh so dry. The contrast of light was way down, and physical things seemed to lose their distinctness. I doubled over, gasping.

"It's not that bad." Alicia took a deep breath. "You'll get used to it." She sounded far away.

Another breath, right in my ear, sucking in the heavy air. I realized it was my breath. My lungs were desperately fighting to draw in and push out air, vicious against the constrictive atmosphere.

Alicia's voice came again, distant. "This is the slipstream. Time without space. A deeper place. Just under the fabric of. The universe." Her lungs were fighting too, but they were clearly more familiar with the battle. "Whenever warp energy. Is used. Some of it trickles down. Down here. Becomes dusk energy. I change it back. Revitalize it. Use it to. Shape these formless. Things. Into what I want. Then. Then when I return to. Normal space. The changes stick. Become permanent."

She walked a few paces from me, her footsteps imprinting in the half-real floor. She swept her arms up like a conductor of an orchestra and traced out the form of a table, a dark image of her design slashed against reality. She created chairs, a pitcher, two cups, and a plate of food.

I sank to my knees. It was too much, too oppressive. This slipstream was hostile as if the dark forms around me of people and bookcases and pillars wanted to crush me, to squeeze out the warp energy I had. To convert me down into its own lower energy but simply couldn't.

"Ali-Ali-Alicia." I choked out the word, past my parched mouth and what felt like shadows in my throat. I felt as if a great axe or weight was hanging over me, ready to fall. "H-help. *Help.*" I pressed my hands to the floor, trying to keep myself from falling completely. My skin tingled from the contact and the floor shifted color around my hands, brightening into a white outline of them.

"Why can't you. Stand it?" Alicia placed a hand on my shoulder and the slipstream was over. I could breathe again.

With great gasps I filled my lungs with true air again, air that had never felt nor tasted so sweet. I looked up at Alicia, but she had already turned away, striding over to a newly created table laden with food.

"We weren't even in for a minute. Come sit down and have a drink of water. You'll be fine."

"N-no." I pushed myself up to my feet. My balance wavered a moment, but I was able to steady myself.

"Yes, you will be fine. The queasiness will wear off momentarily."

"That's not what I mean."

"What's the matter then?"

"I, I need to go. Bye, just... bye." I created a doorway next to me. I grasped the handle and leaned my whole weight onto it, tumbling through the passage and almost falling down onto the grounds outside the Grand Library. I snapped a bar into existence hanging in the air just in front of me which I grabbed before more than my knees could hit the ground.

I kicked the door shut. It disappeared and I formed another, connecting to the first place that came to mind. I got up, stumbled through, and arrived in the Restaurant. It was empty aside from Bot behind the counter.

"She's insane. Absolutely insane."

Bot remained motionless as I flopped down on a stool by the counter. I created a glass of water and drank the whole thing, then created another and drank it too.

Bot didn't even look over at me.

Suddenly I wondered if Bot was even "on" at the moment. "Are you–?"

"I do not sleep. Alicia. Slipstream. Ego Stage. Go away."

I blinked several times. "...what?"

"Currently running probability algorithms. Do not wish to dedicate any processes to you."

"What probability algorithms? And how did you know where I just came from?"

"I did not. Deductions. Library grounds through door. Physical conditions match slipstream effects. 'Insane' most likely referencing Alicia which would reference Ego Stage, which she is growing close to. Are you happy? Please leave."

"You know she's been using the time loop on herself? How in the world could you possibly–"

Bot's head snapped to me, looking me straight in the eyes. I jump in my chair. "I did not. She has?"

"Uh, yeah."

"How long?"

I did the sum quickly: thirteen years from forty-seven. "Thirty-four years. She's 151 now."

"Is that accurate?"

"Yes. I'm good at remembering things."

"Hmm." Bot was silent several seconds. "It usually bodes poorly when a warper of her power starts time looping themself. Can be specifically self-destructive."

"So should we do something?"

"Take action?"

"Well yeah. Like, intervene or something."

" 'Intervene?' A rare word in warper vocabulary, interestingly enough. Everyone, especially Radcliff, would recommend against it."

"So?"

"*So,* meaning you will not find aid in such an endeavor."

"But why not?"

"Because it is dangerous. Because it is not easy. Because warpers are selfish."

"Well *I'm* not selfish."

"Quite something to claim."

"I'm not."

"You would not say it is selfish to try to dictate another's existence?"

"But you just said it was dangerous to her!"

"I said it *could be* dangerous to her. But that was not what I was referring to. I was referring to being selfish by warping anyone in general."

I gritted my teeth. "Not if it's on accident."

" 'Accident?' What an excuse."

"It's not an excuse. It's already happened. I just found out yesterday that Peter is a similar copy to Kris. I never would have done that on purpose, never would have consciously lied to myself."

"No? Are you so certain? Human desires run far deeper than most ever realize. A veil can be the most comforting thing in the world."

"No. *No.* It's stupid. They don't even work. You can't even completely erase things from other peoples' minds."

"Example?"

"Literally just yesterday I found a painting on my planet that had a cone tree in it that doesn't exist anymore. I wiped them from my planet and from everyone's memory, but there it was. The artist somehow remembered it or reimagined it, or something."

"You sought to dismember, but it was remembered?"

"That's not what dismember means."

"Indeed. But it is one of the facets of the English language that fascinates me."

"Whatever." I wiped my hands down my face.

"So tell me: What are you going to do now?"

"About what?"

"Any of the things you have been complaining about."

"I dunno. I feel like I don't know anything anymore. But since you made a big deal of it I think I will tell Radcliff that Alicia's been using the time loop on herself. Then I'll see if he really won't want to help."

"He will not."

"Why are you so sure?"

"Because I know him. I know the ways in which you both differ. I know what decisions he has made over the last 416 years."

"I dunno." I paused. "But hey, you're talking to me. That's a small victory. What happened to those algorithms?"

"I decided to put them on hold."

"What were they?"

"Nothing really. Just idle amusements."

"And now I'm more amusing?"

For a moment Bot's eyes grew brighter, and I got an uncanny feeling that the gesture was a substitute for smiling. "In a manner of speaking." Then Bot looked away from me, up towards the ceiling. "Did you want any food while you are here?"

I shrugged. "I can't eat right now. This was just the first place I thought of coming to."

"Interesting."

"Is it?"

"I find most things interesting. At least for the first few seconds. Though due to my advanced processors, a few seconds to you are like minutes to me."

"And you're just so proud of that, aren't you? You know, I bet I could make a scientist who could put processors into my brain, then I'd be just as fast as you."

"Would you truly do such a thing though? Remove yourself even further from reality around you? Transcend not only Humans, but warpers as well?"

"I dunno. Probably not. I just wanted to point it out. I *could* be a smartass like you."

"Indeed." Bot's head titled to the side and Bot fell silent.

"I just really, really don't like any of this. Like, I remember I was excited before, back when this started. Kris took me to Io and everything was so amazing for a minute there." I paused. "But everything has just been going downhill since. I even ran into Jett and almost got killed by him."

"Yes. Life would be nothing if not for its trials."

"Thanks, fortune cookie."

"You are welcome, but do not ever call me that again."

I half chuckled. "Fine, fine."

"So, what will you do? What action will you take?"

"I don't know. It seems like everyone has some sort of problem or other, and I just don't know what to do."

"Why do you feel a need to do anything?"

"Hang on, you just asked me what I would do."

"Yes, and non-action is an action, one that has become somewhat standardize. However, you will never be on purpose if you fall into the pattern others have placed for you. If you wish to act, you must choose the action yourself. Doing what you have not chosen carries no value."

"You're talking about two different things now, aren't you?"

Bot chuckled. "Perhaps. Now, if you want anything to eat, go ahead and do so. In the meantime, I am finished talking, though I have no doubt you will return yet again at some point in the future."

"You say that like you don't want me to come back."

"I would recommend always taking my words at face value."

"Why?"

"It will make your life much easier."

Chapter 21
Join Me

Several days later I was hovering over the shattered remains of a planet once known as Sorik. It was the first Rurrian controlled plant to fall to Jett's bombardments. Nothing remained on the surface. Cities were blackened craters of flatsmashed buildings and melted metal that had fused with the ground. Dirt and sand were petrified into cracked clay and glass fields: a heat set terracotta husk. Even the atmosphere had been blown away, and now the ruins would remain forevermore.

It was horrifying. To wipe clean a planet in such a devastating way, just because its people knew they weren't permanent. How could Jett do this? How could he live with creating so much pain?

I clenched my fists. The emptiness of this world made me want to run. To run and run and clamber over mountains, over the sides of buildings. To dig my hands into good earth and feel waves crashing over my feet; just keep going and hitting my soles against grass until my legs burned and my lungs heaved and I knew I was alive.

I dropped, teleporting as I did, and landed in the middle of my house above the ocean. I hurried to my room and snapped up the cell phone Kris had given me. I didn't have a clear idea of what I was going to say, but that didn't stop me as I pressed the plastic against my ear.

It rang thrice and Kris picked up. "Ethan."

"Kris, I... what are you doing right now?"

"Nothing really. What's up?"

"I want to do something. I don't know what to do, but I need to do something."

"Like what?"

"I said I don't know."

"How about Prabble? We haven't gone yet."

I was silent a moment, not sure how to return the conversation.

"Since you're not with Peter anymore. I mean, you aren't with him anymore, right? Since you realized what he is?"

"Kris, that's not what I'm talking about. Have you seen the planets Jett has destroyed?"

"Whoa. Hang on." He appeared beside me. "Why in the universe would you go back there?"

I closed the cell phone. "I haven't been there before."

"I mean go back to where Jett was. What if he had caught you again? You can't go there."

"I was in a different system than the Rurrian's home system. I wasn't gonna get caught." I walked into the kitchen.

"But haven't you learned already?" He followed me. "You almost got *killed*. Why would you go back?"

"I had too."

"No you didn't." He crossed his arms.

"Kris, this isn't even why I called you."

"Then why'd you call me?"

"Because I need... I need something else to think about." I tried to set the phone on the counter, but I wasn't looking and almost dropped it on the floor as I set it on the edge of the marble.

Kris tilted his head to the side. "What?"

"You didn't see them. And you don't know what it's like for there to be *nothing* left. To be so adrift."

He came closer to me and started scratching my back lightly. "I think I might have an idea of it."

We were both silent for a minute or two.

"Let's go somewhere," Kris said. "Somewhere we don't have to worry about things."

"Like where?"

"I did mention Prabble. We should go there."

"And what's Prabble?"

"I'll show you, then you can make up your mind." Kris teleported us. Rushing colors and darkness and we were in space.

The structure floating before us was undoubtedly Prabble. It was a conglomerate of spheres, some large and some small, all of varying colors. Some were domed in glass, and many of the spheres that were not directly touching were connected by enclosed walkways. All of the spheres were arranged in such a way that they made rough suggestions of individual levels within the entire mass. There was no overarching shape to the collection, but the widest levels were about a fourth of the way up from the bottom, and each level above and below those were smaller or branched off erratically.

"What is it?" I asked.

"It's the epicenter of celebrations, the heart of camaraderie, the fount of indulgence. It's every party you've ever wished you could go to but never have. The kind of parties you only hear about but never see. The name is literally 'party' and 'bubble' meshed together, and it's one of the best places in the universe if you want to escape."

I looked on, watching flashing lights through a few of the glass domes. "Is this where you went to all of those parties you talked about before? The one's when everyone was in their partying stage?"

"Yeah, but not all the time." Kris closed his eyes and shook his head. "Those times." He refocused on me. "You wanna go?"

"And what? Just, party?"

"Kinda. You drink and you dance and then you stumble on the party when you're not looking."

"I dunno. It seems kinda," I shrugged, "kinda weird."

"Okay, that wasn't the best way of describing it, but you'll see. Come on, just try it."

"I will, but first I need something from you."

"What?"

"I need you to not disappear."

"Not—? I don't disappear."

"Uh, *yeah*, you do sometimes. If anything is going to have a chance for working with us, I just need you to promise not to run away. If you need time alone or anything like that, that's fine. That's fine. I just need you to not disappear as an answer."

Kris bit his lip and was silent a moment. "Okay." He took my hands in his. "I'll try. I mean, you know, I will. I promise."

"Thank you. Now we can go."

He kissed my right hand, and we flew towards Prabble together. We landed on a balcony that stuck out from one of the widest levels. Kris pushed open the double glass door and held it open as I entered. Inside was a rather plain room with a valet behind a counter and several couches along the opposite walls. A deep thrumming of music was alive through every space in the room, flowing through the floors and up the walls, a conglomerate of beats at ever varying paces. It was waves in the air, in my gut, in my ears. The place was music. It was a shock to the system that made me feel more awake than I had before.

"Any coats or baggage you wish to check in?" the valet asked us. His voice seemed distant, like an afterthought; I was still lost in the initial shock of the place.

"Nope, none you can carry," Kris said. "Thanks."

"Very good."

Kris pulled me further into the raw pulse flowing around us. Down a short hallway, around a corner, and we came out into a huge room, the ceiling vaulting away from us. It was high enough for two balconies to ring the room above us with curving stairs to access them. The music was not coming from this room but from everywhere around the room. This bubble merely had chairs, tables, a bar, and numerous openings to more hallways.

"Where do you wanna go?" Kris asked me.

"I dunno. What do they even have here?"

"Everything. Any kind of party you can imagine, there's a bubble for it. Warpers have been adding them forever, so believe me, *everything* is here. Techno, Z-G, disco, alt rock, counter-rock, metal rock, light rock, Indie rock, paint, foam, water, fire, shadow dance, sex, classical... *anything.*"

"Shit."

Kris nodded. "I know, right? Any preferences?"

"I really dunno."

"Alright. Let's get drinks first, then I'll show you a rave bubble. That's my favorite."

"Drinks?"

"Yeah. You've drunk at parties before, right?"

"Not really. Don't you remember, we've already talked about this."

"We have? Oh, right, I kinda remember. That one night. We'll start you out light."

At the bar Kris slapped his free hand down and spoke loudly, "I'd like an Anita Rose for myself and an Upstate Cabdriver for this one."

The bartender eyed Kris up and down, raising a single brow. "An Anita Rose, ye' said?" He glanced over at me.

"Yeah, for the irony," Kris said.

The bartender just shrugged and produced two glasses from under the counter. With practiced speed and precise movements, he prepared both drinks in thirty seconds flat: ice, pour, pour, shake, pour out, *clink*, repeat.

Kris handed the second drink to me. "This is really good, the Upstate Cabdriver. It's a variant on the Jamaican Cabdriver, 'cause it's only got coconut rum and cranberry juice, but the best part is that it literally tastes just like Jolly Ranchers."

"What are Jolly Ranchers?"

"What? You didn't have Jolly Ranchers on your Earth?"

"No. What are they?"

"Delicious, that's what. They're a hard, fruity candy. I'll show you them later, just have your drink now." He took a long gulp from his own glass.

I slowly sipped my drink, expecting the burn of alcohol I'd tasted on a few occasions before, but to my surprise it never came. The drink was very sweet, and I could only assume this was in fact what Jolly Ranchers tasted like. "This is really good."

"Yeah. Dangerously good."

"What do you mean?"

"Any drink where you can't taste the alcohol can be dangerously good, because you don't realize how much you've drunk 'til after the affects start setting in."

"Oh. I don't think I'll have to worry about that. So what'd you get?"

"Mine's vodka, gin, some grenadine syrup, and a splash of cranberry juice. Wanna try it?" He offered his glass to me.

"Alright." I took a sip. It was way stronger than the drink I had, and I winced as I swallowed.

Kris laughed. "We'll work you up to the stronger stuff."

"Sure. Great."

"Come on then, we've got a rave to get to." He led me down one of the hallways.

It went to another bar bubble, but we passed through it, turning down a hall. Our path continued on like this for several minutes, twisting through and past a plethora of bubbles. Past dance floors and flashing lights, the music rising and falling around us as we traveled through the sea of sources. We were on a gradual ascension the whole time.

We passed a short hallway that led into a moderately sized bubble that was silent and empty aside from a single dancer. She had long black hair and was wearing a black dress, twirling round and round, each spin accompanied by a footfall, moving like a ballerina.

I stopped. "What's that one?"

"That's the Hall of Ghosts. Don't go in there. Some old warper's sick idea of a joke or something."

"Why? What is it?"

"Basically, if you go in, you'll instantly be filleted and all of the tendons ripped from your body."

"You... you're kidding, right?"

"No. I wish. I've seen it. Not pretty."

"Why is that even here then?"

" 'Cause it's warp locked, just like most of the other bubbles here, so there's not much we can do about it. But so long as you know to stay away, you're fine."

"And if you didn't know?"

"Well... then it'd suck to be you." Kris tugged on my hand. "Come on, we're nearly there."

When we had first arrived in Prabble, most everyone I saw was dressed in what I would consider more "normal-casual" attire: graphic tees, jeans, short skirts, tank tops, some nicer pants, and a smattering of jackets. Now that we were several floors higher, much more colorful and flashier attire started to dominate the scene. Neon shirts, fur leg coverings, glowing sunglasses, and beaded necklaces.

I finished my drink as we traveled, and Kris stopped to get me another at a different bar. I sipped the second more slowly. A short distance from there we arrived at a bubble with fog drifting out along the floor.

"Now, there's just two things to remember at a rave: don't stop dancing, and stay hydrated." Kris handed me a water bottle.

"I don't know how to dance," I said.

Kris laughed. "Anyone can dance at a rave. Just follow the crowd." He pulled me in.

Inside the bubble the music slammed against my ears, invading, not giving me a second to focus on anything else. Demanding to be followed. The air was hazy, the smoke thicker around our feet, with strobe lights and laser lights flickering through it. Kris pulled me into a throng of dancers jumping in sync to the beat. Everyone was a waving kaleidoscope of colored fabric and glowing patches of light, more like a roiling ocean than a crowd. Kris started flowing with the crowd, bobbing with the beat, his upper body writhing.

He slipped further into the crowd, moving towards the center of energy. I sipped my drink. The music was so overwhelming it seemed to force a disconnect as if you were floating and not really present. Before I knew it my drink was empty, and I was swaying to the beat. Someone grabbed my shoulder.

I thought it was Kris, but I turned and was met with a girl that seemed familiar. She was smiling and saying something I couldn't hear. She pulled me farther onto the dance floor and I followed. I wasn't completely sure what was going on, but I found that strangely I didn't completely care. It was just the music now, lights flashing bright, dark, bright, and I was jumping up and down. The girl was laughing. I still couldn't place who she was as I stared at her. Several others were in our circle now, and Kris had joined us too. I leaned against him, and it suddenly occurred to me that I had no idea where that water bottle was. Instead I had another drink in my hands. Kris was smiling and we kept dancing, and it was as if it was not me dancing anymore, but someone else standing in the same place as me. In that moment I thought perhaps I understood the reverence Kris had given parties before.

*   *   *

Sometime later, I wasn't completely sure when, the four of

us were together in a hotel room. I didn't remember leaving Prabble, but the exact details didn't bother me. I was tired. We were all sitting on the floor between the two queen size beds, our backs leaning against the mattresses. My head was on Kris's shoulder, eyes closed.

"–exactly what it seems to run into: if, if you want it to be happening, it's not actually *actually* rape anymore," the girl was saying. I had only recently realized that she was so familiar, because she was Lena from the Grand Library. The gold warper pendant was still around her neck.

"I think what you're really saying, really describing is role playing," the guy with Lena said. I still didn't know his name.

"No, no. You couldn't be satisfied. An actual rape fetish couldn't be satisfied by it. By role playing. It would have to be actual rape; but if you actually want it—it, the rape—then it's not actually rape anymore."

"I don't think... I'm pretty sure, pretty sure that'd be a disorder, not a fetish," Kris said. "Don't quote me though. On that."

"Nah, no no, definitely would be role play," the guy said.

Ice cubes clinked against glass, and I opened my eyes. Lena's drink was nearly finished, and she was toying with the pendant between her fingers.

Kris glanced over at me. "Doing alright?" he asked softly.

"Yeah. Fine. Tired." I closed my eyes again.

"What about this then: can you, do you think, can you role play role playing?" Lena asked, her drink rattling again.

"Huh? Explain," Kris said.

"Okay. If your fetish was meta. Meta role playing. Like you pretend extra. Like pretend to be other people pretending to be other people."

"Why? That just, just sounds stupid," the guy said.

"I don't know," Lena said. "Maybe like, maybe you would pretend to be an angry person pretending to be a, you know, um, a soft person. Then everything would be opposite. Would be going against itself. And that 'going against' was what you got off to."

"I still don't get it," Kris said.

For a few seconds I felt like I knew exactly what she was talking about, but then I lost it and was just thinking about how much I wanted a pillow. In the back of my mind I kept thinking over and over again: what a weird night this was.

I heard Lena yawn. "Doesn't really matter, not really. I don't know either. But I should really go. Gotta be at the Library early, early tomorrow. I have to put the final touches on the N-T-, N-P-, no the, uh, uh, the Natural Third Plant, Prerogative, pre-presentation. Ugh." She stood up, her pant legs brushing against each other. "That thing. That mouthful."

"Wanna take some warp extract with you?" Kris asked.

"Oh, that'd be perfect. Please."

"Here. I'll walk you out." Kris voice dropped when he spoke to me again. "Ethan, I need to get up."

"Okay." I lifted my head and opened my eyes. Lena and the guy were both standing, and the guy was whispering something quickly to Lena.

"I'll be back in just a minute," Kris said to me.

They left the room and I slumped over on the floor. I felt like I could sleep right there all night. I almost did; seemingly seconds later, Kris was shaking me lightly.

"Hey, Ethan, you don't want to sleep on the floor do you?"

"Yes," I mumbled.

Kris chuckled. "You know, did I ever tell you you're adorable? You're especially adorable right now."

I grunted. "Stop it." I covered my face with my hands.

"Hey, I will lift you up. I will lift you up with my magic powers if you don't get up yourself."

I just grunted again.

"Okay, I guess, I guess that *did* sound more like incentive than an actual threat. Fine, here it goes."

I started as I was suddenly lifted off the ground, now much more awake.

Kris laughed and set me down on the bed.

"Geez, thanks a lot." I sat up and rubbed my eyes.

"I warned you. Didn't I warn you?" He sat down on the opposite bed.

"Pssh." I dropped my hands and just looked at him for a few moments. "No excuse."

"You're the one trying to give them here. The excuses. Not me." He smiled.

"Whatever." I fell on my back and kicked off my shoes.

"You wanna sleep?"

"Yeah."

"Alright." Kris stood. "I'll see you in the morning. Call me. When you wake up." With a quick flick of his wrist, a cell phone appeared a few centimeters away from the night stand and fell to the floor. "Oops."

"Don't worry. I don't need it. I already have one."

"I know. Just wanted to make it easier for you. Go to sleep now." He leaned down and kissed me, then walked to the door.

I smiled. "Night."

"Yeah. Later." Kris turned off the light and disappeared.

Chapter 22
Of a Beloved Friend

The next morning I awoke with a piercing headache. It was as if a dozen little shards of glass had been inserted into my skull. Luckily a bit of warp extract cleared it up quite quickly. I lied in bed a few minutes longer and realized I was still in Prabble. A far off *doo doo doo doo* trembled up through the walls, pounding like a smashgrinder in some overly elaborate conveyer belt death trap. It reminded me of the Hall of Hostile Hosts, and I smiled to myself.

The constant thrum was distracting though, so I soundproofed the walls. Instantly the room was rendered silent, a silence more absolute than anything I had experienced before. The total lack of auditory input made me feel almost crushingly alone as if this room was the only room in all of existence. I shuttered and removed the soundproofing.

I sighed and got up. I showered, made a fresh set of clothes, and wanted to check the time. The problem was when you have a huge building floating in space there is practically nothing to check the time against. Instead I made a watch that was synced with my time zone on my Earth. It was a little past noon.

As I walked out of the bathroom I wondered when I had fallen asleep last night and if Kris was awake yet. I made a cheat sheet, and it answered respectively: *2:43am* and *Moose*.

I would just call him then. I grabbed the phone off the floor and pushed the single button. It ringed longer than any previous time I had called him, but he finally picked up.

"Hullo?" His voice was groggy.

"You know, that was quite a night, but I don't think I really want to ever drink alcohol again."

The line was silent a moment. "What?"

"I said it was a good night, and I don't want to drink alcohol again."

"What? That, that last part... *what?*"

I sighed. "I. Don't. Want. To–"

"No. I heard it. You're craaa-zy." The last word got stretched out in a yawn. "Hang on." Kris hung up.

He appeared in the room shrouded in a purple blanket and proceeded to crawl into the other bed before saying anything else. "What's this alcohol abuse I'm hearing?" He made several more pillows and lied on his side facing me.

"It didn't seem to really do much for me, and it just gave me a headache."

"You didn't stay properly hydrated."

I shook my head. "Anyways. I did want to talk about us."

"Oh? What about?"

I took a deep breath. "We both know about Peter now, and I'm still really not cool with the fact that I made a copy of you. Not because the copy was of *you*, but because it was a copy at all. It negates what Peter was, and I really don't like that."

"It doesn't negate him," Kris said softly.

"Really? You're the one who was always saying he wasn't real."

Kris propped himself up with an elbow. "I know. But, well, he still happened. He's not gone. He's just, not continued."

"Yeah, he still happened, but I feel like he's negated, because what he stood for was never true. But anyways, I'm gonna need some time to get over him. I still find myself thinking about him at times. Not a ton, but enough I guess. Bottom line: I do want to try us out, but I'm gonna need it to be slow. Especially because I really don't like the idea of us being arranged or forced. I don't feel like our powers matching is enough of a basis to go on. I want to make sure we can work together as people, you know? You and I. If we can really work together, then we'll go from there. Everything is just strange right now, and it's gonna take some time for me to work through it."

"Good thing we're strange too then. We're in our element," Kris said.

"Heh, I guess so." I half smiled.

"So how will you know if we work?"

"I dunno. I just need time to see. I mean, I like you. You have your moments. I just want to make sure first."

Kris closed his eyes and was very still. I worried he might disappear again, but then he spoke. "So what now?"

"Huh?"

"What now? What do we do in the meantime? Where do we stand?"

"Well, it's kind of the same as before. I want to spend time with you, but right now we won't be boyfriends."

"We'll be 'just friends?' "

"No. We're more than friends right now. We're, I guess, potentials. Yeah. You're my potential." I smiled.

Kris laughed, and it was genuine. "Never heard that term before."

"I think I just made it up."

"I doubt it. When you've got a whole universe of planets, someone's always already made at least one of everything."

"You think so?"

"Yeah."

"Well. Way to steal my thunder."

Kris smirked. "You're welcome, potential."

"Yeah, yeah. Sure." I stood up and kissed him, leaning over him as he lied in in his cocooned blanket.

He smiled. "Thanks."

I just nodded and sat down next to him. "So. Why does Prabble have hotel rooms?"

"To be self-sufficient. Anyone can use them, but mostly it's just the permanent partygoers here that do."

"And who restocks at all the drinks and food here?"

"It's automatic. It's a warp trick where you set up a flow of energy to keep doing the same thing. Like digging a side stream to a river and making water keep flowing where you want it. It's the only way warp vending machines can work. Though it needs time to 'recharge,' so to say."

"That's convenient."

"By the way." He sat up. "I can't believe you gave a Gold Mark to Lena. She said you two had only met once before."

"A what?"

"A Gold Mark, that pendant you gave her. It's kind of a

really big deal for Warper Born. It singles her out as having your favor and puts her a rank above everyone else. Like, she could make district rep or even *continent* rep like *that* now," Kris snapped his fingers, "if she wanted to. The rest of any career she takes up is pretty much set."

"Oh. I didn't know."

"Did she tell you about how to make it?"

"Yeah, but, I offered her something. I didn't know that pendant was so big though."

"Don't worry about it."

"Should I have not given it to her?"

Kris shrugged. "Maybe, maybe not. They're more symbolic than anything. She seems like a nice person. Besides, as soon as she tells people you gave it to her they'll know you're just a new warper. No offence."

I was silent a minute; I felt concerned, and a little used, though I didn't want to admit it. "How did she even get here? Since she's not a warper?"

"There's teleporter pads on Ven and Riktor, and they link up here too. Any of the Warper Born can come here whenever they want." He paused a moment. "So, what would you like to do with the rest of the day? Head downstairs for round two?"

"No thanks. I mean, it was cool and all, but I don't think these parties are really my kind of thing."

"Oh come on. Why not?"

"I dunno. It just seemed silly. Like that wasn't even dancing. It was just jumping up and down."

Kris laughed. "Okay, then what would you call dancing?"

"I don't know. I've never actually been dancing before. I guess something more like in a movie. Something more classical."

"Oh? Oh? Raves aren't classical enough for you?"

"I'm pretty sure they can't be considered 'classical' by any stretch of the word."

"Just wait a few centuries." Kris chuckled. "But that means you need to try out the other stuff. Here, I'll show you some classical dances. Let me just get dressed." He stood up and he was only wearing a pair of blue briefs. He created some pants and pulled them on. "There's a lot of really good ones that aren't boring."

"Like what?"

He created a shirt and put that on too. "We can do the waltz, the cha-cha-cha, tango maybe? Or we could foxtrot or my favorite: Victoria's pax." With each name he moved his torso side to side, demonstrating rhythms I didn't catch.

"You actually know all of those?"

"That's just a fraction." He smiled. "Quick, stand up." He pulled me away from the beds, next to the far wall. With a snap of his fingers the beds and carpeted floor disappeared, replaced with hard wood flooring and elegant drapes hung around the walls. A small chandelier appeared hanging from the ceiling, accompanied by a small table with a phonograph atop it.

"Now then." Kris held up my hand. "What shall we dance?"

"I dunno."

"Just pick one."

"How about tango then. Reminds me of spies."

Kris smirked. "Spies? That's something I can get behind. Alright. Stand here, in front of me." He took me by the hips and positioned me so we were facing each other. "Now, I know you've seen this stance before. Just put your right hand on my shoulder and we lift our other hands here." His right hand clasped my left and he raised them shoulder height as he put the other on my hip. "You got it."

"This feels so ridiculous."

"Hey, you're the one who wanted some classical dancing."

"I know, I know. But that doesn't mean I actually want to do it now."

"*Pshaw.* Now, I'll lead. You'll step back, back, back, pause, out and over, then back together, and repeat."

"Huh?"

"You'll get the swing of it."

Kris winked and the phonograph clicked on, a festive melody of trumpets and drums with the beat clapped out by recorded hands. He immediately jumped right into it, his right foot crashing directly into my shin.

"Ah! What was that?" I broke away from him, rubbing my leg. "Ow."

"I said: back, back, back, pause—"

"I know, but I didn't know what you meant."

"It couldn't have hurt that much."

"That's not the point."

"Okay, okay. I'm sorry. Let's try again. Just step backwards this time. We have to move as one."

We resumed our positions and Kris started the music over again. This time I watched his feet and was able to avoid another collision. However, after the three steps back, I took another instead of going to the side. We started over and finally completed a round of tango steps.

"Now do it this time without looking down," Kris said

"I doubt that'll work."

"Have more faith in yourself."

"Okay."

We began another round and on the first step I didn't go back far enough, and Kris's foot landed right on my toes. I yelped and tried to jump back, but it didn't quite work. I fell to the floor.

I remained sitting there and crossed my arms. "This is hard."

"Of course it is. We just started." He sat down on his legs in front of me.

"Let's just chalk this up to me not being a dancer, hm?"

"Or just giving up too soon." He poked my chest.

"Whatever." My gaze drifted away to the wall and up towards the ceiling.

"We're gonna do this another time." Kris sprawled out on his back next to me and stopped the music.

"Okay."

I listened to the far off beat of some dance room below us. I wondered absently what the upkeep of something like Prabble would be if it was more real.

"Whatcha thinkin' about?" Kris asked.

"Prabble."

"What about it?"

"Nothing really." I paused. "Actually. You said you've been here lots of times before, right?"

"Yeah."

"How many of those times were with Tavin?"

"Most of them."

"Was he a dancer?"

"Even more than me." A quick smile tugged at Kris's lips.

"Hmm."

There was silence for about half a minute.

Kris rolled to his side, facing me. "Why do you ask?"

"Just wondering."

"Well, I'm not trying to get you to dance just because he did, you know. It really is a good thing. Dancing, that is. It's cardio. And fun."

"I know."

"Good." He returned to his back.

"There's something else I was wondering."

"What?"

I debated whether or not now would be the best time to bring it up. I decided there probably wouldn't be a perfect time to ask at all, so I might as well ask now. "Um, this is something that's kinda been skirted around before. Radcliff said I should ask you about it directly."

Kris rolled to face me again. "What is it? Just ask. You're making it sound really heavy."

"It is though. I mean, probably. Yeah, definitely."

"Just ask it already." He slapped a palm on the floor.

"Okay." I took a deep breath and sighed. "How did Tavin die?"

Kris opened his mouth partway and furrowed his eyebrows. He returned to lying on his back: staring up at the ceiling with his left hand over his mouth. After a minute passed I feared be might not answer at all.

"I'm sorry," I said. "You don't have to—"

"No."

I waited. "Huh?"

"No. It... it's okay." He sighed. "You probably should know anyways." He kept his eyes fixed on the ceiling, and his words were muffled slightly by his hand. "It was the Dark Agencies."

"Really?"

"Yeah. I don't, we don't... I don't even know exactly what happened. He was off doing his own thing one week, like normal, but then, then Alicia called me."

"Alicia did?"

"Yeah. Let me, let me just tell the story. Okay? Just, ask me anything after I'm done."

"Okay. Sorry."

"Don't worry. So... she called me. I remember exactly what I was doing too. I was at this mega mall, because I had decided to put together a new wardrobe. Something that was more colorful, not all white and black. I had just taken off my t-shirt, just about to try on this pink button up, when my palm started to warm up. The t-shirt was still in my hand so I tossed it aside, and there it was, the palm ring glowing brighter than normal. I usually left it on back them. I answered, and... and the first thing Alicia said, the very first thing was, 'Where are you?'

"Something in her voice, something in it set me off instantly. I can't remember ever quite hearing that tone in it before. It was so, so subtle though. So underneath the words. I ask her what was up, and she just asked me where I was again. She said this was urgent, that we needed to talk in person. So I teleported to her, to the Archives, and Radcliff was with her. Raine wasn't there though. She was only about eight back then.

"Now I was really nervous. Alicia said something, something like, 'there's no easy way to tell you this,' and she held up her left hand. I didn't realize what I was looking at at first, but then I realized. I realized that the circle on her palm was broken. Missing a slice. Someone was dead. And then it clicked. Why else would they call me? Only me?" Kris paused a moment. "I think I started crying. I don't really remember.

"They asked me when the last time I saw him was. We tried to figure out where he might be. Well, where the body might be. To figure out how he died. We had, we had been on a bad bend lately, Tavin and I. Not seeing each other. And I know it's not my fault it, it, you know, happened. But still, sometimes..." He shook his head. "I can't even remember what the last thing we said to each other was. It was probably bad."

I licked my lips and waited for him to continue again. I wanted to cut in, wanted to say something soothing, but I didn't know the words. If I was there again, reliving my life, with all the experience I know now, I wouldn't have worried about saying anything. I would have simply hugged him and given him all of my support. One of the things I regret the most is that I didn't do anything for him in that moment.

"We eventually did find him though," Kris continued. "His body. He was on his home planet, in his house in the city. It was this mansion literally on top of a skyscraper. He was there, out in the back garden, down on his stomach. Nókrutar had killed him. A few of them were still in the house, lingering around a few warp locked pieces of art. We killed them. I killed them. I obliterated them. But that, well, that didn't help, of course.

"He had the most horrible look on his face too. Radcliff tried to stop me, tried to stop me from looking, but I did anyways. His skin color was all off, but the worst part was the look on his face. His mouth, it, it was in this twistified grimace. Like he, I guess like he was trying to scream, but couldn't open it all the way. I especially remember his lips. Kinda, curled inwards, and split in a few places. Like they were too dry. But then his eyes... his eyes were all wrong too.

"They were only half open, but I could still see everything. They weren't even his eyes anymore. They were like some... *fake eyes*, put in his skull. They were so empty. So... just *so* empty. I don't even know how to describe it. Like, hollowed out. Not literally empty or hollow, you know. But... just gone. Gone."

"Hollowed out," I whispered.

"Yeah."

I was half surprised he even heard me. I was still sitting on the floor, but I had pulled my legs up against my chest and wrapped my arms around them. Kris's gaze was still fixed on the ceiling, one arm lying back on the floor near his head, a single fingernail sliding side to side on the wood floor.

"What, um, what happened then?" I asked.

"What do you mean?"

"I mean... what did you do? How long did it take to recover?"

"Recover?" Kris sighed. "I dunno. *Do* you ever recover?"

"I wouldn't know.

Kris sat up and poked my shoulder. "But it's okay, right? We have each other. That's, that's how it goes."

I nodded and we were silent for a few minutes.

"I need to show you something," he said.

"What?"

"At my house, another picture."

He took my hand and we appeared in his house's living

room. Outside the windows was a deep forest, light filtering down green and brown through the canopy. Kris led me upstairs, up to his bedroom which was still so lacking in furniture. We stopped in front of the wall hanging covered with cloth.

"This is it." Kris pulled off the cloth and revealed an aerial photograph of a city.

"What is it?"

"Tavin's city. Kravis. The same, the same one he died in. He always thought it was his greatest accomplishment. And it moves, the picture, if you stand in front of it and think for it to move. So you can see more of the detail." He took my by the shoulders and positioned me in front of it. "Look."

Nothing happened at first, but as I focused on an interesting building the image zoomed in and shifted its angle to provide the best view of the structure. I looked to the edges of the frame, following a sidewalk, and the image moved too. The layout of the city was so intricate, so elegantly designed. Nothing looked cramped or out of place. The roads fit in perfectly and efficiently, maximizing traffic flow without being confusing. Bridges over the roads were common to create safe walkways, even with some places completely covering the road with elevated parks between buildings.

"This is incredible," I said.

"It's so amazing. Maybe, maybe we can go sometime. But later. A lot later."

"Yeah."

"Potential." Kris gave a small smile.

"Heh." I worried for a moment that he was trying to be ironic, but as I looked at him, looked into his eyes, I didn't believe that was the case. "Potential." I nodded.

Chapter 23
Dearest

I walked along a sidewalk in the suburbs of my home town. The summer heat pressed around me, even now after the sun had set, its faint traces of purple still smudged along the western horizon. Cars drove by: their headlights brightening the street, then fading. Everything felt so unreal. Everything felt so far away. Disconnected.

This was the last thing I had to do on my planet. I felt like I was walking through a movie set and every single thing around me was just a prop. I hated it. In that very moment, I hated it so much. The next car that drove past me—*shhwwwh* behind me, casting my shadow far ahead—I shoved my hand violently out at it. It burst into flames, screeching sideways, topped over into the median and exploded. I stopped walking.

Almost a week had passed since Kris and I had been at Prabble. Restless nights in which I could hardly think of anything besides him and Peter and what they meant. I had wanted to work on making a new house, but that had never happened. I clenched my fists and held myself very still for several seconds. At last I released the air from my lungs and took a deep breath. I recreated the car I had destroyed. It drove away, and I continued walking towards Peter's house.

The easiest thing to do would be to simply erase the whole planet, but I couldn't do that. I couldn't erase Peter and I couldn't even erase just his memories. I couldn't bear the thought of ripping away all our time and leaving him without even knowing he had a hole in his life. It would feel like a betrayal, even worse than non-existence.

A new idea had come to me last night and it seemed viable. Perhaps even inevitable. It bothered me on a fundamental level though, and I felt that to do it would be a certain point-of-no-return. It was, in fact, a perfect idea. It let me eat my cake and have it to, in a sense. It still irked me nonetheless, like carrying around a mousetrap snapped on my finger.

I couldn't put it off any longer. I made a doorway into Peter's bedroom. So familiar. The movie posters; the double bed; his desk scattered with papers, pens, wallet, keys, gum, a candle; his overstuffed shelves; a book by M. R. Trammel on the bed; a few shirts on the floor. Peter. It was dark in the room; the only light came from the street lights outside or spilled in from the connected bathroom. Peter was inside there, towel around his waist as he prepared his toothbrush.

"I'll be out in just a minute," he called.

"Okay," I whispered as I sat down on his bed.

I picked up the book and flipped through it. One of the pages was torn and I mended it. Inside the bathroom Peter finished brushing his teeth, gargled, spat into the sink. He walked out.

"What's the matter?" he asked.

"Huh?"

"You look upset."

I shrugged. "I guess."

"Well... what is it?"

I stood up and wrapped my arms around him, squeezing him tight. "Don't worry about it, okay? It's nothing." And with that, I made him sleep.

His body went limp in my arms, and I levitated him to the bed. I pulled away the wet towel and tucked him under the covers.

"I loved you."

I sighed and scratched the back of my neck. I assumed this next step would be tricky, because I had never done it before. But then again, how difficult could it really be? I pressed my hands together, closed my eyes, and concentrated. Focused on myself. But not exactly myself. A mirror of myself. That was the easiest way to visualize it: a mirror, but more accurately: a double reflection so the image wasn't reversed. I reached down, inward, and touched the core of my being. The warp energy flowed out, flowed out, and created form. I opened my eyes and looked into my doppelganger's eyes. A perfect copy.

"Hello." He smiled. He, my own doppelganger, another Ethan standing naked before me.

"I did it."

"Yeah. No problem at all, was it?"

"I guess not." I forced a laugh. It was too strange, too uncanny, too insane.

"You're getting a weird vibe to?" he asked.

"Yeah. Shit. Yeah." I shook my head.

"It'll be fine though, I think. We think."

I glanced over at Peter. "You'll take care of him?"

"You don't even need to ask. I must be the mate, and I'm still you. He'll be in the exact same hands."

"But... you're not *me*."

"Oh come on, you've already worried and debated and kept yourself awake over this. You know as well as I do that I am not you, but I am still Ethan. Just as you are."

"Fucking hell. I must have made you stronger." I looked away: at the ceiling, at the walls, anywhere but him. "You must not be weirded out by this at all."

"Oh, no, I sure as hell am weirded out by this, but you put more determination into me. Or I think it's more accurate to say you locked more determination in me." He looked down at his hands. "I remember all my worries from before, but now, now I don't feel like they're really important. I feel like I know exactly what I'm doing."

"Damn, and you're already a different person, even after a few minutes."

My doppelganger laughed. "I guess so."

I looked at him now, looking at myself in a way even more clear than a mirror could ever offer. My hair, my shoulders, the way I stood, my whole body. So strange to actually see it; see it like others see it.

I laughed.

"What?" he asked.

"Nothing. Nothing. Just something stupid."

"That you wanted to kiss me?" He grinned.

"W-what?"

"I am you, remember? You can't hide from me."

"Okay, yeah, I guess I would call myself out like that," I said.

"I want to also–"

"–just to try it?"

"Yeah." He nodded.

"Aw, this is stupid," I said. "Making out isn't part of my plan for tonight."

"So? Just one."

"I do want to–"

"I know." He step forward and placed his hands on my hips.

We leaned into each other and kissed. It was the strangest thing I'd ever done. That either of us had ever done, really. We only kissed a few times before we stopped. We hesitated together, lips still close but not touching. Then my doppelganger stepped back and let his arms fall to his sides.

"So..." I said.

"Yeah..."

"I think we should just stick to other people. That was too, bizarre." The way my own movement matched me too exactly. It made something exciting into something expected.

"Probably a good idea," he said.

I walked back to the bed and brushed my hand over Peter's forehead, moving back his bangs. I always loved his face when he slept.

"You'll miss him," the other Ethan said behind me.

"Yeah. I, I will."

"You could always come visit..."

"No. You know I promised I wouldn't. Not after tonight."

"Sorry."

"It's fine." I leaned over and kissed Peter's forehead. One last time. I turned back to my doppelganger.

"You don't have warping, so now I just have to make you forget and everything will be the exact same for you and him. As if I had never gotten this power. You're not... worried, are you?"

"No." He shook his head. "I don't think I really can be. You made me for this plan, and I want to follow through."

"I dunno if I should be glad or disturbed at that." I placed my hands together again.

"Don't think about it then."

"I'm never making flying pigs, just so you know, I'm never ever making flying pigs after this."

He chuckled. "Just get it over with. Make me forget."

"Don't you two break up."

"You can ensure that."

"I don't want to."

"Okay."

I closed my eyes and reached out into my other mind, isolated the memories and tugged them away. No knowledge of warping, or other worlds, or Kris. Only him and Peter as it had been. And when it was done, my doppelganger slept. I laid him down next to Peter, created a set of cloths in pile on the floor for the morning, and tucked him in. The doppelganger Ethan rolled to his side and placed an arm over Peter.

It was done. It was right again. Peter would be happy. I would be happy.

I forced myself to look away from the couple in bed as a few tears started welling up in my eyes. I took a shuttering breath and walked out of the room through a doorway floating high above the Amazon rainforest. It closed behind me and disappeared.

The sun had set hours ago here, and the dark of night was total. It suddenly occurred to me that even this place, a whole separate continent and hemisphere, was still too close to Peter. I flew up, through the clouds, out into space. I arced around the planet and perched upon the Moon. My feet kicked up a fine mist of gray dust which slowly settled again. Directly in front of me—like a circle of blue, green, and brown on a black canvas—was my Earth of origin.

I raised my hands to it, touching both thumbs and both forefingers together, making a sudo-circle around the planet. I felt its presence: so much rock and water and life. I disallowed it to change. I weaved the warp energy over it, around it, forcing it to keep its shape, locking the entirety of the planet.

"Goodbye," I whispered.

Behind me I created another door, one that was completely random. I step through to an unknown point in space and began constructing a new solar system for a new Earth. My new Earth.

Chapter 24
To Inherit Silence

Several days later I was showing Kris around my new home: a tower at the western edge of the Amazon on my new Earth. He leaned over the pool, peering through the water at the foliage below. The pool had a clear bottom and was set within a balcony that jutted straight out from the side of the tower at a ninety degree angle. It was over a hundred meters before you'd even hit the highest leaves.

"Nice pool. Were you inspired by anything?" Kris asked.

"Maybe." I smiled. "Mostly I just thought it was cool."

I continued the tour to the main living room. It was a mostly circular space with the center sunk a few steps into the floor. A bright crystalline shard about the size of a mini fridge and glowing white was fixed to the ceiling. Kris immediately hopped down the steps in a single bound and walked between the semi-circle couches, touching the corners at random.

"Meeting room of some sort?" Kris asked.

"Not really. I just though this looked cool too."

"Is that your reasoning for this whole thing?"

"No." I crossed my arms. "Well... maybe I shouldn't show you the bedroom."

"Ha! Like that's gonna work. Now you have to."

"No I don't."

"Yeah you do. Cliff hangers like that aren't allowed to be left open. It's a rule somewhere or something. Besides, the bedroom's the most important part."

"Whatever. I'll just show you now to get it over with." I lead him down a hallway.

"You seem to be implying that this is gonna be really weird."

"I don't think it's weird."

"Maybe you're implying you're weird." Kris laughed.

I stopped in front of the doorway to my room. "I think it's awesome." I opened the door.

"Oh. Shit." Kris walked inside, mouth agape.

The floor, the curved walls, the domed ceiling; all was glass in a delicate, square-separating framework of metal. The room hung off the side of the tower like a soap bubble, and it only had a bed inside. Two other doors led to the walk-in closet and the bathroom.

"The bed faces east so the sun wakes you up," I said.

Kris stood in the center of the room, hands on his hips. "Does this mean you're an exhibitionist?"

"Really, Kris? No. You can't even see in from the outside, and even if you could, no one's around."

Kris laughed and held up his hands. "Just checking."

"So then. What do you think of it?"

"I dunno." Kris spun around slowly, taking a final look. "The only reason the glass floor isn't bothering me is because I'm not looking at it. I dunno if I could sleep in here."

"Well you better get used to it them."

"Is that an invitation?" Kris looked at me out of the corner of his eye.

"No. *That* wasn't." I sat down on the bed and patted the spot next to me.

Kris chuckled and flopped down beside me, lying back and looking up at the sky though the ceiling.

We stayed there in silence for a minute or two before I spoke again. "So were you really–?"

"What's that?" Kris asked.

"Huh?"

"That." He pointed up. "That star."

In the afternoon sky, almost directly above us, was a star glowing faintly against the blue.

"It's just a really bright star," I said.

"This isn't the same Earth."

"Uh, no. It isn't. I said that."

"No you didn't."

"Yeah I did. I said that was my new Earth when I brought you here."

"But that could just mean you redid the place. It doesn't necessarily mean you got a whole new planet."

"Okay fine. Kris, this is a whole new planet. Happy?"

"Why?"

"Why what?"

"Why'd you make a new Earth?"

"I just thought it was for the best." I paused. "You know. Moving on."

"Moving on?"

"Yeah. You know, because of Peter."

Kris propped himself up on an elbow and looked at me. "You made him forget you?"

"No."

Kris furrowed his eyebrows. "What did you do then? When you called me you said he was all set now."

"Yeah, he is. I made a doppelganger of myself for him. He won't be alone now."

Kris blinked and didn't say anything. He let himself fall onto his back again.

"This will keep me from worrying about him, you know? It helped me let him go, knowing that a 'me' is still with him. Of course I'm not gonna just instantly forget him, but I–"

"No."

I waited, confused, but Kris didn't say anything else. "What?"

"Nothing." Kris stood up. "I should– I need– I... I'll be back. Later. I'm sorry. I'll see you later."

He disappeared.

I sat for a moment, then processed what had happened. I jumped up. "Kris!" At first I couldn't even articulate more words. "Y-you promised you wouldn't do this again!"

An itching sensation ran up my arms, and I hurried back into the living room. I knew he wasn't here anymore, but a small part of me hope I'd find in another room just beyond a closed door. I continued through several more rooms, not stopping when I saw them empty. I realized I was subconsciously continuing the interrupted tour. I sighed and headed straight to the top. The roof was a small, circular open terrace. A slight breeze rushed past me as I looked out over the rainforest. Why had he run again?

I held out my hand and the phone that called only Kris appeared in it. I pressed the button and waited. He didn't pick up. I called again, but still nothing. I wouldn't let him run away. Not this time. I asked where Kris was, and made a cheat sheet.

Moose.

"Goddammit," I muttered.

How had he always been able to know where I was? It wasn't Alicia; she had said that the rings only worked if the individual in question had theirs activated. How did he track me, I asked, and made another sheet.

Moose.

Why aren't you useful?

Moose.

I tossed the papers over the side and watched them fly away on the wind. I looked down at the phone in my hand and suddenly it struck me. The phone itself. Kris literally told me a few weeks ago that he could know where I was if I had the phone with me. But how?

I called Kris again and focused on the ringing, focused on the signal being sent. I could feel it, ever so faintly. A subtle pull in the warp energy around me, like a bit of fishing string trailed across the surface of water. It was just as Jett had once said: things can be made with shortcuts, made inherently reliant on the energy. The phone's whole existence was wrapped up in warp energy: powered by it, working with it, riding on it. Shooting warp bound sounds across unimaginable distances. I grasped at that small stirring string and followed it.

Upon opening my eyes I found myself floating in a dark corner of space. Nothing was around me besides far-off stars. The trail ended here though. I surveyed the area, confused. True, I couldn't find the exact end of the string, but I knew it had to be right around here. Somewhere. Was there something invisible here? How could I find something invisible?

I continued floating, pondering this new dilemma. None of the constellations surrounding me looked at all familiar, though I wasn't surprised by the fact. I was just about to make a cheat sheet asking where I was when I glanced down and saw complete darkness beneath my feet. There were no stars; there was no light. There was nothing below me at all but a huge circle of void.

My heart jumped and for several seconds I was afraid it was a black hole beneath me and that I might already be trapped within its pull. I quickly realized that wasn't the case, because I wasn't moving. The hell was it then? I created a pair of super night vision goggles. It was a moon—or rather a would-be moon—drifting alone in space. It looked much the same as Earth's Moon: empty and full of craters. I noticed one variance on its surface. There was some sort of structure in the crater directly beneath me.

It wasn't very large, a cylinder wider than it was tall with a convex roof that couldn't quite be called a dome. I flew towards it and soon I could see a few red lights glowing faintly around the rim of the structure. Aside from the lights there were no markings or entry points.

Clearly the only way in was to teleport, and teleport I did.

There were flashing lights, blaring music, and people all around me. A club? Had I just found a hidden moon club? That's what it had to be, but why in the world did it exist? There was a dance floor, a few bars, tables. I turned my head this way and that, taking in everything, utterly speechless. As the discovery sunk in I slowly realized that a hidden moon club made more or less perfect sense for Kris to run away to. But why?

"I don't recognize you. How'd you get here?" someone asked from behind me.

But, that voice. Something about that voice. I turned around. Jett. It was Jett standing right before me, holding a glass in his hand, wearing a fedora, and sporting a slightly confused expression on his face.

I gasped and took a step backwards. "Jett!"

"You know me?" He squinted his eyes. "Who are you?"

"Of course I know you. You gave me this!" I held up my arm and pointed to the two small circular scars.

"It's too dark. I can't see."

"Why are you even here? I thought you were fighting the Rurrians!"

"Fighting the–?" His eyes widened. "Oh. *Oh.* You, you're Ethan? Right?"

"Yeah. That's me. There's no way you could possibly have forgotten what happened."

"I never knew 'what happened' in the first place. Hmm. You should probably just come see Kris." He grabbed my wrist to lead me through the throng of people.

I pulled my hand out of his grasp.

"Fine, fine." Jett raised his hand. "Just go yourself. There, at the bar." He pointed to one of the bars about twelve meters away.

Something about Jett seemed off. Different. Was this the alternate personality? Why was he with Kris? What was going on?

"Yeah, yeah. I'm just gonna go talk to Kris." I took a few steps back, watching Jett, then turned and quickly pushed my way through the crowd.

Kris was leaning back on one of the stools, shaking a mug around as he sang with the others around him. His phone was sitting alone on the counter.

"–wine's all gone but it ain't strong / so take a shot with me. // Don't hesitate to top it off, / don't water down the ale. / We're drinking far past tipsy now, / of this we cannot fail."

The song continued into the next verse as I tapped Kris on the shoulder.

He turned around, beaming, but instantly his smile flattened as the mug slipped from his fingers. It *klunked* against the floor, sloshing beer over my left pant leg.

"What the fuck, Ethan! What the fuck!" He put his hands on my shoulders and tried to stand up, but he almost fell and I caught him. "Why are you *here*, Ethan? How did you, how did you even get *here*?" His words were slurred.

"I just followed the phone. What's going on? Why's Jett here?" I had to hold his arms tightly; he seemed in constant danger of toppling over.

"What? Shit. Thought that, thought that was one way. Or some, shit." His eyes drifted past my face. "No! Shit!" He lurched away from me.

I turned with him, losing my grip on him, and he stumbled into a woman's arms.

"Tell, tell him not to come. Tell him, tell him not to," Kris said to the woman.

"I'm sorry, he's drunk." I tried to pull him away.

"Of course I know he's drunk, and who the hell are you?" She shoved me, and I almost fell backwards but caught myself on a bar stool.

That was when I really looked at her. She had green hair spiked into a mohawk, with a silver ring pieced through the bridge of her nose. Was that really? "*Alicia?*"

"How do you know who I am?"

This was the same Alicia from that photograph. I realized Jett had looked the same as picture as well.

"What's going on? What is this?" I asked.

Kris knocked back a vial of warp extract as I spoke. He turned to me. "Hang on a tick. Hang on." He turned back to Alicia. "Please go tell him not to come. For the love of everything, *please.*"

"Alright, alright. But I'm coming right back so you can tell me who this joker is." She disappeared into the crowd.

Kris turned back to me. "Ethan. Why are you here? *Why* are you *here?*"

"I was just trying to find you. You promised you wouldn't run off again. What's going on?"

"Dammit. Dammit, this was *literally* the last time. You don't even know. We need to just go now. This is just stupid stuff, no big deal. Let's go." He pulled on my arm.

"No. Tell me what this is first."

"I can't, okay? I just can't. Not now. Later. Now let's *go.*" He tugged on my arm.

"What's going on?" A new voice.

"I'm sorry, Kris, I couldn't stop him." Alicia came up to us behind someone else.

"Fuck." Kris covered his face with his hands.

The new person put his arm around Kris's waist and pulled him away from me. "What are you doing to Kris?"

"No! Stop, stop. It's not– stop." Kris pushed the arm away.

I couldn't believe it, but there was no mistaking it. Everything fit. Now I understood. The rest of the picture. "T-Tavin," I stuttered.

"Yeah, what's it to you?" he asked.

"They're doppelgangers? Aren't they?" I asked.

Kris looked at the floor and remained silent.

"You're a warper then. You here to hurt Kris?" Tavin asked.

Jett put a hand on Tavin's shoulder. "Tavin. This is Ethan."

Less than a second passed, hardly enough time for a heartbeat. Tavin's eyes widened. "Oh..." The syllable fell, dragged out, became a ringing echo of memory.

Kris struck his arms out to both sides as if trying to throw water droplets off his fingers. Everyone disappeared and the club fell silent. The lighting was still dim and flashing, and I stood agape, processing the event.

"I'm sorry." Kris rubbed both his hands down his face.

"Kris..."

"I–" He looked up at me with such mangled eyes, hesitated, and swallowed. "I... this really, *really* was the last time. I swear. I was going to get rid of them tonight."

"Was everyone here?"

"Huh?"

"Everyone? Radcliff and Erika too?"

"Oh. Yeah... yeah, they were here too."

"Why?"

"I dunno." He looked at the floor. "I never wanted you to know about this."

"Kris, just..." I put my arm around his shoulders. "Come here." I led him to one of the booths and we sat down. "It's okay."

"No it isn't."

"Why not?"

"This isn't okay. Aren't you mad?"

"A little bit, but mostly because you ran away again. As for all this, I mean, yeah, this is really weird. Like *really* weird. But, well, I think I kinda understand. Probably."

"But this wasn't fair for you. Always coming here. Coming to, to see... Tavin. Over and over again."

"Is this where you always went when you ran away?"

"Usually." He leaned against me.

"Does anyone else know about this place?"

"No."

I hesitated a moment, thinking. "Okay. Let's start at the top. Why did you make this?"

"I dunno."

"You have to know."

Kris sighed. "I guess."

I waited.

"I missed them," he finally said.

"Who?"

"Everyone. How everyone used to be. Back when Radcliff was cool. Back before Jett and Erika went loco. Back when Alicia was the life of the party. Back with, with Tavin. But that's the real problem. You're here now. I shouldn't have, needed, Tavin."

"I did brush you off at first."

"But I was trying to be focused on you. I really was. But... I just wished nothing had changed. I wished nothing changed at all."

I thought about Peter. "I think we were doing the same thing."

"But you did it better."

"Huh?"

"You let Peter go. You didn't make a doppelganger of Peter. You made one of yourself."

"Kris, it's okay. Let's not compare anything. I think we both did some stupid stuff, so I think maybe what we both really need is to start over fresh. Again, I guess."

"But how do we do that then?"

"Well. I let Peter go. You let Tavin go. It'll just be me and you, and we can go from there."

Kris was silent for several minutes. "I still wish you just hadn't seen this at all. I feel so stupid. So embarrassing."

"Don't worry, it'll be okay. Really."

Kris just sighed.

The club around us seemed so strange empty. The glowing dance floor still slowly pulsed through its different color sets. But all was silent. It created a creeping eeriness that encroached around us, and I wished Kris hadn't gotten rid of everyone and the music. If the party had still been happening this place could have easily passed as a room in Prabble.

"He wasn't really like that, you know," Kris said.

"What?"

"Tavin. He wasn't always so rawry. Like literally. Never. He was just, defensive. I think we all were back then. Defensive of each other."

"I was surprised when Alicia shoved me like that."

"They just didn't know who you were."

"Jett did."

"Yeah." Kris paused a moment. "Did you talk to him before you came up to me?"

I nodded. "He freaked me out too. I didn't even know where I was when I stumbled in here, and then he showed up, and well, you know the last time I saw him."

"Yeah."

"I guess he recognized me after I told him he was supposed to be out fighting the Rurrians."

"Would make sense," Kris said.

"How much did they know? Those doppelgangers?"

"Some things. They knew deep down that there were doppelgangers, but it wasn't a big deal for them. They knew a little about current events, usually just stuff I complained to them about. So when you mentioned the Rurrians, Jett must have been able to put three and three together."

"What did your Jett think of what the real Jett is doing?"

"I dunno." Kris was silent a moment. "He never really said anything about it. He probably tried not to think about it."

"And what about the Alicia doppelganger? What did she think about what her real self is doing?"

Kris looked at me. "What do you mean? What's Alicia doing?"

I remembered I hadn't told anyone yet, and I didn't want to get into the topic of Alicia now. "Nothing exactly. The last time I talked to her she seemed different. Bot seemed concerned too."

"Wait. Bot? Bot from the Restaurant? Concerned? *What?*"

"Yeah. I was talking to Bot a little while ago, and when I told Bot about Alicia, Bot said it was concerning."

"Okay, hang on, hang on." Kris sat up. "Bot talks to you? As in actually talks to you? Not just backhanding everything you say?"

"Well yeah. I mean, Bot still doesn't always have much patience, but yeah. Bot talks to me."

"But, but, *how?* Bot doesn't talk to *anyone.*"

The first real conversation I'd ever had with Bot flashed through my mind. "I... I dunno." I glanced away.

Kris's mouth hung open, like he was trying to find the words to fill it. "You... you're so weird, you know that? You don't act like a warper." Kris leaned back and crossed his arms.

"Well I'm still just in the 'Initiation Stage,' aren't I?"

"I guess." He paused. "So what did you tell Bot about Alicia that got Bot 'concerned?' "

I tapped a finger on the table. I guess we were getting into this now. "Basically, it was just that she'd been using her time looping on herself."

Kris leaned forward again. "What do you mean?"

"To read books. All of the books, apparently. She said she's 151 now."

"Uh, that... that's probably really not good."

"Bot thought the same." I sighed. I felt so tired now. So drained. "Why does everyone seem so lost?"

"I dunno. I really don't know. But there's nothing we can do about it."

"No." I closed my eyes, remembering things. The moment Alicia knelt down and brushed a strand of hair behind Raine's ear. The wavering of Jett's voice as he screamed in a white room. Something fallen behind Erika's eyes when she could not avoid what she was seeing. These were not endings. "We could do something about it. I know we could. I think we should."

"Like what?"

"Help them. Somehow."

"We can't help them. We don't interfere like that. Alicia says we shouldn't, and so does Radcliff. We can't do anything."

"But I can."

Intermission II

One time I was skinny-dipping in my pool, quite well relaxed, when Kris came bursting through the doors as he was oft to do in those days.

"We must go to the Queen of the GEK! I've had like seven cups, five cups of coffee today, so I am ready! So ready!" he pronounced.

I treaded water for a moment, staring at him. "The what? What?"

"The GEK, the Greater European Kingdom. It's on a planet where the British were able to take over all of Europe, and the Queen is holding an important luncheon and we must attend."

"A luncheon? Really?" I swam to the edge of the pool and climbed out. "The Queen of Europe is holding a luncheon?"

"Well, when I say 'luncheon,' I really mean a super formal dinner feast for the annual holiday of Unification. It's in Berlin, and we're going to be secret agents. We've received intel that there's plans for an assassination attempt. We have to prevent it!" He dashed forward and grabbed my wrist. He teleported us to his bedroom within his house.

"Kris, I didn't even get my towel." I held out my arms as water dripped on the carpet.

"What will we ever do?" He laughed as he created a towel and tossed it to me. Then he summon his Reality Converter and plugged it in.

I started drying off. "I thought you said we were going to see the Queen."

"We are, but we can't go like this, and you definitely can't go naked. We need to be really nice and formal." He pulled open his closet and took out a tuxedo. "See? White bow ties and everything." He draped his suit across a chair and created another one. "This one should fit you perfectly." He handed it to me.

"Thanks? I've never worn one of these before."

"It's just like anything else you wear." He started stripping down to his underwear. "I'll help you with the cuff links and bow tie."

I finished drying off and dressed. When it came to the cufflinks I kept fumbling with them as Kris fastened his. I couldn't keep a good enough hold on the sleeve to get the link through all the way.

"Here, here." Kris took the cufflink. "Don't try to do both at the same time. Just stick it through the top hole first, then wrap the cuff over to link it together." He demonstrated as he spoke.

I watched and I was able to fasten the second one with much more ease.

"I'll get your bow tie now." He pulled the length of fabric around my neck and started wrapping it over and under.

"Hey, Kris."

"Yeah?"

"There's something I've been wondering about."

"What?"

I hesitated a moment. "Are we gods?"

He chuckled. "Gods." He pulled the bow tie firm but not tight. "That depends on your definition of a god. If god is an omnipotent being, then we are almost god. If god never begins and never ends, then our powers are god. If god is something that exists outside of the universe, then we are not god. If god is merely energy, then the question would be who is not god? If god is just an idea, then we are not god. If there is not one god, but many gods, then we certainly are gods. And if god isn't a constant, but some ever-changing thing, then we might be god. It all depends. What *is* god?"

I stared at him for a few moments. "I thought you said you weren't in the 'booking it up' stage yet?"

Kris laughed. "Well what were you expecting? I don't know."

"What about when we die?"

"The warping power goes to the next conceived person."

"But what about *us*? You know, as a person. Me." I put a hand on my chest.

Kris just shrugged. "I dunno. No one knows. But the powers come through us, not for us. We're not actually special, we just happened to be conceived at the right time."

"Oh great, thanks a lot."

"Hey, it wasn't a dig on you. Just saying." He had finished with the bow tie a minute ago, but his hands were still against my collarbone. "I think you're special though."

"Heh, thanks."

Kris just smiled, then leaned forward and kissed me. "Now, let's get going. Don't want to be late for the Queen."

I nodded. Kris took my arm in his and teleported us to a long promenade in front of a fancy palace; the whole front of it was lined with pillars and windows that stretched from the bottom of the building to the edge of the roof. Several people dressed as equally formally as us—or even a few more formally dressed—gasped and pointed at our sudden appearance. Kris snapped his fingers, and they all continued as if nothing had happened. It was late in the evening and the sun was close to the horizon.

"Right, so we just go in, mingle for a bit, and try to figure out who the assassins are and stop them before the meal starts proper," Kris said as we walked towards the building.

"Fighting assassins?"

"Yeah, I know. Exciting." He grinned wildly.

"And this is just a game, right?"

"My dear Ethan, *everything* is a game, but that doesn't make it not real."

I shook my head. "And you said we're secret agents?"

"Yep. We're the two head representatives from the Bureau of Woodland Expansion Under Urbanization on the Greater English Isles."

"The what?"

"BWEUUGEI.[1] Don't worry about it. If anyone asks you anything, just make up some bullshit about trees. Or say it's classified."

" 'Cause that'll totally work."

---

[1] Pronounced: **bwee**-jee, rhymes with "squeegee."

"You'd be surprised here."

We walked right into the ornate place, and Kris explained that the security checks were at the fence around the perimeter. Inside people were milling about several large ballrooms and each room had a small live orchestra playing light music.

"I bet it's one of the violinists, and one of those cases aren't empty," I said.

"And what do you base that claim on?"

I glanced at Kris, and he was smoking a pipe. "Really? A pipe?"

"We *are* detectives after all."

"I thought you said we're secret agents?"

"Yes, but this part's detective work. We're both." He blew a smoke ring into the air.

"You're crazy."

"Thank you."

We reached the final ballroom, and it was larger than the three previous rooms combined. A huge table stretched from one end to the other between two rows of columns. Waiters were walking slowly through the crowd, deftly carrying platters of hors d'oeuvres or cocktails.

As one of them passed by Kris grabbed a cocktail and handed it to me. "You mingle, scope things out. I'll go meet our contact."

"Contact? Who's our con–"

"Shh, shh, shh." Kris touched his nose. "Remember. *Secret* agents."

"Wow, so much help you are."

"You just aren't enjoying it properly yet." He smiled, raised his pipe to me, and faded into the crowd.

I sighed and tugged at my collar with three fingers. How in the world are you even supposed to find an assassin in a crowd? My first thought was to make a cheat sheet, but that felt like it would literally be cheating, so I withheld myself. I took a sip of the cocktail and coughed. It wasn't very good, and I had no idea what it was. It was mostly clear with a hint of gold color and three olives on a spear.

Just then a man with black, slicked back hair and a few medals upon his jacket stepped in front of me. "Well hello, I don't think I've met you before." He was in perhaps his late twenties or early thirties, and he had the most peculiar way of talking. His teeth always remained touching, no matter what words he was pronouncing.

I blinked several times, waiting to hear his voice again.

"Oh you're not deaf, are you?" His voice was a cascade. It reverberating deep within his throat and rolled over the words with a relaxed ease, stretching out the ones he emphasized.

"No, s-sorry. Just, wow. The way you talk. That's really cool."

"Oh really? So easily amused. Hmm. No matter, I am Stanly Richardson III, Baron of Winchester. And you are?"

"I'm Ethan. Stroud. Ethan Stroud."

Richardson waited a moment. "And what's your title?"

"Oh. I, don't have one."

"Then why, pray tell, are you here?"

"Well, okay, I don't have a title, per say, but I am one of the head representatives of BWEUUGEI."

"Of what?"

"The Bureau of Woodland Expansion Under... well, basically we handle trees."

"Trees?"

"Yeah. Like planting them and stuff." I licked my lips, then added in a quieter tone, "Also it's classified."

He stared at me, his eyebrows low. "Is that so?" He turned and walked off.

"Ah!" I was aghast. "Oh, yeah, that was polite. I could have the Queen's ear and you just wrote me off. We'll see how long you get to keep your barondom!"

A few people nearby stopped their conversations and stared at me. I smiled. This was kinda fun. I turned to a small cluster of dignified looking individuals.

"Did you see the nerve of that guy?"

They just looked at me for several moments, then a lady in a green dress with a thin mesh draped across the top of her face spoke up. She was smoking a cigarette through a long jade holder with one hand and holding a glass of red punch in another. "No darling, I didn't. Why are you even here? The invitations specifically said no *children*."

"Actually, I represent BWEUUGEI. From—" I started to say.

"Dear, they didn't say that." A man next to her placed a hand on her elbow.

"They should have." She curled her upper lip.

The man looked at me. "Please forgive her. She's had too much punch."

"It's just punch," she said.

"I asked one of the waiters. He said there is alcohol in it."

"Always such a crimp on my days out." She tugged her arm away from him, sloshing some punch on her wrist. She directed her attention back to me. "BWEUUGEI, you say? What in the spirits in that?"

"It's pretty important, I can't actually talk about it much," I said.

"Does that have anything to do with those Oweegee boards?"

"It's pronounced Ouija, dear," the man said.

"Don't correct me, John. I wanted to see what he'd say."

"No," I said. "Why would we have anything to do with them? They're just child's toys."

A slight ripple went through the small group as they shifted on their feet or looked down into their drinks.

I glanced between them. "What is it?"

Another man at the edge of the group cleared his throat. "If those are child's toys, I'd hate to hear what you think is actually a serious subject."

"W-well, I mean, who can take them seriously? Talking to ghosts, really? That's so..." I couldn't think of a fitting word. "Rudimentary?"

The man put a hand over his chest and leaned back. "If you'll excuse me." He walked away briskly.

"We should, probably go as well." John put his arm around his wife's waist and led her away.

The few remnants of the group spread out and were absorbed by other circles. I remained standing where I was, baffled as I watched them all move away. I looked down at my suit then back up at the people around me.

"Ah! There you are!" It was Kris.

I turned around and saw him approach me just seconds before he clasped me on the shoulder. My arm jittered and some of the cocktail splashed down my front.

"Kris, dammit," I said in an undertone.

"Oh, oh, here." He produced a handkerchief from one of his sleeves and wiped at the spill, warping it away as he did so. "There! No harm, no foul, isn't that right, boys?" He turned back around, pulling me gently with him. "This is my comrade-in-arms, if you don't mind such a phrase." He laughed.

Before me was a small group of men, all of them in pristine suits with a haze of smoke drifting above them. Many of them seemed anxious to some degree, one of the men in the back of the group was blotting his face with a handkerchief. An older gentleman holding a fresh cigar and with a balding head seemed to be leading the entourage.

"Ah, the other representative?" The older gentleman asked.

"Indeed," Kris replied.

"Hi." I raised my arm to offer a hand shake. "Ethan Stroud."

The group of men were silent for a mere second, then the older gentleman laughed and the rest followed. "No need for that, my good Mr. Stroud. For you, I would *willingly* be an open book through my words." He smiled widely, but it did not reach his eyes.

"O...kay." I lowered my arm.

Kris took a small step forward. "Never fear my good men, never fear. We have no need of that today. But!" His eyes widened. "But, I think one of you is in disbelief, mayhaps?"

They all looked at each other, and a few of them laughed nervously while most of them muttered lines such as, "Not I" or "I'm highly patriotic."

"Ah! But I have just the thing." Kris raised a hand high above his head and waved for someone to come hither.

Several moments passed while I stared at Kris in bewilderment. Finally a waiter arrived with a single glass half filled with water and a thin stool that was a meter tall. He set the glass upon it, bowed, and backed away.

"Observe." Kris held out a hand to the glass and closed his eyes.

Nothing happened at first, but he made an act of exerting more and more effort, tensing his face and shaking his hand slightly. The glass hopped from the stool, the bottom smashed apart with a pop, and the remaining top nine-tenths of the glass rocketed into the air. The whole room went quiet in time to hear the glass fall back to the floor and shatter.

About six seconds passed, then the older gentleman raised his hands and started a slow clap. The rest of the men join in, and soon the whole room was filled with a round of hesitant applause that ended quickly.

"Good show, man. Good show." The older gentleman nodded his head. "I need be going."

The other men were quick to follow him.

Once they had gone I asked, "Okay, what was that?"

"Shock and awe tactics. Shock and awe. They saw me talking to my informant, so I had to divert their interest."

The waiter returned with a small broom and dustbin and started cleaning up the mess.

"By blowing up a glass? How did they just accept that? Why didn't they freak out?"

"They think I'm a psychic now. Or more accurately, they actually believe it now." He grabbed a glass of punch from a waiter who walked by and downed half of it in a single gulp.

"Psychics? Why do they believe in psychics? Wait... there were some people babbling about ghost things earlier."

"This is such good punch. And yes, ghosty things. This is one of the more interesting Earths."

"You know that stuff has alcohol in it, right?" I pointed at his glass.

"Really?" He drank the rest of it and licked his lips. "Shit. This is my fourth one. This is dangerously good punch."

I shook my head. "Oh, Kris."

"Anyways!" His face brightened. "My informant told me that the assassins are both female. Female *ninja* assassins."

"What? *What*? Hang on, did that really just happen? Did you just now make them into ninjas to make this more exciting?"

"No, of course not. I set this event ahead of time." He raised his pipe to his mouth and muttered, "Questioning ninjas."

"Okay, fine. Fine. Whatever. Now what's this about psychics and ghosts?"

"Oh, didn't I mention? There's a bit of a 'psychic cold war' happening on this planet. Very exciting." His eyes widened.

"No. No, you did *not* mention that."

"Ah. Well there is. Now you know. Also, the ninjas might be psychic. They might be reading our minds right now."

"Can they even do that?"

"Um, Ethan." Kris snatched the pipe from his mouth and tilted his head, raising an eyebrow as he stared at me. "Do you not know what 'psychic' means?"

"Of course I do. Do *you*? It can mean a whole lot more than just mind reading. Are they even that kind of a psychic? Like that trick you just did, that would be telekinesis, not telepathy."

"But the old man was afraid you'd read his mind. Ah-ha." He pointed a finger at me.

"Yeah, I guess so, but through touch. Keyword, *touch*. Also, we're warpers. Even if they can read minds, can they read ours?"

"Doesn't matter. Ninjas, that are probably psychic. We have to focus on that and focus on protecting the Queen."

"She's not even my Queen."

"Oh just play aloooong." Kris rolled his head and glared at me.

"I am. I decided I'm a defector from whatever that opposite side is."

"W-what? You can't do that."

"I just did." I smiled and crossed my arms. "I'm expecting a huge monetary reward after this assignment, but there are still underlying suspicious of my true motives."

Kris grinned. "Well then that's complicated by your feelings for the operative you were assigned to work with. It was love at first sight the moment you saw him."

"Oh really?" I raised my eyebrows. "Well that's extra complicated for you, because you can tell that the defector has feelings for you, but you know from his file that he brutally murdered his last known romantic partner with psychic energy for reasons unknown."

"Wow. What a sudden and macabre turn."

I laughed. "So what do we do now? How do we stop these ninjas?"

"Don't know. We don't have enough information yet. We just have to keep going through the motions of the luncheon to make sure the ninjas don't realize we're on to them. We'll be sitting down soon, and if that happens before we catch the ninjas then the fallback plan will be initiated."

"And what's that?"

"Ambush the ninjas. We'll get a note when we need to move into position."

"Ambush, great. If you had told me about this beforehand, I would have brought smoke bombs."

"We can still have smoke bombs." Kris opened his jacket and showed as a small canister appeared in one of the pockets.

"Isn't that cheating though? I thought this was like the temple of doom?"

"Eh. Kinda-sorta." He rotated his hand up and down.

We continued searching through the crowd, looking for any suspicious ladies. It was by no means easy, considering how incomplete the informant's information had been. Very soon a small bell was rung six times, and everyone started to cluster around the great table to find their seats. Some had already located their seat and sat down immediately. Others had not had such foresight and had to circle halfway around to find their place. Kris led me to ours near the head of the table. I didn't see either Richardson or the other group I had bumped into anywhere near us. The gentlemen who had been on Kris were less than a dozen seats ahead of us.

Kris leaned over and whispered to me, "Why would they even assign a defector to help protect the Queen herself?"

"Because of his incredible psychic power rating. Also they believe you can handle him since you're one of the Queen's top agents. They're expecting you to use any means necessary to keep me in check," I whispered back.

"Oo, I like that."

After everyone was seated a set of double doors in the wall behind the head of the table opened and two lines of attendants streamed out. Once they were in position, the Queen, several of her highest ranking officials, and yet more attendants entered the ballroom. Everyone at the table stood immediately, and no one sat again until the Queen took her seat.

Even once the Queen had sat she was still higher than anyone else, due to a slight upward slant that had been built into the end of the table, and her regal chair rose above every other chair. She held up her hands and started signing out a message to the table. An attendant standing next to her cleared his throat and spoke the words aloud.

"I, as your Queen, Queen Elaine II, welcome all most warmly to this feast. It gives me the greatest pleasure to visit the most pristine city of Berlin in the province of Germany. Even now, in this hour so clouded by suspicion and doubt with our neighbors..."

I leaned over to Kris and whispered, "She's mute?"

"Yep."

"Is she deaf too?"

"No. She can hear perfectly well for her age, or at least that's what I've heard."

"Ugh, rumors." I created a cheat sheet. "There. Concrete proof. She can hear just fine." I passed it to him.

"Ah, yes. I see." He folded the paper and slipped it into his jacket.

The attendant continued speaking for the Queen until at last she bade everyone eat. Countless carts of food were wheeled to the table, laden with chicken, pork cutlets, and beef, along with gravies, whipped potatoes, baked potatoes, countless vegetables, candied pecans, jams, cheeses, bread rolls, trout, pike, and even caviar. The drinks had changed to wines, beers, ports, and ciders.

"Holy balls," I whispered to Kris. "This is insane."

"Welcome to royalty." He took a hefty swig from his glass of chianti.

I helped myself to a plate of whipped potatoes and drowned them in gravy.

"Aren't you going to have some meat? This pork looks fantastic." He was in the process of scooping some onto his plate as he spoke.

"Maybe. But, more importantly, what about those assassins?"

"The ninja assassins?"

"Yeah, yeah. Whatever."

"Dunno. We haven't been summoned yet."

"How will we know when they need us?"

"We'll know."

"Hmm." I paused. "The defector is starting to question the reality of the situation."

"What now?"

"He has become suspicious of you and is wondering if this is actually a real assignment, or if this is just an overly elaborate way to sneak him out into a dinner date."

"Oh come on. The queen's top agent is hurt. If he was going to take you on a date, he'd just tell you so." Kris smiled.

I just nodded, still skeptical.

We were only a short while into the meal, perhaps twelve minutes or so, when a waiter refilled Kris's wine glass and discreetly dropped a small fold of paper on the table next to his plate.

"Ah! Oh!" Kris quickly took a drink to wash down the food in his mouth, then unfolded the paper. "See."

"What is it?" I asked quietly, leaning over.

"Here." He handed it to me.

It was a small, thin rectangle upon which "EZUGSFZUKYNBSPTGN" was printed in precise penmanship.

"What's it say?"

"I dunno. I don't remember the code, but it's time to go." Kris wiped his mouth with his napkin, tossed it over his dish, and stood.

I followed him as we ducked into a door off to the side of the large room and started running down a side hall.

"Where are we going exactly?" I called out.

"Towards the royal suite. In about three minutes the Queen will dismiss herself and head towards her room. That's when the ninjas will attack, and we've gotta intercept them." He reached the end of the hallway and skidded to a halt.

I ran into him. "Kris, give me a warning next time you stop."

"Shh, we can't be so loud."

"What?" I tried to keep my voice reigned in. "You were the one yelling just *three* seconds ago."

He was peeking around the corner. "But now we're much closer to the ambush zone."

"Your logic, Kris. Your logic. I just, I just can't right now. Seriously."

"Then just focus on our upcoming fight with ninjas instead. Come on." He waved his hand forward and took off again.

We ran down a shorter hallway, turned another corner, and entered a hallway that ran along a side of the building. The wall on the left was a row of windows and the wall on the right had pillars halfway extending out of the wall in half circles every three meters. Kris pressed up against the hall behind one of the pillars, and I did the same next to him.

"Now what?" I asked.

"Wait." He looked down at his watch. "Less than a minute to go I think."

I waited. The hall was silent, and I wondered exactly how far away from the main ballroom we were. Kris grabbed my wrist, and I peeked around the pillar. Quite a ways down the hallway two ladies in black dresses were walking towards us, almost quickly enough to be jogging. As they approached they unzipped their dresses at the waist and let the fabric fall away, revealing tight combat fatigues with several weapons strapped to their legs. Kris reached into his jacket for the smoke bomb, moving very quietly. Then I felt it. My ears started ringing and the hairs on the back of my neck rose. I looked at Kris; he was already looking at me. We both turned out heads to the window across from us and saw a black blur racing through the air towards us.

"Get down!" Kris shoved me as he dived in the other direction.

The Nókrutar crashed through the window and collided with the wall. A hollow *thud* and tinkling glass echoed down the hallway. The Agency was partway embedded in a newly formed dent in the wall, pulling itself free from the physical object it had collided with like a shadow pealing itself out of a painting. Perfectly silent, glowing blue-white eyes, reaching out for me, straining against the wall.

"We've been found out! Run!" The assassins fled, but neither I nor Kris were paying the least bit of attention to them.

Kris rolled over just as the Nókrutar pulled free of the wall. I raised my arms and was only able to let out a half gasping scream before it collided with me. It was unlike any attack I had ever suffered before. The Dark Agency it passed through my skin, a freeze rending through my body. It was in the same space as me, inside me, dragging through my body. My lungs stopped, I think my heart stopped. Everything cramped up, dried up. My skin pulled tight as my arms were forcefolded inwards. My vision was dark and I could barely hear Kris's screams. The only thing in my mind was it and the pain.

Suddenly I was free, gasping for air as several explosions reverberated dully through my ears. I was in a fetal position, staring down at the ground, shaking uncontrollably. A few more flashes of light and the last of the rumbling explosions ebbed into silence.

Kris straddled over me, his hands on both of my cheeks as he turned my head gently. He was just a blurry double-imposed image. I thought maybe I could see his mouth moving, but I could hear nothing that sounded like words. I felt something smooth pressed against my lips and almost choked as liquid ran down my throat. I coughed, turning my head to spit out the drink. My vision was coming back together. The smoothness was at my lips again, and this time I was able to drink.

"–you fucking, dammit. Don't you *fucking* dare," Kris was saying.

"K-K-Kris," I sputtered.

"Oh fucking thank you." He leaned forward and wrapped his arms around my head. "Oh, thank *god*."

My head was still throbbing, and I didn't want to move my limbs. "That... that wasn't, part of this... was it?"

"No, not at all. That was totally *not* supposed to happen."

The room was spinning now, so I closed my eyes. "Good thing it was just one then, huh?"

"The loners are always the worst."

"They are?"

"Yeah. Always the most aggressive. And maybe that's why they're alone. But I'm just so glad you're okay."

He was still lying on top of me, but it was comforting, knowing he was there. I still hadn't opened my eyes, afraid I might throw up if I did. "I think I need a little more warp extract."

"Sure. Here." Kris readied another vial, and I drank from it.

I felt close to perfect now. I glanced to my right, where the explosions had come from, and saw a huge portion of the palace was destroyed. The damage was so extensive that there was a crater in the ground as well.

"Wasn't that a bit, a bit of overkill?" I asked.

"Maybe. I might have accidently blown up the Queen myself." Kris bit his lower lip.

I forced a laugh. "So the best agent was the traitor all along."

Kris shook his head. "Who would've thunk?"

Chapter 25
From the Clutches of Darkness

I really hoped Kris wouldn't find the backpack full of grenades under my bed. I was probably worrying a lot more than I had needed too, but it was the main thing on the forefront of my mind. We had spent most of the day raising robot Dragons on a Mars that was just being colonized, tweaking the trajectories of two colliding galaxies to collapse them into a sub-point kessler nova, and trying to solve a single action puzzle planet where a coastal city called New Diablo was under invasion and we had to stop the domino effect leading to a New World Order.

Through it all, Kris kept intermittently asking me if I was okay. I was distracted, but trying to hide it, so I kept telling him I was fine. In the end we gave up on the puzzle planet only after a few tries and returned to my tower. We were laying in my bed now, gazing up at dark sky, his arm over my chest and neither of us saying anything. I was waiting for him to fall asleep.

I knew he wouldn't like what I was going to do tonight. No one wanted to get involved with Erika and Jett, and that was exactly what I was about to do. I had a plan for both of them. A way to hopefully help. Even if nothing could be done about what Stage they were in, I had an idea of how to work around it.

"Hey, Ethan?"

"Yeah?"

"Whatcha thinking about?"

I was silent a moment. "Not much of anything."

"Mmm."

He started tracing spirals on my chest and I felt guilty. I had actually expected this whole thing to be a lot more dramatic. That he would somehow know to look under the bed, and he'd find the backpack and would instantly figure out what I was going to do. Then we'd start yelling and he'd try to stop me, and it'd all come down to one line to which I had the perfect response.

"I'll follow you!"

"I know. I'm sorry. I'll be back, I promise."

If only I had put that much thought into my exact plans after that scene in my room. But no. Instead we were just lying on my bed, and he was tracing spirals with a single finger. The fabric of my shirt bunched up under his touch and stretched a little side to side. I think that was the first time I realized I loved him.

Kris fell asleep quickly; his mouth open, his breathing slow. There was no chance for me to fall asleep anytime soon, my nerves twisted up so. I waited. Twelve minutes. Sixteen minutes. After thirty minutes I eased out of bed, trying to jostle him as little as possible. I crouched beside the bed and grabbed the backpack beneath it. I teleported silently to my tower's roof.

I created a new pair of pants and shoes and put them on and was ready to go. I looked up at the sky for a moment. Half clouds, half stars. It'd be just a few hours. Just a few hours. I'd be right back. I made a doorway and walked through it.

It lead to Erika's prison-palace, just three meters from the warp shell that surrounded it. Much in the fashion of the single action puzzles, I had thought for quite a while on the best approach to untangling Erika and Jett from their self-made mazes. I had come to the conclusion that Erika would be the easier of the two: she simply needed to be removed from her captivity. And the rules of her captivity would work to my advantage. If she didn't want to leave, I could just drag her out.

I walked through the warp shell and teleported right outside her room. I knocked. I waited. The door opened.

Erika stared at me. For a moment her face seemed vacant and so empty, then I saw an almost hopeless surprise. "Ethan?"

"Hi."

"*Ethan?*"

"Uh, yeah. It's me."

She was wearing sweat pants and only a bra; her long hair hung about her face more tangled and still unwashed. I looked up at the ceiling, feeling awkward. Only a single one of the bipedal robots hid behind her leg.

Erika reached out and touched my cheek. "Are you really...?"

"Really?" I looked back at her. "Really what?"

"Really... here?"

"Well, yeah. Yeah, I'm really here."

"Why?"

I took her hand in my own. "I want to help you."

"Help, me?"

"Yeah."

For a moment she was silent, staring into my eyes. She spun around and walked back into the room, the small robot behind her. I hesitated before following.

The room was much worse than before. Papers were strewn everywhere and many of them had ragged edges, suggesting they had been ripped from books. Countless jellybeans were smashed into the carpet or smeared across pages creating dull, disjointed rainbows. Several of the tables were flipped over and scrawled writings covered every centimeter of the walls and even parts of the ceiling. A few of the robots lied motionless on the floor and a few lied on the tables. Only the one following Erika was still alive. The fireplaces were black, unlit abysses.

"What, what happened?" I asked.

"Happened?" Erika leaned back, looking up at the ceiling, then rolled her head to the side and regarded me out of the corner of an eye. "A mouse ran through here. A mouse squeaking and screaming and biting and skittering." She spun around and ran right up to me, grabbing my shoulders. "You *can't* help me."

She was squeezing too hard, her fingers clawing into me. "Erika, *stop*." I tried to push her arms away.

She instantly let go and sat down on the floor. I waited, but she said nothing. All she did was pick up a crushed jellybean and place it in her mouth. She didn't chew. It just sat on her tongue.

I crouched down. "Erika. I don't understand. Last time we were here you'd been here nineteen years and the place was a mess, sure. But now, hardly two months later, and the place is a disaster. Why? What happened?"

She mumbled something softly. The jellybean fell out of her mouth.

"What?"

"J-Jett. Never... never came. No one." She started scratching at the top of her head very quickly. "This is not yours!"

I leaned back. "Wha-what are you talking about?"

"I don't know. Why did I do this? I can't solve anything here. I can't do anything here!" She covered her eyes with both hands. "Go away."

"Why do you want me to–?"

"No. Not you."

"Who?"

"You can't help me, just leave. I don't know why you're here."

"I said I'm going to help."

"How?"

"Um." I had had this conversation thought through a bit, though I had certainly expected her to be more lucid. The plan had basically been to make her focus on finishing her work on the old language, slip her past the warp shell, and take her directly to the Yorrlak standing stones. I wasn't sure if that approach would still work.

"You can't stay here," I said.

"Yes I can."

"But... why?"

"Because."

Dammit, she needed to give me more to work with. "Because what?"

"Because everyone wants me here. I want me here. I won't let myself destroy people or places during my Ego Stage. I *won't* make that pain. You can't convince me to leave. I won't break the lock."

"Break the lock?"

"No!"

"Okay, okay."

"Now you're just playing nice."

"Uh, not really. I'm just..." I took a deep breath. "If you stay here, you're going to kill yourself. Like literally, I bet. You need to get out."

"*No!* I won't be like Jett! I won't be like Radcliff! I won't kill people! Stop trying to convince me to give in!" She jumped up and ran to a corner of the room. The robot scampered after her, but tripped and fell before continuing.

I followed her.

"You can't, you can't. I won't. I've said no so many times. No, no, no no no no." She was wringing her hands against her chest, forehead pressed to the corner where the walls met.

"Erika?" I paused. "I'm not going to hurt you."

She spun around again, her eyebrows tight together, staring so intently at me. She opened her mouth and her lip quivered. She shook her head. "No."

"Erika, it's me. Ethan. It's just me. Ethan."

"Stop! Stop!" She clutched her head.

What could I do now? Maybe I should just grab her and pull her out now. But before I could make up my mind she darted off again; this time running the full length of the room and into her bedroom. She turned the corner and disappeared from view, not bothering to shut the doors. I considered for several more seconds, but my thoughts were interrupted by a bell ringing.

Ding-da-ding. Ding-da-ding ding.

I didn't move, waiting to see what would happen. At first there was nothing, then a door hidden in the wall opened and the butler walked into the room carrying a tray with a small covered dish, a tea pot, a cup, a blue vial, and a few other small things on it. He regarded me for a moment but continued past me, walking briskly into Erika's bedroom. I followed.

Within the next room Erika was crumpled in a corner, knees against her chest. The robot rubbed against her ankle as if trying to help wake her. The butler had set the tray down on a desk and was mixing up a drink. He poured a bit of the blue liquid—warp extract, I assumed—into the tea pot and filled the cup from the pot.

"What are you making?" I asked.

"A tonic, of sorts." He scooped a spoon of sugar from a small container and stirred it into the cup.

"What's wrong with Erika?"

"Her mind. I'm afraid she's particularly clouded today. I do wish you had announced your presence here."

He didn't say anything as he crouched down and offered the cup to Erika. She just stared blankly, not looking at anything specific.

"Does it help? The warp extract?"

"Enough." He lifted the cup to Erika's lips, and she took a small sip. "What's in that backpack you're wearing?"

I was silent a moment. "Puzzle pieces."

"Is that so?" He looked anything but amused. "Why are you here?"

"I want to help."

"You are not doing a very good job."

"I didn't know this was happening."

"Excuses." He tipped the cup to Erika again, and she drank more.

I blinked. "Well, at least I'm *here*. No one else is."

"Indeed. But at the moment she cannot even properly appreciate your presence."

"What are you talking about? She knows I'm here."

"Ethan. I cannot lie and I am in tune with her mind. Her mind has been assailing itself, and I fear your actions have been too boorish. You may very well need to leave." He gave her more of the drink. "Perhaps you can return later."

I closed my eyes. "No."

"Excuse me?"

"I came to help her, and I know how to help her. I'm taking her out of here and that's simply what I'm going to do. You can't stop me."

He set the cup down in its saucer and placed both upon the tray. He stood and turned to me. "I must be the protector. As long as she wishes to leave, the shell will not permit her. As long as she does not wish to leave, I will keep her here."

"What–? Are you, are you serious?" I almost laughed. "What are you even going to possibly *do*? I'm a warper, and this place isn't–"

With blinding speed the butler extracted a flintlock pistol from his coat and a deafening *crack* shattered the air as smoke drifted up from the barrel. I reeled backwards from shock, shock that he had just shot at me. The gun was pointed directly between my eyes.

My ears were ringing as I looked down at my body and

glanced behind me. I definitely wasn't in pain; I definitely hadn't been hit. I didn't see a bullet hole behind me either. When I turned back, the butler looked just as confused as I did. A bead of sweat slid down the side of his face.

"Don't," a small voice said.

It was Erika. She still sat slumped in the corner, but her hand was raised with the Ad Infinitum Fork in it.

"Mistress?" The butler turned to her.

"Don't, shoot, Ethan."

"M-mistress, I apologize. I truly and sincerely apologize, but he threatened to–"

"I know. I heard."

"But then you know I was duty bound–"

"I know. You're dismissed."

His jaw dropped and he reached out to her, but promptly faded out of existence.

Erika had erased the bullet before it hit me. She stood up, her legs wobbling slightly as she clutched the desk for support, knocking the tray to the floor. She muttered something and walked to me, the robot hopping around her feet. She grabbed my shoulders and looked straight into my eyes. "Do you know who made the warp locked shell around here?"

"Uh, no. No, I don't."

"Tavin did. He had to. That was the plan. If I had made it, I could just remove it. But because he made it, I had to stick to it. But he died, and now you're here." She sucked in a shuttering breath. "I d-don't, don't want to leave. I can't leave. I have to believe it. I do believe it. I cannot leave. *I mustn't leave!*" She shook me.

The fear rose up in me again, but it couldn't get a proper grasp on me. She kept staring into my eyes, never breaking contact. It was time, but neither of us could think it. Neither of us could know it. I wrapped my arms around her and grabbed the small robot with the warp energy and shot all three of us straight upwards, smashing a path through the wood above us. Through the ceiling, through floors and rooms, through the attic, through the roof and shingles. Into space. Through the shell around the fortress. Free.

We just drifted in space for a bit, sixty meters away from the feudal prison. Erika looked over at me and smiled. I smiled back. I had done it. I had gotten her free. My hands were shaking.

"Thank you," she whispered.

I smiled. "Yeah. No problem. I– I'm just glad it worked."

"Now what?"

"What do you mean?"

"Do the others know you came here to free me?"

"Not yet."

"They'll be mad."

"Let them be."

A small smile pressed the corners of her lips up, and she looked away. The little robot was kicking its feet in space, panicking that it had nothing to stand on.

"But right now, my original plan ended here." I teleported us three to the Yorrlak standing stones.

Erika chuckled. "The standing stones..." She looked over her shoulder at me. "What made you decide to bring me here?"

"Well, you did mention wanting to study them. Radcliff told me why you couldn't, and I thought maybe they could help. You know, help you crack the old warper languages."

Erika was silent for several long moments, then she threw her head back and laughed. It was a laugh unlike any I had ever heard her give; it was exuberant and rose through her entire body. The robot jumped up and down in place. She skipped to the third stone and pressed both hands against the smooth surface.

"So... I guessed right?" I stepped forward.

Erika spun around on one heel, Ad Infinitum Fork in her hand. She struck it against the stone behind her and the vibration chimed out, spread, engulfed the entire platform, and was gone. Tables and shelves filled the space now with books and papers in neat piles organized upon them.

"Yes," she said. "I *will* finish my work."

I just nodded; it was all I could do in that moment. I felt overwhelmed. I knew I had done the right thing.

*   *   *

Jett was a different story. I knew it as I floated in space sixty kilometers away from his fleet of starships. I was surely too small to be detected by any scanners, but just to be safe I had made a lens in front of me that I could see through but would mask my presence. I was watching the ships through a spyglass, and I had determined which one was Jett's flagship.

I had decided during my contemplations that the best way to stop Jett and whatever was going on with the Rurrians would be to simply stop the attacks. I figured that no more attacks would solve the problem regardless of what the problem was. If it truly was the Rurrians defending, then they could return to peace. If it was Jett fighting against himself, then this would break the cycle. I had the grenades; all I needed now was an accomplice. And who better than myself? I created another doppelganger.

He looked down at his hands, up to me, and smiled. "I know kung fu."

I forced a quick laugh. "Okay, seriously, we really don't have time for this. I'm already shaking and I really just want to get this done."

"I know. Just thought I might try to lighten things up. Also, holy crap, you should invest in some actual classes yourself."

"Yeah, yeah. Later, maybe. Right now let's just focus on Step Two."

"Fun with grenades. Got it," he answered with a smile.

I made a doorway. "Good. Here's your door. As soon as you go I'll move in. Be fast."

"Hey, I must be the infiltrator. Of course I'll be fast." He opened it and stepped into the flagship.

I erased both the doorway and the lens and flew straight at Jett's fleet.

The plan was rather simple. I, the actual warper, would distract Jett long enough for my doppelganger to hide the grenades at key points throughout Jett's flag ship. The trick was that the grenades were perfectly normal grenades except for one very important point: the pins, and only the pins, were warp locked. To that end, when Jett copied his flagship to rebuild his fleet, not even a minute would pass before the copied ship exploded into smithereens. Every new ship would explode, because every new ship would have the grenades sans pins. The icing on the cake was the extensive stealth and martial arts expertise I had made my doppelganger with. Given that and the tools I had sent him in with, he should be able to plant all the grenades unnoticed and escape through a timed doorway that would appear in exactly twenty minutes. It would take him to a hidden base on the Pluto in my original solar system. Everything was set.

To say I was worried was only marginally accurate. "Terrified" was slightly more accurate, but as I soared nearer to the starships the terror slowly trickled into exhilaration. I had shields all around me just to be safe. They had extra warp energy folded into them, so even if I got put in a warp lock they would still last. This was it. Just run interference for twenty minutes. There would be zero communication between myself and my doppelganger for fear of it being traced and him discovered. I would only know if he was successful after I left here and went to the hidden base myself.

Before I had even gotten close enough to distinguish individual windows on the ships unaided, half a dozen missiles launched from Jett's flagship and came straight at me. I dipped down to avoid them, but they curved and followed. They were more agile than I had imagined, so I tried to erase them. They were warp locked. I gritted my teeth and forced myself to ignore them as I continued towards the fleet. I simply had to have faith in my shield making handiwork.

They exploded against my defenses behind me. I felt it. A deep pulling vibration, rupturing my being, shaking straight down to my core. A huge chunk of warp energy was instantly ripped out of the shields: muting the blow, saving my skin. My vision blurred and I tumbled forward, but was able to recover. I kept flying towards the ships, my fear growing again as the excitement faded, and I wondered how many more hits like that I could take. Before I could find out I crashed into an invisible wall.

Again my shields took the brunt of the impact, but I still felt the energy strike against my whole body. I felt flattened. I stopped flying and simply floated. My chest hurt, my arms hurt, my face hurt. Everything hurt. These shields were really not working as I had hoped they would.

I shook my head and assessed the situation. I was in a level two warp locked box. Trapped. Jett was here, standing a meter away from me.

"Esta baboso," he muttered.

"W-what?"

He sighed. "I've found that having trigger-happy gunmen is usually a good thing when assaulting a planet, but not when it comes to targets like you." Jett started circling me slowly.

"What are you going to do?"

"That depends." He was silent as he walk all the way around and back to his original position. "What are you doing here?"

"Um... just trying to talk to you."

"Really? There are much easier ways to accomplish that than flying right at me."

"Like how?"

"You're not a buffoon. You could have thought of something. The thing is, I don't believe you've come to talk to me. However, you were doing nothing offensive. Yet. Only shields and attempted dodging. But why? Why not simply do something easier?"

This new warp lock was very troubling, but if I could just get him to keep talking then my doppelganger would still be able to plant the grenades. I'd work out the rest later.

"Well, here's the thing," I started, "I did think of doing some other things, like maybe a giant space billboard, but I was worried that you'd think it was a trap. I thought it'd be best to be as direct as possible."

"Hmph. Maybe you're lying, or maybe you're actually just stupid. I've heard before to never underestimate just how stupid people can be, but I'm really not sure." He rubbed his chin. "You're no threat, for the moment. No exploding Reality Generators to save you this time. If you really want to talk, you've got it." He started flying towards his flag ship, pulling the box I was trapped in behind him.

Upon reaching the ship, Jett waved away a wall and brought me directly into the bridge. It was mostly rectangular with rows of screens along both side walls and a large window across the front. There was a raised computer console near the center, and two rows of command stations were sunk into the floor with six crew members working in each one. Jett created a comfortable armchair and set the box down on it, so the chair entered the box.

"Please sit," he said.

"You know, um, this warp lock is preventing me from turning off these shields I made. So could you–?"

"No."

"Well, I can't sit then." I took a step forward, and the chair scraped against the floor as my shield pushed it.

"They'll dissipate when your shields run out of reserved energy," Jett said absently as he adjusted the collar of his jacket.

"Fine then." I crossed my arms. What in the world was I going to do? Maybe I could convince him to drop me off somewhere when he thought I had said everything I came to say.

"So, what did you want to discuss?" he asked.

"First." I held up a hand. "I just want you to know that I believe you."

"Believe me?"

"About the Rurrians. Everyone else doesn't believe that the Rurrians could possibly be building up faster than you can attack them. Radcliff even said you could've developed a split personality or something. But I've seen them. I mean, I haven't seen them building things, but I have seen the Rurrians. I don't think you're crazy."

Jett narrowed his eyes and walked up to the edge of the invisible box, staring at me. "I still don't know if I *believe* you," he said softly.

"Why not? Have I ever lied to you before?"

"I threatened your life. I rattled the whole lot of you. Why would you want to ever see me again?"

"Well..." I hesitated a moment. I felt the reserves of warp energy slowly fading out of the shields. "This'll probably sound crazy, but I don't need to like you in order to try to save you."

"Ha. Cute." He turned and walked to a black orb floating in the air. He hovered his hand over it. The orb wavered and started flickering in an out of existence, like a continuous image wipe between one photo in which it was there and one photo in which it was not.

"What, what are you doing?"

"This is an orb of osmium." Jett looked back at me over his shoulder. "Once I store up enough warp energy, I'll make my

326

final assault on the Rurrians. With the knowledge you inadvertently provided me, I'll finally be able to crush them."

"That stuff about the Reality Generators and warp locks?"

"Yes. I will replenish my forces on the field and continue pressing the assault without needing to retreat. They will have no time to rebuild."

"But you don't need to kill them."

"Why not?"

"They've never done anything to you."

"It's what they're going to do."

"But they haven't done it, so there's no way you can know that they will try to take over the universe. Your attacks might be what pushes them to do the very thing–"

"Shut up," Jett said. "Is this all you came here to say?"

"No, no, wait. Listen. I found out something very recently about my own life that shook everything I knew. Before I was realized as I warper I was with this guy, Peter, but I discovered that I had somehow actually made him like a copy of Kris. Before I had even met Kris I made someone like him. The warp energy is so insane, how can you really know for sure what is going on with the Rurrians? What if you really are doing it yourself? Have you even thought about that? Even considered that nothing you think is going on is really going on?"

Jett was very still. For nearly a minute he stood, staring at the orb, then he turned to me. "No. I have to do this. I'm the only one who can see where the Rurrian threat will lead us. I'm the only one who will step up to keep everyone safe."

"Really?"

"Yes."

"And what about putting that bomb on my arm then? Huh? What about that?" My voice rose.

"That was a calculated cost, for the highest reward."

"Really? *Really*? From what I remember, it seemed like you were enjoying the whole thing. Taunting me the whole time. You weren't nearly detached enough to make that a purely *logical* decision."

"*Exactly*." Faster than any Human I had ever seen, Jett came right up to the edge of the box, staring me down, his teeth bared. "So why? Are you? Here? I *can't* believe you're trying to help me."

I shook my head. "But I am! You know, Kris vouched for you!" I quickly racked my brain, trying to remember when exactly that happened, but I couldn't remember the details, because of the pressure so I just kept going. "Erika too! After that hologram thing was shut off. But, but we didn't do anything, because, because we didn't know what to do! We didn't want to fight the Rurrians, but you wouldn't listen to us. And, also..." I swallowed. The shields were almost completely drained now. "I meet– I mean, Kris told me all about you. About how you used to be. I can't believe that how you used to be is simply gone. Just stop fighting the Rurrians. Please. Come home."

Jett's upper lip twitched, and he turned away from me so I couldn't see his face. "Home?" he asked, a slight quiver to his voice. "I don't believe it."

"Look. The other warpers are only afraid, because you're so... extreme. All they need is to see that you've calmed down, then they'll listen and they'll accept you again."

Jett chuckled. "No. No. You're just talking about the Wisdom Stage now. They won't believe I'm in it."

"So? Who cares about the Stages?"

"Everyone cares about the Stages! If they still think I'm in my Ego Stage, they won't have anything to do with me."

"Do you think you're in the Ego Stage?"

Jett was silent for several seconds, then turned back to me. "I suppose I am."

"That's stupid." I crossed my arms again. "Go to the next Stage then."

"You can't do that. You can't just go into another Stage."

"Then fake it 'til you make it."

Jett's mouth fell open as he leaned back. "Fake it? What? Do you even– you don't even understand the reality of this, do you? The Stages are absolute. There's no avoiding them."

"I thought we made–"

"Jett. Sir." One of the crewmembers in the closer sunken command station turned in her chair. "You need to see this."

"Don't go anywhere." Jett hopped down and walked over to the crewmember.

She whispered in his ear and pointed at a monitor in her station.

Jett leaned forward and instantly stood straight up again. "Bring him here immediately!" He jumped back up and smashed his fists into the box, tipping it backwards with warp energy onto another side, sending me and the chair sprawling on the floor. "You lying, subterfuging, wildcard! *What* are you thinking? Did Radcliff put you up to this? Or Alicia! *Why?* What are you doing!"

For several seconds I found myself floating half a meter off the ground, my shields suspending me. But my own weight was pressing against them as they pressed against the ground. My ears started buzzing, and the shield shattered as their energy gave out. With a *thud* I hit the ground, dazed. I blinked several times. Jett was still screaming, and my doppelganger had been dragged in by two crewmembers. I winced and sat up, the buzzing fading slowly.

"—working alone! No one else had anything to do with this! They don't even know we're here," my doppelganger was saying. "We're the only ones who did this, and we were only trying to help!"

"Help by blowing me up! How is that *helping?*"

"Can't you feel it yourself? The pins are warp locked. They only would have blown up the copied ships, not you!"

"Shut up! Why am I even talking to you?" With a wave of his arm, Jett erased my doppelganger. He turned back to me and threw the grenade in his hand at me. It bounced off the box and clattered harmlessly across the floor. "You don't even understand what this would have done to me! If I had replenished my fleet on the battlefield with your sabotage, they would have blown up and not only probably damaged my ship here but also could have left me in a situation in which I could not escape, because I had expected to have backup! This very well could have killed me!"

"I didn't know you were going to be making ships while fighting them! My only plan was for you to run yourself out when you were away from the battle, and then you'd have to stop."

"Pitiful plan. This is unacceptable on every level. You've lied to me, you've tried to trick me, you've almost gotten me killed, but worse, you keep meddling! Why won't you do what you're supposed to do? You're supposed to be *learning*, not *crusading.*" He turned around, looking to his crew members. Many were standing and the crewmembers that had brought in my doppelganger had remained, uncertain of the current situation. Jett waved them all way. "Back to your stations. Everything is fine now."

Slowly everyone left and returned to what they were doing, leaving Jett standing near the center console: his eyes closed, cracking each of his fingers individually. Several minutes passed before he finally spoke again. "I've decided what to do with you. You have to be eliminated. You are out of conduct, and you are now a constant threat to my plan. Your successor will likely be much better, or, even if not, he won't be around for a while."

"You, you can't kill me."

"Yes I can."

"The other warpers won't stand for it! What, what about Kris? You're going to make him lose *two* people now?"

"They won't know; I've already thought of the way to do it. And it is a pity about Kris, but that can't be helped. He'll get over it. He only knew you for a few months anyways. Hardly enough time to be meaningful."

"Of course that's enough time! He, he'll murder you." My arms were shaking. "I, I could see him doing that."

"Compared to almost a century? I think not. But I could certainly see him leveling his vengeance at me, which is why I'm just going to throw you to the Nókrutar. No proof then that I had anything to do with you."

I felt as if I couldn't get enough oxygen into my lungs. "Kris knows I came here."

"Is that so?" Jett took a slow, deep breath. "I don't think I believe you. Your doppelganger said no one else was involved, and Kris would have come and helped you if he knew. If not earlier, then certainly now. I'm just going to chuck you into the Dark Zone near your home planet. If he does know you came here, then why would you be there?" He grinned.

"Don't do this, Jett, please. If you do this none of them will have any sympathy for you when they find out! *Erika* won't even have sympathy for you."

"They'll never know. Alicia is going to be surprised to see the circle break in just a few minutes though."

"Please. Please no!" All that was running through my mind was the description of how Tavin had died, the crushing feeling of the slipstream, the attack at the Queen's palace, and the absolute darkness of their beings.

Jett simply raised his left arm and shot me with a drugged flechette from his wrist controller.

"Ah!" I crumpled inwards, tugging it from my skin, but it was too late. Instantly my muscles uncoiled and my eyes drooped. I fell prone.

"Don't worry. This sedative will be gone from your system by the time you're found." Jett removed the warp lock, but I couldn't do anything at all. He took me by the wrist and we appeared in space, not far from the Dark Zone. "I'll make sure you survive the fall, and the Nókrutar will do the rest. So nice of them to have inhabited a level two warp locked planet as well."

Jett gave me a little shove, and I sailed towards the planet. He shrank from my vision and soon I passed through the protective network of defense crystals. Breathing became difficult and my vision faded.

Chapter 26
Of a Great Man

Sometime later, sometime uncountably later, I woke up.

I was on my back and for several disorienting seconds I thought the stars were falling from the sky, huge purple stars about to bombard the planet. Slowly I remembered and realized I was staring up at the defense network of crystals that kept the Nókrutar trapped. They were the only lights in the pure black sky. I shut my eyes tight, bracing myself for when they all descended upon me. I knew it would hurt.

But nothing happened. I waited, and nothing happened. I opened one eye and slowly turned my head to the side, hair brushing through the dirt. They were there. Countless Nókrutar conglomerates like a vat of darkness all around me. Their glowing dark purple eyes were multitude and non-symmetrical, strange bunches flecked near each other or amassed into a singular huge off-circle eye bleeding at the edges like watercolor. Everything else was so dark and so dry. I shut my eyes again.

Still nothing. It was so silent too. My whole body was shaking, and I wasn't sure if it was because of my fear or the cold. Probably both. I opened my eyes and looked at them. The masses of darkness stayed where they were. I forced myself to turn my head to the other side, to keep looking around. There were more of them on my right side as well. Just staring at me.

What were they doing? Were they messing with me? Waiting to drive home the fear before all crushing upon me like a held back flood? That wasn't something they seemed completely capable of doing. Should I sit up? Would *that* provoke them? Did they think I was already dead?

After several more minutes of waiting and debating with

myself, I decided it couldn't possibly make things any worse. I rose. Slowly at first as I pulled myself from the ground, then I was up. I sat, knees lifted, looking at the shadows around me. The Nókrutar stayed where they were. A slight shifting ripple seemed to pass through them, but they did nothing beyond that.

I tried to say something, but I couldn't even manage a whisper. A swallowed a few times, pressing the lump in my throat down, trying to fight through the dryness of my mouth.

"H-hey," I rasped.

I received no response.

I really needed some water, and my eyes were starting to burn as well. Everything was too dry. If the planet wasn't warp locked I could make some water, but then I realized. I could *feel* the warp energy. It was hardly more than a trickle and not very near to me, but enough to know that I *wasn't* in a warp lock. But how? The manual and Kris had both said this planet was warp locked. But it wasn't. They had been wrong. I half chuckled as I realized I wasn't completely surprised. Slowly I collected the warp energy unto myself, straining to scrape it from my surroundings, and created a small glass of water. I drank it slowly, keeping my eyes on the Nókrutar.

They stood in a ring around me, a constant three meters in all directions. I could have teleported away immediately, but I was curious. I stood up slowly. They remained as they were. I threw the empty glass at the group of them, and it passed through the clustered darkness, smashing against the ground. *Ktch.*

I felt more bold, but was still hesitant, afraid this was too tenuous a balance to safely push at. I pushed anyways. I pulled more energy to me, dredging it up like a rock through thick mud. Once I had enough, I created an orb of pure warp energy smaller than a golf ball. It glowed brightly, illuminating the black ground and the shadow figures around me. I got ready to teleport, and threw the warp energy into the mass of Agencies. It exploded and disintegrated a piece of the mass, and a few individuals of the conglomerate near the explosion broke off and circled around in the air before settling back down into the group as if nothing had happened. They maintained the circle around me.

"What are you doing?" I yelled out, my voice lost in the sea of darkness.

I was still shaking. I took a few deep breaths to calm myself, and I took a step forward. The wall of Nókrutar in that direction moved back, keeping the same distance from me. I glanced behind me. It appeared the mass behind me had moved forward. I took another step and the same happened: the perimeter was maintained.

"Okay, okay, *this* is the weirdest thing I've ever seen. What in the hell are you guys *doing*?" I expected no response; I was simply too confused to remain silent.

I really wished they would stop staring at me. I almost felt a need to constantly spin around so I could continually check all of them. A new singular Nókrutar was rising up from the ground, pulling itself free as it was spawned from darkness. I watched it, but it simply rose up and was absorbed into the mass directly behind it, its eyes joining a small cluster nearby.

So the warp lock was gone, but why? Or had there never been a warp lock in the first place? I recalled everything I knew about Nókrutar and came up with a hypothesis. I pulled more warp energy down. I had to reach farther up, because the area around me was practically depleted. I created a three cementer cube of level two warp lock in front of me. It floated for a minute as I made sure it was stable, then I sent it forward.

It was invisible like all warp locks—just a change in the way the energy flows—but I knew where it was. I could sense it. The cube drifted towards the line of Nókrutar, and as it came near the mass all the eyes bulged towards it a little, focused on the lock. The cube passed through them and into the sea of Nókrutar. Within a minute I felt the lock start to break down and fade from existence.

"Holy shit," I whispered. "They can kill warp locks."

This was really big; no one knew this. I trembled and this time I knew it wasn't from the cold. Could I use this to my advantage? I could swoop right in with these guys killing warp locks and snatch Jett away from the Rurrians without any fuss at all. Of course I wasn't completely sure to what degree their lock breaking worked, but I could test it once I had a Nókrutar outside the Dark Zone.

To do that though, I supposed I'd have to cage one. That'd

be interesting. I wanted to have a single Nókrutar instead of a whole conglomerate of them, and I wondered if making a cage within a mass of Nókrutar would force them to break apart. Either way, I'd need quite a bit more warp energy to do it. It took twelve minutes to draw it all down and direct it at a Nókrutar conglomerate nearby. A rectangle of glass formed inside the edge of the darkness. For a moment nothing happened. I walked towards the cage, and the Agency mass attempted to float back. For a moment the darkness remained attached to the cage, then it snapped, leaving the cage standing in empty space. The Nókrutar within was just a blob of shadow for a moment before it formed into a singular Humanoid shape and also tried to retreat. It bumped into the glass wall and ceased moving.

I stood at the glass cage, looking in, wondering if the Nókrutar would do anything else. So far it did nothing besides stare at me. It was... a strange moment. Something so dangerous so close to me, and it wasn't doing a thing. Dread trickled down my spine, and I snapped my head to the side, looking over my shoulder. The other Nókrutar were still keeping their distance.

I sighed. I had what I needed, now I needed to get out of here. A normal doorway would be too small for the caged Nókrutar, so I knew I'd have to make something larger. I laboriously pulled down yet more warp energy and spun it out into a circular gate with a closed iris door, its counterpart set at the edge of the Rurrian warp lock. Now it would just be a simple matter of levitating the cage through. I held up my hand and the gate's iris slid open.

The whole sea of Nókrutar surged forward, bottlenecking the gate, dashing through me with such haste they knocked me to the ground. They weren't attacking; they were flying, flying away from this Dark Zone and into freedom. I could hardly see anything as they continued to swarm above me; this wasn't supposed to happen. I pushed myself over, to my side, reached up, and fought through the darkness. I forced the warp energy to the door and shut the gate. The rushing stopped. The masses of Nókrutar froze for a moment or two, then floated away from me, reforming the circular perimeter. I could breathe again.

I was so drained. I stopped holding myself up by my arm

and rolled on my stomach, my eyes closed; I might have slept for a few minutes, or maybe just stopped thinking. Finally I groaned and pushed myself up. I tried to create another glass of water, but the energy was so far from me, all of it nearby had been used up.

The Nókrutar in the glass cage had forced itself halfway out, phased through the glass to its midsection and now merely floated there, listless. This wasn't going to work. If I couldn't keep one in a cage, how was I supposed to use one in a fight? I was so thirsty.

I teleported away from the surface, back into space outside the Dark Zone's crystal containment grid. The warp energy washed over me like a refreshing breeze, and I sighed in relief. I drank a glass of water and considered what I needed to do next: destroy the Nókrutar I let out and stop Jett, again.

I made a doorway to the same location at the edge of the Rurrian warp lock where the warp gate had led to, but there were no Nókrutar to be found. Something in my gut started sinking as I looked this way and that, unable to located the Agencies. They must have gone into the warp lock, rushing towards its source. That was bad, right? New step in the plan: find the Nókrutar, destroy them, then stop Jett. Those went right after the "figure out how to stop Jett" step.

To stop him I'd need to stop his ships, and probably stop his crew as well, so I could get at Jett and talk to him. However, I'd probably end up having to subdue him. How in the world could I stop his fleet without bring a whole fleet of my own and making it a huge bloody fight? In the back of my mind I thought about the first spaceship I'd ever created and how the Rurrians had taken over it, then I realized: malware! I could malware his fleet! Then I realized I had no idea how to do that.

But I could make someone who did.

I pressed my hands together and envisioned an AI that could stop entire fleets, reorder commands, overcome any sort of software, work better than any computer, and know everything I was trying to do. The warp energy quickly started rushing through me, building and building, not ceasing. The creation took more energy than I had expected, stretched me further than I could have known. I strained through it, gritting my teeth, forcing myself to endure. Finally it congealed and with a small pop, began to exist. It was simply a small black box with a microphone on top and speakers on all four sides.

"Oh! Wow, I'm alive," the AI said, its voice slightly scratchy through the speakers. "Wow. That's a tall order. Oh wow, space."

"Rob?"

"Is that my name?"

"Yeah. Sure. First thing that came to mind."

"Oh. Rob. Delightful. I'm Rob. And you're Ethan. Ships. We're gonna go stop ships."

I smiled. "We are, aren't we?" I almost laughed but was feeling too nervous. "I still don't know how though."

"We can safely guess Jett has a lot of hacky defenses, but I'm sure I can overcome it. Just so long as he doesn't have an AI too."

"I didn't see one when I was on his ship."

"I know. But what about the other ships in his fleet?"

"What about them?"

"I can't hack them from afar. I need to be touching them. I need to caress their circuits with my sweet, sweet overrides."

"Why? Don't you have wi-fi or something?"

"Because of the way you created me. I don't actually have physical processors. Processors. Or really anything corporeal. *Corporeal*. Oo, that's a good word. Anyways, basically, I run on warp energy and that's why I can work better than anything else out there. But to interact with the physical world I'm limited to this instance of myself, which is this box you're talking to. I'm like a ghost, except absolutely nothing like a ghost. You'll need to make other instances of me and send them to the other ships if you want them all decommissioned."

"Um, okay. Easy enough I guess. Then you can take over his other ships and make them fly away while we land on Jett's flagship and stop him."

"Hands on. Yes. How will we keep in touch?"

I thought a moment, wanting to create something that I couldn't lose in the warp lock. I could make some sort of mental device that was linked to my brain, but warping a microchip or something similar into my brain sounded like a really quick way to probably kill myself. Instead I created a nanite on the tip of my finger, almost invisible to the naked eye.

"Aw man..." I muttered.

"What? What?"

"I'm gonna let this crawl up my ear, but I'm already having second thoughts."

"Why?"

"It's gonna feel so weird, I know it." I hesitated another moment, but I really didn't have time to spare. "Dammit."

I tilted my head to the side and tipped the finger over my ear. The nanite fell near the external canal, and it immediately marched inward. My whole body shuttered as an itching-tickling sensation flared up, followed by an overwhelming scritching sound. It slipped past my eardrum, and the noise slowly died away. I twisted the tip of a finger in my ear and groaned.

A few seconds later Rob said, "It's working. I can hear your *brain*."

"Good. That's set, at least. Now I gotta make a ship, make instances of you, and get–"

"–get defense crystals for the Nókrutar!" Rob finished for me.

I blinked. "Yeah, yeah *I* was about to say that."

"Sorry. Just got excited. It's like telepathy. Like I have superpowers."

"Are, are you sure you're up for this?" I was slightly concerned I might not have made this AI right.

"No! No! You made me right! Let's go, let's go!" Its module started doing slow somersaults in the zero gravity.

"Okay. Just take care of his ships, and I'll do the rest."

"Don't worry. I've got this like entropy's got heat loss. Loss."

I didn't respond. Instead I simply created a high powered telescope to see how many of Jett's ships I would be dealing with. It looked like both his fleet and the Rurrian fleet were still engaged in battle above the planet; however, this information was an hour old. He might have already destroyed the planet by now. What's worse, it'd still take me an hour to reach him.

"You get it?" Rob asked after my lack of response. " 'Cause entropy always has heat loss, so I've *always* got this."

"Okay, okay. Explain the joke on the way, we don't have time. I'll be right back." I didn't make a doorway, I just teleported above Cosmos. I snatched thirty defense crystals and teleported back in an instant.

"Make more of me now!" Rob cried.

"Hang on, hang on. I'm not even sure how many of you I need."

"Better over guess. There were at least fifty of his ships at Rur an hour ago, and he could potentially have made more since then. Make ninety-nine more of me to be safe."

"So, how do I make more of you? Just copy you?"

"No, not exactly. Make shells, that I can be in, that are like my box, but that I'm not in. Not yet."

"Um, okay."

I did as it asked and made shells. They came easier, shaping into the same form as Rob's box. The warp energy slid between them and Rob with ease like so many interconnected pipes and hubs.

"It worked. I didn't doubt you," they all said at the same time.

"Now there's a hundred of you? A hundred Robs?"

"No." Only the original Rob spoke. "All of 'them' are just the other instances of me, and now I'm in more than one place at a time. Time. Kind of like bilocation, except right now it's hectolocation."

"Just so long as it works. That's the important part."

I started drafting up a spaceship that could take us through the warp lock at near-light speed and be able to deploy both the defense crystals and Rob's instances. It ended up being a rather simple craft: mostly cylindrical with the crystals loaded up front under the cockpit to be launched out like torpedoes and the instances in small pods all around the hull in the middle that could detach in unison and fly out like a swarm.

"You should add some shields too and slap their generator on the back," Rob said.

"If everything goes according to the plan we won't even need shields."

"Ethan. Ethan. We all know this scramble-made plan is going to go to shit, so you might as well try to cover all your bases."

"Wow, Rob, so much confidence in me." I crossed my arms. "I don't even know what to say to that."

"Maybe 'I'll put some shields on it now, so we have a smaller chance of dying?'"

"Having doubts there?"

"Never. Call me Frosty. Frosty, Barron of Shields and All Things That Make Us Die Less."

"I'm putting shields on it now." I attached a generator.

"Good. Considering you also made me your acting consultant on this, you would be defeating your own intentions by not listening to me."

"Okay, okay, I got it. We're ready now, come on."

At least I was able to fool myself enough to believe we were ready. I teleported both of us into the cockpit and took flight immediately. From our perspective it wouldn't take too long to arrive at Rur, but it was still more than enough time for butterflies breed in my stomach and agitated the supports of my resolve. I started pacing around the cockpit, Rob sitting on a counter nearby.

"Ethan?" it asked.

"What?"

"Why exactly are you doing this?"

I stopped pacing. "You can read my thoughts, why are you asking?"

"Because mindreading something deep isn't easy. Also your thoughts are really jumbled like... how does that line go? 'Papers strewn to the winds, / kin to currents in the seas?' Seas. That's what they feel like when it comes to the reason."

I was silent a moment; I didn't know how to explain it. "I just... No one else will. Jett shouldn't be trying to kill the Rurrians." I paused. "Jett needs, not punishment or anything, but, direction. Direction, I guess."

"Direction to what?"

"To not killing people."

Rob chuckled. "Circular logic is circular."

I walked back to the pilot seat and fell into it with a sigh. "Doesn't matter. I know I need to do this. What's happening isn't right. I can feel it."

"Feel it?"

"Yeah." I held up my hand as if I was about to grasp a small sphere floating in the air. "It's the same problem as always: when things are non-continuous." I rotated my hand, spinning my fingers around the sphere that wasn't there. "All my life things have always changed and the good parts never... *kept.* And the one really good part, Peter, well, he was just a copy. And Jett. I've seen kind of what he was like before, and I've heard from Kris how things used to be. I just want some stability for once in my life."

"For things to stop changing in ways that hurt."

"...yeah."

"But how exactly does stopping Jett do that?"

I was silent.

"I think I can discern what you're thinking," Rob said slowly, his speakers scratching more than normal, the words filled with thin cracks. "You can change anything, but that is not stable. Stable. You can force permanence, but that is not stable. There are so few things you cannot control, but that control is so slippery and full of echoes and unstable and it makes your teeth want to bite your hair. If you could only control something you cannot, even for just a moment, especially something that has controlled you, it will make you feel like you can force the world to listen to you. Force everything to–"

"Stop." My eyes were shut tight. "I'm not..."

"Oh! I'm sorry!" Rob's box jerked forward a few centimeters, scooting closer to me. "I was just following and I didn't know where I was going and I–!"

"It's okay," I whispered. "I'm really... really not. I'm doing this, because it should be done." I paused. "Because they know they can be changed, and they don't deserve to die for that. They don't deserve to live their whole life afraid."

We both stayed silent after that, my gut still churning, Rob unable to shiver. We sunk into a strange desire for the journey to end while still dreading the destination we'd reach.

Soon we could see Rur and Jett's fleet assaulting it. The battle in space was over. There was no more Rurrian fleet, there were no more intact space stations, and the partial planet armor had fragmented into several large sections that were crashing into an ocean below. Jett's fleet was bombarding the planet: red glowing missiles and quad-lasers burning from the tips of the wings exploding against an energy shield which was the only thing still keeping the Rurrians alive.

"Where are the Nókrutar?" Rob asked.

"Did we overtake them?"

"Maybe?"

I edged forward in my seat. "I guess we did. We were going really fast." I paused. "I dunno though; I don't like not knowing where they are. We should probably just play it safe." I started rotating the ship around.

"The crystals are just gonna start orbiting Rur if you fire them now," Rob said.

"I know, but I'll feel safer." I launched the crystals back in the direction we had come, and they flew away. "Can you tell if Jett's seen us yet?"

"Visually, probably not. Radar tracking though, probably yes."

"Then this is it." I reoriented the ship and throttled up, an instant blast rocketing us towards Jett's flagship. "Launch all your instances as soon as possible!"

"Ready. Firing in six seconds. But what about Jett's crew?"

"Oh. Right." A tingling ran up my spine. "Umm..."

"I could open some airlocks once I take control."

The flagship was looming ever closer. It continued firing upon the planet, and I started to believe we'd make it before Jett could retaliate. Rob's ninety-nine instances launched and cruised towards the other ships in the fleet.

"We don't really have time to waste, Ethan," Rob said.

"I know, I know. Just wait until we latch on and you take over, then tell me what my options are."

"Okay. They might be limited at that point."

"I know."

Seconds before impact my ship slowed as to not pulverize the both of us. With a jolt and scraping of metal my ship skidded along the side of Jett's and finally latched on via magnetic anchors.

"Hacking commenced!" Rob said, his voice bubbling with pleasure.

"How long will it take?"

"Don't know. Just do the hatch boring now."

"Okay, okay."

I flipped a switched and a high powered laser on the underside of my ship started cutting a circular opening into the hull of Jett's flagship. It extended a connecting duct as it dug down and soon a safe path between the two ships was created. I started receiving mental reports from Rob's other instances of successful ship incapacitations. They starting flying them away from Rur, pulling them to anywhere but here.

"Do you have it?" I asked Rob.

"No, no. Not this one. Jett's fighting me."

"Does-does he have an AI?"

"No. He's fighting me manually. I'm trying to get a datahold."

I crouched down over the hatch in the floor, readying myself for when I'd have to plunge into the flagship. "How much longer?"

"I dunno, I dunno. Hang on." Rob paused. "Ha! Shorted out the terminal he was working at. That'll give me just the few seconds I need." He was silent again for three seconds. "There. I'm basically in now. Locking down all doors. There's still crew in the hallways though; they'll stop you. Want me to flush them?"

My hands were shaking. I clenched them into fists.

"Ethan! Should I flush them or not?"

"Fine, fine. Fuck. Flush them out."

"Airlocks opening now. Count to six and go."

My eyes were closed, and I kept telling myself that it was okay. Jett had made the crew. They weren't losing anything; no one was losing them. It was to save the Rurrians. Save the Rurrians.

"Ethan! Go!"

"Going." I pulled the hatch up and over, swinging it outwards, and climbed down.

The short tube had cut diagonally into a hallway below. A little more than halfway down gravity shifted as I left one ship for the other, and the ladder was now on the top of the slanted tube. Surprised, I lost my grip and tumbled out into the hallway, hitting the metal floor hard. Pain throbbed up from my ankle as I fell to my side.

"Ah! Fu– ah!" I rolled on my back and reached down to grab my foot. I must have twisted it, or sprained it, or something. I wasn't sure. I couldn't even remember what the difference was between a twisted ankle and a sprained ankle.

"<They mean the same thing. Are you okay?>" Rob asked me in my mind through the telepathic connection.

"I'm fine. I'll manage," I muttered out loud as I pulled myself up by a door handle nearby, and tested the foot. It hurt to put pressure on it, and I cursed myself for not having thought to bring along some warp extract. There was nothing I could do now; I was too far in to stop. I gritted my teeth and limped down the hallway using the walls as support.

"<Ethan! Good news. I just found something really good. You remember how the crew stations on the bridge were sunk into the floor?>"

"Yeah."

"<I found an emergency extendy panel. Panel. It covers them up so they can't get blown out if the bridge is breached. I'm closing them now. You'll be able to deal with Jett without interference.>"

"Great. Yeah. Still gotta deal with Jett."

"<Panel,>" Rob said again. "<That is a good word. Such force in that sound.>"

I ignored Rob and continued limping down the hallway. I came to an intersection and realized I had no idea where I was going. "Rob."

"<Yes?>"

"Where do I go?"

"<Where are you?>"

"I dunno. Can't you find me?"

"<Maybe. Jett's trying to get back in again and– oh.>"

All the lights in the hallway flicked off. Not even a door switch glowed in the new absolute darkness.

"Rob?"

No response.

"Rob!"

New lights started coming on. They didn't all turn on at the same time, instead they sequentially turned on down the hallway, one red light after another until the whole place was awash crimson. A vaguely female automated voice sounded over the intercoms.

"*Emergency systems activated. Running complete diagnostic now. Diagnostic running. Major errors will be reported as found. Full diagnostic will be reported when finished.*"

A cold panic washed through my chest. "Is that an AI!"

"<No. No. Just automated systems. Wow. Jett's good at this. Oh. Hang on.>"

"Are you gonna stop those emergency systems?"

"<Nope. They're a separate system. Harmless. Need to stay focused on Jett. Also. Found you on the cameras. Cameras. Go left, first right, straight until you see a lift on the left, go up to deck D, left after exiting the lift, and straight ahead. Type in 'robrox' with an 'x' and no caps on the double doors. See you there.>" He spoke very quickly and cut off instantly after.

I sighed and was thankful I could remember things well. I hobbled off in the direction I had been told. The ride on the elevator took only a minute, and the double doors to the bridge were visible down the hallway once I exited. I typed in the password and they slid open.

Jett was typing away at the computer console near the center of the bridge, his back to me. He was almost smashing the keyboard with the force he was applying. The three consoles to his immediate left were shorted out. Some of the crew in the sunken command stations were pounding on the metal cover shields, but Jett was ignoring them. The doors shut behind me, and I stood by the wall, using it as support to hide my injured ankle.

"Jett."

He froze. A second later he turned, his eyes squinted, his mouth part way open. "H-how? How are you still alive? How are you *still alive!*"

"Apparently Nókrutar just want a little balance in the world." I shrugged.

Jett shook his head. "You did this then." He pointed behind him. "I was afraid the Rurrians– you though. You and some stupid AI!"

"Oi! I am *not* stupid!" Rob said over the intercoms.

"Goddammit!" Jett glanced at the computer screen behind him and back at me.

"Yeah, I only need a few seconds to really get into these things," Rob said. "Great distraction tactics, Ethan. We're such a team! Team."

"Jett, it's over," I said. "Your ships are gone, and Rob has control of this one. Stop fighting the Rurrians. Come *home.*"

"No! How can you *not* understand? There won't be a home if the Rurrians aren't destroyed. They'll come. Maybe not when we're alive, but eventually. Eventually they'll come. They'll kill us all."

"No they won't."

The ship's automated voice cut in. *"Unknown craft detected attached to the outer hull at 2-10, off deck F. Containment and Elimination procedures initiated. All available crew converge."*

"Perfect," Jett said. He pulled back his sleeve and pressed a button on his wrist controller.

The whole ship went dark and silent. I hadn't noticed it before, but there had been a slight vibration pulsing through the floor that was gone now. I began to feel like I was falling as the artificial gravity disappeared too. I grabbed a bar in the wall to the left, the sudden movement lifting me off my feet. The only light on the bridge was the dim glow of Rur through the large window.

"Jett, what did you do?"

"I shut everything down."

"<Um. Ethan.>"

"No engines."

"<Everything's gone.>"

"No generators."

"<I don't know what I did.>"

"No fans."

"<Did I die?>"

"Not even life support. There's nothing for your AI to run on."

"(Rob, shut up,)" I thought. "(Jett just turned everything off.)"

"<Oh. Good. Not my fault then. And oh. I see it now. I'll just turn everything back on.>"

Jett had remained where he was since he had not made any major movements yet. He glanced down at his wrist controller. "That 'Rob' is already trying to fight through the activation codes, but I'm confident my crew will reach your ship before he can get back in."

"But all the doors won't even open now, will they?"

"Most of them have manual overrides in the event of a loss of power. And they'll just cut through the ones that don't. Do not worry. They will make it out to your ship and destroy whatever is keeping your craft linked to mine. You. Won't. Stop me."

I warned Rob mentally about the incoming crew.

"<But things were going so well!>"

"But why? Why, Jett?" I asked. "Your fleet is *gone*. What do you plan to do even if you do get this one ship working again?"

"I can still win. All I have to do is destroy one more generator, then I'll have more ships. And kill you of course." Jett stretched out his arm. "You remember my flechettes, right?"

"Even if you drug me Rob can still take over the ship fast enough to end this."

"I doubt it. And I'm not going to drug you. I'm going to blow you up. Don't you remember? I do have explosive flechettes in this."

"Explo–! No. Stop. Listen, Rob can tell everyone else if you kill me. You won't get away with it."

"I'm prepared to sacrifice myself at this point." He paused. "Yes, yes I think I am."

The warp lock distorted for a mere instant, and a flash of white and blue sparks lit the room. I flinched, my arms half raised, my body frozen. It was surprisingly less painful than I had expected. Then I heard the beeping. Beeping. I opened my eyes, and I wasn't dead. I was still on the bridge and something new had appeared to the right, something egg shaped with a blinking red point of light that flicked on with each beep it produced. And each beep came faster than the one before it.

"Fuck!" Jett wheeled around and fired two flechettes at the bridge's window.

For a sickening second the flechettes hung in the window, inactive, then they detonated, blasting a wide chunk from the window, the bomb instantly jettisoned into space as the air whooshed out. I was pulled forward and crashed against the center console, the blow knocking the last breath from my lungs. My hands grabbed the two things closest to them as I stared out through the open fissure. Everything became perfectly silent and serene as I floated in the vacuum.

"<Ethan! Don't try to breath! Close your eyes!>"

The thing my right hand had grabbed started shuffling, and

I realized it was Jett. He took a moment to punch me. In the dim light he was only able to hit my shoulder, but it was still unexpected.

"<Now you're probably gonna die, because the ships is shut down and the doors–"

The jettisoned bomb exploded off the upper front of the ship. There was no heat, no shockwave, only a blinding light that quickly faded. Jett reached up and fired two more flechettes. Their explosion crumbled the doors in, and the metal didn't hold. The pressure forced them back out towards us as they were blown into the room. The doors flew over our heads, and one disappeared into space as the other crunched against the hole in the window, precariously held up by the edges. New air screamed past us. I could breathe but was pressed against the console as the last shards of metal bombarded me.

"Holy shit! Holy shit! I don't even know how we're still alive!" I said as I kept holding onto Jett's jacket.

"Because you don't fucking know anything about space!"

Jett kicked me, and I slid to my side at the edge of the console. He started climbing up along the floor, and I noticed there were small holes covering the floor that fingers could easily fit into.

"<He's right. There are a lot of technicalities about space, most of them due to the vacuum. Ironically, some things are a whole lot less–>"

"Not now, Rob! Get this ship back on!"

"<Right! Sorry. The ship. Especially since the crew is probably still coming. I won't be able to see them, because there's no cameras outside our ship.>"

Jett looked back and saw me sitting up. He turned awkwardly, reaching his left arm back to aim over his right shoulder at me. He hit the button with his chin, and I rolled over as a flechette impaled itself a millimeter into the console before being dislodged by the rushing air and blown away. I lunged forward, grabbed Jett's ankle, and pulled him back down. He crashed atop me and tried to aim his wrist controller at my face. I grabbed his arm, pushing it aside as he launched another flechette up at the ceiling.

I clamped my hand over his, forcing his finger to hit the fire button several more times and two last drugged flechettes whizzed harmlessly away from me. He punched me on the cheek. I fell back, dazed, as he started climbing up the floor again.

"<Ethan! I think someone is banging on our ship. Also, I think I have the engines working again!>"

A deep rumble vibrated through the ship as the engines fired at full thrust.

"What is your AI *doing*?" Jett yelled.

"<Good test, good test. Stop. Stop now!>" Rob was silent a moment, and the engines became still again. "<Ah, good. Okay. Good news, engines are almost a go. Bad news, our orbit may now be decaying. Decaying.>"

"(Are you kidding me!)"

"<I, I could lie if you'd like me to.>"

"Jett! We're going to die!" I yelled at him.

"No. *I* won't. My crew should almost be at your ship."

"Then what?"

He didn't respond. He had reached the destroyed door frame and climbed out into the hallway. I started climbing after him, my ascent slowed by my injured foot.

"<Also, the banging stopped. I don't know why the banging stopped.>"

I gritted my teeth as I climbed, grateful I at least didn't have to put much weight on my sprained ankle. It was difficult pulling myself up against the torrent of air, and I wondered exactly how much we had left in the ship.

"Jett!" I called up to him as I climbed. "I really think you need to rethink this air problem. If Rob doesn't get the ship back on in time we'll all suffocate." I reached the broken doorway and pulled myself into the hallway.

In the darkness I could just make out Jett's outline, his right arm looped around a bar attached to the wall. "You backed me into a corner. However, your AI won't be a problem any longer."

Rob started screaming in my mind. Jett raised his left arm and shot me twice straight in the chest with two regular, non-drugged flechettes.

"<Our ship's blown up! Our ship's blown up!>"

I gasped, lost my grip, and curled inwards. My visions blurred as my eyes filled with tears, and I was pulled back into bridge and flew towards the broken window. I hit the precariously balanced door on my back, the pain making it hard to think. I could hardly breathe; the air was thin and I couldn't take in a full breath.

"<We are so both very dead! Our ship's engines are gone and I'm crashing towards the planet and I can't stop. I'll see you planet side. Maybe. If you survive, and I survive the crash. I'm sorry I couldn't help more. Please don't die.>"

My mental connection to Rob slowly faded until it snapped as he drifted out of range. I gritted my teeth as each breath sent a new wave of pain across my chest. One flechette had hit me a few centimeters under my right collar bone close to the sternum, and the other just above my right nipple.

Jett leaned over the open doorway and fired the two last regular flechettes at me. One ricocheted off the metal next to me, and the other pierced my left shoulder as I cried out in pain. I rolled to my side, trying to protect myself, but the flechettes shifted inside me. The one next to my sternum caught on bone and tore my flesh where it had entered. I could barely think of anything besides the pain.

Jett dropped into the bridge, perched on the center console. He pressed a few buttons on his wrist controller, and red lights turned on in the room and all down the hallway behind him. The whole ship vibrated momentarily. A blast shield started sliding down over the outside of the broken window.

Once it closed the air in the room stabilized, and I could mostly breathe again. I tried to fill my lungs, but instead I felt dizzy and coughed up blood. The field of red droplets misted in front of my face, slowly floating away. The metal shields over the sunken command station slid away.

"What happened?" one of them asked Jett.

"He did." Jett pointed at me. "Get him away from that door. The gravity is running up, and I don't want him crushed and killed just yet. Everyone else get this ship ready to go the moment the startup procedures have finished. We need to stabilize our orbit."

Two of the crew pulled me away from the door hanging in the air, bringing me next to Jett as I left a small stream of blood behind me in the air. We slowly drifted towards the floor as the gravity grew until I was resting on my back and the others were standing. The crumpled door teetered for a moment on its side and fell with an echoing *thud*.

"We're at the cusp of the atmosphere," a crew member said from within one of the recesses. "And... and we appear to be *under* the planet's energy shield."

"Under the shield? How?" Jett jumped down to see the screen himself.

"I don't know, sir."

Jett stroked his beard. "We'll worry about it later. Tell me about the planet. Is anything else coming for us?"

"No, sir. Our scans aren't picking up anything."

"Keep scanning. I don't want to be surprised." He climbed back up. "What's the status of the ship?"

"Air levels are at 63%. All breaches have been sealed, and all systems are running at normal."

"Seal storage and get everyone out of the crew quarters and seal those too. Vent that air into the rest of the ship. And you," he pointed to a crew member, "get one of each flechette clip. I need to reload. Everyone else continue the attack. Find the closest Reality Generator on the surface and destroy it."

The crew hurried to their duties and Jett crouched down over me. "Looks like I've won. Just think, all I had to do was turn off my ship and shoot you with a few flechettes. It's almost funny."

I didn't respond; I was still in too much pain.

Jett took hold of a flechette and pulled it out with a slight twist. I moaned, my voice breaking, eyes pressed shut as tight as they could. I tried to push him away, but he grabbed my wrist and wouldn't let go.

"Don't worry, Ethan. Bleeding out is a very peaceful death. It's a small token I will grant you in defeat."

My shirt was soaked with blood that dribbled to my sides, running into a few of the small holes in the floor. I didn't want to die like this. "P-p-ple...ple..."

" 'Please?' Ethan, don't you think–" He paused and looked up. "Wait... I can *feel* them!"

I pulled my arm away from him, and he let it go. I pressed both hands over the hole in my chest.

"Sir?" The nearest crew member asked.

Jett jumped to his feet. "Their Generator network! I can feel it now. We've never been this close before. I... I can end this *right now*. I can erase them all! Ha!" He started laughing and turned to his crew. "I can feel a cluster of them right now, almost directly beneath us."

"We're passing over several coastal cities now," a crew member said.

"Target all of them."

"Yes, sir."

The bridge fell silent aside from my periodic coughing. A trail of blood was flowing out from the corner of my mouth, and I felt like I would never want to move for the rest of my life. In the haze of pain I still remembered why I was here though, still remembered that I had to stop Jett. I held a half formed plan in the front of my mind, desperately clinging to it even as the room seemed to start spinning.

"Firing now," the crew member said.

"This is it, ladies and gentlemen. The final victory over the Rurrians," Jett said.

My thoughts wouldn't stay straight. They wobbled and my body shivered and I struggled to remember what to do. I could feel the Reality Generators now too. The trick to feeling them was to open up a chance to let their flickers of far off energy flow into you, and I couldn't block them out now. The whole network beneath us glowed in my mind, searing a web across my thoughts. Slowly I reached out one hand, but not towards the Generators.

The missiles hit. In an instant the raging band of disrupted warp energy charged through space, rushing around us like a wave. And in that moment, we both made our moves.

Jett cackled with delight, his face split wide into a grin, his eyes almost squinted shut. "At last I–!" The grin disappeared. "N-no! I, I felt them go! I erased them! I erased them *all*! Why am I *still–*?" He took a step forward and ran flat into the wall of the warp lock I had put around him.

"Sir!" Several crew members stood and turned towards him.

"It's Ethan! Don't let him die, or this box around me will be permanent! Get a med team in here! Now! *Now*!"

I smiled to myself; I hadn't even considered that aspect of the warp lock. The crew jumped to my assistance, elevating my feet and compressing the wound without a flechette. Within a minute a small med team arrived and set up next to me. They cut off my shirt and stuck a blood transfusion into my arm. The blood wasn't working fast enough though as everything continued to dim.

"Don't let him get consciousness either!" Jett yelled. "Keep him alive but keep him under!"

"We're trying!" one of the doctors yelled back. Even though he was next to me his voice still sounded so far away. "He's suffered massive trauma. We need another blood bag!"

I wasn't gone yet. This wasn't happening.

"S...stop..." I whispered.

Everyone froze. I was lying on broken metal and concrete. I was bumping along in a van, and I wasn't here at all. I opened my mouth and warp extract poured into it out of thin air. I tried to swallow, but choked and twisted to my side, spitting out red and blue. I convulsed, my body tightening into a ball, the flechettes gone, everything burning. A voice was still yelling.

I turned my head, sucking in more extract, the liquid overflowing past my lips, over my chin. I finally opened my eyes again. Half a dozen faces and a dozen hands were around me, all of them statues: unchanging. I looked down and saw the holes still open in my chest. Slowly I reached over them, slathering them in uneven streaks of bio foam.

"I'm... not..." I mumbled. I raised a vial to my lips and drank. Once it was empty I let my arm fall and let it go, the glass rolling across the floor. I closed my eyes and didn't move.

Jett was pounding his fists on the warp lock around him. "Damn you, Ethan! Damn you!"

"Shut up... Jett..." I said slowly and opened my eyes.

A small group of new crew members were running towards the bridge. I created a metal wall covering the hole of the missing door. With a groan I slowly sat up and pushed a few crew members away from me. All of them inside the bridge had been frozen.

"Fucking darts," I said.

"My crew is going to kill you! Do you understand? They are going to *murder* you."

"But then you'll be trapped forever." I took a deep breath and sighed. "So they won't actually."

The crew outside pounded on the metal wall a few times, but I ignored them. I stood and attempted to take control of the ship but discovered it was warp locked. I frowned, but a better idea a popped in my mind. I created a small box with speakers all around the side and a microphone on top.

"Ethan!" Rob cried out. "You're not dead!"

"*Fuck.*" Jett hit his forehead against the warp lock.

"Surprisingly not. Is your other instance on the planet now?" I created a new shirt and pulled it on.

"Nope. Or at least, I don't think so. I overheated during entry and shut down, so I don't know what happened."

"Well you're back now. Could you take over the ship again? I want to land and talk to the Rurrians."

"Aye, aye! Also, report of my other instances: I'm flying the rest of Jett's fleet at near-light speed away from Rur. What would you like me to do with them?"

"Just take them somewhere far away where they can't hurt the Rurrians."

"Got it. These ships have jump drives, and now that the warp lock is gone I can use them. I'll take them to a nice planet in some other galaxy, give them enough time to evacuate the ships, then I detonate the cores."

"Sounds good." I turned to Jett. "Now it's actually all over. I'm gonna tell the Rurrians that they're not in danger anymore, then I'm taking you back with me."

Jett just snarled, curling his lips and baring his teeth.

"Have you even tried talking to the Rurrians before?" I asked.

"How do you think I found out their exact plan?"

"I have a feeling those weren't the kinds of talks I'm referring to."

Jett just crossed his arms.

"We're entering the atmosphere now," Rob said. "We're going to need a custom landing pad though. The ship's shape is kind of awkward. Awkward. I don't think it was ever designed to actually land."

"I'll make it. Just tell me where." I created a monitor floating in the air above me that provided a view outside the broken and covered window.

"The Rurrians will kill you," Jett said softly.

"I doubt it."

He sat down cross-legged and placed both palms flat against the metal floor.

We dipped under the clouds and flew over a city. Several dozen missile batteries fired surface-to-air missiles at us, but I erased them before they even made it halfway. The ship approached an open field, and I created a landing platform that would support Jett's flagship perfectly. We landed smoothly, and Rob shut down the ship.

"What are you going to say to them?" Rob asked.

"I'm not sure. I guess I'll ad-lib."

I took a deep breath to prepare myself, then created a camera on a tripod in front of me. It started broadcasting my image to every video screen on the planet, everything from TV's to monitors to cell phones were receiving my image. Even ones that had been off were automatically turned on for my presentation.

"Hey! Hi, everyone. Um, wow, you know, this is really weird. I've never talked to more than like thirty people at one time before, so I'm really glad I can't see you, because I kinda feel like I'm gonna trip over all of my words in just a second here."

Jett groaned. "How the fuck did this happen?"

I ignored him. "Anyways. So. I'm Ethan Stroud, and yes, I'm a warper. But I'm here to help. Honest." I put my right hand over my heart and raised my left. "I hope most of you speak English. Actually, why don't I just make some auto translators." I snapped my fingers. "There. If I did that right my words will be automatically translated as they're broadcasted to the most common language of the area they're being received in. It should've worked at least.

"Anyways, like I was saying I want to help. Jett here was the one attacking you." I motioned behind me. "I stopped him though. He was attacking because you all know about us warpers, and Jett believed you were a threat. I don't believe that though. I don't believe you really want to kill us. The way I see it, it looks like you're just defend–"

There was a flash at the floor a meter from me, and another small egg shaped, shiny metal device with a red blinking light appeared in a shower of blue crackling sparks.

"Oh shit!" I jumped in place and frantically swiped my arms at the bomb, erasing it from existence. "Whoa! Fuck. *Not cool*, guys. Not cool."

"Don't really want to kill us, huh?" Jett asked.

"Okay. Uh, um, okay. I know you guys are probably really scared right now." I turned around in a slow circle as I spoke, securing the area. I put up an explosion shield around us and created a level two warp lock within, so nothing else could be teleported to us. "I remember how scared the people on the space station seemed last time I was here. But look, your warp lock is down. If I wanted to kill you I would have already."

"Goddammit, Ethan, you're making a fool of us warpers!" Jett banged his fists against the floor. "How are two bombs not proof enough? Do you need a *third*? You're trying to talk to them, and they're still trying to kill us. Can't you admit I was *right*?"

"No. I still don't believe it. They're scared. People do stupid things when they're scared." I looked straight into the camera. "I think we really need to make this into more of a two-way conversation. And I mean two-way with words." I temporarily unlocked a small bubble before me and created a cheat sheet within it that had the location of the Rurrian leaders. "I'm coming to talk to your leaders now. I'll be there in a minute."

I turned the camera off and walked up to Jett. "I'll come back when I'm done. You'll be safe here and so will your crew."

"Oh joy." He wouldn't meet my eyes.

"Just hang tight. Rob, hold the fort down."

"Roger. I got this."

I made another temporary unlocked area and created a doorway that lead to the council room of the Rurrian leaders. I pushed it open part way.

"Hey, surprise doorway," I said through the crack. "Don't shoot me please."

I opened the door the rest of the way. Within was a small room with unadorned walls and a semi-circle table with seven people sitting. Three of them were men, the other four women, and they all bore grim expressions. In front of them were three rows of fully geared military soldiers wearing full facemasks of black fabric and black tinted goggles. They had their rifles trained on me, but none of them fired.

I walked in slowly, my hands raised. I had made a shield in front of me to be safe. This place was out of range of my mental connection to Rob.

"I hope you all heard what I was saying a few minutes ago. The most important parts were the 'I come in peace' part and me trying to explain that Jett was the one attacking. You see, it's a little complex, but we go through these Stages..."

As I spoke I let the door close and disappear behind me. That was when I felt it. I trailed off, blinking. It felt like a warper was right behind me. It was that subtle pull, a subtle shift. Like feeling a depression in a mattress from someone sitting close to you. But who? Who?

I wheeled around. In the wall behind me was a window into a huge cylindrical room with a ceiling too high to see. There, in the center of it, was the machine. A great pronged looking device: three pointed towers at equal spots around the side of a metal platform that had controls and screens across the side of it. Between the towers pure warp energy crackled like lightning, flashing blue-white light as the bolts arced up and dissipated. At the very center of the machine, upon the metal platform, was a wired brain in a glass dome. The brain was "alive," the machine was not, but the whole of it could warp like any living warper. I was dead sure of it.

"What, *is* this?" I asked slowly.

The room remained silent, and I turned back to face them.

"I'll just find out, you know. I can do that." I held out my hand and a cheat sheet appeared in it. I read it quickly. "A 'Warp Node?' A *'Warp Node?'* That's what that is? How in the world does this thing even exist? I thought, I thought we were... the only ones."

"You're not." An elderly lady said at the far right of the table. "This is this crux of our strength. This is why we will *not* be conquered." She stood and pointed at me. "I don't know if you truly mean us well or if this is some sort of ruse, but by the fabric of reality, we will not be extinguished."

The other leaders nodded in agreement, and one of the men started clapping. He stopped after only a few seconds.

"I don't want to conquer you. You all are in *no* threat of being conquered now. I'm going to take Jett away from here, to the other warpers, and we'll figure out–"

"How many warpers are there?" She asked quickly.

"Six."

She nodded. "Shoot him."

I flinched and back stepped, expecting spikes of strain as bullets cascaded against my shield. But no one fired.

"Wha-what are you waiting for? Shoot him! In the name of all Rurrians and in defense of your planet, shoot him!"

In my mind I was frantically thinking of how much Jett needed to *not* know this happened. They were just afraid. I knew that was it. I could see it in their eyes, at least from the leaders' eyes. I couldn't tell from the soldiers, because of their goggles, but I assumed they were scared too. Still nothing happened though. One of the soldiers near the center of the first line stepped forward and pulled off his mask and goggles.

"He said he doesn't want to harm us." This soldier was young, surprisingly young. He hardly looked as old as myself.

"I will have you for insubordination! All of you!" she yelled.

"With respect, High Councilor Agnete, we all know the Reality Generators are gone. If he wanted to kill us, we'd already be dead," the soldier said.

"Yes! You understand!" I said. "This is perfect, this is exactly the kind of person I need as an example for Jett! What's your name?"

"Don't tell him," High Councilor Agnete commanded.

"Markus."

"Cool, okay. Markus, you've got it exactly. Without a warp lock I can literally do anything I want. But you know that, because you guys have got your own warp machine right here. How do you even *have it*?"

"Rediscovered technology. We've had it working for almost six years now," Markus said.

Many of the soldiers had lowered their weapons. The other leaders stood and looked fearfully among themselves.

"*What*? Okay, okay, you'll have to tell me about that later. Right now, quick, I just need to know more about you. I need to use you to support my case that you guys don't really want to kill us." I made a cheat sheet with the highlights of Markus's personality and background.

Markus grinned halfway. "She just ordered us to shoot you," he said.

"I know, I know. And Agnete, look, all of you Councilors here, look. Just, please, you have to believe me. None of us warpers want you dead. Jett's going through his Ego Stage, which is something we just go through. Can be very destructive, can be very bad, but I don't believe it has to be. I think with the right direction it could be harmless, even if it really is unavoidable. Look, I'll come back later, after I sort out everything with Jett. First, I need to go get him and–"

"I'm already here."

I didn't breath for a second as a termer washed through my hands. I turned and Jett was indeed here. He stood looking through the window at the Warp Node.

"This makes so much sense now," he said.

"How did you, how did you get out?" I asked.

"Incompetence on your part. You neglected to make a barrier at the bottom of my box since you assumed the floor would make a strong enough sixth wall. When my crew arrived and destroyed Rob, I told them to cut through the ceiling of the deck below, and then, like magic, I'm free and here."

"It was a trick!" High Councilor Agnete yelled.

"No! No, it wasn't. I *swear*." I looked down at my list of information about Markus and started rushing through my words. "Jett, listen, listen. Look, Markus here believes me. He doesn't want us dead. He's here defending the leaders, because they have so few people left. They sent all their strongest to be the first line of defense. He's lost a lot of his extended family already, and he actually loves liver and onions. He writes poetry in his spare time, and he–"

"Shut up, Ethan. Just shut up. This has gone on too long. Far, far too long." Jett snapped his fingers and every Rurrian in the room clutched their chest, screamed, and fell to the floor convulsing. "I'm going to glass this entire planet, because erasing this lot will be too good for them. Not after all the sweat and blood you've put me through. And I'll do that right after I kill you." He clapped his hands together and drew them apart, creating an orb of warp energy between them. He started stretching his arms out to fire it at me.

"No!" A trick jumped instantly to my mind, something simple, something I had seen in a cartoon before.

I spun the floor Jett was standing on and the beam of

energy exploded against the wall to my left and continued a quick path along the wall as Jett continued to spin. It shattered the window, toppled a tower, and struck the brain within the Warp Node.

A flash of blue light flooded the world mono-color, and the explosion imploded first. Not even a second of darkness, then out again. Blue light burning, ears ringing. The blast did not move anything. We both remained on our feet—arms raised in protection—and the bodies remained where they had fallen. Through the opening between the fabric of my sleeves, I saw squares. Squares. Nothing remained where the Warp Node had been. Literally nothing. Now it was a rift through which I could see sparks of light and an ocean of square tiles writhing and cascading away from the blow in a movement that reminded me vaguely of dominos. And several squares were floating freely, floating out from the rift. One headed straight towards me.

All these things I barely perceiving in the seconds of the explosion, then the square collided with me. I started to fall backwards but never hit the ground.

Chapter 27
Flashbys

A million and one places passed before my eyes. My mind was cascading over minds. Over worlds. Through lights and through spaces I could not see. Each thing I alighted upon mixed, and there were no lines. No borders. I took some of them. They took some of me.

A woman gasping in a mirror as I stood behind her. The heart monitor beeping. Beeping. Beeping.

A great explosion of heat as a sun flattened and shimmered, being drowned in water.

I stretched further than I could ever stretch. My toes in the sand, my face in the not so empty space past a universe. Or so I thought. Great elongated flying became my life, no, my existence. The name "Ethan" fell away from me and for a great length of time I knew myself as no thing.

But it was the time of a dream and the knowledge of a dream. The sort of time and knowledge that merely presented itself from no source but was still irrevocably understood as true. As a thing that merely was. Not known. Just was. It was. I knew it to be so even without going through the motions. Even without going through the countless millennia. Millennia. Mill any after.

A father reaching out for his child. I give the child the last few centimeters she needed.

Always an ocean beneath me. Always I was in the ocean even as I came to different shores. Shores abroad, shores abroad. But a shore I still stayed in as well. I was no where. No place.

I paced for ages around a smoky table. Its edges wavered whenever the oscillating fan turned back to us.

We sat on a sill, still we were eating. Above the expanse of a city bubbling with foam and froth, bubbling with the things it was striving to be without conscious direction.

But I could feel the direction. I could feel wayward collectors consuming, consuming as well. Never enough. I fled from those shores even as they tried to follow.

Laid to rest in my chest was a gem of density once. Too great to encompasses with my palms. Too heavy to encompasses with my eyes.

The shores were devoid of trees. The shores were not trees. The sand had tress, and the water wetted the sand and flowed between the great spaces between each individual grain.

A shower of water over a yellow flower as it spun like a top in a fast-motion uncurling, flattening bloom.

I sat across from a boy, floating behind him. I was only a light, and he tried to tell me things. Things. How could he be so certain?

Sure. Sure. Dance with me, stars, dance with me. The spinning is not pulling. I knew there were strings on which they swung, and within the strings were vibrant life and great swellings of water. Water always merely trickling through my fingers; too pure, too pure.

I remembered bloom. I remembered bright lights, remembered from before I swam through light. I remembered. After so much time I remembered. I sank back, ever so slowly. Like a body being lowered within a dark cave by a thin stream of light that pierced through its chest. Lowered into another body that was the same body without color. Slowly, slowly. Lowered on its back. Lower, lower. Arms hung back, head hung back, looking up at the stars through the ocean. I remembered.

I forgot.

And these fragments are all I can ever recall.

Chapter 28
Overhead

My head struck the ground as I fell onto my back. I laid there for a minute or so, blinking repeatedly up at the ceiling. My thoughts were a jumble of yarn; I could not remember where I was or what was happening. I pushed up with both arms and looked around.

The room was blackened: the walls scorched, the floor dusted with ash. I had none on myself though. I coughed and stood up on wobbling legs, slowly becoming more steady, brushing streaks through the ash. Everything was coming back to me. The last thing I could remember was an explosion and... and the knowledge that there was some lapse within my mind. The room where the Warp Node had stood was now gone, caved in with dirt from above.

The Rurrians still lied motionless. Jett was sprawled on the ground as well, also devoid of ash. He had slid his arms up above his head on the floor, wiping clear a trail in the ash like halfway making an ash angle. His fingers gasped at air. Then he lifted himself, floating above the floor, and stared at me.

"What happened?" he asked.

"I don't remember."

His eyes narrowed and he snarled. He whipped his left arm up and shot several flechettes at me, striking me in the chest.

With a *whof* I doubled over and clutched at them. "Dammit, Juh... Juh..." My jaw went slack and my legs gave out. I fell to the floor and felt a warp locked box slam down around me.

"Now stop me, Ethan! Now do it! Defy the warp locks again. Do something *clever*. Stop me now! Stop me *now!*" Jett howled with laugher.

Fuck, I though. I couldn't move at all. I couldn't even move my eyes. I was stuck staring slightly down at the ground, Jett only partially in my vision.

"You can't can you? Of course not! Not this time, little one, not *this* time. There's no half measures here, no cracks you can squirm through." He drew a long knife from his boot. "And no one to help you."

Was there anything I could do now? Anything at all? I didn't think so. Not a single thing. In hindsight my mind started devising an automated warp extract dispenser that I could wear on my arm, or maybe as a belt. Yeah, that would have been a really good idea. I wished I could at least close my eyes. No one was here. Everyone else was dead and I was alone. So alone.

But then I remembered. Alicia. I could always contact Alicia! I had no idea if there would be enough time, or if the circle on my palm was even activated since I couldn't see my hands, but I started screaming out with my mind. Alicia! Alicia! Alicia! Help! In the back of my mind I knew it was a last ditch effort.

"You just kept on breaking the warp locks, you just kept on breaking the rules. You can't escape now. Not this time, not while I'm watching your paralyzed body. I don't know how you always found a way out of the warp locks before, but I know you can't this time! Now you are going to die, and I am going to do it myself. I have you trapped now, and you won't get out of the warp lock this time. Not, this, time! I don't know how you've done it before, but now you've finally hit a lock you can't wiggle out from. This is the end of the line for you; the paralysis is ensuring that. How does it feel, Ethan? A warp lock you can't escape? Won't you tell...?"

I was confused now. The fear was still throbbing at the front of my mind, but I hadn't expected him to rant this long. Especially not so repetitively. Jett was raving on but hadn't even taken a step forward. I heard footsteps between us, and I felt a surge within me that would have been a smile if I hadn't been paralyzed.

"What have you gotten yourself into?" Alicia asked. "Last I saw you, you had pulled a classic Kris and simply ran away without explanation. Now it seems you've pulled what is becoming a classic Ethan: getting tangled up in all the *mierda*."

She sighed. "All of the problems. *All* of them. Just couldn't leave well enough alone, and now we're pulling you out of the fire again. Well, more accurately, *I'm* pulling you out of the fire this time, though I haven't quite made up my mind about that yet."

She walked over to Jett and stood in front of him. He was still yelling about me and warp locks, unable to see her.

Alicia had to speak loud to be heard over him. "You know, I think this is probably terribly ironic, but I feel the truth depth of it is lost to me." She approached me, couched down, and lifted my head to look at her. She grinned like a lioness looking down at prey. "I was originally going to put you both in a time loop while I assessed the situation, but alas, this little warp lock has shielded you. Now you get to hear all my debating, and I'll feel slightly worse if you do end up being the one to die today."

She released my head and it fell to the floor, my forehead knocking against the cement. I really wished I could say something. I tried communicating with her mentally through the palm ring.

"Oh stop it," Alicia said. "All I'm getting is a general distressed feeling from you." She paced back to Jett and considered him. "I have no love for Jett, as you know. He used to be a good person, but not so much anymore."

"...because this time you can't even move, not to mention warp. I finally have you, and this will be the end of it all. I'm going to..."

Alicia pulled a loose hair off Jett's shirt. "If I let him kill you, then he'll kill the Rurrians, and we'll never have to hear about them again. That would be so much more relaxing, and I'd get to put off dealing with a childish warper for another nineteen-almost years. But on the other hand, I doubt Kris would get over losing another person, but honestly, if he can't toughen up and just deal with it then he doesn't really deserve any sympathy, don't you think? However, the problem then would still be with Jett. Maybe he will proceed to attack the Warper Born, and maybe not. He's never did actually say he wants to kill the Warper Born. But does that really matter? The truth is, after all, what you make it.

"But. But, but my hypothesis was not completely baseless.

He *did* say he wanted to kill all non-warpers who knew about us. Do I want to take that chance though? I would rather like for Raine to have a nice childhood. Maybe I could just kill both of you. That would solve everything. Yes." She was silent a moment as she bit the tip of her pinky. "*But.* But, but, but. You are so strange, you know that? And in an indirect way, you were protecting my Raine by standing up to Jett. I suppose I should take that into consideration."

She paced back and forth for almost a minute. "I'm curious. I think what I will do is merely even the playing field." She crouched before me again. "I'm going to cure your paralysis, but no more. I do hope you understand my musings from before. One does have to consider all of the angles before acting, don't you think?" She smiled and injected my arm with warp extract, then stood. "Ta-ta. Do make good use of the element of surprise." Alicia disappeared and time resumed as normal.

"...is the last time." Jett walked forward and crouched over me. "It's a bit disappointing that no one will get to witness my final victory. Maybe, actually, maybe I'll let you watch me glass the planet first. Just to show how much you failed, hmm? Like that idea?"

"Nope!" I sprung up and barreled into him. Before we even hit the ground I had teleported us to a random planet far, far away.

"*E-than!*" Jett twisted the name in his scream. "*How? How?*"

I rolled away from him and jumped to my feet, erased the knife, and prepared to block oncoming attacks. I noticed without paying much attention to the fact that we had appeared in an empty lot within a large city, skyscrapers rising all around us.

"I guess I just get really–" I stopped as soon as I saw what Jett was doing.

He had raised his arms above his head and was forming an enormous orb of purest black with a silhouette of gray around it. Instantly I recognized it was anti-matter. He was forming it larger and larger, any second it would collide with the buildings around us.

"Jett!" There was nothing I could do but brace myself.

I stepped back, arms up, my footing sure, and created the

opaque shield around me that would protect against anti-matter. I waited, expecting Jett to dispel the anti-matter and start pounding against the shield directly. But that didn't happen. Everything remained quiet within my small protected space. Calm.

Several minutes passed, and I still didn't drop my stance. Several more minutes. I bit my lip. Was he baiting me? Or...? I created a small monitor in my grasp and a floating camera outside the shield.

"Oh. Oh no." I dropped the shield. I was standing on a small circle of ground in empty space. The planet was gone; the anti-matter had done its job.

"Jett!" I screamed. "Jett! No!"

But even as I screamed, I knew the sound went no farther than the air bubble around myself and was lost to the silence of space.

Chapter 29
With Great Uplifting Movement

Dead. Was Jett truly dead?

The only person who could know for certain was Alicia. I hesitated a moment, considering all she had just said to me in the time loop. But I didn't care. I had to know. I took deep breath and made a doorway to the Grand Library, arriving outside Alicia's house. I pounded my fist on her door. Alicia opened it.

"Is he dead?" I demanded.

"And hello to you too, Ethan the Victorious."

"He's–?"

Alicia held up her hand. The white circle glowed softly but was broken, a sixth of it missing. "Congratulations."

"No."

"Tell me, how did you do it? Something direct, like poison? Or did you get a little more creative? I personally would have driven a train into him. Very unexpected."

"No. No, he blew himself up. With anti-matter."

Alicia raised her eyebrows. "Oh? How foolish of him. Then he deserved it. Isn't that right, Raine?" She glanced back over her shoulder.

She was sitting cross legged on a cushion in the center of the living room, the small purple ball in her hands. "Yes. Right as can be."

"That's my girl," Alicia said softly.

I could only shake my head. "I– I'll see you."

I took several steps back and made another doorway. I slammed it shut and let it disappear as quickly as possible. I was on the Moon of my home planet. Breathing still wasn't coming easy, and my hands were halfway numb. This wasn't supposed to happen. This wasn't supposed to happen. I needed to talk to someone, but I didn't know if I could speak at all. The list was short: Radcliff or Kris. I went to the Restaurant instead.

I went straight to the counter and fell into one of the chairs. My heart was still racing, and it was all I could do to keep my hands pressed flat and steady on the counter. Bot seemed to be ignoring me, simply staring over my shoulder. That didn't bother me though; I knew how Bot normally acted and was perfectly happy with having a few minutes to try to compose myself. I leaned forward, resting my forehead against the cool marble counter.

"I just cleaned that," said Bot.

"Really? Really?" I rolled my head to the side. "I've never seen you clean anything in here."

"That does not mean I do not do it."

"Ugh. Sorry." I lifted my head.

"I can see you are exhausted though, so I will let it pass."

"Oh, now you tell me?" I placed my head against the counter again.

"Yes. And I can tell your exhaustion is not something so mundane as running or lifting chairs. You have been in battle."

"What do you know about battle?"

"Probably more than you think."

"Well, well," I licked my lips, "do you want to know what just happened to me?"

"I will entertain the hypothetical."

I paused, considering what Bot said for a second. "Well, basically, I guess I just traded a whole planet of people for... aw shit, I didn't even save Markus!" I stood up but suddenly felt faint. I leaned against the counter.

"Who?"

"A Rurrian Jett killed. I need to go back."

"A Rurrian?" Bot's head turned to me. "Stop. You are in no state to go anywhere."

Maybe not. I sank back into the chair. "It's all ruined."

"What are you babbling about?"

"I tried to stop Jett, well, I did stop Jett, but not how I wanted too. And he killed some Rurrians—he killed Markus— and I forgot to remake them when I teleported Jett and myself away and then Jett blew himself up and Alicia is even more insane!" I pressed my forehead against the counter again and covered my head with my arms."

"If you actually want to involve me in the conversation I need you to start at the beginning and actually explain everything."

"You never normally need me to do that, Mr. Deductor."

"I will not accept that title."

I grunted and we were both silent for a time.

Finally I lifted my arms and turned my head. "I stopped his fleet from attacking the planet. I had Jett trapped for a bit, but then he got out and almost killed me, but Alicia rescued me. I teleported Jett away, but he blew himself up with anti-matter."

"Does not sound too complicated."

"It was a bit more involved. Honestly, I'm not really sure how I survived, I–" I stopped and squinted my eyes.

"What?"

"I dunno. I kinda, I almost thought I remembered something for a moment there. Like a dream. But... no, I don't remember anything."

Bot leaned forward. "When?"

"Just now."

"No. When do you think you remember having a dream?"

"Oh. Um, I dunno. Before Alicia rescued me."

"Interesting." Bot straightened.

"Why?"

"Nothing. Tell me though, why do you feel so worn out by this battle if you won?"

I sat up slowly. "I, I don't think I won."

"Why not?"

"Because Jett's dead."

"Is that not what battle is?"

"I guess... but I didn't want to kill Jett. I thought I could avoid it. I thought I could get him to stop attacking the Rurrians and save him and them."

"And why did you want to save the Rurrians?"

"Because they know they're not real."

Bot leaned forward slightly. "Elaborate."

"Well, like, the Rurrians knew about us, so they knew they could be erased or meddled with or changed. They knew. They knew they weren't solid. When Jett blew himself up, he blew up a whole planet too. I didn't even remake that planet. I didn't care about them. And I didn't care, because they didn't know. But the Rurrians knew. And Markus knew, but I forgot him."

"An interesting qualifier to determine importance."

"It seems like the only qualifier that matters."

"Who exactly is Markus?"

"One of the soldiers in the Rurrians' bunker. The soldiers wouldn't shoot me, even when order to. And he stood up for me. But Jett kill him and everyone else in there too. I need to go back and save him."

"How do you save someone who is dead?"

"He'll only really be dead if I never remake him."

"So he will never truly be dead so long as you remember him?"

"Uh, yeah. I guess."

"Then why remake him?"

"So he won't be dead. I just said that."

"Is that a good idea though?"

"Why wouldn't it be?"

"I am asking you."

I hesitated. "But I can save him."

"Then why not do so right here? Right now? Remake him here and he will be saved."

"But... I, no. I need to be *there*. Where his body is."

"Why?"

"Because. Because." I raised my arms and dropped them. "That's where he died, and where he's supposed to be, and everything."

"Ethan. You are having such trouble answering these questions, because you are not acknowledging that it is irrelevant if Markus is alive or dead or if he is here or there. He did die. If you remake him he will still know he is unreal, because he will know he died. And if you remake him such to the extent that he does not know he is unreal, then by your own measurements you will not have saved him. You cannot save Markus if you want him to remain true."

"But... but..." I was shaking.

"When last we talked, you told me you were making a doppelganger for Peter."

"Yeah, so?"

"Tell me, why did you let Peter go in that manner?"

"Because it was the best way to do it."

"Yes, but *why*. Remember what your exact reasoning was."

"It would have betrayed him if I had done anything else. Betrayed who he was and betrayed the time we had together."

"Exactly. It is the same with Markus. His death happened. It will forever be a true event. To undo it would be to betray his past and betray his reality, even if it saves his life. The mantel of godhood is the most painful of all."

"But then... I failed. Completely."

"Failed? Please. Tell me, how have you failed?"

"I didn't save anyone."

"You saved a whole planet, or did you forget?"

"But Jett."

"You were not the sole author of his fate. His destruction was brought predominantly by his own hand."

"It doesn't feel like that."

"Tell me this then: Do you think you took the correct actions?"

"In what?"

"In trying to stop Jett and the ways you tried to accomplish that goal?"

I thought a moment. "Yeah. Yeah, I think so."

"Then it was noble."

"So I did the right thing?"

"No. I said it was noble, not that it was right. Why do you Humans always intertwine virtues so quickly?"

"But, wouldn't 'noble' imply–?"

"No. It would not. It would imply that you were trying to do the right thing, even if you did not in fact do the right thing. Being noble easily includes doing the wrong thing for the right reason."

"So did I do the wrong thing then?"

"I did not say that."

"Then what are you saying?"

"I am saying that you took noble actions. The consequences are what they are and sound to have been predominantly out of your control."

"I don't feel like you're really helping here." I slumped the head against the counter again with a soft thud. "Ow." I had slumped a bit faster than I had intended.

"You could go talk to Kris. I am sure he would say exactly what you want to hear."

"I doubt it. He's gonna be really mad when he hears about this."

"Why do you suppose that?"

"Because I snuck out and got into so much danger. He won't like how close I came to dying. And then there's the whole problem with Alicia. If I tell Kris and Radcliff about what she did, that'll be a mess as well."

"What did she do?"

"She debated whether it would be best for her to kill me, kill Jett, or kill both of us. She decided to just leave it up to chance."

Bot was silent for several moments. "I thought you said Alicia *rescued* you?"

"Well, yeah, it wasn't the best rescue. Not by any stretch. But if she hadn't shown up, me and the Rurrians would all be dead now for sure. I'm really worried about Raine though. I just saw her and she seems... different. Too much like Alicia."

"In what way?"

"Like, just as cold as her mom. She wasn't like that at all when I first met her. But then again, neither was Alicia."

"Alicia's change can easily be accounted for, but not Raines. This is perplexing."

"Yeah... it's fucking shit." I groaned. "Powers beyond measure and I still feel like I can't do anything."

"You do not always have to do something. You do not always have to intervene."

"I know. I know. But, still." I paused a moment. "Oh. Oh, and you won't believe this. The Rurrians had a Warp Node."

"They *did*? You are *certain*?"

"Whoa. Yeah. You... you know what that is?"

"No. No. I can merely draw conjecture from your statement that it was not a good thing. Nor expected. Also from its name it is safe to assume it affects reality in some direct way." He kept his eyes dead on me. "Elaborate."

"Well, it was like three giant prongs with a brain in the center. It was a machine that could reality warp. Just like us."

"Did they ever use it?"

"I guess so. I never actually saw it used directly, but that would really explain how they teleported bombs to us, or why Jett thought they were rebuilding too quickly. I dunno why they didn't use it when I was down in their bunker. The leaders seemed really bent on killing me."

"With *precise* detail, tell me when, how, and what number of bombs they teleported to attack you with."

"Just twice." I leaned back in my chair. "Once in space after I had stopped Jett's ships and again after we had landed."

"How much time was between both of those incidents?"

"I really don't know. The ship was crashing and Jett was almost killing me." It seemed to have happened so long ago. "Damn, I never would've thought I could even live through something like that."

"At least give me your best guess."

I shook my head. "Sixteen, twenty minutes? Half an hour? I really don't know. *Why?*"

"When did you go to their bunker?"

"A few minutes after the second bomb. Are you gonna explain these questions or what?"

Bot was silent a moment. "Given what you have told me, I would assume that the Rurrians did not use the Warp Node against you further, because they were unable to do so. Machine made warping would take an incredible amount of energy. It wouldn't be so quickly reactivated."

I grunted. "I still can't believe that's possible. How could a machine *possibly* use reality warping?"

"I would not know."

"It had a brain. Well, a brain in a jar. Literally. And when Jett's beam hit it that's..." My eyes drifted to the side. "It was, gone."

"The brain?"

"No. The machine. There– there must have been an explosion. The room was collapsed with dirt afterwards. But I can't remember it."

Bot remained silent.

"Oh, I suppose you're gonna tell me how you're superior again, being a robot and all."

"No. I was not about to say that."

"Then what were you about to say?"

"Nothing."

I stared at Bot for a minute, my lips pursed. I broke the stare with a sigh and a shaking of my head. "I guess I need to go face the fallout now."

"What fallout?"

"Like I said, I need to go tell Radcliff and Kris what happened. And, Erika. I, I have to tell her too." I was starting to feel so tired. It was certainly well past my relative midnight.

"That Jett is dead?"

"Yeah." I stood, my chair scraping against the floor. "Later." I walked away from the counter and made a doorway.

"Ethan."

I looked back.

"Be... Do not do anything stupid. Would be a shame to lose you after you have survived so much."

I smiled. "Bot. Did you just admit to actually caring?"

"No. It was merely a directive."

"Sure, sure. Thanks." And I left.

I was back on the roof of my tower. I was so exhausted now. Even standing was too much effort, and I let myself fall forward as I created a dense cloud to catch me. I lied there on my stomach for who knows how long. What had I done? Did I really do the right thing?

I groaned and rolled over, extending the cloud so I wouldn't fall. The sky was still mostly cloudy with stars breaking through here and there. Finally I got up and teleported back into my bedroom. Kris was still there asleep. He was on his side, curled up a bit. Like I hadn't left at all. Like nothing had happened.

I stepped out of my shoes and crawled up next to him, running my fingers through his hair. I didn't want to wake him, but I didn't want to be alone either. Putting my arm over Kris, I curled up as close to him as I could and kissed the side of his neck. It was strange how you could be so close to someone yet still feel so alone. I felt some tears in my eyes, and I started sniffing as quietly as I could. My crying woke him anyways. Kris, I'm still really sorry that I couldn't have saved it for morning, but you were so good about it too. I guess I'm feeling nostalgic as I write this.

He twitched a little and turned his head without opening his eyes, and mumbled something before clearing his throat and finally asked, "What's happening? What's wrong?"

"I messed it up. I messed it all up. I tried to help but... and you all said to stay away."

"What? What are you talking about?"

I hesitated for the longest time. Kris turned over and opened his eyes, staring into mine. He didn't push me, he just waited and put his arms around me.

"Jett's dead."

"What?"

"I tried to help. I tried to stop him from fighting the Rurrians, but it didn't work and now he's dead and I was really trying for that to not happen. Really, really trying." I shook my head.

"Whoa whoa whoa. Whoa. It's okay. You're gonna be fine." He pressed his forehead against mine. "Was it a dream?"

"No."

Kris was silent a moment. "Jett's dead?"

"Yeah."

"How?"

"Blew himself up. Trying to kill me."

His hand squeezed my shoulder, and he pushed his forehead a bit harder against mine. "When? Are you hurt."

"No. I'm not hurt. I'm... It was just... an hour ago. Or something."

He didn't say anything then. He just held me.

"I don't know what to do," I said.

"Shh. Nothing now. I have you. Later. Later."

Thank you, Kris.

Chapter 30
Godly Yet Creaturely

"Dead?" Radcliff asked.

"Yeah. Jett's dead," I said.

No one spoke again for a minute or two. He, Kris, and I were in the Archive, in one of the green carpeted lounges. Kris and I sat on a couch, him leaning against me.

"I can't believe this. Do you understand now why I said we need to leave those who are in their Ego State alone?" Radcliff asked.

"Maybe."

Radcliff wiped a hand over his forehead and walked over to a counter. He pulled the steeping tea out from his cup that was next to plate of chips and gravy. He hadn't touched them since I had started recounting the incident to him. "I suppose, out of all of the possible outcomes, this one is far from the worst. It's by no means favorable, but by no means the worst. Jett is gone, but I think the foremost consequence of that will lie with Erika. I'm very worried how she will react."

"Me too," I said.

"I think I should be the one to tell her," Radcliff continued.

"Why?"

"Because I know her better than you, and I can weigh my words better as well. And if she does become furious, she will not be able to immediately direct it at you. I do not want to subject you to any further possibly of danger while I can still intercede."

"Just let Radcliff do it," Kris said.

"Um, about that... she's not in her fortress anymore," I said.

Radcliff sat in an armchair and looked up at the ceiling. "What?"

"I got her out."

"Out? You got her *out?*" He looked back at me. "How in the universe did you get her out?"

"I guess I just found a loophole, because she wasn't the one who actually took herself out."

Radcliff sighed. "Where is she now?"

"At the Yorrlak standing stones. Or at least that's where I last saw her."

"Then I will have to try to find her. Hopefully she'll still be there. It'll be one more thing to talk to her about."

"What do you mean?"

"I mean I'm going to ask her what her plans are now. What she's going to do with her re-found freedom, if she yet has plans."

"Oh." I looked down at the ground. "When will you go?"

"I'm not sure. Within a few days for certain. I will need time to prepare my words, but the sooner she knows, the better it will be I think."

"Fine." I wasn't going to try arguing with him.

"As for the rest of your recounting of the events, I simply cannot understand your account of the Warp Node. But even more so, your account of the Nókrutar."

"Me either." I shook my head.

"Are you one hundred percent certain that what you told us is accurate? Jett threw you into the Dark Zone? And he didn't leave a shield around you? Didn't make you hallucinate?"

"No, it *really* happened. I was on a Nókrutar planet."

Kris shifted on the couch next to me. I glanced at him. His eyes were closed, and he had crossed his arms. I place a hand on his elbow and stoked his arm with my thumb.

"And you're certain they saw you? That they knew you were there?" Radcliff continued.

"Yes. They were all staring right at me. I even blew some of them up."

"Then I do not understand how you are still here."

"I don't either. The lack of a warp lock sure helped."

"Which is equally incredible. You are absolutely *certain* they can destroy warp locks?"

"Yes." I shook my head. "I even tested it, like I told you."

Radcliff was silent. "It was not the most empirical test." He blew on his tea before taking a small sip. "Perhaps you made the warp lock cube flawed, or you weren't able to properly maintain it due to the lack of ambient warp energy."

"But warp locks never need ambient warp energy," Kris said.

"I know," Radcliff said. "But if Ethan had created the lock with a flaw it might have required warp energy."

"I didn't make it wrong." I looked away from him, eager to finish the conversation and leave. I had known this would be unpleasant, but now it was just frustrating me.

Kris leaned forward. "What about the Rurrians? What do we do about them now?"

"Nothing. Nothing has changed," Radcliff said.

"But they actually *did* have reality warping machines," Kris said.

"Apparently. And only one, which is gone, as Ethan said." Radcliff motioned with his teacup at me.

"I want to go talk to them again," I said. "Tell them the news about Jett. Let them know that they're safe, because of how things turned out." I paused. "I think they could trust us eventually."

"Why are you still so concerned about them? They are a singular group of Humans, insignificant when compared to the countless masses in the universe."

"But they're not insignificant. They *know*. They know about us, and they know reality is shaky at best. They think we're a threat to them." I pointed off at a random direction. "I wanted them to know we aren't and that they don't have to be afraid. We won't change them."

"And why do we have to explain all of this to them if we are not going to be affecting them?"

For a moment I considered telling him about Markus, but that part of the story seemed too personal in some way. Like it would be a waste to tell him; as if Radcliff wouldn't be able to fully appreciate what had happened. "I think it's the right thing to do."

"Not a very logical answer." Radcliff took a long drink of tea. "I know I can't stop you, but I must strongly recommend against it. Everything is easier when we don't have to concern ourselves with every other being in the universe. Just let them have their little solar system and ignore them. Now though, I'm going to need some peace to myself to reflect on these happenings and decide on my words for Erika."

Kris stood up.

"Wait." I also stood, but I held Kris's arm so he wouldn't leave yet. "There's one other thing that happened after Jett blew himself up, when I went to Alicia to make sure if he was really dead or not. You already know how Alicia acted, but I think the real problem is Raine. She, she was almost the same as Alicia. Like she didn't care about anyone anymore either." I stopped a moment, looking for words. "I think– I think your daughter needs our help."

"Ethan." Radcliff rubbed one of his temples. "Ethan, Ethan. I... know about this."

"And you're just going to let it happen?"

"No. Ethan, you *need* to trust me. You were incredibly lucky with Jett, but there is no way you could pull off the same feat if Alicia were to consider you an enemy."

"Fine." I looked away from him.

Radcliff must have seen something in my eyes before turning away, or he deciphered some clue from my posture or tone. He stood and put a hand on my shoulder. "Kris, I need to talk to Ethan in private for a few minutes."

"About what?" he asked.

"Why he *must not* interfere with Alicia." Radcliff turned to me. "If nothing else, you must listen to me now."

Kris and I shared a glance, and he understood. He took a step away. "Fine. Ethan, I'll meet you at your house." He disappeared.

I looked back to Radcliff. "So what is it?"

"I need to show you it." He teleported us.

We appeared in a short tunnel of metal and concrete. I had no idea where we were, but it look reminiscent of the bunker Raine had been in when we had gone to the audience with Erika. All I could sense around me was a sea of churning warp energy creating a sphere around us. And the sphere was huge, perhaps around the size of a small moon. I could sense nothing beyond it.

"Where are we?" I asked.

"Within the planet we were just on, Cosmos. I did mention

it was a bastion of warp energy, but it's a little more than that. I can hide certain things behind the obfuscating energies stored within the core here." He started walking down the tunnel. It branched off at various intersections. There were a few doors in the walls as well, but none were close together.

"Obfuscated?"

"Hidden. Like in a fog of light as I'm sure you can feel."

"I know what it means, but why do you need to hide anything here?"

"There are reasons. Some things are too dangerous." He stopped at a metal door "Now, this is incredibly important. What I am about to show you, you mustn't tell *anyone*. Not even Kris. I had thought after you discovered what Peter was, you'd fall into the normal pattern of a new warper, but you haven't really. I can't have you crusading against Alicia when there is no need to."

"How did you know about Peter before I did?"

"After meeting you I thought it would be prudent to look into your background, so I could better understand where you had come from and where you might go."

I crossed my arms. "Well thanks for spying on me. And how can you possibly say there is no need to help Raine?"

Radcliff shook his head. "See for yourself."

He opened the metal door, and it swung inwards silently, revealing a cozy room with a loft. The walls were wood, the floor carpeted, and well-trimmed furniture filled out the space. The contrast was so jarring to the cold hall outside. Then I saw who was inside.

"R-Raine?" I asked.

She looked up from a book she was reading. "Ethan?" She glanced at Radcliff. "I thought you weren't going to let anyone know about this?"

"I wasn't, but I was afraid of what Ethan would do if he didn't know."

"What do you mean?" Raine glanced at me.

"I'll tell you the whole story later," Radcliff said. "The simple explanation is that he ran into your doppelganger and was very concerned. I had to put those concerns at ease."

"Raine's been a doppelganger this *whole time*?" I asked.

"No. Not the whole time," Radcliff said.

Raine set her book aside and hopped off the couch. "Dad did a switch back when you all went to Erika's place and talked to Jett."

"Basically. I have you to thank for it actually, Ethan. Your discovery of making doorways allowed me a new tool. Before the audience I made a doppelganger of myself and another of Raine, but the extra Raine doppelganger—the one that is with Alicia now—doesn't know she's a doppelganger. My doppelganger took a timed doorway to the bunker Alicia had created and made the switch. The end result: Alicia has a Raine that will completely mold to her will and keep my real daughter safe."

"Oh. Wow." I rubbed my arm. "You were way ahead of me then."

"Yes. I told you to trust me," he said.

"Then what now?" I asked.

"What do you mean?" Raine asked.

"Are we going to do anything else then? To help Alicia?"

"No. We... we have to leave her be," Radcliff said.

"But, why? Can't we at least try to talk to her? Try to do something?"

"There's nothing to do," Radcliff said. "If she continues as she is now, then her Ego Stage will merely be centered on Raine and probably trying to give her reality warping. It's already about as controlled of an Ego Stage as possible. She will remain with the doppelganger until she leaves the Stage. If anything dire should happen, well, Raine will be safe." He ran a hand through her hair. "And maybe it will be enough to shock her from the Ego Stage early."

"Same hands off approach then, huh?" I crossed my arms.

"Yes, because the only action necessary has already been taken, and your 'hands on approach' was so successful."

I grimaced and looked away. "I *tried*."

There was a moment of silence, then Raine asked, "What happened?"

"Jett's dead," Radcliff said slowly. "Accidental. He blew himself up."

"And you were there?" Raine asked me.

"Yeah."

"Why?"

"I was trying to stop him. I thought I could help. I thought, I really thought that if I could just break his attack on the Rurrians then I could get him to stop. I was just trying to help, I really was."

She reached out and touched my wrist. "It's okay."

I met her eyes, and it was the strangest thing. I could see her, not as the child she looked like, but as the adult she was. Her words carried weight. "Thanks," I murmured.

"Now, Ethan, remember. I only shared this with you, because I thought it could save your life. Absolutely no one else must know about Raine being here, do you understand? It's the only way this ruse will keep her safe."

"Don't worry, I won't tell."

"Good. Now I'll take you out." He turned back to Raine. "Is there anything you need?"

"No. I'm good for now," she said. "But, does this mean Ethan can visit me now?"

Radcliff was silent a moment. "I suppose. With the proper precautions."

She smiled. "Cool."

"But we must go now," Radcliff continued. "Kris is waiting for Ethan."

"I'll come back soon," I said.

She nodded and waved. "Until then."

Radcliff took me back out into the hallway and closed the door.

"Hang on," I said.

He leaned forward a bit, waiting for me to continue.

"Why did you do something for her but not for the others?" I asked.

"I don't think I follow."

"With Raine and Alicia. Why did you do something to help Alicia's Ego Stage but not with Erika or Jett?"

"Oh." He took in a deep breath, glancing away. "There was nothing so simple."

"*Really*? You know, all I had to do to help Erika was get her out of that prison of hers. That was really simple."

"Was it?"

"Well, yeah." I thought of the butler momentarily. I hadn't mentioned him before, so I wasn't about to now.

"And how are you so certain it was successful? Have you seen Erika since you let her out?"

"No, not yet."

"Then how do you know it was successful?"

I thought a moment, groping for the words. "I– I'm *sure* it worked. You weren't there. You didn't see her after she was out. You know, I think you just cared more in this situation than–"

He grabbed me by the shoulders. "*Of course* I cared more. I love Alicia and Raine." I thought he was about to shake me, but he didn't. "Raine is my *daughter*, and for all intents and purposes, Alicia is my wife. Yes, I care more about them than anyone, but, *but* that will not stop me from trying to help anyone else I *can* help.

"Erika put herself in her prison, so I thought it would be best to leave her in peace, especially considering her significant other was going through his Ego Stage at the same time. You barely survived your encounter with Jett, what makes you think I could have done any better? He probably would have attacked me outright." He shook his head slowly and released my shoulders. "There was simply nothing I could do."

I was stunned. I hadn't completely considered his perspective before, and I was just about to apologize, but he said one last thing.

"Maybe you'll understand... when Kris goes through his Ego Stage."

My eyes narrowed. "Maybe. Maybe I will understand exactly what you're talking about, but I doubt it'll change anything."

"You'll see." Radcliff held out his hand. "I'll take you back out. If you don't know the way through the energy currents they can deposit you right inside the magma."

*   *   *

Not even a full twenty-four hours later I was in my glass bedroom pacing back and forth, looking out over the rainforest. Kris was lying on our bed. His head was hanging off the edge, and he watched me pacing even as the blood rushed to his skull and built pressure in his ears.

"I made a new type of satin. I didn't get to tell you yet," Kris said.

His words filled in the gaps of silence between my footfalls. I wasn't completely paying attention though.

"It's even softer than regular satin, but doesn't have that weird slippery feel. I did some research, and I made it from a blend of cotton and *klis*, which is a not-silk fiber I made up. I still need a name for the new fabric though." He waited a second. "You really should try sleeping on a bed of it."

I stopped and stood still, looking down past my feet and through the glass floor. An ocelot was prowling around the base of my tower.

"Ethan?"

"Huh?" I looked up at him.

"Did you even hear what I said?"

"Oh. No." I took in a deep breath and sighed. "No. Sorry."

Kris got up from the bed. He wrapped his arms around me and rested his head against my shoulder. "It's okay."

"What's this?" I asked.

"Nothing. I just wanted to tell you how much I care about you and how glad I am that you got back alright." He paused. "I'm so glad you're here. I wanted to make sure you knew that."

"I... Kris. Kris, thank you." I hugged him back.

"Just don't, don't do that again. Okay? Please."

"Do what?"

"Leave me behind."

"Oh." I paused. "I didn't want you in the middle of a crossfire. I thought I'd be best if I just went alone."

"Well you're not doing it again, you understand? That's a pretty selfish way of looking at things. If you're going off on a crazy adventure, I'm coming with you."

"But if it's dangerous–"

"Especially if it's dangerous. You only didn't die because Alicia decided to help you. If I was there–"

"You would've been paralyzed in the warp lock right by me."

"Nu-huh. There's *no way* you can know that."

"Maybe not." I walked away along the glass wall, my eyes slowly passing over the horizon.

"Why are you doing this?" Kris asked.

"What?"

"You're so restless. You haven't stayed still all day."

"Oh." I stopped. I stood still. I realized it took effort to do so. "I dunno."

"Ethan, look, it's over." He followed me. "You don't need to be so anxious anymore."

"I know, I know." I rubbed my forehead and walked another few paces. "I don't know what it is."

"Well look, you almost died. That's enough to frazzle anyone. But it's okay. It's *over* now."

"But, but it's *not*. There's still..."

"Still? Still what?"

"Erika. The Rurrians. They..." I paused, thinking. "I need to be the one to talk to Erika, not Radcliff." I took a step towards the door.

"Whoa, whoa, no!" Kris grabbed my arm. "I'm coming with, remember?"

I was silent, thinking for several moments. "As opposed to trying to stop me from going? Radcliff did say I shouldn't."

"When have either of us really listened to Radcliff?" He forced a small chuckle. "I'm coming with you, and that's it."

I nodded. "Alright. Alright, come on."

"Good."

"We need to go to the Rurrians after that."

"What are we gonna do there?"

"I have to go finish talking to them, and I guess it would be good if you came too. Let them meet another warper that doesn't want to kill them."

"Okay, but before we go, I do want to say that talking to Erika could be really dangerous. Are you sure you wanna do this?"

"Yeah. I feel like *I* need tell her. Tell her first, I mean. It is... Jett dying was my fault."

"No it wasn't. He did it, not you."

"Whichever way. I was still there, so I feel like I should tell her."

"Well... I can't talk you out of this, can I?"

"Nope."

He smirked. "Well, I guess that's a good thing at its root. Let's go."

"She's probably still at Yorrlak." I made a doorway.

Just beyond it was the dais on which the Yorrlak standing stones resided. The tables and bookshelves still filled the space, but now near the center of the platform several dozen new standing stones were clustered around the original Yorrlak stones. Erika was in the middle of it all, scribbling into a notebook near one of the stones, three of the bipedal robots lingering around her. They saw us first and ran up to me.

"Erika?" I called out.

She wheeled around, pencil flying out of her hand. "Ethan! I hadn't expected to see you again so soon. And Kris, you're here too. Fantastic! Come look at this!" She waved her hand vigorously for us to come forward.

"What is it?" I asked.

"It's so simple! I can't believe we never realized it before. These standing stones, the Yorrlak standing stones, they're the key to unlocking the warper language from the Third Era!"

"How? What do you mean?" Kris walked forward, and the small robots avoided him.

I crouched down, and they stared up at me with their big camera eyes. I held out a hand, and one of them jumped into it. I smiled.

"Look! Look!" Erika was flipping through her notebook and held an open page up to Kris. "This diagram shows it. The text on the back of the stones! Individual words line up with the images on the front side! Hand, foot, planet, stars, eyes, exhausted, reaching, teacher, disciple, anticipation. They're all right here." She pointed at the pages, tracing lines between two sketched images of the standing stones. "It's a pictorial lesson."

Kris squinted at the upheld notebook.

I glanced up at them. "Is that... how it works?" I stood, still cradling the robot in my hands.

"Of course!" She threw her arms wide. "I've almost finished cataloging all the words, then I'm going to start translating these ancient texts!"

"Well." Kris straightened and glanced at me. "Quite a lot of work here. Quite a lot of excitement." He walked few paces until he was behind Erika. Hidden from her view, he waved a flattened hand in front of his neck and nodded to leave.

I sighed. "No." It was only a whisper.

"These other standing stones are from the Third Era as well, from a few other sites, and I'm going to trying reading them first," Erika said.

I approached her, and the other two robots followed me. "Listen, Erika. This is great, but I have some really bad news to tell you." I reached out and placed a hand over her notebook. "It's the same thing Radcliff's gonna come tell you in a day or two, but I thought I should tell you first."

Her eyes would not stay on me. They darted side to side: to the stones, to me, to the notebook. "What?"

I swallowed. "Jett. Jett's..." I held my breath a moment, worried. "I'm sorry. Jett's dead."

Her eyes froze. She did not move. The notebook started to slip from her hands, but I caught it.

"I'm really sorry, Erika. Really. I really am. He... it was an accident. Anti-matter. He blew up a whole planet and, well, he didn't get out. I'm really so sorry. It was my fault, but I was trying to help him. I promise, I was trying to—"

She said something too quiet and too quick for me to understand. The robot jumped out of my hand.

I blinked. "W-what?"

"No." The word was merely a breath of air and just as difficult to catch.

"Erika..." I reach out to clasp her shoulder, but she struck her hand up quickly, knocking my arm away.

"You saved me just to *break* me."

"No! Erika, he was hell-bent on—"

"Shut up! Get out!" She backed away from Kris and I, colliding into one of the standing stones. The three robots scattered as well, hiding behind the stones.

"Erika, I heard the whole story," Kris said. "There really wasn't—"

"Get out!" She screamed. The Ad Infinitum Fork was suddenly in her hand, raised at both of us.

"Okay, okay." I dropped her notebook and raised my hands as I started backing away from her.

Kris stepped in front of me and grabbed my arms. "Ethan." He teleported us away. "You've really got to get your movement instincts updated."

We were floating somewhere in space. "Where are we?"

"About a hundred light years away. I just jumped us in a random direction."

"What in the world are *movement instincts*?"

"Teleporting instead of running." He placed his hands on his hips. "Radcliff might have been a better candidate for this."

"She's gonna react the same. But later it should be better, I think. If I were her twenty years from now, I know I would be glad to have been told personally."

"That's a really hard thing to know for sure. And now you'll have to deal with Radcliff being upset with you again when he finds out you already told her."

"I'm not really concerned about that." I looked away, off into space, wondering what she was doing now.

Kris shrugged. "So now the Rurrians?"

"Yeah. I'll make the doorway." I set the energy in motion, but nothing happened. The energy was blocked. "Huh?"

"What is it?"

"I can't make a doorway on their planet." I imagined the destination further back, several thousand kilometers from the planet, but still could not place the door. "Or outside of it."

"Warp lock?"

"No... it, it can't be." I kept imaging the doorway further and further from the planet but still to no avail. "Can it?" I started to worry, but finally, ten light-minutes away from Rur, I was able to place a doorway. I ran through it and found myself at the edge of a warp lock.

Kris came up behind me and rubbed my back. "It is."

I shook my head. "But *why*? I was coming back for them."

"Maybe that is why."

I clenched my fists. "Dammit! But Markus!" I slipped down, sitting on my legs now.

"Who's Markus?"

My head was lowered, my eyes closed. I didn't respond. I just waved a hand up and created Markus standing beside us.

He gasped, clutched at his chest, but stopped and realized he was okay. He looked down at his hands.

"Markus?" Kris asked.

"Yes... I, I'm Markus."

"Who are you?"

"I'm dead."

I stood up, but wouldn't look Markus in the face. "Listen," I said. "Listen. I already know what you're going to say. I already know it, because it's the only way this can go at all. But I have to hear it. You have to say it. I won't believe it otherwise."

"What? What do you want me to say?" Markus asked. "What's happening?"

"Just, just answer this. Are you... are you real?"

He blinked and was silent for a moment. "No, not anymore," he whispered. "I'm supposed to be dead. I remember dying. You brought me back."

"Yeah. Yeah, I did."

"Why?"

"I wanted to make a difference. I wanted to help. But I don't think I did. Rur's locked again. They don't want us to come to them. I'm giving you a choice. I can return you to Rur, or I can take you somewhere else, any planet you'd like. Or you can go... you know, back."

"The Rurrians will never accept me. They'll think I'm some sort of spy or trick if they know I died."

"Ethan." Kris touched my shoulder. "This is like talking to ghosts."

"I know! Markus, I'm so sorry. I know the only way you can stay real is if you stay dead, but I wanted to give you the choice. I can let you live. I can. I can make you forget and put you anywhere you want. Please. Just tell me what you want."

Very slowly, agonizingly slowly, Markus shook his head. "I am Rurrian. 'We know the face of the universe and of gods themselves. We know the nature twisted and the relics lost. We proclaim ourselves unchanged, and we won't blind ourselves to lies. We are Rurrian.' Let me die."

I closed my hand into a fist and pressed it over my face. I wanted to fight him, to change him, to make him not so stubborn, to save him. I didn't though. I didn't fight him.

But I did save him.

Epilogue

By Earth measurements it has been 96 years, 4 months, 3 weeks, 6 days, 12 hours, and 53 minutes since Ethan first stepped into my Restaurant. Now he is stepping into it again. The Humans all move so slowly, but to be accurate, this is merely my perception created by my exceedingly quick thinking time. Ethan is just now turning around to close the door.

I had been running several battle simulations of an ancient war from the days before the planet was called Rur and before the fighters were called Rurrians. I always find their choice of names to be so amusing. This is a war from a time when peoples were led by kings and blood was spilt over the best soil to till. Times not gone quickly enough. The door is just now closing. I will be able to run the simulation a few times over before he reaches the counter.

I try to focus, but this is truly such a bother. I already have to ignore Erika and Andrew in one of the tables against a wall; they are making fools of themselves as they feed each other French fries. By the powers that be, I wish they would stop.

Ethan has taken three steps now. It is grating on my mind just how much I cannot ignore him. Why do they have to come so frequently? Why cannot they come every other year. Now that would be bearable. Maybe.

I continue running through the simulation, currently engrossed in the exact difference the change of wind direction by one degree can have on a battle in which arrows can be such a deciding factor. The outcome is close to my expectations. Pitiful arrows, they are no match for the wind itself. Ethan is talking to me now, but I let a subprogram dictate my responses. I cannot be expected to give him my full attention every time he talks to me. Apparently he has written a sort of auto-biography, and he wants me to read it. Joy. As if I really want to know about his sex life.

He continues on, but my subprogram starts saying something I cannot choke down. I cut in just in time to change the sentence. "Letting the warper beans out in such a– what? Stop. Repeat everything you just told me." He has gotten my attention again. Maybe that is why I so dread when he comes to my Restaurant.

"Weren't you listening?"

"No."

He blinks. Why does he always have to hesitate and blink? Why can he not just speak quickly?

"I said I wrote a book about when I first became a warper. And about the whole Jett incident. It's part of my plan to let everyone know about us."

"And why do you think that is a good idea?"

"I already said. From all my research into philosophy, religion, even politics, I truly believe that if Humans at large knew about us and the existential implications, they would be less inclined to be so frivolous. Not to mention the questions we can answer that have been plaguing most planets since the dawn of their civilizations."

"I think your logic has more holes in it than I can point out in a week."

"Just read the book, okay? I think you'll understand when you do. You're in it, you know."

"Why am I in your book?"

"Because of all those conversations we had, remember? I learned a lot from you."

Was that a compliment? "Perhaps I will read it."

"Good. Thanks. When Kris was reading the rough drafts he was complaining that he wasn't in it enough."

Maybe that means there will not be sex scenes. "And what does Radcliff think?"

"Radcliff doesn't like it much, but Raine really likes it."

"Am I the last to read this book?"

"No. I mean that's how they reacted to the idea. I'm handing out all the copies now, then I'll go start planting them on planets." He sets the book on the counter.

"*Warp World*? How droll."

"Hey, it's alliteration. Everyone loves alliteration."

"Sounds more like you should have called it *Look How Damn Clever I Am: The Book*."

"Oh come on, there's a lot more to it than just the title."

"Very well. I will read it went I have time."

" 'Have time?' What do you even do besides stand there?"

"I will not honor that question with an answer."

"Okay, whatever. I'll come back in a week or so to see what you think of it so far." He turns to leave but stops. "Oh, one more thing."

"Yeeees?" I draw the word out.

"Thanks. In advance. For reading it, that is."

"Your words of premature gratitude will not force me to read your book."

"I know, but I think your curiosity will." He laughs and waves. "See ya later." He goes over to Erika and Andrew, no doubt badgering them to read his book as well.

Humans.

An idea pops into my mind. If he is going to practically force me to read his book, at least I can find some amusement in it. I wait until he leaves the Restaurant and call upon the warp energy that resides deep within me. The warp energy I so rarely use. It flows in. It flows out. And the change is made.

I open the book from the back, skip right to the epilogue, and read aloud, "I wonder what Ethan will think when he sees I have added this to his book."

If I had the ability to smile I would have done so now as I flip the book shut.

Jacob H Ramm

is very pleased to bring you this story, and he hopes you enjoyed it. He is currently unmarried, has no pets, and believes we really, really need to get into space already. Ramm is, in fact, a full supporter of Penny4NASA. You can find Ramm at Morhawven.tumblr.com. He is currently working on his next book which will be a horror novel.

A word on the categorization of this book.

"A Concordant Book" is the categorization of this book in relation to all my other (future) books. The Concordant Books are independent of each other unless otherwise stated in their sub-categorization.

"Unsettled Realm" is the sub-categorization describing the world the book is set in. Any books set in the same Realm are part of the same story. In other books, such as the Entwined Books, this line will list the date when the story happens.

"Single" refers to this book being a standalone novel. If there was a series then the placement of the book in the series would be listed here.

31393581R00249

Made in the USA
Lexington, KY
10 April 2014